SANDRO MARTINI

Sandro Martini is a seasoned journalist who has worked in three continents. He has spent years researching the facts and creating a story which tells us much about men, their addiction to speed and the love of the machine at a particular time in European history.

Published in the UK by Aurora Metro Books.
67 Grove Avenue, Twickenham, TW1 4HX
www.aurorametro.com   info@aurorametro.com

Editors: Cheryl Robson and Stephanie Charamnac
Aurora Metro Books would like to thank: Simon Smith, Neil
Gregory, Richard Turk, Suzanne Mooney.

Printed in the UK by Ashford Colour Press, Fareham,
Hants.

ISBN: 978-1-906582-43-2

TRACKS

RACING THE SUN

BY

SANDRO MARTINI

AURORA METRO BOOKS

This book is for Natalie.

Thanks to:
Hans Etzrodt, and Aldo Zana for their kind responses to my thick-headed questions, Birgitta Fella for her diligence, and Jon Denton for his motor-racing knowledge.

And finally, thank you to Sarah Gadd for her patience and love: This is as much yours as it is mine.

PART ONE
THE ITALIANS

We declare that the splendour of the world has been enriched by a novel beauty: the beauty of speed. A racing automobile with its bonnet adorned with great tubes like serpents with explosive breath ... a roaring motor car which seems to run on machine-gun fire, is more beautiful than the Victory of Samothrace.

— The Futurist Manifesto, F. T. Marinetti, 1909

THE ISOLATION OF SPEED

L'Isola Del Lido, February 14th, 1968

'So why are you here?'

'As I explained in my letters – '

'It's all been told already.'

'Not all – not everything.'

'And your interest is what, precisely?'

'There are dead ends that I hoped you could – '

'You said you were writing a book? On Varzi?'

'Varzi, yes, and – '

'But not about me.'

'Well, you do come into it, of course.'

'But not much?'

'Well that depends, I suppose…'

'On what?'

'On what you tell me.'

'And what role would you have in mind for me, should I help you with your dead ends?'

'I – hadn't thought about it. Why, what did you have in mind?'

Lunch in the hotel restaurant where the waiter in jeans and white shirt escorts us through an archipelago of forsaken tables rising from a well-worn carpet to his table, this elderly man who I'd spotted easily enough in the lobby this morning, sunk into a deep leather chair with a brown suit swimming over a frail body and his long, bony nose pointing down into a pink sports newspaper. He'd mumbled sit, not even raising his eyes as I'd launched myself into the seat opposite, the rucksack on my lap making me feel like a homeless refugee. Fidgeting nervously, I'd glanced about the hotel lobby, a once-swanky place now fallen into disrepair and – if the dozy woman sitting alone by the door in her cheap low cut dress was any indication – disrepute.

'So you're the journalist who's come all the way from New York to hear my stories,' he'd said, folding the newspaper in half with one crisp flick of the wrists, a gesture well-worn with age. His eyes – brown and glossy – had lifted with casual reluctance to meet mine, but if there was an appraisal, it was well-guarded.

'Joe Deutsch,' I'd said, and held his cold hand in mine.

'Hotels are like families,' he tells me now as we sit in the dining room with the last glimmer of the afternoon sun fading fast. 'Some generations prosper, others toss it all to the dogs.' He looks down at the menu. 'Still, they do have their ghosts.'

'If walls could talk,' I say, regretting my inanity instantly. He looks at me coldly with his dark Italian eyes.

'If walls could talk,' he says, 'room 102 would be the ones you'd want to listen to.'

'You mean Varzi – '

'I mean the lassie back there,' he interrupts dismissively. 'Rather noisy at her job that one – they tell me she's Albanian.' He takes a sip of his blood-red Campari and soda, licks lips with purple tongue and gazes down at the menu once more. 'So tell me, where does your – narrative begin?'

'I – I'd planned to begin when Nuvolari and Varzi first raced each other, back in '26 – ' I watch his head bob about with the delusion of expectation. 'But where,' I ask uncertainly, 'would you begin?'

'No one cares about the back-story, I'll tell you that for free,' he replies, his goaded eyes watching thoughtfully as I draw a Norelco Carry-Corder 150 from my rucksack. I plonk it on the table, and he waits for me to peel the microphone out and extend it across to him. 'But if it's Varzi you care about,' he continues after I click the record button on the mike, 'the winter of 1930 is as good a place to begin as any. I was working for the *Gazzetta* back then ...'

○

I was standing in my office staring out at the smog, thinking of that face, with its grimace of a smile, ever since I'd read the telegraph from Libya with its headline screaming, 'The Death of Count Brilli-Peri'.

One of our stringers had covered the Libyan Grand Prix – a minor event out in Imperial Italy – and his terse report had landed on my desk that Monday morning. I'd read it with a mounting sense of bewilderment. During Saturday practice, the reigning Italian champion Brilli-Peri had been setting-up his Talbot when he'd come unstuck at the quick left-hand turn that led into the village of Suq al Jum'ah. It was just past midday and two miles out of Tripoli at 180kph when Brilli-Peri's Talbot 1700 had flicked into a slide; correcting it, Brilli-Peri had borrowed too much and lost it all when the car speared into a stone wall. Thrown from his Talbot at full speed face-first into the wall of an abandoned house, Brilli-Peri had been killed outright.

I recalled my own impressions of Africa from my time there after the war: heat, filth, sand, disease. The memory of the desiccated heads of camels lining the market stalls teeming with flies suddenly came to me, and I imagined those blow-flies finding Brilli-Peri long before the marshals ever did, poor bastard.

How to write about it was the issue. The Death of a Champion perspective, I knew, would only enrage my editor for whom cliché was ample justification for the pink slip. National Tragedy had its merits, but I'd done that for Materassi at Monza back in '28 when he'd misjudged a pass on Foresti and careened through a series of straw bales into the crowd killing himself and twenty-two spectators. Just before he'd lost control, he'd been battling against Nuvolari and Varzi, still seething that his protest against both before the race had fallen on deaf ears. I turned from the window and sat behind my desk, inserted a clean sheet of paper into the Littoria typewriter, and stared at it.

The Italian desert, the oasis of Mussolini's delusion, Marshal Badoglio's new world, Italy's African empire, the curse of the first ever scuderia founded by Brilli-Peri and Materassi, all of it flooded before me and none of it would discharge from my fingers onto the virginal whiteness of that page ... where to begin? In 1925, when the young nobleman, Count Gastone Brilli-Peri, had won the first-ever Monza Grand Prix? Or perhaps – the shrill tring of the phone interrupted my deliberations and a voice rasped, 'Finestrini?' into my ear.

'This is he,' I replied, searching for my cigarette pack on the cluttered desk.

'This is Varzi, Achille Varzi.'

'Varzi.' The pack of Camel revealed itself beneath the soft pages of that morning's *Corriere*. 'Have you heard?'

'Yes. A tragedy. I'm sure you'll convey this to your readers in tomorrow's 'paper.' One was always unsure with Varzi: Was it contempt in his voice? 'I'm at the Pidocchio,' he announced, 'come have lunch.'

'I have a deadline.'

'An unfortunate turn of phrase, Finestrini. I heard his girlfriend left him the day before he died.'

'Really?'

'Come past in about an hour. That should give you enough time to type-up the curse of Materassi, death in Imperial Africa nonsense. I have,' he added, his voice distracted, 'an idea for your comic strip.'

I abandoned my story, grabbed my new loden overcoat from the rack and headed out into the smog. Perhaps Varzi had a point: Brilli-Peri deserved more than a national hero dying for the patria epitaph.

I bought a copy of *Avanti!* and paged through it on the damp tram that trundled its way through the fog and mounting sleet. *Avanti!* had reprinted a story from the *New York Times* verbatim: "Fears Moron Types Will People Nation: Dr. Wiggan Says Democracy Will Not Outlast Century Unless The Intelligent

Reproduce".

The Duce's almost completed Milano Centrale railway station hovering in a cloud of steam acted as a beacon for me to jump off the tram. A shower of icy hail stung my face as I made my way towards The Pidocchio.

Inside all was grimly quiet; a table near the back, shrouded by cigarette smoke in which shadowed faces emitted hushed words, offered the only sign of life. I was headed deeper into the restaurant when a firm hand, on my shoulder, slowed me in my tracks.

A face, behind me, lingered alone in the dankness. Achille Varzi. I'd never really stared at Varzi's eyes long enough to notice their exact shade – to me they were the tint of black ice, and not even his smile – that smile that contracted like a spasm across his lips – could disguise their vapid appearance, a guise of terror veiled by raw nerves. I took the rough hand that was stabbed into my abdomen and allowed this man in the charcoal double-breasted suit to escort me to the modest bar where a single blood-red Campari and soda sweated ice beneath the pale damp light.

'Johnnie Walker, black, straight-up, for Johnny Finestrini,' Varzi told the guy behind the bar, 'the *Gazzetta*'s best motor-sport journalist.'

The barman placed the glass on the bar and stole a fleeting glance at my face. I'd been around men like Varzi long enough not to be overcome by the veneration that surrounded him and, by extension, those permitted into his circle. ' ... tell me about Brill-Peri,' Varzi was saying.

'He hit a wall,' I replied.

'Dead on impact?'

I glanced up from my glass. What could I say to a man who could meet the same fate next week at the Mille Miglia? The fear was there in his eyes when I turned to face him. He lit a Lucky, blowing a curtain of smoke in my face.

'Yes,' I replied, breathing in the smoke. 'Dead on impact.'

'Quick then.'

'Quick – yes.'

'In life and in death.' I watched his face break into a smile, (a face that had been reconstructed after a shunt at Livorno in '25 when he'd hit a wall rather than a boy crossing the track). 'Perhaps you ought to try that line, I don't think you've done that one yet. And don't forget to mention that bloody whistle he used to carry with him. Sonofabitch would blow that thing like a referee – almost had me off at Spa last year, frightened the crap out of me.'

I looked away uncertainly.

'Are you hungry, Finestrini?'

'No. No, I had a late breakfast.'

'Yes.' He lifted his Campari, considered it, then rested it decisively back down on the bar. 'You realize of course,' he said, running a finger over the brim of the glass, 'what this means.'

'I'm not with you.'

'Have you spoken to Jano?'

'Jano?'

'Jano, yes. You know, Viktor János, aka Vittorio Jano, the world's foremost racecar designer. You have heard of him, no?' He looked at me with his head slightly tilted as if deciding whether I was merely being coy or demonstrating some form of mental retardation. 'Have you?' he insisted.

'Of course I've heard of him,' I said, swallowing whisky.

'Talked to him,' said Varzi. 'Have you talked to him yet?'

'About *what?*'

Varzi's eyes focused on my lips as if the echo of my words had confirmed something in his mind. 'About Nuvolari, for Christ's sakes. About Nuvolari taking Brilli-Peri's car for the Mille Miglia.'

◼

Finestrini taps on his menu and looks up at me. 'Polenta with liver is what I'd recommend. For a water-locked people,' he says, glancing at the Carry-Corder between my elbows, 'the Venetians are vile with fish. But that's often the case with people who are tight with money – and believe me, you couldn't squeeze a dime up a Venetian's ass – they prefer their food rich and their wine white.'

'But why Brilli-Peri? Why would you start with his death?'

11

'Because it started a sequence of events that would lead to Varzi's downfall – and Nuvolari's legacy.'

'You mean their rivalry?'

He frowns.

'Legend has it,' I tell him, 'that it was you who … how shall I put this … ?'

'However you like, it won't change the answer, Deutsch.'

'Joe, please. Did you invent their so-called "rivalry"?'

'Journalists don't invent, Deutsch; they refine. That rivalry existed, going all the way back to their motorcycling days in the mid-'20s – that's a matter of record.'

'So tell me then, exactly how did Brilli-Peri's death lead to Varzi's downfall?'

'Because his death,' Finestrini replies, 'freed up a seat on the Alfa Romeo works team that had dominated grand prix racing since Vittorio Jano had designed the Alfa P2 in '24 – that car was, as you Americans say, a game-changer, yes? And on the back of an exceptional self-financed season in '29, Varzi had been signed up as a full works driver for 1930, and now Nuvolari would join him. Italy's two greatest prospects about to do battle in the same team driving the same all-dominant Italian cars – we couldn't sell enough newspapers in the days leading up to the Mille Miglia.'

'Was Varzi angry? To find Nuvolari on his team?'

'Angry?' Finestrini pretends to consider this, embarrassed perhaps on my behalf as he shuffles his glass around the white linen tablecloth. 'No, you're not listening – it was *his* idea to have Nuvolari on the team; it was Varzi who persuaded Jano to give Nuvolari the drive. It's why he'd called me to the Pidocchio that morning; he wanted me to sell Nuvolari to Jano, asked me to write an editorial extolling the virtues of *Il Mantovano Volante*, the Flying Mantuan. No easy task that, I can tell you – Jano was not the world's biggest Nuvolari fan, not since he'd written-off one of Jano's P2s.'

'When was that?'

'Back in '26. Nuvolari had been invited to test for the Alfa works after Ascari had died in the fall of '25. Alfa was in need of a new star – not that they came bigger than Ascari – and Jano went out on a limb with Nuvolari, went against the advice of his own board – Nuvolari's reputation as a wild man did not sit well with them, or Nicola Romeo who was still heading up the company. I was at Monza for that test – I'd been at the *Gazzetta* for less than a year then. Nuvolari was told to take it easy, not to rev' over 5400rpm, the usual rookie stuff, you know, and while he went out, Jano invited us to lunch at the Levati restaurant which was pretty much smack-dab in the middle of the Monza autodrome in those days.

'We could hear the Alfa go out into the early afternoon, hear the engine rise and fall through the trees. Two, three laps, all sounded fine, the engine echoing delightfully with our panzarotti. And then … ' Finestrini looks for words up on the ceiling, up there where a peeling fresco of an inland mountain scene stares down at us, 'it's odd, you know, but there's always a – a lull of sorts before an accident. A silence. We heard the engine note alter pitch, rising, rising, screaming, then tyres squealing before,' Finestrini slams one palm onto a fist. 'All of us were running then, I can tell you – it sounded like a big one. We found him in the trees just beyond the second Lesmo slumped over in the cockpit screaming like a demon, blood everywhere, the P2 lying in a ditch with its spine broken.'

'His gearbox had apparently seized on a downshift blocking the rear tyres solid and plunging him into the scenery. He spent three days in hospital with broken ribs and a pretty nasty concussion. Jano, meanwhile, had been made to look a fool when the mechanics found the tell-tale rev'-needle hovering at over 6200rpm. You understand, Alfa built maybe a half-dozen P2s in a decade. Those cars were expensive to fabricate, hand-built, and Nuvolari had just written one off in what was meant to have been a test session. You can imagine my astonishment then when I arrived that Sunday to cover the most lucrative bike-race of the season – the Grand Prix of Nations at Monza – to find Nuvolari on the grid with his body, from shoulders down to his knees, sheathed in bandages and plaster of Paris. He'd had the doctors set them so that he was in the riding position, and I'll never forget the wild ovation from the grandstands when his mechanics lifted the little man like a plastic toy and dumped him onto his Bianchi with his belly on the fuel cell. I'm sure he'd have waved if he could have, but all he could do was sit on that bike and ride the damn' thing. If he came to a stop, he'd have simply toppled over, and Christ alone knows what would have happened had he come off, he'd have had no chance of breaking his fall. As it turned out, strapped on that machine for 500 kilometres, he won the race by over thirty seconds – against the best riders on the planet. When I asked him how he'd done it, he replied, "A man rides a bike with his belly, not his ass".'

'The Mummy Rider.' I watch the waiter come up toward the table. 'That was your headline.'

'Yes,' Finestrini meets the waiter's eyes, '*La Mummia*. I remember chancing upon Jano at the Alfa factory a couple of weeks later and he was still livid. That Nuvolari had enhanced his legend at the cost of one of his beloved P2s was just adding insult to injury.' Finestrini orders for both of us, staring at the waiter's pen scrawling indifferently on a notebook. 'That race made him a household name – kids were pedalling their bikes all over Italy wearing bandages like Nuvolari for months after that. But as far as Jano was concerned, Nuvolari would never again drive for the Alfa works.'

I sip on water, warm and dust-speckled. 'I still don't follow – why would Varzi have wanted Nuvolari on his team?'

Finestrini considers his reply. 'At the time, I saw it as self-interest. Alfa Romeo, that year, were running two teams for the Mille Miglia, pretty much an A- and B-team. Brilli-Peri had been on the A team, Varzi – only twenty-six and in his rookie year as a works driver – on the B. His idea was to get Nuvolari into the team as his own replacement while he – Varzi – would be promoted into the A.'

The waiter pours our wine, a careless Merlot from the Veneto. 'At the time?'

'I beg your pardon?'

'You said "at the time". What do you think now?'

He sips the wine. 'Naturally it was self-interest. There was no doubt that the eventual winner of the Mille Miglia would come from the A team – but there was something – something … he opened the door to his own betrayal,' Finestrini says, his eyes rising and meeting mine. 'Do you see? He let the devil in at the Mille Miglia. And I'm not convinced, not anymore, that it was entirely unintentional.'

'What do you mean by that?' I ask, glancing down at the Carry-Corder.

◙

The Fascists loved the Mille Miglia. After the first race in '27, it was obvious that this throwback to the city-to-city races of our youth would become the sporting event of the spring. Hardly surprising given its character – one thousand miles, from Brescia to Rome and back again, all run on public roads left open to regular traffic. The race not only offered a passionate trial for driver and car – the type of challenge that manufacturers welcomed, this being the days when a win on Sunday meant a sale on Monday – but an adventure of the heart that the racing world (not to mention the Party) wholeheartedly embraced. I had written an editorial (my first for the *Gazzetta*) in which I'd likened the organization of the event to a military exercise: 'A mobilization for sport today, tomorrow a mobilization for other conquests in other fields.' Rome had eaten that up, and the race was granted a permanent date in April.

For the fourth Mille Miglia (or the IV Mille Miglia as our style sheets from the Ministry of Propaganda insisted numbers were to be written now that we were living in the II Roman empire), the Party itself had mobilized over 24,000 soldiers to patrol and monitor the course, and they re-named the trophy the Mussolini Cup.

All of which seemed to act as some sort of provocation for my editor, Cristoferi, who spent the weeks leading up to the race pestering me for decent copy since my first filed article had been returned with – in the boldest red imaginable – MEANINGLESS DRIVEL scrawled across the page. Bordoni, the 'horse guy' with whom I'd shared a desk for my first six months at the *Gazzetta*, had it that, when Cristoferi was particularly disgusted, he would slice his thumb with a knife and bleed on the copy before sending it back. 'Don't you understand, people don't want to know, don't *care* about cars! They care about *people*! If a sport can't be individualized to people, it's meaningless, like reading about chess tournaments. Give me *people*, Finestrini, make me *care* for them. Make me *hate* them,' he'd growled at our Christmas party while I nodded back my grappa, too drunk to blush. 'You should see what he said about my horses,' Bordoni confided when the two of us – both single and without family – welcomed in Christmas morning together in a bar in il salotto di Milano. We convinced ourselves that night that it was only Cristoferi's need for filler for the slow Tuesday issues of the *Gazzetta* that kept us employed.

Nuvolari versus Varzi had changed all of that. I'd stumbled onto the most popular sports story of the decade, and as their rivalry rose from the back pages of the sports dailys to the front page of the news dailys, so had Cristoferi's interest in my work until, with two weeks remaining before the IV Mille Miglia, he had summoned me up to his office on the fourth floor, sat me down before his desk with a cup of grappa and, with what he must have thought was a passable imitation of an ingratiating smile, assured me that, 'Not even you can fuck this up.' And then, slapping me lightly on the way out, he'd added, 'So don't,' while pinching my stinging cheek.

I spent an anxious few days working the phone, calling every contact in my address book in a hunt for quotes. Cristoferi had asked for a daily 300-word column that would run until the eve of the Mille Miglia, and I began with Varzi who, as always, didn't let me down when I called him in his suite in Milan on the Sunday before the race.

'A thousand mile race decided in fifty,' he'd said.

Up through the Raticosa and Futa, he'd maintained, in those desolate stretches of mountain passes that rose and fell 900 metres winding through the Apennines linking Bologna to Florence on dusty, narrow roads jagged like a serrated knife and just as deadly, with orchards and olive groves, vineyards and ancient cypress trees on one side and terrifying ravines on the other, those were

16

the roads that led a man to victory in Brescia 800 miles away.

Convinced of this, Varzi had been leaving his suite at the Hotel Cinque on the Piazza Fontana in the cold of dawn along with his lover Norma to head south to Bologna before climbing up into the Raticosa. Norma, by then, would have stirred from her dozing, sipping coffee from a thermos, endlessly lighting cigarettes for Varzi. He'd driven the Raticosa dozens of times, he told me when we spoke that Sunday evening, not concerning himself with speed but with memorizing as much of the layout as he could. To aid him, Norma – holding a can of red paint – would climb from the FIAT to deface road-markers and trees and cliff overhangs with a red-painted V. At speed, Varzi would use these markers to warn him of danger – of a particularly menacing turn, bump, or ravine. On many, he would instruct Norma to paint the V over the symbols already scrawled by his rivals, the TN of Nuvolari, the B of Biondetti, the GC of Campari.

Before he'd hung up, Varzi had invited me for lunch at the Guattari on Tuesday. Pintacuda had discovered the cosy tavern with its views over the Apennines back in '27, and it had since become the favored 'pitstop' for the top names in the weeks leading up to the race; Brilli-Peri, Materassi, Biondetti, Campari, all had enjoyed leisurely lunches of roasted boar and gnocchi at the Guattari, and I was delighted to accept the invitation, thinking it would make an excellent filler for the Wednesday edition.

On the Monday evening, I spoke with Enzo Ferrari – a Modena-based tuner who was preparing Alfa's racecars and who'd founded his own scuderia on the eve of the Crash (the one on Wall Street) – hoping to get a little insight into the Zagato-styled models that Alfa would bring to the Mille Miglia. In passing, I mentioned my invitation to the Guattari with Varzi and Norma Colombo.

'Norma Colombo?' he asked. *The* Norma Colombo?'

'I think so.'

'And you say she's now with Varzi?'

'Indeed, *Ingegnere*.'

'I thought she was with Meazza.'

''Fraid not, *Ingegnere*.' I glanced down at the front page of the *Gazzetta* where Peppino Meazza's face stared back diffidently with

17

that street-urchin smile of his. Meazza, the prodigious Inter Milan trequartista (who'd slept with more women than he'd scored goals) had just become the first footballer to sign a contract with a personal sponsor – at twenty years of age. The scandal had evoked pages of comment and editorials (mostly concerning the end of football now that commercial interests had interceded in the purity of the sport).

'She's been with Varzi for a month or two,' I elaborated, recalling Meazza at the San Siro in March when I'd watched Juventus play Inter – that chilly afternoon he'd scored probably the greatest goal I'd ever seen, skinning centre-backs Rosetta and Ferrero before nutmegging the 'keeper Combi and running the ball into the net. Italy's greatest-ever talent, the *Gazzetta* maintained, and I was in no position to argue.

'Incredible,' said Ferrari. Then silence.

'*Ingegnere?*'

'Pick me up from my house at 7am, Finestrini. We'll go together. Don't be late.'

On the road out of Modena with the early morning sun scorching away a silver film of mist, Enzo Ferrari sipped from a thermos flask of espresso laced with grappa, his hooded brown eyes gazing out of the dirty windows of my Bianchi as we followed the route taken by the Mille Miglia to gently wind our way up and across the spine of our blessed peninsula.

'Back in '28,' he said, perhaps affected by the astonishing beauty that surrounded us, 'I was coming up here with Campari – for practice, you understand – and the *Negher* was pushing like a bastard – still had that ridiculous square moustache of his, you remember that? – when suddenly I felt this spray of liquid hit my face. I look down at the floor of the car and notice some sort of fluid dripping between Campari's enormous feet. "We need to stop, Campa'!" I shouted, "something's leaking!" – maybe brake fluid, right? No reply. So I lean forward – you can imagine, right, my head's down near that damn fat belly of his, and I'm trying to see where the leak's coming from – no easy feat this, you know Campari's an animal when he's on it, and we're going round the turns in these enormous drifts, and I'm holding on with one hand to the damn door for fear of being thrown out knowing full-well the bastard won't stop if I do, and then I notice that the liquid's oozing out from under his pant-leg. "*Campa'! Ma che cazzo fai?*" I shout. "*Ohè*," he replies, "you don't want me to stop while I'm in training, do you? I gotta practise pissing myself!" ' I made sure not to smile when Ferrari glanced sideways at me.

The Guattari, when we crunched up into its dirt parking lot just gone noon, was not much to look at, just a wood-and-stone tavern with a terrace out-back leaning over an olive grove. The view, though, was postcard-perfect when we stepped in to find Norma Colombo suffused in a swathe of that delicate gold-sprinkled spring sunshine one finds in no place on earth but this, the land of Fra Angelico. She said something to us, I could see those luscious lips moving, but I wasn't listening. Varzi, beside her at their table, looked up without a trace of emotion.

'*Ingegnere* Ferrari,' he said, fixing me a look. 'What a pleasant surprise.'

Ferrari, bowing, thrust his hand out at Norma, ensnaring hers. He was an odd-looking creature, Ferrari, with that square head and self-conscious smile.

Over lunch, Varzi spoke of the challenge of the Mille Miglia. 'I'll do this race until I win it, then never again,' he said. 'It's madness – whoever thought it up was a sadist.' Varzi was on his third espresso by then, his hands, as they fiddled with a Lucky, trembling with anxious energy. 'But really, Finestrini, you do your newspaper an injustice. You sit here with the great *Ingegnere* Ferrari, and you have yet to ask him who he believes will win.' He stood up then, Norma at his side.

Ferrari knocked over a cup in his haste to stand and get his purple lips on Norma's hand. 'Doesn't much matter either way,' he said, gazing into her hazel eyes. 'To me, Varzi, you've already won the greatest prize.'

◘

I watch Finestrini stick a piece of ripe juicy liver between his lips. He indulges me with a gently masticating mouth. 'Varzi would have won that race too, you know.'

I check the rolling cassette cartridge in the Carry-Corder. 'Would have?'

'Would have, Deustch,' confirms Finestrini, 'had it not been for what Varzi would always believe was Jano's betrayal.'

A spiteful April rain fell without respite over the drivers, cars, and crush of spectators on the imposing Viale Venezia, all huddled together before Attillio Teruzzi, Chief of the Militia, as he prepared to address the crowd. The Blackshirts – volunteers, patriots, and war-hero Teruzzi's charges – had been assigned the responsibility of keeping order over the race, and their leader had come well-preened for his close-up in the flickering sun of a hundred flashbulbs going off like grenades.

'Brrrrrrr,' he began before, clearly unhappy with the sound, jumping onto a crate and grabbing a megaphone that he jammed into his face. 'Brrrrrrilli-Perrrrrrrrrri!' he hollered with his high-pitched voice echoing through the rain and delicate mist hovering over the medieval piazza and its colonnades, still as soldiers. 'Brilli-Peri!'

'Presente!' the fans and drivers shouted back.

'You love it, don't you,' the voice whispered in my ear. 'This love of tragedy of yours: you bastards will have us all dead just to get a chance to glorify our fucking tombs.' Varzi, beneath a hefty black golf umbrella, had materialized beside my shoulder. He wore a pale gray suit over which, to protect him from the chill, a brown leather jacket was draped. In his gloved hand – Fowler gloves, handmade for him, I'd been told by Jano, in England – he held the official programme of the IV Mille Miglia. It wilted beneath the icy rain. 'You see I'm scheduled to start at 1:12 p.m.'

I nodded.

'And Nuvolari,' he continued, staring at me as if I was somehow to blame, 'he leaves ten minutes after me, at 1:22 p.m.'

'Yes,' I said, watching his cigarette smoke blend into the mist.

'If Jano had been good to his word, I'd have started behind

Nuvolari. As it stands, I'll become the hunted. Nuvolari will know the gap, will be able to manage his race accordingly. He'll be able to track me while I, I'll have to run like a rabbit. Jano wants Nuvolari to win – he thinks it will ingratiate him with your mates over there.' His jaw jutted out toward Teruzzi, stumbling off his crate with his leather coat sweating a glitzy sheen. 'That would make you happy too, wouldn't it? ... Well I'll tell you what,' he continued over my weak protestation, 'you'll all be drinking white wine in sixteen hours.'

After a *frittata* in a café just off the piazza, I returned to the Viale Venezia in time to watch Varzi's Zagato-styled Tipo 6C 1750GS Alfa, polished blood-red by the rain, rise to the starting platform beneath the TEXACO and Goodrich billboards. The crowd was held back by a column of Blackshirts eager to crack some skulls, and I recalled that these were the men who, in 1920, had broken up the strike at the Alfa Romeo factory in Milan which had signalled both the rise of Mussolini's Fascisti and the demise of Italy's socialist movement. But what Mussolini took with one hand he always repaid with the other; after all, Alfa would have gone bust after the Crash of '29 had it not been for the Party. And without Alfa, I'd have been covering bottom of the league football in Trentino...

Varzi, smoking in the narrow confines of his open cockpit, waited for one of the Mille Miglia's founders, the amiable Aymo Maggi, to begin the countdown. Canavesi, Varzi's mechanic, waved at the cheering crowds from within his piddling dogseat. Varzi rested his hands delicately on the slick wooden steering-wheel, his goggled-eyes staring fixedly into the gloom of that miserable April afternoon.

The smaller cars had all left by then, and the crowd had swelled now that the favorites were stacked up in a haphazard row behind Achille Varzi, his Alfa's long brooding nose pointed at the Viale Venezia that snaked between the mob standing ten, twenty deep, an apron of black umbrellas beneath a dull, wintry sky. Maggi strobed an arm down between the pop of flashbulbs. Varzi, ever the stylist, accelerated serenely away into the rain, and it was easy to imagine him shifting gears with two silken fingers.

Behind him, Tazio Nuvolari, in an identical Alfa and wearing a leather jacket and red leather skullcap, rolled up to the starting platform with a stuttering right foot. He acknowledged the throng that had taken up a chant of *Nivola! Nivola!* behind a series of excited engine-shrieks. Beside him his mechanic Guidotti was looking distinctly nervous, holding for grim life onto a leather strap, and I could well imagine his fear. When you went out with Nuvolari, you went knowing that returning uninjured – or even alive – was not his top priority. I wondered, as the enormous clock above the starting ramp ticked ever closer to 13:22, whether Guidotti was aware that, beneath that leather cap, Nuvolari had stapled an Italian flag along with a photo of the Madonna. But perhaps Guidotti, with his lips moving and eyes firmly shut, was already invoking otherworldly favors. He looked terrified, poor man, sitting there under the rain waiting for the countdown to end and Nuvolari to drop the clutch and power away with a surge that seemed almost a release from his barely contained savagery, the rear of the Alfa fishtailing testily.

Nuvolari couldn't have cared less: The throttle he kept floored, the power through the rear-wheels flattening the car out before he heaved it into a turn with an exaggerated powerslide, the crush of spectators parting to his sheer virility like the water beneath his sturdy rubber tyres. Ever the showman, the echo of his name convulsed through the soggy air between the arcades and porticos long after he'd bounced over the railway track and hit the open road south of Brescia.

The race was on: Sixteen hours it would take them, an interminable time for us, for them – for these warriors engaged in a struggle between victory and exhaustion (for neither Nuvolari or Varzi would allow their mechanics to even lay a finger on the wheel) – time would flow in accordance to the race, furious up into the mountains and then coning into itself as they headed down to Rome before inching their way back up the Adriatic on endless stretches of narrow, unlit back roads. As always, Maggi – an old friend from Brescia – and I would cut across to Ancona, that city on the Adriatic which was roughly the half-way point of the race, and wait for them there.

The Alfa team had strung a red plastic tarpaulin across an abandoned stone farmhouse a mile south of Ancona that served as an awning beneath which tyres, fuel, and spare parts took up every conceivable inch of space. The fuel was stored in sizeable rusted barrels beneath the plastic canopy that slapped in the wind and rain. Vittorio Jano, in a gray flannel suit and rubber fedora, chain-smoked beside the drums. He glanced from beneath the awning when we arrived and offered a curt nod that warned me to stay well away from him and his men, and it wasn't long before, breaking over the horizon, three distinctive lights – forming a triangle – pierced the nebulous murk: unmistakably one of Jano's cars. The mechanics were snapped out of their reverie by Jano's barked commands. He edged out onto the road with a flailing flashlight, the mechanics grabbing tyres and fuel urns, preparing for the approaching Alfa whose headlights fell swiftly upon us. The local militia struggled to contain a small but passionate group of spectators across the narrow road who'd lit a bonfire that crackled stubbornly and forlornly in the rain.

Varzi and Canavesi. We could see their faces in the cockpit as the mud-soaked, oil-splattered Alfa pulled-up beneath the awning, guided there by Jano and his flashlight. Varzi killed his engine, lowered his goggles over his neck (where he wore an extra pair), found a smoke from his top pocket and slid it between his lips. Canavesi lit him up. In that light I saw Varzi's face; it glistened with the filthy lustre of a newborn. The mechanics frenetically drained fuel into a metal urn jammed into the Alfa's fuel tank. Varzi's face was drawn; smeared with oil and dirt except for around the eyes, he carried the appearance of a startled owl caught in the moonlight. Jano leaned toward him, and I strained to catch what he said.

'You're up by two minutes, Varzi. I need you to slow the pace. Nuvolari is second, Campari third – we have this race all sewn up. No need to push: Let's just get to Brescia in that order.'

Varzi swapped his goggles, sliding the new pair up and securing them before his eyes searched Jano's face in the murk. Varzi said something, words which Jano seemed to ignore for his attention was drawn instead to three mechanics fitting the final tyre onto the Alfa.

'Clear, clear!' Jano shouted, pushing the mechanics away from the dirty-red 6C. Varzi lifted one arm for the mechanic up-front to fire-up the engine. First gear was engaged, the clutch about to dip beneath one judicious foot when his head turned and I swear those eyes fell upon me. Just for the briefest of moments, enough for me to wonder, and then he was away, the engine smooth and free as he accelerated north up the coast for Rimini, his engine audible long after the red tail lights had been lost to us in the ocean of a moonless night.

◘

Finestrini watches the waiter walk away with our dirty plates. He sips his water, his eyes adrift.

'Go on, please,' I murmur, not wanting to break the spell.

Finestrini considers his stained napkin for a moment. 'Varzi had to skirt the coast all the way up the Adriatic to Venice before turning west while Maggi and I shot inland,' he says. 'By Rimini, where the midnight streets were speckled with fans waiting to cheer those red Alfas flash by on their lonely way to Brescia, Varzi had stabilized the lead. He powered through Cesena, Forlì, Faenza, Imola, then back to Bologna and onto the flatlands through Ferrara, Rovigo, and Padua with the bonfires giving off the glimmer of a false dawn, drawing ever closer to the tens of thousands – and the glory – that awaited him in Brescia.'

Finestrini gestures for the waiter to bring the bill before resting his eyes on me and continuing.

'It was somewhere between Feltre and Bassano del Grappa when Canavesi first saw them. He had turned in his seat and stared back into the chasing darkness streaking away at 180kph, straining his eyes into the horizon that was no further than the rear of the Alfa. He told me years later, he'd felt as if touched on the shoulder by a presence he could not describe. They were there; at first he had to blink as a man does on the ocean when gazing at a far-away beacon, but soon no straining of the eyes was required; it was no mirage, no imagining of a tired mind. He

24

turned away from them bewildered, about to speak of the three distinctive lights he'd seen back there chasing through the night, ripping through that fabric of nothingness when Varzi had said, "it's him. We're done for."

'Canavesi leaned back in that little seat of his and hung his head down. If they could see Nuvolari's headlights, it meant the Mantuan was maybe a minute behind, two at the most. Since he had started ten minutes after Varzi, he was up by no less than eight full minutes. How had this happened? The lights had appeared from nowhere: one moment there had been nothing back there but the certainty of the dark, the fulfilment of an empty night, and the next ... could Nuvolari really have been chasing them with his lights out, using only Varzi's brake-lights as a guide while he inexorably crept up toward them like a murderer? Could he really have raced through the rain in the pitch dark at over 180kph?'

'Is the legend true then?' I ask. 'Did Nuvolari really chase Varzi through the night without any headlights; did he actually do the run from Rimini to Feltre with no lights save those on Varzi's rear?'

'Guidotti said it happened that way.'

'And Nuvolari?'

'Never said a word about it. Not to me, anyway.'

'Not to anyone else, either,' I reply. 'But is it true?'

'Do you want it to be?'

I glance down at the Carry-Corder, at the white sound meter needle flipping about.

'On the flatlands of the Veneto, in an identical car to Nuvolari, Varzi knew the race was lost. On the run through Peschiera del Garda, on the shores of that wintry green lake and less than fifty miles out of Brescia, Nuvolari made his move, his coup de grâce, slipstreaming Varzi out of the fishing village that crept up the cragged shoreline before ambling past with a wave of his fist. Varzi raised an arm in acknowledgment. The battle was decided. Nuvolari had triumphed, entering Brescia at just past 7 a.m.'

My rucksack is on the floor. I lift it up onto my lap and unzip it. Within its bowels is a thick pink folder that I draw out and place onto the table. I find the cut-out article taken from the *Gazzetta* and slide it over the table. It is dated April 15th – Anno IX.

Finestrini looks at it, flattens it on the table amidst the breadcrumbs and reads.

'You make no mention in your race report,' I tell him, 'about Jano and Varzi. About the betrayal.'

Finestrini waits for the waiter to place two shot-size glasses of Limoncello before us along with the bill. He watches me insert four notes into the leather bill holder.

'Betrayal, Deutsch,' he tells me when the waiter steps away, 'is not a – how do you Americans put it? – a quantifiable phenomenon. It doesn't much matter whether Varzi was betrayed or not; what matters is that Varzi believed Jano had betrayed him. And what's more, he believed it was his own decency, his own chivalry that had exposed him to such treachery. Hadn't he fought for Nuvolari to get the Brilli-Peri drive? And hadn't he been the loyal team-player when he'd obeyed Jano's command to slow the pace of the race?'

'So the betrayal, you're suggesting, was self-inflicted?'

Finestrini downs the urine-coloured drink. 'You'll find that every betrayal – after the first one, when a man should learn his lesson – is self-inflicted.'

I glance down at my notes. 'Did you speak to Varzi? After the race?'

Finestrini licks his lips, tasting the sickly-sweet liquor. 'I didn't need to. I knew full well what he was thinking.' He places his hands on the table, preparing to lift himself to his feet.

'Varzi was after revenge.'

◙

I'd hardly been in my office five minutes when Cristoferi had stormed in waving the morning's *Corriere* in my face. Who are these people, he'd demanded. Was it true that this Varzi was a Count? And what of Tazio Nuvolari and his deal with the devil? This is the rivalry of a generation, he'd snarled, and you – pointing that rolled up *Corriere* at me – you have let our readers down, left them in the lurch, betrayed the sacred trust, the duty of the journalist.

'What duty?' I asked, unsure of whether I ought to stand for the abuse or simply remain seated there behind my desk.

'What we need,' he said, spanking my desk with the *Corriere*, 'is a background story on these men. Before the next race. When is that, by the way?'

'On Sunday.'

'Sunday? *Porco can*', that gives you less than two days. You're up against it, *figliolo*. I want it by Friday morning, 3,000 words, all wrapped-up nice and pretty like a sausage. Make me care for these men, Finestrini. Make me *love* them.'

Love, I thought, sitting at the schoolhouse desk in my apartment staring at the sheet of paper in the typewriter littered with letters – Christ almighty, love? The banker's-lamp shone its vaporous-green dullness over the clock that clipped toward 5 a.m. Words have a particular scent when they've been stamped out through the night – an odour inlaid with blood-warm ink and the smell of a man's sweating soul. I took a long sip of Merlot, sank back on my chair with the sound of the leather scraping familiarly under my weight, and lifted a fistful of typed pages from beside the typewriter.

◾

'Is this the one?' I ask him, producing a yellowed newspaper clipping from my bag.

He leans forward and accepts it. 'Why don't you read it to me,' he suggests, sitting back in his seat and throwing the clipping back on the table, 'and I'll get us a drink.'

"Motor-racing," I read, "is the only modern sport: Yes, like other sports it pits man against man and the spiteful and often willful spirit of Fortune, but it is, ultimately, man's vainglorious attempt at defeating that which he has created in his own image – by nature, both violent and fast – that defines our sport as modern. Motor-racing is the metaphor of our age. Life, death, and fate enmeshed in that most human belief of a better tomorrow despite the dead-sure knowledge that a machine has no pity, feels no remorse, and will kill the brave and the the good and the cowardly and the evil with equal indifference.

"We in Italy invented the automobile, both word and concept. It was in the 14th Century that the Siennese artist and engineer Simone Martini conceived of a 4-wheeled vehicle – powered by men – he dubbed an *auto* (from the Greek for "self") *mobile* (from the Latin for "to move"). It may have taken us a further three hundred years, but eventually we got around to translating Martini's fantasy into reality with the first motorized automobile, too. That honour falls, depending on your way of thinking, either to Murnigotti in 1876, or to Enrico Bernardi who, in 1880, affixed an internal combustion engine to his son's tricycle."

'Yes, yes,' says Finestrini, who'd summoned the waiter and now orders two Camparis. 'Cut to the chase, Deutsch,' he tells me. I scan the article and begin again.

"Varzi is disciplined and organized, shrewd and precise. He is, like Felice Nazzaro, the consummate professional. To see him drive is to witness the fluidity between man and machine that is a seamless metaphor of modernity. His method emboldens the future – scientific, methodical, devoid of emotion, focused solely on the result. Behind the wheel he is calmness personified, never phased, never rushed, always smooth, always soft. But where Achille Varzi is technique, Tazio Nuvolari remains – being his natural antithesis – pure reaction. The survivor of multiple shunts that would have seen a man of lesser providence dead (and a man of lesser fortitude retired), he has developed a tail-happy style in the tradition of Vincenzo Lancia and yet uniquely his own: His furious drifts allied to a consistently attacking demeanour does not capture, it is true, the spirit of the modern, but neither does it reflect back to the past despite his firm Catholic belief and traditional way of life: He is a force of nature, fearless and committed, a metaphor not of modernity, but of modern Italy."

'A tale of two men,' Finestrini tells me, 'one a champion, and one a hero.'

I scribble that line down. The windows dappled by viscous velvet curtains surrender nothing of the late afternoon outside, the light into which Finestrini merges pale and listless. 'Varzi's revenge,' I venture when Finestrini offers me a silent toast with his newly-arrived Campari, 'was that in Alessandria when he and

Nuvolari smashed into each other – '

'Partly, I suppose,' Finestrini concedes. 'But really, it was at the Targa that Varzi would have his pound of Jano's flesh.'

He sits back and folds his arms and legs and waits for my full attention.

I'd made the mistake of taking the night ferry from Genoa in May of that year and had arrived in Palermo with the dawn along with the full Alfa works team. Varzi's glazed P2 was in the process of being winched down from the boat onto a dock crammed with crates marked ALFA ROMEO MILANO, its wheels sagging in the damp air like talons, when I set about trying to find a taxi. The P2 was the only car that had travelled with us on the ferry, the rest having been dispatched to Sicily weeks earlier along with a skeleton crew of mechanics and test-drivers, and Varzi's decision, to run the P2 he'd used to win at Alessandria the weekend before and not the short wheel-based 1750 which had been gunning up and down the Madonie for a month, had apparently gone down about as well with Jano as my dinner had with me.

The taxi mounted the hills in the gathering day to the town of Cerda, and from my hotel room in the foothills of the purple-shrouded Madonie Mountains, out there on a terracotta-tiled terrace sipping on a warm Peroni, I sucked down lung fulls of warm, African air and considered the folly that was the Targa Florio.

Up here in Cerda all was spring and blooming, jade-like meadows lolling serenely beneath a sweet breeze dipping over carpets of wild flowers draped against a backdrop of silver saw-toothed peaks. I loved it up there despite being cut off from the teams and drivers and the rest of the international press corps down at the Termini Imerese hotel a few miles out of Palermo. I was comfortable there, away from the noise and bustle and damp heat of the coast, relaxed and warm on my terrace. Snow was still discernible on the Pizzo della Principessa, the highest peak of the Madonie, and it struck me that it was madness having a race here – I thought it then as I'd thought it when first I'd come to watch the race in '19 as an unemployed convalescing War-vet' on my forlorn way to Africa. That was the year Giulio Masetti had conquered the Madonie on the 108 kilometre layout that had run from Campofelice on the coast up into the mountains before doubling back through the Saracen-founded towns of Cefalù, Pollina, Castelbuono, Sclafani Bagni, Caltavuturo, and finally down to Cerda.

They'd done four laps then; this year, the race had been increased to five – 540 kilometres of exquisite folly. Vincenzo Florio's folly, the eccentric land-baron who'd first conceived of the race back in '06. That first event had been an epic thing that twisted through 148 kilometres of torturous roads and through villages that had never, until that day in the early spring, ever even seen a motor-car. It was a throwback to the pioneering days of grand prix racing that had come to an end with the 1903 Paris–Madrid massacre in which Marcel Renault and eight others had perished before they'd even reached the outskirts of Bordeaux. But that was France and this was Sicily, and here in the foothills of Africa, life was worth that little less.

Folly and madness, that was the Targa Florio alright. The roads up in the Madonie were nothing more than mule tracks twisting over ravines and craggy valleys suspended up there where only eagles dared to soar above fatal chasms, hungry wolves, and angst-ridden bandits. Masetti himself had taken me up for a practice run in '26 – I was then a few weeks into my career at the *Gazzetta* and still sharing an office with the 'horse guy', Bordoni – and he'd advised me to bring a warm coat despite the searing heat down in Palermo that hung about like a wet diaper. By the time we'd grasped the upper reaches of the Madonie, the rain had been falling as if we'd left Sicily entirely, a cold drizzle that had transformed the roads into trenches and stung our faces like wasp-bites. The turns up there had come relentlessly one after the other, and no one had ever counted – or agreed – as to their exact number. What the drivers could agree on was that they engaged second gear on the way up, third on the way down, and did nothing but steer this and react that way for hour upon hour as they threaded their cars between walls of frozen rock and gulleys of certain death.

The oldest existing race in the world, the Targa Florio, and each year the world's finest manufacturers came to Palermo with the spring to send out their cars and test-drivers into the heat, day after miserable day, searching for technical solutions for shredded tyres, smashed transmissions, cracked axles, sand-ruined engines, slaughtered wolves, and the occasional ransom demand for car, driver, or both.

I'd felt sick that day up in the Madonie with Masetti. I'd gone up with the intention of counting the turns, but the nausea had risen with us to the summit, and Masetti – testing a new suspension element – had refused to slow. Counting the turns was like counting the waves on an ocean as we tore back down toward the coast. Masetti had told me at the hotel that evening that in '21 his lead had been such that he'd spent the last lap counting the bends in an effort not to lose focus, and he'd got up to 1,205. Who knows, maybe he was doing the same in '26 when he went up and never came back down; they found him a day later in a ravine … what was left of him anyway.

'He went into the artichokes,' the locals had explained when the police came looking, and his number thirteen would never again appear on a car at the Targa. That was the year Bordino – riding along with Werner – had retired mid-race with his shirt drenched in vomit, and I'd since seen many of the greats pull out of the race feeling sick, dizzy and disorientated as they slalomed down those mountain roads. But for the drivers, each departing from Palermo every fifteen seconds, winning the Targa and the Mille Miglia was the Holy Grail of a career, and every year they and the works teams came to do battle against one another, but mostly against the Madonie.

It all made for great copy too for the press corps which arrived en masse in the first week of May, filing their hastily put-together stories: how Rudi Caracciola had camouflaged his German white Mercedes Italian-red after he'd been pelted with stones the first time he'd gone up into those mountains; how Campari had snapped the cable to his throttle only for a bandoleer to use the

SANDRO MARTINI

string from his instrument as a crude replacement chord while Campari sang *O Sole Mio*; how Elisabeth Junek had led the race in '28 in her blue Bugatti until, with four miserable miles left, her brakes had faded – she'd dominated the best in Europe that day, Divo, Campari, even Nuvolari.

Out there on my terrace I could track the path on which the cars would race into the shadows of the mountains, climbing up, ever up through hundreds of razor-sharp curves made slick by the donkey-crap that'd been ground into the earth for centuries. The eight kilometre straight that arrowed along the coast, the Retilineo di Bonfornello and its rows of grandstands, flags, officials, and fanfare I could just make out under the twinkling lights of Palermo when darkness fell upon me like an illness.

I slipped out my Moleskine notebook and balanced it on my knees to jot down ideas. Jano, I wrote, was under pressure this year from his board in Milan who'd tired of being ritually spanked at the Targa by Bugatti, winners of the last five editions. He'd come fully-armed with an all-star line-up – Campari, Nuvolari, and Varzi – and a new car, the short wheel-based 1750 that had dominated the Mille Miglia. And then Varzi had come along and stuck a wrench into the works: Varzi and his grand prix P2. The car, admittedly, was up 50bhp on the 1750s, but Jano was right – to take a grand prix car up into the Madonie was madness, the kind that one readily found at the Targa; it was as if a fever claimed these men the moment they set foot on the island, to take part in this Sicilian race that was a heady narcotic of wine, fear, sunshine, and paranoia.

I spent a restful evening writing my copy for Cristoferi down in the hotel restaurant eating sausages and eggs before turning in early. The next morning saw me head down the mountain to Palermo and the start–finish line where loudspeakers pushed out pulsating Arab-flavored folk music into the damp, humid air. By the time I'd arrived back at the hotel with the night – having, in my excitement, foregone watching the race from Cerda for the first time since '26 – I was armed with a splendid story that I simply had to set down immediately on paper, abandoning all thoughts of dinner in my haste to file what was a stirring chapter in Varzi's year of infamy.

◼

Finestrini sips on his Campari, eyes milky in the musky shade of the hotel. I notice that my Carry-Corder has stopped recording, and I quickly flip the Philips C.90 cassette over as Finestrini observes with a smile playing on the edge of his lips.

'Varzi conquered the Madonie that day,' he says. 'It was madness, of course, just the craziest race. Chiron versus Varzi and no one else had a look-in, much to Jano's consternation. And then they embarked on that final lap, Varzi trailing Chiron by a few seconds as they went up into the mountains. Somewhere up there Varzi decided he needed to lighten the car, so he had Canavesi, his mechanic, rip off the spare wheel. In his haste, Canavesi managed to rupture the fuel tank. Chiron, meanwhile, had hired a local boy to ride as his mechanic – the mechanic wasn't needed except to comply with a technical regulation, and the kid was the lightest body he could find – and the boy had become violently ill. So there they were, Chiron with his mechanic unconscious on his lap, and Varzi running out of fuel, racing down the mountain towards the chequered flag in Palermo.

'On the run down from Cerda, Varzi ordered Canavesi to refuel the car. Which Canavesi did – while Varzi kept his foot down. Poor Canavesi was riding the back of that Alfa like Tom Mix, jerry-can in hand, and somehow he contrived to feed enough fuel into the tank to get them over the line. Unfortunately, he managed to spill the rest onto the exhaust which promptly ignited and then exploded.

'That Alfa,' Finestrini laughs at the thought, 'was like a comet, I swear; Canavesi was standing in the cockpit fighting the flames with his scat seat when they hit the Retilineo, Varzi all curled-up over the wheel with the wind and Canavesi the only things keeping that inferno at bay. They whizzed over the line mere seconds ahead of Chiron, by which time Varzi's clothes were on fire, *he* was on fire as he jumped out of the cockpit and ran about chased by his mechanics with buckets of water and blankets.

'What a scene, only at the Targa, I tell you. I fought my way through the mob toward Varzi, and by the time I got near him, he

33

was smoking his Lucky Strike with this manic grin on his face and his clothes still smoldering as if he'd just wandered out of hell, contemplating the burnt Alfa's chassis which resembled the white ribs of a carcass. As I got to his shoulder I saw Jano closing in.'

Finestrini lowers his glass and measures the distance between us with a hand. 'As close as you are from me, that's how close I was when Varzi accepted Jano's hand, Jano's praise. "That was," Jano said, "about the most astonishing thing I've ever seen." His face singed oil-black, Varzi's eyes, like fat white oysters, had settled on Jano. There he was at the peak of his career with the world's greatest race car designer and team in his thrall having just won the legendary Targa Florio in a way that was guaranteed to make front page news across the globe and what did Varzi do? He leaned forward and, loud enough for everyone crowded around him to hear, said, "I'm sorry about the car, Mr. Jano. I suppose it's a blessing I won't be driving for Alfa Romeo again."

'Just like that – cold as you like, no regrets. Turning away before Varzi's words had quite penetrated the layers of his distracted mind, Jano froze. I remember him turning back to Varzi who had, no doubt, planned for this moment since Brescia in April. I could see Jano chewing on his words, but whatever he saw there in Varzi's face silenced him like a stiletto to the heart.'

'Revenge,' I murmur.

Finestrini rotates his Campari on its coaster and considers the Carry-Corder microphone before him. 'You know, I don't think that it was about that in the end.' He watches me light a cigarette. 'It may have started like that, but it ended simply as a good old-fashioned,' he gestures upwards with his middle-finger. 'You understand?'

'Varzi left the team after that race, yes?'

'Yes.'

'And went on to win the Italian Championship.'

Finestrini nods. 'In a Maserati, the 26M that Alfieri Maserati had designed for the new formula introduced in 1930. It was an evil car, that one. Maserati was pretty much just a tuning-shop in Bologna until Varzi put them on the map by manhandling that car all year. Anyway, after Monza, Varzi cleaned-up at the Coppa

Acerbo in Pescara, and then secured the championship with another win at San Sebastian in Spain. It was there that I asked him for a quote for the *Gazzetta* – '

' "Jano is served", ' I interject.

'Yes, exactly. Jano is served. But Varzi knew which way the wind was blowing. Maserati had lucked onto a winning car for 1930, what with Jano's P2 now half a decade old and Bugatti still running their ancient T35s. By 1931, though, Jano had developed the world's first single-seater, and Bugatti had the T54, both of which promised to consign the Maserati 26M to the scrapheap. Alfieri designed the V4 in response, but it was an abortion, and Varzi, ever the shrewd professional, secured himself a works drive with Bugatti for '31. But you see, that's what it was like with Varzi: he liked the game. Winning, for Varzi, was rarely about himself, it was about making others aware of their own loss, their own failure – I think that motivated him more than his own triumphs.'

'How do you mean exactly?'

I remember Cristoferi was shouting, 'That damned Varzi, he's signed for the French.' He looked at me then, perhaps to see if I was suitably outraged as I cowered behind my desk.

'The bloody *French*, Finestrini.' I was about to remind him that Bugatti was himself an Italian ex-pat from Milan, but Cristoferi had found his rhythm now, slapping a series of typed pages onto my uncluttered and shamefully clean desk. 'It's a loss of faith for Varzi to have signed for Bugatti – for foreigners. This is a man who places his own interests above that of his team – above that of his nation. He's not a patriot, he's an individualist, and I will not give this bastard one square inch in my 'paper, do you understand me?'

'It's January,' I said, mesmerized by the speed of Cristoferi's fingers tearing my profile of Bugatti into so much confetti, 'stories don't exactly fall from the trees.'

The man's pale blue eyes lifted to my face. 'Was that a metaphor?'

I blinked.

'Focus on Tazio Nuvolari,' he said, my tattered words falling like rain to the linoleum floor. 'Focus on Italy.'

Patriotism: La patria. Sitting on my desk that morning was the *Gazzetta*'s edited style sheet along with a crisp memo from the Ministry of Propaganda via the editorial department stating that all names appearing in print had, from this week on, to be Italianized. Not, the memo reiterated, *italicized*.

It took three phone-calls to persuade Nuvolari to allow me into his villa on the Viale Delle Rimembranze in Mantua for what I described as a profile on 'Italy's best-loved sportsman'. Nuvolari, unconvinced, had put me on to his wife Carolina. She came across as direct and confrontational, but she'd eventually consented. Three days later, in his home, I realized why he'd been so reluctant. I found myself grinding through one boring day after the next surrounded by the most tedious domestic bliss: Cycling was about the only subject – outside of motor-racing – that held any interest for Tazio, his uncle having been a semi-professional in the early years of the century (he showed me a sepia photograph of the man that he carried in his brown leather wallet, along with photos of his wife, children, and, naturally, an Italian flag).

Other than that, the man was a sensitive and ridiculously patient father, hopelessly sentimental husband, patriotic citizen, bone-deep Catholic, and totally content in the cradle of a family who loved and cherished his presence. It couldn't have been worse, and I was soon skulking about the immaculate villa desperate for any shred of a story.

By the end of February, I'd written the profile, and it numbered two hundred words, half of which were synonyms for warrior, patriot, and patria, and the other hundred comprised of a brief conversation we'd had one morning over breakfast when I'd asked him, 'Tazio, it's always said about you that you desire nothing more than dying in a racecar.'

'What of it?' he'd asked with his long face staring down distractedly at the morning's *Gazzetta*.

'Well, I don't understand – I mean, knowing this, how do you even get into a racecar? If that's your destiny?'

He'd looked up at me with a deep frown. 'And you, do you think you will die in bed?'

I acknowledged that there was a high probability of that.

'And yet,' he said, returning to his 'paper, 'you climb into bed every night. That seems far more courageous than what I do – at least I have some form of control over my racecar.'

Nuvolari was convinced fresh air (no matter how bloody fresh) was crucial to his fitness – and one afternoon, on the terrace of a restaurant on the shores of the half-frozen Garda lake, a crowd had begun to assemble about us. The throng gradually swelled to hundreds, all these strange faces milling about us in a wretched hush and every single one staring shamelessly at Tazio Nuvolari. They didn't speak, they didn't address him – they just stood there and gawked. None asked for an autograph, content, it appeared, just to be close to him, almost as if here was some form of religious icon. Nuvolari was oblivious to it all, just went on talking about this and that, nibbling away at his fish as if the crowd didn't exist, focused entirely on the plate of fish-bones discarded at his elbow.

That whole scene had proven instrumental to the story I handed in to Cristoferi, written mostly on the train back to Milan, titled, 'The Ancient Face of Modern Italy: Tazio Nuvolari'. I'd found my angle. Nuvolari, I wrote, was Fascist Italy's talisman.

◼

'How did he react to that?' I ask.

Finestrini fixes me a lengthy stare. 'There was no shame in it,' he tells me, slowly placing his glass on the table. 'Not then, and not for Nuvolari. Not for any of us involved in motor racing. You can ask Ferrari about that.'

'Tell me about him, about Enzo Ferrari … you knew him too, didn't you?'

Finestrini smiles and casts a weary eye on the Carry-Corder. 'Ferrari,' he says, 'was a natural.'

'A natural?'

'A natural bastard,' he says laughing. 'The most skilled bastard I ever met. He created a legend out of a mudfield because he is the coldest son of a bitch you will ever meet.'

'What do you mean by that?'

◉

I next caught up with Ferrari in Trieste, I think it was.

'Finestrini,' he said, rising to shake my hand. 'I hear Nuvolari's taking you up today, is that right?' said Ferrari. He nodded his head at the Stelvio Pass that rose into a frozen dawn.

Nuvolari was standing beneath a makeshift awning that hung from the back of the fuel truck amidst Engelbert tyres and tools, laughing along with Baconin Borzacchini, a young, good-looking lad wearing a black beret who was having his arm repeatedly punched by Campari. Borzacchini was, I deduced, yet again the willing victim of a Campari joke. Despite his almost painful shyness, though, Borzacchini held the world record for the flying mile achieved in a Maserati back in '29. He was also the only driver who'd never consented to an interview for the *Gazzetta*.

'You know,' Ferrari led me away from the rattling shards of engine with an elbow wrapped intimately about mine, 'I did a run with Nuvolari at the Circuito Tre Province in Bagni di Poretta – you know the track, right?' I nodded. 'I shat myself, Finestrini.' Ferrari grabbed my elbow tighter and offered me a staid look.

'That man,' he jutted his jaw at Nuvolari who was now standing over the 8C with the mechanic Compagnoli, 'was born without fear. He races for Ferrari like the Alpini fought for Italy, you understand? For the homeland, for freedom.' He waited for me to nod before adding, 'you should write that down, you should quote me'. We stepped back to the Alfa, squat and long and as crimson as the rising sun. Nuvolari had climbed in by now and was waiting impatiently with his tongue stuck out of the side of his mouth, his head titled as he listened to the engine respond to his nervous foot. Borzacchini was squatting beside the car pointing something out when I stepped beside him.

'Finestrini,' Nuvolari said, patting the seat beside him, 'climb in, *forza* – I have some news for your comic strip.'

Borzacchini accepted my hand and shook it weakly, smiling a timid hullo. An awkward man he was, seemingly oblivious to his good looks or to the fact that he was one of the top race drivers in the world.

'Borzacchini over here,' Nuvolari was saying, and I noticed Borzacchini visibly cringe, 'has gone and changed his name.' Borzacchini's face registered a combination of shame, embarrassment and fright. 'You know where he got his name from, right?' Nuvolari continued. 'You know the origin of *Baconin?*'

I shook my head not really listening, my attention drawn to that minuscule 'mechanic's seat' beside Nuvolari. How, I wondered, did anyone survive a journey on that scat seat bolted to the metal floor no more than eight inches wide? 'No,' I said eventually, looking down at Nuvolari who was staring up at me with an expression that seemed curiously mystified.

'From the Russian, Mikhail Bukanin. The *communist,*' he added, and I noticed Borzacchini's cheeks burn crimson. 'Isn't that right, comrade Baconin?'

Borzacchini stared at me with wide, pleading eyes. 'Christ,' he whispered, 'he wasn't a communist.' His voice was almost pleading. 'He was an-an-anarchist.'

'There,' said Nuvolari, 'that's even worse, isn't it, Finestrini? Which do we hate more, anarchists or communists?' He pointed at a gap beneath the dash' and the metal floor through which I was meant to slide my legs. 'Why aren't you writing this down? This is news!'

'Fucking hell,' whispered Borzacchini, 'you'll have m-m-me shot Tazio!'

'Shot?' Nuvolari patted the dogseat beside him with a hint of impatience. 'Who would shoot you, Borza', now that you've changed your name and dispensed with your Russian forefathers?'

'Changed it to what?' I asked, one foot inside the cockpit as if I were testing the temperature of a bathtub.

'Mario,' whispered Borzacchini, face down and staring at his calf-leather driving shoes. 'Mario Um-Umberto.'

Nuvolari broke into a howl of laughter. I was in the car by then, the engine vibrating under my buttocks. Seated lower than

Nuvolari, I could see down beneath the wheel to where his foot engaged the clutch. With the engine balanced and still laughing, he glanced at me with a curious expression.

'So, you ready?' Whatever reply I croaked was drowned by an engine that rose and peaked at 4000rpm before he dumped the clutch and left my head behind along with half my soul. We tore off into a bracing cold morning with me clinging onto a worn leather cord for grim life. The chassis was stiff, and I could feel every bump punching my kidneys – how the hell, I wondered, did Compagnoli sit like this for 1,000 miles? By the time we'd come out of that first turn, my question was answered: He had no time to think about his discomfort, nor anything else except to say his prayers. 'Sweet God sweet Jesus Mother of God … '

The night before, I'd studied the monumental Stelvio Pass on a topographic map, had sat there with a whisky counting the sixty hairpin turns and endless jagged switchbacks rising 3,000 metres into the Eastern Alps, and as we headed up, I began counting off the bends, counting them off as a man does bullets fired at him from a six-shooter. Nuvolari was a study in focus and determination, his hands twisted about the wheel held close to his chest like a wrench, for that grip was all that kept him from being thrown out of the cockpit, his legs stretched down below it manipulating the pedals with jarring thuds.

He was a twisted, fully-occupied halo of energy, the 8C a part of his being, dominated, tamed, and disposed to his commands. Thrown this way and that, my shoulders, knees and arms crashed about in the tight confines, the pain postponed by the rushing adrenaline. They say that when a man's heart-rate reaches 170bpm, the middle brain – that ancient lump of unevolved brain-scrap – takes over, and man reverts to beast, no smarter than a dog. I realized, as Nuvolari locked-up brakes into an urgent scrappy right-hander with the frozen day yawning before us in the chasm of a thousand metre drop, that dogs prayed far more than I'd ever given them credit for. It was clear he was operating in a time-warp, his mind perceiving, experiencing time in a different way than I.

To me it was all a blur, his feet and hands operating levers and turning the wheel in a furious rhythm until suddenly we were out of the turn with the rear snapping away impetuously, inches from going over into the crevasse. I was still thinking about screaming when that long face turned to me in a toothy grin. '*Ola*,' he said, correcting the power slide with one casual tug, 'I forgot about that one!'

'Bloody hell,' I shouted above the din of the engine that screamed its torment at 5600rpm, 'there are thirty-four turns left! Do you want me to count them off for you?'

He was still laughing when we entered a terrifyingly quick section of switchbacks, left, right, left, right again; with swift, confident tugs of the wheel, Nuvolari, all rhythm, danced his way into the turns to the tune of screeching tyres, and I noticed how tranquil he was when the car entered into a slide: his reaction to the car's loss of balance was early, correcting almost before the tyres lost grip.

'I read that polemic you wrote, about Varzi and his patriotic duty. Finestrini. Varzi is a sensitive soul,' he shouted on full counter-lock, 'you need to be careful with that shit.' He glanced over at me with the car balanced in a neat four wheel drift.

'You're telling *me* to be careful?' I shouted back.

Nuvolari laughed at that and roared on into the dawn.

◘

'These men,' Finestrini tells me, 'were intoxicated by speed, and I saw many overcome by that senseless joy spreading through their hearts and giving them the wings of angels until it was clear they were about to fall. And yet they couldn't turn from it; it was like morphine, the addiction always demanded more, ever faster until they were devoured.

'Guys like Nuvolari, war-veterans, they needed the adrenaline junk like other survivors needed silence, a physical need, a rage of the spirit stilled only by the wind slapping their empty heads about at top speed. Men like this drove a car not to their own paltry human limits, but to the car's mechanical limits.' He glances at his expensive wrist-watch. 'I think maybe it's time for a walk, Deutsch,' he announces, standing slowly. I follow him toward the

41

lobby mentally checking all my belongings – jetlag and amnesia. The waiter has vanished and we are, I realize, completely alone in the wet light.

'They'll put the drinks on your room,' he says when we reach the lobby, our footsteps echoing vainly in the vast emptiness of the espresso-coloured marble-expanse.

From a coat rack Finestrini drags a gray ankle-length coat and accepts my aid when he slips his arms through the rough fabric. We step out of the hotel onto the promenade lapping beside the Laguna Veneta. Venice sits there across the oily channel under a halo of light that plays on the dark waters of the lagoon in the early evening, cold on my flesh as I button-up my parka and stride alongside the old man. Finestrini stares out at a gondola gliding over the lagoon below us, a tiny red light suspended on its black silhouette, a coffin drifting into the netherworld somewhere south of the isle of La Giudecca. He considers the lagoon and the sliver of island in the frigid dusk.

'Were you ever,' I ask, 'uncomfortable with what you wrote?'

'I'm sorry?'

'Glorifying fascism – by making drivers out to be political symbols.'

'In Italy, in 1931,' he says, his eyes drawn to the lit campanile of San Giorgio Maggiore, 'nothing was political because everything was political. In '28, like every other journalist, I'd made my moral bed when I chose the Party over exile. As a reward, I got to keep working, and I got to write about and befriend the greats of that era.' He slows his stride and looks at me for a moment. 'The credo of Fascism, Mussolini said, was heroism, and Nuvolari was the perfect embodiment of this. The Futurists, like the Fascists, were obsessed with bloodshed, with the inhumanity of the machine. And what could demonstrate the dazzling potential of that savagery more absolutely than a fearless man hurtling through life in a metal bathtub sloshing with gasoline? In motor racing, Fascism had found its natural expression. Speed, violence, and the machine allied to the heroic superman charging through history for nothing other than the glory of the nation. And it was my place to bring this history to life on Monday mornings in the summers before it all ended in annihilation. For history is only created, isn't it, when a man writes of it.' Finestrini pinches his nose, inspects the tips of his fingers and shivers in the cold as a mist hovers spectrally an inch above the black grave of the Laguna Veneta. 'Bordoni once told me that we journalists taught people not how to live as Fascists, but how to die as Fascists.'

'And a lot of these drivers did die. Nearly every race.'

'They died gloriously. Because in the end, death isn't news, is it? We're all dying. It's how you die that matters, Deutsch,' he tells me. 'And sometimes, where.'

'I don't understand.'

'Better to die in the Targa than in some pisshole town in Switzerland is what I mean. And there were plenty who did just that; I remember the Targa of 1931…'

◉

Sicily had been hit by a week of ferocious storms that had washed away roads and bridges up in the Madonie, forcing Vincenzo Florio to alter the course of the circuit. He had reverted back to the original route (the Grande Madonie) that had been used until 1911. It was a larger circuit, but one that cut out many of the mountain passes and ran 148 kilometres, forty longer than the track on which Varzi had triumphed the year before.

This natural catastrophe had come as somewhat of a surprise to me. Up in Milan, the only natural disasters we were accustomed to reading about were those hungry storms that rolled across America's dust-bowl. As a consequence, Bugatti had decided against sending a works team to the Targa because the nature of the Grande Madonie heavily favored the more powerful Alfas and Maseratis. With the race thrown into chaos, I decided to head over to the Imerese Hotel down in Palermo, where I sat in the plush lobby with a map of Sicily spread on the table before me, tracing out the new route with a pencil. The drivers were coming and going – Campari led by his belly, Borzacchini and that faded cowhide briefcase of his, Caracciola in a guarded conversation with Mercedes' racing chief Alfred Neubauer, and just as I was about to sip my cappuccino, I noticed a familiar figure walking towards me. It was Varzi, accompanied by a thin, short man in a white three-piece suit.

'Ciao, Finestrini. This is Viganò,' Varzi said, indicating the man beside him. 'My secretary.'

I nodded, he nodded, and Varzi nodded him away.

'I'm surprised to see you here,' I said, standing and holding out my hand. 'Have you come to watch the race?'

'Watch? Who watches races? No, Finestrini, I'm here to race. And to win.'

'I don't understand. I thought Bugatti had pulled out?'

Viganò was waving a set of keys from the reception desk.

'I have to go, Finestrini,' said Varzi. 'See you at the race, eh?'

I watched the two men stride into the elevator. As the bronze doors were about to meet, Varzi lifted his head and fixed me, I was almost sure, with an amused smirk.

My calls to Molsheim and Bugatti HQ went unanswered. When I called up to Jano's room, he had little to offer other than a diatribe that lasted ten minutes. 'That cretin Ferrari can't win a race with my car – and you know why? Because he's decided to piss about with the engine, him and that idiot Bazzi – I've told them, if they want to win the Targa, they'd better stick some mudguards on that 8C, it'll be like a mudslide this year up in the Madonie, but will they listen? Talking to those two is like spanking a bloody drum!'

As for Louis Chiron, Varzi's team-mate at Bugatti, he was at his apartment in Paris with his lover Baby Hoffman. She answered the phone and informed me that Bugatti's race-team boss Meo Constantini had dined with them the night before and had no plans to travel to Palermo. The desk-clerk, meanwhile, assured me that he had no Bugatti personnel or drivers booked in at the Imerese aside from Achille Varzi in room 110, and he wasn't accepting any calls.

I had a story burning in my gut with no confirmation and no leads – rather like suspecting one's lover is playing the field – but I'd been a journalist long enough to know where to sniff out the truth, fabricated or otherwise: the nearest swanky hotel bar.

I'd hardly ordered a whisky when a foreign voice drawled, 'Ah, speak of the devil!' It belonged to a flush-faced guy in a creased linen suit.

'Bradley,' he announced, offering me his clammy hand, 'we met in Belfast in '24 after the T.T. You do remember of course, don't you Minestroni?'

'But of course,' I said, shaking the hand distastefully. 'How charming to meet you again.'

'Yes, isn't it just?' He grabbed the stool next to mine and climbed on it as if he were scaling a peak. My thoughts flew back to 1924 when Varzi had entered the oldest bike-race in the world, the T.T. He was riding his DOT 350, winning his class comfortably when, at Signpost, he had drifted out to find the narrowed exit obstructed by a fallen rider. The man was attempting to right himself when Varzi had shot out of the blind bend committed to his line. In that instant he was left with two options: slam into the stricken rider or find a way to avoid him. A simple decision – except that avoidance meant rotating his bike into a stone wall on the outside of the bend. His decision, I'd always maintained, was an indication of what lay dormant in Varzi's core: he had thrown the DOT into the wall, over which he was launched into an uncertain destiny. The marshals eventually found him sitting under a tree, surrounded by a cloud of cigarette smoke, with a splintered cheekbone and a few cracked ribs.

'I just had a chat with your man,' Bradley said, bringing me back to the present.

'My man?'

'Varzi, old boy, Varzi. Your man, yes?'

'Ah.'

'Yes. The crazy bastard has entered the Targa as a privateer, brought his own Bugatti for the occasion, painted Italian red he tells me.'

I sipped my whisky. 'Buy you one, Bradley?'

'Go on then, be a sport and make it a double. So who do you reckon's the best, eh? I heard you were the one who coined that wonderful phrase, is it true?'

'I'm sorry?'

45

'You said, "Caracciola will tell you he's the best; Varzi no doubt thinks he's the best; Tazio, however, *knows* he's the best". Was that you? Damn good, I'll grant you.' He came in closer, leading with his breath. 'I read that piece you wrote on Nazzaro – needless to say, I lifted most of it for *Auto Week*.' He watched the barman pour him the golden nectar with oily, red eyes. 'Listen, old boy, I have a favour to ask you … '

Auto Week had sent Bradley to the Targa to write a profile on Tazio Nuvolari, but he was having a hard time getting the Italian to meet him, much less consent to an interview. 'What I really need,' Bradley admitted after another round of drinks, 'is for Nuvolari to take me up into the Madonie with him.'

I pumped him for as much information on Varzi as I could. Varzi, I learnt, had paid for a dozen local men to operate as his 'team' for the race, and he'd personally spent the week training them up in Castelbuono where he'd been holed up. He'd been running the Bugatti in secret too, in the evenings, and wasn't it fantastic, Bradley said, how the roads and signs had all been painted with large VV Varzi and VV Nivola, and was it true the locals would throw flowers at the drivers during the race from their apartments, and he'd talked half my ear off by the time I'd dragged him to the lobby and called Nuvolari's room. It took five minutes to impress upon Nuvolari the commercial benefits of an international reputation before he consented to taking Bradley up into the mountains.

'Tell him I'll call on him in his room,' he said, sounding bored at the idea.

Bradley shook my hand, giving me his best impersonation of a smile. 'You know, Varzi gave me quite a droll quote when we spoke this afternoon. "Nuvolari is the boldest – the most skillful – madman of us all".'

Typical Varzi, I thought, leaving Bradley to return to the bar while I headed for my room. I spent a listless evening writing out the story that appeared in Saturday's *Gazzetta*, a copy of which was being crumpled in Varzi's fist when I came down to breakfast the next morning. He was sitting in the hotel lobby with his secretary Viganò and with Bradley; the Englishman was yawning into a cup of tea and frothy milk. Viganò … who could have known then what destiny had planned for the pair of us?

'Finestrini,' Varzi called, his voice like that of a schoolmaster, 'come join us.' He placed the *Gazzetta* on the table, and I could see the headline of my story proclaiming: "Varzi, Alone, Challenges the Might of Italy".

'This is Mr. Bradley,' he said as I sat down, 'another foreigner, like me.'

Bradley cast his bloodshot eyes in my direction and groaned. Between his elbows was a plate of eggs and salami which Varzi watched him eat with a faint air of disgust.

'Nuvolari called on me last night,' Bradley said between bites.

'Did he take you up into the Madonie?' I asked, all too aware of Varzi's intense gaze.

Bradley wiped food from his lips with the back of his hand. 'All the way up, Minestrini. But that's not the issue.'

'I'm sorry?'

'The question, dear boy, is why the bloody hell did he take me up at two in the morning.'

'Two *a.m.*? Did you ask him?'

Bradley, with one hand shovelling food into his mouth, slipped out a notebook from his mud-stained white jacket and flipped through the pages. 'I quote: "Sicily is full of bandits – imagine how much they could get for the world's greatest racing driver".'

'Imagine,' said Varzi, trying to catch my eye. 'How much do you think the world's greatest man would be worth if he were kidnapped by bandits, Minestrini?'

I avoided the question by glancing about for a waiter. 'So how was your drive anyway, Bradley?'

'Haven't a clue, old chap. It was pitch black up there, even if I had kept my eyes open.'

■

'I watched that race from the terrace of my hotel room,' Finestrini says. 'I remember, like it was yesterday, watching Varzi buzz past in a whirlpool of black dust and sand, chased by the three *fratellini*,

SANDRO MARTINI

Nuvolari, Campari, and Borzacchini, all of them racing up into the Madonie for one final lap and separated by seconds. It was here in Cerda that the Alfa team had set up their pit for that year's race, and I watched an unusually animated Jano signal frantically to Nuvolari as he roared past. I couldn't see what he was trying to convey with those anxiously gesticulating hands of his, but I could well imagine, for up in the Madonie, a big, ominous rain cloud had descended over the peaks, and when it burst, the sodden roads were quickly transformed into impenetrable rivers of mud.

'Thirteen drivers raced up the mountain on that last lap, but only six came back down. Biondetti in his Maserati, Dreyfus, and Emilio Romano all went off, and were lucky to have come back down alive. Up there in the Madonie, Varzi struggled to keep a grip on his grand prix Bugatti, and to add to his woes, vast amounts of mud was being flung into his cockpit. His plight became so desperate that he was forced to throw off his goggles to keep going, his eyes caked in the stuff, his feet slipping off the filth-laden pedals.

'It was the mud that sealed Varzi's fate. After nearly nine hours of racing, he could no longer respond to the chasing pack of Alfas behind him, each one equipped with a humble device that would prove to be crucial: mudguards. A simple oversight on Varzi's part ultimately decided the Targa Florio that year. First Nuvolari, then Borzacchini passed him on their way down to Cerda. And that's how they finished down in Palermo: Nuvolari, Borzacchini, Varzi, Campari.

'Varzi, you know, had taken on the entire might of the state-subsidized Alfa-Romeo team and had come within an hour of beating them. Had the storm held off for twenty minutes, victory would have been his. Instead, his Bugatti had been a tub full of mud when he'd entered Palermo, his face and body caked in the stuff. My stringer told me they were laughing on the streets of Palermo when Varzi climbed out of his cockpit oozing that foul-smelling muck.

'That evening, at the victory dinner in the Imerese's ballroom, Jano offered a toast to the absent Varzi. He could barely suppress the delight in his voice. "Last year Johnny Finestrini wrote that Varzi had devoured the Madonie. This year Varzi went one better. He actually *ate* the mountain!"'

Finestrini shakes his head. 'It was humiliating,' he tells me, staring out at the lagoon. 'He resembled the character from that Jewish legend, Deutsch, what's it called – '

'The Golem?'

'Yes, that's it. This was not just a defeat. This was humiliation. Varzi had come to Sicily convinced he could defeat the might of Alfa and Nuvolari on his own. And not only had he failed, he'd made a fool of himself in the bargain. You know he didn't win another race that season, except for Montlhèry, and that was only because Chiron did most of the driving that day.'

'So what do you think happened to Varzi after the Targa?'

Finestrini leads me back down the promenade toward the hotel. 'His life took over. What was it that Lukacs said? "Living the life of the bon vivant in the Grand Hotel on the edge of the abyss"? That was the generally held view, anyway. Personally, I've always believed he lost a part of himself up in the Madonie that day, and I don't think he ever quite found it again. Not really.'

'Or maybe,' I venture, 'he found something on his way down.'

'And what would that be, Deutsch?' Finestrini asks.

'Shame.'

We enter the lobby of the hotel. The desk clerk watches us step past him towards the elevator. 'Tomorrow,' Finestrini says to me, 'we can carry on if you like. We can start with Alfa Romeo's withdrawal from racing, and how Italy lost its Golden Generation in one afternoon.'

I accompany him to the elevator and we go up until I reach my floor. Finestrini offers me a tired smile as the doors shut, leaving me alone in a dim hallway. I step to my room, insert the key, push the door open and illuminate the room. On the bed I dump my rucksack and lie beside it in the buzzing static-hush. The number I know by heart, and I dial it on the phone.

'*Ja?* Hallo?'

'Hi, it's me.'

'Joe, finally, I've been sitting here all day waiting. Have you met him?'

'Yes.'

'And?'

'He is as you led me to expect.'

'He must be seventy now, if not a day. How does he look?'

'Old.'

'And have you asked him? Have you spoken about – '

'No, not yet. We're meeting again tomorrow.'

'Tomorrow.'

'Yes. Look, I haven't had the opportunity of asking him, about – about – '

'Yes, I understand, Joe.'

'How are you feeling?'

'Doctor Muller was here earlier. He says I'm still alive. Will you call me, as soon as you, as soon as he – '

'Of course.'

'Thank you. … You must be tired.'

'I am, yes, the flight was long.'

'You'll need your rest. Don't be drawn in by his, his – '

'I know. I won't … Goodnight.'

'Goodnight, Joe.'

PART TWO
THE BORA SCURA

We want to celebrate the man at the wheel, the ideal axis of which crosses the earth, itself hurled along the track of its orbit.

– The Futurist Manifesto, F. T. Marinetti, 1909

SIGNORI SENZA QUATRINI

L'Isola Del Lido, February 15th, 1968

The Bora scura had come in the night like a fever. The wind lashes against the windows of the hotel's bar in gusting claws of rage and rain, all somehow connected fibrously to my nerves that recoil in horror. Finestrini sits beside a window in the dining room, the fleshy curtains slit like a throat. Venice, across the choppy white-capped lagoon, feels unmoored from us now, a hollow city adrift on a sea of inky water whipped by the northern wind that carries with it the scent of rot. He has a boiled egg before him, Finestrini, the shell cockroaches on a napkin beside his hand, a glass of water held to his flaky lips when I pull up a seat and slide on in.

'You look tired, Deutsch,' he tells me.

I place an open notebook on the table between us. 'The wind,' I reply. His eyes stray to the notebook where I have jotted down a single name: Ciano. He quickly looks away and probes at his breakfast with a fork.

'The north wind,' he observes between bites, 'has never been kind to us. As a people we long for the south – despite our conviction that strength always comes from the north.'

I fiddle with my pen, not meeting his eyes. 'I was hoping to talk to you about Galeazzo Ciano.'

'I see. Why?'

I have the answer, I'd rehearsed it so often, but all that stammers from my mouth is, 'I need to … I mean, I'd like to … understand what impact Ciano had on your writing.'

Finestrini seems amused at my discomfort. 'Ciano had absolutely no influence on my writing. As you know, he was Mussolini's son-in-law; a gambler, a playboy, and as vain as a peacock. But during his stint as the Minister of Press and Propaganda, he never influenced anything I wrote.' Finestrini laughs gruffly. 'I was a motor-sport writer for God's sake.'

'Ciano did ask you to speak to Varzi and Nuvolari, didn't he? In early 1932?'

Finestrini is visibly tense when I look back up at him. Turning his pallid face away from me as I set the Carry-Corder to record, he stares out at the raging wind and slowly starts to speak.

◎

In the cold spring of 1932 I was still in Milan, having missed Varzi's season-opening win for Bugatti in Tunis. The prospect of meeting up with him – and the warmth of a Sunday afternoon on the Côte d'Azur – had me up late that night, anticipating the journey and the season to come. I'd exhausted myself that winter trying to avoid an incessantly choleric Cristoferi. One of these years, I kept thinking, the bastard was going to fire me in November or, worse still, force me to file Serie C1 football recaps. I could picture myself shivering on the touchline of some minor match in Pavia, and it was this prospect that had inspired me to write a preview of the '32 season for the *Gazzetta* in which I'd predicted yet another year of intense rivalry between Varzi and Nuvolari.

Who would triumph this season? Bugatti's new T54 had already proven itself as quick as winter testing had suggested while Jano's Alfa Monza was suffering birth pangs: Would Varzi be able to stretch his championship lead before Jano sorted the new Alfa and while the three *fratellini* fretted over their new team-mate Rudi

Caracciola, poached from Mercedes after their withdrawal from GP racing in the winter of '31?

Cristoferi had not said much when I'd filed the story: Still, I'd earned my crust, filled the back page, and a summer of racing lay ahead somewhere beyond my couch. The clock over the spent fireplace showed a little after 11pm.

'Who is it?' I enquired, standing some distance behind the locked door.

'We're from the ministry,' came the reply.

'I'm not in the habit of handing out donations at this time of night.'

'Ministry of the Press,' said a curt voice.

I opened the door. Two men stood on the threshold. By the look of them, I figured reading wasn't high on their hobby list – which, I suppose, made them the ideal demographic for the *Gazzetta*. I had them down as *squadristi* for sure, and my stomach clenched. It took a certain type of man to function at the Ministry of Propaganda, where a good beating always trumped a better argument.

'You're coming with us,' said one of the men, and I couldn't help but notice his bald, scarred head.

'Where?'

He pointed toward the ill-lit corridor. On his lapel, a pin marked him as a survivor of the Battle of Caporetto.

'Can I get my jacket?'

'This won't take long,' said the man's companion, a six foot blond guy with a menacing brow.

I stepped out of the apartment in my pyjamas and slippers. We avoided the elevator and headed down the stairs, the *squadristi's* boots slapping against the marble. Together we walked out into the chilly night. A huge black FIAT was lying in wait outside my palazzo, exhaling a wispy trail of smoke into the stillness. A tallish man, impeccably dressed in an ankle-length, flesh-coloured coat and black hat, eased himself out of the car. Even by the pale light of the nearby streetlamp, I could recognize the face of Galeazzo Ciano.

'Let's take a walk,' he said, brushing past me without a pause.

'I've just had the most contemptible dinner, and at my age it all tends to stick to my butt as if I'd literally glued the damn risotto on there.'

I fell in step with him, wondering if Edda – his wife and Mussolini's first and most beloved daughter – would really care all that much about his fat butt, but before I could ponder this any further, Ciano was lighting a cigarette and offering me one.

'From China,' he said when I bent over the trembling flame in his cupped hands. 'I became addicted while I was in Shanghai. Miserable place, Finestrini. The shit those people eat – *porco Dio.*'

So he knew my name. I felt a wave of panic wash over me.

'I was reading your column in the *Gazzetta* today,' he continued in a casual tone. 'Or, more to the point, I was instructed to do so.'

'Oh,' I said, taking a hesitant drag and meeting his dark eyes. He was a good-looking man in a cruel sort of way, his lips hovering on the edge of a smile.

'I've always believed our best writers to be sports writers. The purity of a sporting endeavour always seems to attract romantics – and motor-sport is an ideal substitute for war, don't you think?' My thoughts, I knew, were best kept to myself: He was working up to something, and all I could do was wait. I sensed his power instinctively, as a gazelle senses a lion's. This man, I knew, could end my life without hesitation or consequence. 'This weather is bloody miserable,' he said, stalling his walk to appraise my pyjamas with a frown. 'You must be looking forward to Monaco, yes? I ask because Il Duce has a personal request to make of you.'

'I – of me?' I fumbled for words, suddenly conscious of the tattered leather slippers on my feet.

'Yes, indeed,' he said, in a tone that almost sounded benevolent. 'Of you. I trust that you appreciate the urgency and importance of the matter, given that Il Duce has chosen you as an intermediary?'

'God yes,' I replied. 'Of course.' Ciano remained silent, so I hastily added: 'I'm honored to be of service to Il Duce in any way I can.'

'Of course you are, Finestrini. As we all are when called upon.' He turned from me and began walking back towards my palazzo. 'Il Duce believes the ongoing hostility between Varzi and Nuvolari to be – well, it just isn't seemly for our two top sportsmen to be involved in a so-called "blood feud". It doesn't reflect well on the Italian people, do you understand? It fulfils all the clichés of our friends to the north, and it shames us. We don't like to be shamed. Il Duce has asked that you intercede on his behalf; he wants you to enlighten those two imbeciles on the importance of national unity, of a united front against the common enemy. It's unacceptable for those two idiots to be fighting each other while the Germans win all the bloody races – like that halfwit Caracciola did at the Mille Miglia. Il Duce was enraged by that colossal fuck-up – did you know that he almost cancelled the race? A bloody German holding the Mussolini Cup, for God's sake! It was all I could do to persuade him not to cancel the race right then and there. Do I need to remind you, Finestrini, of how much the Italian motor industry owes to Il Duce's generosity?'

I shook my head with what I hoped was fervent passion.

'Precisely. Where I come from, we have a saying: "The only winner between two men is the whore".' We were at my building again; Ciano flipped his cigarette butt onto the sidewalk and crushed it underfoot. He snapped his fingers impatiently and the blond *squadrista* came forward, holding out an envelope. I reached out to accept it, but Ciano was quicker on the draw, snatching it with an admonishing click of his tongue.

'This letter,' he said, shaking it in my face, 'is from Il Duce himself.' He paused to let the importance of that fact sink in. 'You're to make sure those two cretins read it, do you understand me, Finestrini?'

I nodded, and he handed me the envelope bearing Mussolini's official seal.

'Il Duce expects, Finestrini. Do you understand?'

'Yes, of course.'

'You understand what is being asked of you?'

'Yes, *sir.* '

Ciano clapped me on the shoulder. 'Good man. Now you'd best get warm – nothing worse than catching a cold in April. My God, man, you northerners and your constitutions – you could at least have worn a coat!'

◘

The sound of the wind is an engine out there as it sweeps out over the frothy lagoon. 'I had the most ruinous cold during my weekend stay in Monaco. But that was the least of my problems.'

'Did you deliver the note then?'

'Oh yes,' Finestrini replies with a smile. 'Oh Lord yes.'

'What did it say?'

' "Put national honour before personal ambition: Fight for Italy's glory, not your own." Varzi read the whole letter out loud before tossing it in my face when I showed it to him at the bar in the Hermitage Hotel. "What does Nuvolari have to say about this?" he asked. "I haven't spoken to him yet," I confessed. "Well, go and convince that idiot then," Varzi had replied, incensed that I had come to see him first. "When he decides to let me win, I'll certainly put national glory before my own." '

'And what did Nuvolari say?' I ask.

'Pretty much the same thing, only there was a lot more swearing. It was an impossible situation, of course – Mussolini was essentially asking for one of them to let the other win, and that was never going to happen. I spent most of that weekend trying to plead my case, extolling the virtues of patria before finally breaking down and explaining that if Il Duce's request was denied, I would almost certainly get shipped off to Lipari Island for a protracted vacation alongside Malaparte.'

' "Good," was Varzi's sentiment. "It might improve that cold of yours." It got even worse when Alfa's consigliere, Giovannini, found out about the note. He raked me over the coals on the morning of the Grand Prix, standing over me with one finger wagging in my face. "If you ever pull a stunt like this again," he yelled, "I will personally guarantee that no one at Alfa will ever speak to you again. *No one!* Do you think those two give the smallest fuck about Mussolini or his fucking letters? They'll end up killing each other just to make their point! And then it'll be on your head – yours and that miserable prick Ciano's. All you've done is piss them off – you know Varzi! He's busy telling anyone who'll listen that Tazio needs state intervention to beat him, and as for Nuvolari – if he hears of it, you know he'll drive Varzi into a wall. What were you thinking, Finestrini?" '

'You must,' I tell Finestrini, 'have been relieved at the outcome of the race then.'

'I think you can say that, Deutsch,' he replies. 'The race was a straight fight between Nuvolari and Caracciola, and thank God for providence, my friend, because I later heard that Ciano had come to Monaco with Edda to personally report on the Varzi-Nuvolari situation. I went out of my way to get a photographer to snap a shot of them shaking hands before the start, and I begged Cristoferi to run the image in the *Gazzetta* with the caption: "Competition, friendship, national pride".'

I find a clipping in my file and slide it over to Finestrini. 'From *Auto Week*,' I clarify. 'From their race correspondent at Monaco in '32: he watched the race at Rascasse.'

Finestrini retrieves a pair of gold-rimmed spectacles from his blazer, and starts to read.

"Nuvolari   is talking to himself. Naturally, nothing can be heard above the noise of the exhaust, but his lips are moving, and one can imagine the full-throated words they are emitting. As the end of the race approaches, he becomes excited, hitting the side of the car with his right hand, gesticulating wildly – oblivious to everything that is happening in the outside world. His fuel supply is very low. Perhaps he is beseeching the Madonna to make it last till the end."

'Caracciola gifted Nuvolari that win,' Finestrini says, nodding at the words. 'Sat on Tazio's tail-pipe all afternoon and played the role of number two with his usual quiet dignity. It must have really gnawed at him, especially when the crowd cottoned on to what was happening and began hurling more than just abuse at the poor bastard. But Rudi didn't have much of a choice: Alfa was the only game in town that year. Not that it changed anything; when Alfa pulled out of grand prix racing and sold their race cars to Ferrari at the end of the year, Caracciola was yet again out of a job. But that's for another time.' Finestrini points at my bag there on the floor. 'Do you have the manuscript for your book in there?'

'A draft,' I acknowledge, glancing down at the pages within their pink folder.

'Why don't you show it to me?'

I look at his face. He shows no emotion, casually staring at me. I take a sip of the espresso; 'Perhaps another time,' I whisper, and to deflect my hesitation, I snap open the cassette-housing and fiddle with the cassette on the Carry-Corder.

'Bit secretive are we, Deutsch?' he asks. If he is mocking me, it does not reflect in his smiling face.

'Actually,' I reply, 'that does lead us nicely to Libya, 1933.'

'What does?'

'Secrets.'

Finestrini hunts my eyes down and laughs. 'There were certainly enough of those to go around in Libya, I'll give you that,' he admits sitting back in his chair with a cheerful smile.

It was a slow Tuesday in April of 1933. The *Corriere* lay open on my desk proclaiming that Italy was still strong. This was a reassuring thought, given that the *Gazzetta* had just laid off a dozen staff writers that morning. My column had survived, but this victory had come with a pay cut and a reduced word count. Still, I was grateful enough. As I sat at my desk revising my world-exclusive article on the upcoming Libyan Grand Prix, my thoughts wandered back to the genesis of this unlikely motor race.

Back in June 1932, I had been invited out to lunch by Egidio Sforza, the president of the Auto Club. Sforza and Galeazzo Ciano had come up with the idea of holding an international motor race in Libya – our place in the sun, as dear Benito never tired of telling us. Il Duce had had enough of Italians immigrating to the Americas. A great power, he believed, did not export its own people; they sent them, instead, to their colonies. The problem, however, was that Italy's poor saw nothing in Libya but more dirt and poverty, and so Ciano had decided that a world-class motor race in Tripoli would be a great advert in selling Libya's potential. According to Sforza, they had already found a number of financial backers, and this new racing track would be the fastest and most advanced circuit ever conceived. There was, however, one minor snag: how to attract the world's best drivers and teams to Libya?

'Finestrini,' he'd said, plying me with fine wine, 'you, the world's greatest motoring journalist, what would you suggest?'

'Money,' I'd replied.

Sforza had gone quiet as if embarrased. 'There is no money in Libya,' he'd explained patiently. 'Look, what we need is an angle, something that will make this race stand out so that no important driver or manufacturer would ever dream of missing it.'

I promised Sforza that I'd look into it, but the truth was obvious: the motor racing circus had even less interest in heading off to North Africa than the dirt farmers of Calabria. And that's how it would have ended, too, had it not been for an extraordinary event in September of 1932, when a local gang of *squadristi* had broken into the *Gazzetta*'s office hunting for my colleague Bordoni, who had dared to compare a local Party overseer to a horse's ass. Bordoni had sought refuge behind a printing press where they'd eventually found him all curled up and crying like a child. They'd forced him to drink a litre of raw castor oil before dragging him out to the street by his hair and beating him senseless. Bordoni had lain on the sidewalk for a long time before he'd crawled away into the dusk.

We never did see Bordoni again – but his sorry fate significantly improved my fortunes. Cristoferi had assigned me all his unfinished articles, including one on the Irish Sweepstakes, and it was while reading through his notes on that horse race that I had stumbled upon the idea that would save the Libyan Grand Prix. Sforza had been delighted by my idea, and he had set my plan in motion with the help of Italy's Minister of Colonial Affairs, Emilio De Bono.

Two months later, it was announced that the Libyan state would be making tens of millions of lottery tickets available until April 1933. The official draw would then select thirty-three winning tickets, each corresponding to one of the thirty-three drivers entered for the Libyan Grand Prix on May 7, 1933. I had helped turn this improbable race into a reality.

But before Libya, there was the Monaco Grand Prix. I had missed Rudi Caracciola's massive shunt during Thursday's practice while debuting with his own team, the Scuderia CC, that he'd founded with his friend, Louis Chiron. His Alfa had apparently pinched its rear-brakes out of the tunnel and hammered into the stone wall down by the promenade. It was still unclear whether Caracciola had broken his legs or his hips, but from what Varzi had told me over the phone, it seemed that Rudi's career was pretty much done. There was talk of infection, amputation, and even death.

By the time I arrived at Casino Square that Sunday, the Monaco Grand Prix was already an hour in, and the large crowd was enraptured by a ferocious contest of wills between Achille Varzi's sky-blue Bugatti T54 and Tazio Nuvolari's 2.3-litre Alfa Monza.

I had arranged to meet with Bradley from *Auto Week* and with Mr. Noghes, the race's founder, in the delightful gardens of the Hotel de Paris. Noghes had mastered the art of ensuring a constant supply of champagne, and I accepted a chilled glass before ambling over to Bradley who was standing none too confidently in the shade of a palm tree.

'About time you showed up, old sport,' he said. 'Been busy with the press then?'

'I'm sorry?' I asked, watching him down a glass of champagne.

'Your scoop – I read it in this morning's *Gazzetta*. How fabulous for the Libyans. So where've you been?'

'With Caracciola,' I replied.

Noghes glanced at me through the pink sunshine. 'How is he?' he asked, sipping his chilled champagne. 'Have they amputated?'

I thought of telling them about his drugged up state, about his wife Charly, crying silently beside his bed. Instead I said: 'Professor Putti just arrived from Bologna as I left.'

I watched Nuvolari and Varzi roar past us on the turn just beyond the hotel garden. 'So what did I miss?'

'What did you miss?' Bradley downed another glass of champagne with the swiftness of an expert. 'Only the best race of the decade.'

I listened as Bradley slurred his way through the story of the first thirty laps. Up and down the track, I could see the candy-striped kiosks – Pari Mutuels – where spectators were placing their bets. Given the wide gap between the first two drivers and the rest of the field (almost a full minute), I doubted the bookies were seeing a lot of action on any other drivers but Varzi and Nuvolari. From the balconies of the modern apartments that flanked the track curling down past the gated nightclubs to the rocky hillside below the Palace of the Grimaldis (the only place where spectators could view the race – albeit with binoculars – for free), from row boats on the harbour at La Condamine to the rooftops of the hotels down by the sea, people stood transfixed by the spectacle served up by our two Italian champions.

After a few too many glasses of champagne, I gladly accepted Bradley's invitation to tour the track. We started to walk down the hill, past the nightclubs and towards the train station. It took us perhaps ten minutes, and in that time Varzi and Nuvolari had raced past us four times, Nuvolari leading for three laps, Varzi for one. All around us – anywhere where they could build and where an access road could take the public – the organizers had set up temporary bleachers. The Monaco Grand Prix was often called the race of a thousand turns, and ever since its debut in 1929, the fans had complained of a lack of overtaking; but it certainly didn't apply to the two Italian drivers on this particular day. As they came speeding past us, I could see Nuvolari (who was trailing Varzi) slap the side of his car, furious to have let the Bugatti through. He needn't have worried; as we stood at the entrance to the station, there where the hill sweeping down from Casino Square turned into an impossibly tight hairpin bend, Nuvolari forced his way back into the lead with all tyres locked-up under braking. Varzi could have tried to make an issue of it, but Nuvolari was so committed that any attempt to do so would surely have resulted in an accident.

We watched them descend sharply from the hairpin, twisting and turning between the walls of elegant hotels and windswept villas, until the road flattened out beneath a stone viaduct. Bradley and I followed the cars down under the viaduct and out onto the seaside promenade. By then Varzi had managed to edge past

Nuvolari, and he clung on stubbornly for five laps. Bradley and I continued our walk along the cobbled promenade, following the native arc of the bay before we arrived at *l'épingle du Gazomètre*, a tricky right hander that required a sharp drop in speed from 230kph to about thirty. It was in this very spot that Nuvolari got ahead; meanwhile, the enormous scoreboard in the harbour indicated that we were on lap sixty-five.

The Gazomètre hairpin fed the cars back past the clay tennis courts and onto the main straight. Grandstands overlooked the pits, unfolding beyond a row of palmetto trees that formed a barrier between the track and the promenade. It was on lap seventy-five, after we had found an ideal spot behind the pits, that Nuvolari shattered the lap record, dipping down to an arresting two minutes. We watched him rattle past the start-finish line, and for the first time in nearly four hours of racing, the gap between the two Italians had stretched out to just over three seconds. By lap eighty, Nuvolari was up by five seconds – the largest gap he had enjoyed all day. We were standing so close to the track that we could have reached out and touched the cars that howled past us. After working out a rough lapchart, we estimated that Varzi had led for thirty-three laps and Nuvolari for forty-seven, with twenty laps remaining.

For the next ten laps, Varzi seemed cowed by Nuvolari's pace. But as I watched them attack the hill at Sainte Devote on lap ninety, I sensed that Varzi still had some fight left in him. With eight laps to go, Bradley's stopwatch confirmed it: Varzi had narrowed the gap to less than a second and had become the first man to lap Monaco in under two minutes. He followed that up with three more laps that all came under the two minute mark.

'Two laps left,' said Bradley as Nuvolari's Alfa flashed by. 'It's now or never for Varzi – and I'll bet good money Nuvolari's not about to let him pass.'

It was an odd thing I said then. 'How much good money?'

Bradley raised one delicate eyebrow. 'Ah yes,' he said, 'I forgot about your thing for Varzi.'

I was about to ask what he meant when the crowd in the grandstands suddenly stood as one. We waited for the cars to reach the final sector of the promenade where they would return into our line of sight, and there was Achille Varzi's sky-blue Bugatti, just a few inches ahead of Tazio Nuvolari's crimson Alfa. Nuvolari was practically shunting Varzi, shouting, 'Va! Va!' as his fist thumped the side of his car.

Into the braking zone for Sainte Dévote they raced. That turn was a wicked thing; the exit always felt slow, as if a driver could get on the power earlier, and the inexperienced would inevitably attempt to do just that and wind-up understeering into the wall. Varzi's Bugatti flicked into an ugly tank slapper on the exit as he was harried onto the throttle early by Nuvolari's urgency. The Mantuan was onto the error almost as if he'd anticipated it, positioning the Alfa for a lunge down the inside up at the left-hand sweep on the crest of the hill. Varzi blocked him ruthlessly. Nuvolari, incensed, went wide, up there in the dirt and clag where no one had been foolish enough to run all afternoon. The two cars trail-braked through the left-hander, Varzi on the line, Nuvolari way on the outside. Holding the Alfa in a carnival drift with the rear brushing the concrete bollards and sending spectators scampering up the steps leading to the Hotel de Paris, Nuvolari powered through the left hander before abruptly lifting his foot. The Alfa started spinning, and Nuvolari allowed it to pivot until its nose was aimed into the garden of the Hotel de Paris – then he was on the throttle, opening up that engine and pitching through Casino Square. He had the run on Varzi now, and Varzi, squeezed, had no choice but to launch himself over the bump on the exit of Casino. He came down ahead of Nuvolari, and immediately veered to his right. Nuvolari, not to be denied, was already up the inside and shifting the Bugatti off line, banging wheels shooting up blue-grey gunsmoke. Nuvolari held that lead doggedly as the two cars vanished from sight, before reappearing on the promenade for one final lap. Four hours, ninety-nine laps, and they were separated by nothing more than the paintwork on their dented, oil-stained cars.

'Crikey,' said Bradley.

The crowd's excited screams mingled with the shrill noise emanating from those two stressed engines as Nuvolari led Varzi into Sainte Dévote one final time. Varzi braked late for the gap up the inside. It was suicide trying to pass through there; Nuvolari controlled the corner due to its narrow, awkward entry. But Varzi had no intention of trying to make the pass stick; instead, he wanted Nuvolari to protect his line and, in so doing, compromise his exit. As Nuvolari steered down early to defend the turn, Varzi lunged to the left and hit the apex out of Sainte Dévote. This time it was Varzi who had the momentum. Nuvolari, as Varzi had done a lap earlier, drifted left and forced Varzi up onto the sidewalk. Would Varzi have the guts to try for the outside?

'Listen!' shouted Bradley.

We could hear the two engines climbing up their rev'-range; the Alfa sounded shrill, the Bugatti's tone flatter. Nuvolari shifted into third gear, not even bothering with the clutch. I expected Varzi to do the same, the sound of the Bugatti engine rising in pitch and stuttering as it reached its climax. The shorter gear, combined with Varzi's exit, had the Bugatti pulling ahead as the two cars rushed into the left-hander. Varzi was trail-braking with the rear-end stepping out, way out, but he managed to recover and seized the lead as the two cars went roaring down the hill, And then they were lost to us.

'Bloody hell,' I muttered, and Bradley nodded his head in agreement.

We waited blindly for what felt like an eternity, but was in reality less than a minute. I could imagine the two cars racing through the hairpin bend at the station, then ducking beneath the viaduct to burst through the tunnel and into the chicane until finally we saw them tearing down the promenade. They were side-by-side, Alfa versus Bugatti in the fading afternoon, and we could hear the Alfa strain every mechanical bit as Nuvolari kept his foot planted in third gear. It looked as though Nuvolari had managed to steal the race after all, with the nose of his Alfa just edging past the Bugatti as they sped towards the braking zone for the Gazomètre bend.

'He's got him!' shouted Bradley. As the cars dipped their noses for Gazomètre, Nuvolari's Alfa choked before a pulse of flames flashed from beneath the bonnet. Then the thing just exploded.

An oil pipe had burst loose from his engine, lubricant spraying onto the hot exhaust. We watched Nuvolari jump onto the rear of the car and steer through the hairpin with his feet, flames now a wall of molten heat gaining strength before him.

Achille Varzi buzzed past the line before us with one gloved hand waving excitedly in the air. But he was a side-show. All eyes stared back toward the hairpin where Nuvolari was now pushing his burning Alfa, utterly deaf to the cheers and whistles of the crowd in the grandstands surrounding him. He pushed that Alfa as it burnt away, did the little man, pushed until his mechanics hustled toward him carrying pails of water.

◘

Finestrini smiles at the memory. 'Those two fought some battle that day. On the podium, Varzi and Borzacchini chatted amicably, but both, I think, were all too aware that they were not the focus of the crowd's attention. The spectators only had eyes for one man: "Nivola!" they shouted, "Tazio!"'

'I really did feel for Varzi at that moment: he'd just run the perfect race, and I don't think there was another driver who could have beaten Nuvolari that day. Not a single one. I expect he'd have wanted Nuvolari to be on the podium with him, instead of sulking in the garage after being disqualified for allowing his mechanics to push his car over the line.

'Varzi looked exhausted – and rightly so, after four hours of racing and over a thousand gear shifts. But his exhaustion was more than physical. I'll never forget the way he turned to Prince Rainier – he was a boy then, nine or ten – and rubbed his hair with bloody, blistered fingers, almost as if he needed something to do, something to distract him, you know? As if he was embarrassed to be there, in the midst of a crowd that kept chanting "Nivola, Nivola".'

Finestrini gazes out the window again. 'After the race I went down to the Hermitage to interview Varzi, but he'd already checked out. Perhaps it's because I'm looking at this from a forty year distance, but I don't think we ever saw Varzi race with that

66

kind of desire again. If the Targa in 1931 had made him a man, as humiliation often does, this race had somehow matured him as a professional. He was a different driver after the Monaco Grand Prix of '33; not slower, you understand, and certainly he could turn it on when he needed to, as he would at the Mille Miglia but – he was less committed, less focused, as if that day he had proven something.'

'And what was that?'

'That he was the best driver in the world.' Finestrini nods down toward the rucksack and my manuscript. 'Or do you see it differently, Deutsch?'

'I don't. But I think you do.'

Finestrini looks up at me, his eyes exploring my face as if he were seeing me for the first time. 'Perhaps,' he admits. 'I think Varzi accepted his destiny that day.'

'His destiny?'

'He realized that he would always be a footnote in Nuvolari's legend. Even in defeat, Nuvolari was the hero, and I think Varzi finally accepted that. Varzi was a champion, everyone could agree on that, but Nuvolari was what you Americans call a star. Everyone wanted to be near Tazio: it didn't matter what he did, they just wanted to see him. Varzi just didn't have that kind of magnetism.' Finestrini rubs his lips with his index finger. 'But that's just – what I can tell you for certain is that Varzi's interest in motor-racing began to wane, except to the extent that it could help serve his own interests.'

'Which were?'

'Staying alive,' replies Finestrini. 'And making as much money out of the sport as he could.'

'Which brings us to Libya. To the fraud.'

Finestrini meets my eyes calmly. 'Yes, Libya. I think that maybe it was inevitable, given that the Monaco Grand Prix was such a high point for our sport. It was only a matter of time before we had to pay for our good fortune. But that's life, isn't it?'

'How involved were you?'

'With what?'

'With the biggest swindle in the history of organized sport.'

Finestrini can't help but laugh. 'Fair enough, I suppose. It was an insane idea, I'll tell you that much. But then what could you expect? This was Italy; the way they went about organizing the lottery, it was like sending a whore to a bankers' convention and expecting no one to get fucked. It was badly conceived.'

'But didn't you play an integral role in planning the fraud?'

'No, I certainly did not. Who told you that?' he asks, sitting forward aggressively.

'But it was your idea, wasn't it?' I insist, deflecting the question.

'For the lottery, yes.'

'And who was behind the swindle?'

'I don't know, Deutsch. By the time I got involved, it was already a *fait accompli*.'

'When was that?'

'At Alessandria, after the Bordini GP – Nuvolari sought me out, which was unusual for him, and suggested that we meet in Rome the following week. Later that day I found Varzi, but all he would say to me was: "Make sure that you turn up. You'll be happy to hear what we have planned: It has a direct bearing on that conversation we had at Bergamo".'

'What conversation?'

Finestrini grimaces. 'That race in Monaco,' he says, 'did not go unnoticed in Rome.'

'Ciano?'

Finestrini bites his lip. 'Oh no, far worse than him. I'd barely arrived back in Milan when I got the call.'

○

I'd been working on my Monaco Grand Prix report for hours. Cristoferi had already rejected my first draft, and I was just thinking of a new angle for the article when the phone started ringing. I grabbed the receiver irritably.

'What?'

'Finestrini?'

'Yes. Who is this?'

'*This* is Galeazzo Ciano.'

I felt my stomach clench. 'Oh,' I said, when what I really meant was Dear God forgive me!

'Hold the line,' said Ciano. 'You know what this is about. Don't you?'

I think I may have whimpered. Moments later an all too familiar voice had me sitting up straight in my seat.

'Finestrini.'

'*Duce!*' I found myself shouting.

'How are you today, son?'

'Fine, sir,' I replied, sweating guilt and shame.

'I have something to ask you.'

I noticed that my hands were nervously tidying up the desk.

'It's about the Germans, son.' Mussolini paused. 'Are they considering a return to motor-racing?'

'Sir?' Hearing nothing but silence on the other end, I babbled: 'Sir, with Caracciola all but crippled at Professor Putti's institute in Bologna, it seems unlikely … though I'm aware that Mercedes have been making noises – '

'The Huns are coming,' interrupted Il Duce. 'I'm sure you know that the prestige of our motor-racing heritage is of vital importance to me?'

'Yes sir, and we are blessed with the strongest and best drivers in the world.'

'Be that as it may, the prestige of this great nation depends on our continued dominance of grand prix racing.' I remained silent. 'Ciano tells me you're his go-to man in these matters, and I trust his judgment. Are you a good Italian, Finestrini?'

'Yes, sir!' I said fervently.

'Excellent. Now about those two drivers, Varzi and Nuvolari – '

'They're the world's best, sir. Without a doubt.'

'But are they patriots, Finestrini?'

'Yes sir, of course,' I replied, feeling faint with anxiety.

'Yet they seem unable to race for the glory of Italy. Why do you think that is?'

'Sir – ?'

'The world will be watching us in Libya, son, and I won't

tolerate anyone who seeks to shame us. The time has come for good Italians to fight together against the Hun – as we did at the Battle of Vittorio Veneto. Ferrari is a good man, and our racing heritage is safe in his hands. But Varzi must be persuaded to be a good Italian. His uncle is a senator, isn't he?'

'Yes sir, I believe so.'

'Very well. Ciano was right about you, Finestrini. You'll make us proud, my boy, won't you?'

Mussolini hung up without waiting for a reply, and I was left staring at the receiver in my hand, trying to fight the panic rising in my throat.

The following morning found me sitting in my Bianchi at the side of the autostrada six miles south of Bergamo drowning in the April fog. Varzi's Monaco-blue Bugatti 55 was first to arrive, the yellow glare of headlamps cutting across the valley like jailhouse lights minutes before he rolled up behind me. By the time I'd climbed out into the chill, Nuvolari's Alfa Spyder had muscled up astride the Bugatti. I waited by my car as the two men shook hands and joined me in a huddle by the side of the road with the fog rising to our knees like swamp-water.

'So how are you doing, Achille?' asked Nuvolari.

Varzi lit up what I imagined was his tenth Lucky of the day, despite his bandaged hand. 'Could have done without this,' he said, looking pointedly at me. 'So why are we here, Finestrini? Don't tell me it's this Race of Champions you idiots at the *Gazzetta* dreamed up.'

'That's not going to happen,' said Nuvolari. 'Varzi and I are not racing each other in equal cars, and that's all there is to it.'

Varzi looked at Nuvolari quickly. 'Why not?'

'Because, Achille, if I win, you'll never forget it – and if you win, I'll never accept it. We'd lose our friendship no matter the outcome; and that, in my eyes, would make us both losers.'

Varzi's eyes flashed, but he said nothing.

'Actually, gentlemen,' I said, breaking the silence, 'I'm here on what you might call official business. I was sent by Duce himself.'

The two men stared at me with renewed interest.

'Is he a personal friend of yours, Finestrini?' asked Varzi.

'What?'

'I see you're on a first name basis.'

'Please,' I said. 'No jokes. Look, Il Duce believes the two of you are bringing shame and dishonour to our nation and our empire.' I tried to ignore Varzi's mocking smile. 'You aren't doing anything to demonstrate national unity to our people, and while the two of you keep squabbling like schoolgirls, others are taking advantage and enjoying the prestige that rightly belongs to us. And on top of all that, the two of you are endangering your own lives. Where will it end?' I asked suddenly, skipping ahead to the conclusion of my prepared speech. 'Does it end with one of you lying dead in a ditch? Or maimed, like Caracciola?'

There was a brief, oppressive silence before Varzi said: 'I didn't realize that we even had an empire.'

Nuvolari snorted. 'He has a point though, Achille. You realize how much money we've lost throughout the years?'

Varzi's eyes shifted from me to Nuvolari, and I knew he was wondering if we had somehow concocted an elaborate plan to trap him.

'Varzi,' I said, trying to catch his eye, 'please listen to me. You remember Ciano's letter last year? This time the message was delivered by Il Duce himself. Jesus. Just consider the shit I find myself in – because of the two of you!'

Varzi seemed to consider my plea. 'So what, precisely, does your pal expect us to do? Manipulate races?' Nuvolari's head snapped up at these words, and he gave Varzi a surprised look. Varzi gazed back at him with a smile that spoke many words – but not to me, not then. 'And who should win all the races, according to Il Duce?' he continued. 'Does he favour me, or Italy's great hero over there?'

'Oh stop it,' I whispered. 'Varzi, please, no one is talking about fixing races. Just give each other some breathing room, that's all. Race like the champions you are. Race with honour, with respect – help each other!'

Nuvolari slapped Varzi on the back. 'What do you say, Achille?' Varzi glanced down at the proffered hand and shook it reluctanctly.

'Very well, Tazio.'

'Thank you,' I said. 'For the honour of Italy!'

'And our bank accounts,' said Nuvolari.

'Indeed,' agreed Varzi, releasing Tazio's hand and wincing slightly. I looked down and saw that Varzi's white bandage was stained with fresh blood.

◼

'*Did* you go? To Rome, I mean?'

Finestrini nods. 'Didn't have a choice, did I?'

'Did you have any suspicions?'

'Truthfully?' He smiles. 'Of course I did. But what was I going to do?'

◉

It was summertime in Rome and the breezy sunshine felt a bit like paradise beneath the fabric on my flesh, my core thawing after another fog-laden Milan winter. I treated myself to a leisurely lunch at a café on the Via Cavour and idly paged through the morning's *La Stampa*. The pages were dominated by the upcoming 'Race of Millions', and they'd printed a photograph of the official draw that had been held at Miramare Castle three days earlier, Sforza and a sour-faced De Bono staring at the camera with tentative eyes. Odd, I thought, considering the cash-cow the lottery had turned into for the Party and its patrons. As for me, I'd not done too badly out of the deal: But then this was Italy, the land of milk and subsidy, and this was Rome, wasn't it? A city I'd always detested, with its hills like the gnarled-knuckled threat of a fist that did little to keep my nerves in check.

I sauntered round the corner to the Massimo D'Azeglio, a boutique hotel in the shadow of the Basilica di Santa Maria Maggiore. The five storey, stolid edifice had been in the Bettoja family for over half a century, and it'd sheltered many of Italy's most celebrated including Duce himself and, during the war, Francesco Baracca, the fallen fighter ace whose prancing stallion emblem, the Cavallino Rampante, had adorned Enzo Ferrari's

Alfas since Spa in '32. The hotel was now owned and run by Ettore Bettoja, a fair-headed man who'd enjoyed something of a reputation as a rising star on the grand prix scene in the '20s before he'd packed it all in for the family business. We'd had occasion to share a drink or few in those days, and he welcomed me into the lobby with an embrace, noting, as he did, that I'd lost some weight since last we'd met. He – I assured him in that cavernous lobby – had not. He laughed politely and informed me the six were waiting upstairs.

'The six?' I asked, puzzled, following Bettoja to a suite on the fifth floor.

Varzi, Nuvolari, and Borzacchini, along with three strangers, were playing scopa with tiny Mediano cards around a mahogany table. They all looked up when Bettoja accompanied me through the cream-coloured door.

'Finally,' Nuvolari said. 'Where have you been, Finestrini? The morning train came in three hours ago.'

'I was having lunch,' I explained, all too aware that everyone in the room was staring at me. Bettoja retired discreetly, sealing the door behind him.

Nuvolari threw down his cards and stood up. 'This,' he said, tapping the shoulder of a balding man, 'is Alberto Donati. The luckiest man in Italy. Not only is Signor Donati one of the thirty-three ticket holders for the Race of Millions, but he also happens to hold my ticket. Do you follow, Finestrini?'

'Three million lira,' I said, adding up the sums.

'More than I've made in my entire career,' said Varzi, tossing his cards face-down on the table.

'And this fine chap is Ardvino Sampoli – he has Varzi's ticket,' said Nuvolari, nodding towards a man with a wildly eccentric moustache.

'Which makes him the second luckiest man in the world,' said Varzi. 'Isn't that right, Tazio?'

'And I'm Alessandro Rosina,' said the final stranger. 'I'm sure you can guess who my ticket belongs to.'

I glanced at Borzacchini. He studiously ignored me, staring at his cards with a grim determination. We stood in silence in that handsomely appointed suite – Borzacchini hiding behind his cards, Varzi leaning back in his chair smoking, and Nuvolari pushing down on Donati's shoulders as if the man were pumped with helium.

'Well, gentlemen,' I said when it became clear that no one else was going to speak, 'I doubt this little meeting is illegal but it's certainly not something the race's organizers would be happy to publicize – which is, I assume, why you called me here? For a human interest piece, perhaps, or – '

'Jesus, Finestrini,' snapped Varzi. 'Sit down and stop playing stupid. We're in need of your help here.'

I grabbed the back of a chair. 'May I ask, why me?'

Nuvolari grinned at me. 'What do you mean "why me"? This was your idea.'

'My idea?'

'Remember our chat? In Bergamo?'

'Oh no, you are not playing that fucking card on me,' I said, trying not to smile at the sheer audacity of it all.

Nuvolari looked at me with what I hoped was feigned innocence. 'But we're doing precisely as you asked. For the patria. For you, Johnny.'

'Think of your country,' Varzi said, and he suddenly broke into a passable rendition of *La Giovinezza*. '*E per Benito Mussolini,*' he sang, '*e per la nostra Patria bella* – '

'You want me to help you *fix* the race, is that it?' I interrupted.

'Of-of-of course not,' hissed Borzacchini, finally looking up from his cards. 'Tell him, Tazio.'

'Tell me what? And hello to you too, Mario Umberto.'

Borzacchini's eyes met mine fleetingly before taking refuge in his cards again.

Nuvolari offered me a glass of whisky. 'The reason why you're here, Finestrini, is that we need you to find some sporting regulations that might work in our favour.'

'You want to fix the race in a legal way, is that what you're asking?'

'The plan is for the six of us here to walk away with one million lira each,' said Varzi calmly.

'Impossible,' I replied.

'Why?'

'Because there's less than six million on the table.'

'Don't be a pedant, Finestrini.' Varzi snatched the glass from my hand and refilled it. 'This is serious business.'

'Crime is always serious business,' I retorted.

'This isn't a c-c-crime,' said Borzacchini sharply, but I could sense his uncertainty.

'Of course it isn't,' said Donati. 'I won the ticket fair and square – we all did.'

'Well,' I said, walking over to the couch, 'even if it isn't illegal, it's certainly against the spirit of fair play.'

'Fair play?' Varzi sneered. 'Getting rich and staying alive, Finestrini, that's fair play. Or would you rather we died tragically for the patria, without a penny – like Brilli-Peri?''

Nuvolari sat down on the couch beside me and laid a consoling hand on my knee. 'How do we do this in a way that doesn't break the rules, Johnny?'

'If you're intending to fix the results of the race, then you're already breaking the rules. It's that simple, Tazio.'

Nuvolari patted my leg patiently with his hand. 'Johnny, you're such an idealist,' he said. 'I'm sure if you think about it –

'He doesn't need to think,' interrupted Varzi. 'He already has the solution. Had it before he even walked through the door.'

'He does?' asked Donati, sitting up straight in his chair.

Varzi blew smoke into the room. 'Out with it, *Johnny*.'

'You understand what you're doing here, I take it?' I said, feeling Nuvolari's hand grip my leg. 'You all appreciate that you're attempting to defraud – '

'Quit the sermon,' said Varzi. 'We won't be defrauding anyone of anything. Not if you help us.'

I sighed in resignation. 'Have all six of you agreed to share the proceeds equally?' I asked.

'Yes,' said Donati. 'That way we have three chances to win rather than one. And if we happen to get a one-two-three finish, we'll have just under six million lira to share.'

'Technically then,' I said, 'you don't need to fix the race at all, do you?'

'I don't follow,' said Nuvolari.

'Because it doesn't matter which one of you actually wins.'

I waited for this to sink in. 'So … we won't decide on a winner,' said Nuvolari slowly. 'That means we should just race normally, right? Except that if one of us has a clear shot at winning, the rest of us won't challenge him.'

'Just as Il Duce asked,' said Varzi.

'I still don't understand,' said Sampoli.

'It's simple,' said Varzi. 'As long as one of us here wins, the net result is the same. So we don't even need to squabble over who should win the race.'

Borzacchini turned to me eagerly. 'So it's legal?'

'It's perfectly legal, Mario Umberto,' I said. 'It's also immoral, unethical, and beneath you – beneath all of you. If this ever comes out, your reputations will be tarnished forever – '

'Finestrini, I don't care what they say about you, you're a genius!' Nuvolari exclaimed, pinching both my cheeks in delight.

◘

'I'm sorry,' I interrupt, spreading out a series of photocopies I've taken from my rucksack on the table.

'Interrupting an old man's memories,' Finestrini tells me, 'is like waking a sleeping baby.' But he still consents to glance at the articles in front of him. 'What am I looking at?' he asks eventually. 'None of these were written by me.'

'Yes, that's the point,' I tap the photocopies with a finger. 'By the time the Libyan Grand Prix came around, it was an open secret that drivers were colluding to fix the results of the race. The French wrote about it, as did the Germans – look, here's Paul Levant's column on the eve of the race – even *Auto Week* had the story! Yet the one journalist who was intimately involved in this affair didn't write a single word about it. Why is that? I understand why you would want to keep it a secret at first, but once the news of this – ' I trail off, struggling to find the right word.

'Agreement,' prompts Finestrini.

'Agreement, okay, once the news of this agreement leaked, why didn't you write about it? It would have been a massive story.'

'Because no one knew.'

I stare at him in disbelief. 'What do you mean? Everyone knew!'

'No,' Finestrini insists. 'People assumed, but no one knew. Not for sure.'

'But *you* knew. So why didn't you reveal the details?'

'Why don't you have a guess?'

I take a deep breath, trying to catch his eye, but Finestrini is still looking at the photocopies. 'I think you were paid,' I tell him.

'Ah,' he says wearily. 'Of course, that's always the motivation, isn't it? How dull, how very dull.'

'So what was it then?'

'Rack your brains,' he suggests dismissively.

'It would be easier if I knew who came up with the idea. Bradley suggested that it was Donati, the man who held Nuvolari's ticket, and yet – I don't understand how someone like that could have managed to assemble three of the most famous racing drivers in the world at such short notice. As for that Sampoli guy – he was a farmer of some sort, is that right? It seems highly improbable that either one of them was the ringleader.'

'I see,' says Finestrini. 'So you're suggesting that someone who had access to the organizers was the secret ringleader, is that it?' I meet his stare. 'It's getting stuffy in here,' he tells me.

'So what *did* happen at Tripoli?'

◉

I came to Africa with a new linen suit that I'd made the error of wearing on the hydroplane over from Rome. It was perhaps my relief at having escaped a night of sea-sickness on the ferry that had led to my optimism: I should have known better, should have known the chilled hydroplane would have led to a sneeze that once exposed to the African heat would ferment into something entirely more sinister that left me shivering in the stench of a spice-scented morning.

Tripoli was a God-forsaken place. The markets were swarming

tents of filth carpeted by maggots and strewn with the severed heads of strange animals in which dark pockets of blow-flies winked evil eyes of glinting green. Feeling increasingly sick, I beat a hasty path back to my hotel room which I vowed not to leave until the grand prix.

That evening, over the phone, Varzi gave me his first impression of the newly-constructed circuit. He said it was the fastest one he had ever raced on; he had been left most impressed by a three-foot-high banked turn that had to be taken at just over 260kph. In return for this information, Varzi suggested that we meet in the morning to chat about our agreement, and I found him at my door just as I'd finished trying to unsuccessfully digest a handful of dried fruit and a glass of lurid warm water. He was dressed for business in a white linen suit immaculately pressed, powder-blue shirt perfectly ironed and hair bristling with brilliantine, centre-path carved like an incision. He stepped into my room, took one look at me, and shook his head disconsolately. 'It's nothing,' I told him as he sat on the wing chair beside my bed. 'I must have caught some sort of bug – not surprising, in all this filth.'

'Eat yoghurt,' he counselled, lighting a cigarette and blowing smoke in my face. 'The local bacteria help your body fight the parasites.' After a slight pause, he said: 'I think that we may have a problem.'

'Nothing good will ever come of this place,' I groaned. 'The filth, Varzi, the filth is everywhere.'

'Yes, you mentioned that already,' he said. 'I was speaking to Birkin over dinner – you know Tim Birkin, right?'

I had met Birkin back in 1930 when he had won at Le Mans in an Alfa Romeo, and I had congratulated him on his terrific win 'for Italy'. He had accepted Bernie Rubin's offer to enter his new 3-litre Maserati 8C for the Race of Millions.

'It turns out that he's bought his own ticket from a chap named Natale Bianchi,' Varzi was saying. 'He thought it was a hoot, buying a lottery ticket from a man named Christmas. It cost him one hundred thousand lira – even if he places third, he'll make almost ten times that much. Apparently Bianchi told him to win for the Empire.'

'What people will do for money,' I said, shielding my eyes from the sunlight pouring into my room.

'God, you're so cynical. Finestrini,' he said, clapping his hands to get my attention. 'Listen, there's another problem. Have you seen this?' Varzi tossed a newspaper onto the bed. I read the headline on the *Corriere's* sports page from the day before, which passed for current news in this remote colonial outpost. "Nivola Swears Revenge For Monaco: Varzi Will Pay."

'What about it?' I asked.

'Are the parasites feeding on your brain, Finestrini? This buffoon is talking about revenge as if the rest of us should just bend to his will and let him win! "Varzi will pay", what does that even mean – '

'So just let him win for fuck's sake!' I shouted, surprising myself.

'That's not the point,' said Varzi coldly after he'd digested my outburst from behind a considered stare. 'That idiot is totally unpredictable once he gets behind the wheel.'

I couldn't argue with that. 'So what do you want me to do about it?'

'Talk to him.'

'Fine, I will.'

'You will?'

'Yes.'

'Do it now.'

I realized that my earlier outburst had stung him – I'd stood up for myself, and now Varzi was going to test how far my newfound insolence extended. He grabbed the telephone and was immediately transferred to Nuvolari's room. 'Here,' he said, waving the receiver in my face. When I held it to my ear, I could hear Nuvolari shouting some native word he'd no doubt picked up at the local bazaar.

'Tazio? It's Finestrini. Can you come to my room? There have been some developments …'

Nuvolari arrived a few minutes later, still wearing his pyjamas. The moment he spotted Varzi standing in the shadows, his eyes narrowed. 'What's going on?' he demanded, slamming the door shut.

'What's all this revenge nonsense in the *Corriere*?' I asked, handing him the newspaper.

Nuvolari studied the sports page in silence.

'Let me guess,' said Varzi. 'They've misquoted you, right?'

Nuvolari ignored him. 'So what's the problem?' he asked nonchalantly.

'The problem,' I explained through gritted teeth, 'is that one of you needs to win this race. And it would be a whole lot easier if you would both just agree to *stop racing against each other*!'

'But that would be against the spirit of our sport,' said Nuvolari with an infuriating smile.

'Christ, do you see what we're dealing with?' snapped Varzi.

'Listen, do either of you actually want the money?' I asked, trying to stay calm. 'If so, you're both going to have to play nice. For three miserable hours. That's all you need to do to become filthy rich. Now how is that so bloody difficult? *How*!'

After a short pause, Varzi said: 'The problem is that Tazio thinks his team-mates are only there to help him win. Believe me,' he added, 'I learnt that lesson the hard way.'

'Why does it matter if I win, anyway?' asked Nuvolari, sitting on the chair beside my bed and thumbing through the newspaper.

'It didn't matter,' said Varzi. 'Until that garbage was printed.' He pointed at the newspaper. 'Now it matters.'

'Why?' asked Nuvolari.

'It just does.'

'Jesus!' I sat up and took a coin from my side table. 'Call it, Tazio,' I said.

'Why him?'

'Do you want to call it, Achille?' asked Nuvolari.

'No,' Varzi replied, 'you go right ahead.'

'No-no,' said Nuvolari, 'really, Achille, I insist – '

'Fine I'll bloody call it,' I hissed impatiently. 'If it's heads, Tazio wins; if it's tails, he loses. Right? Okay?' I tossed the coin high in the air. It spun a few times before plopping on the bed. The two men shuffled closer to examine it.

'Well done, Achille,' said Nuvolari. 'You're always the lucky one.'

Varzi carefully placed the coin into his pocket as Nuvolari tossed the newspaper on my bed. The *Corriere* had printed a photo of Rudi Caracciola in a wheelchair with his entire leg encased in plaster of Paris. The photo had been taken the week before, at Professor Putti's rehab' centre in the hills outside Bologna, and ran a quote attributed to Putti : 'It will be months before we know if Caracciola will ever walk again.'

'Poor bastard,' said Nuvolari.

Varzi turned to me. 'By the way, I've scoped out the perfect place for you to monitor the race.'

'Yes, fine, whatever,' I said, sinking back down onto the bed. 'Now please, please let me get some rest.'

Nuvolari frowned. 'What's wrong with him?' he asked.

'He's being eaten alive by parasites,' said Varzi.

'Seems like they're giving him a backbone.' Nuvolari watched as I reached down for the newspaper on my lap. 'You should eat yoghurt,' he counselled, as both men jostled each other out of the room.

The track had been built around a cobalt-coloured salt basin, and ran from the filthy grime of Tripoli out into the desert to the village of Tajura on the road to the oasis at Mellaha where it circled back on itself, twelve kilometres of specially-treated tarmac and undoubtedly the greatest circuit I'd ever laid eyes on. It had but one straight that dragged on for less than a kilometre, the rest of the circuit linked by a chain of full-throttle sweeps and violently abrupt switchbacks. Brakes were applied but a handful of times, mostly through the tight turns around of the brickhouses of Tajura just beyond which I was to watch the race.

The grandstand across from the pits where I spent the morning trembling under the shade afforded by the bright-white concrete was quite the grandest thing, awash with the colour of Italian officers in their finest mixing with colonial dignitaries in pale linen summer suits, and black-shirted militia sweating under the weight of their destiny. Down on the first tier, in a purpose-built box, the thirty-three lottery winners sat all in a row. I focused my binoculars and caught sight of Rosina with Donati by his side. From up high in the bleachers one could make out Tripoli splayed-out in a mish-mash of modern hotels and apartment buildings emerging from the squat, earth-coloured Arab dwellings, palm trees a verdant olive bowl in which the city marinated a rotten stew of crud, hunger and disease.

The Ghibli had swelled down from the highlands overnight, a hot wind that had deposited blood-red sediment over the track extended like a bullet out into the dust. Just before midday the cars were pushed onto their white-painted starting blocks, bordered by soldiers and hundreds of Italian flags. The drivers, who I'd spent the morning avoiding, stood in a scrum about the Commissioner of the Royal Auto Club, Parisi, who conveyed his final instructions. 'We expect a noble race, gentlemen, in the grandest tradition of Italian endeavour.'

On the road out to Tajura, the organizers had planted boundless rows of date-groves, and the palms reached up now like windmills in an oasis of throbbing calm. The drivers climbed into their machines and mechanics attached the umbilical starters to the engines. With thirty seconds left, the call-to-battle music blaring over the PA was throttled and the announcer began the countdown. Engines rose in pitch as the crowd came to their feet, hypnotized by the rumble. Marshall Pietro Badoglio stood at the head of the grid with his medals glinting like El Dorado. He held the twenty-nine snarling cars as if on a tight leash beneath the Italian flag raised above his shoulder.

I glanced down at the official programme on my desk. Four cars had failed to make the grid, but that did nothing to whittle down what was easily the strongest field ever assembled for a motor race. Varzi, Nuvolari, Borzacchini were the favorites, joined by Ghersi, Fagioli, Biondetti, Campari, Taruffi and, in an Alfa identical to that of Nuvolari, Enzo Ferrari himself, in his first race since his inexplicable retirement from grand prix racing in 1924.

The leash was snapped by the dropped flag, and I looked up to see the field explode away into the haze. It was then that I reluctantly abandoned the grandstand and the rhythmic purr of the overhead fans leaking fetid air on my sweating, fevered brow. On a camel whose head would surely be on a stick by sunset I was led by a local lad toward Tajura. In that syrupy heat, I sweated out a fever, until finally, with my bowels about to rupture, we cantered out just short of the drowsy village the locals called Bab Tajura.

The cars came chattering into the village in a cacophony of sound and trailing chopped images of blurred colour. Leaning into the right-hand bend, Birkin, his trademark black and white polka-dot silk scarf tied like a garrote round his throat, led from Campari's Maserati. Nuvolari came past in third, already gapped by a few seconds by the powerful Maseratis which seemed well-suited to Mellaha. In the crackling of those Maseratis and Alfas I could distinguish the sound of a misfiring engine – Varzi's Bugatti running on seven cylinders and surrendering a position to a hard-charging Enzo Ferrari who was power-sliding out of the turn trailing dirt and dust right there in front of me. He got the rear of that Alfa seriously sideways, and I was impressed when I heard that flat engine note keep rising as Ferrari planted the boot in to his impertinently wriggling car.

In his broken Italian, my guide said, 'I don't understand this at all; they race so fast and yet they don't go anywhere – they are always here.' By then Campari had managed to stumble his way past Birkin. Varzi came through in fifth, his hand coming out of the cockpit to wave at me serenely, and I was reminded of his race at Monza the year before when he'd had his mechanics fit a reserve tank of fuel in order to save himself a pitstop. He'd told me then that he'd developed a misfire when the topped-to-the-brim oil-tank had spilt onto the spark plugs.

Borzacchini, meanwhile, was on a charge, and I suspected he was following orders – the Maserati lump in Campari's car had proven fragile all season, and while Birkin was sensible enough not to offer any resistance, Campari was determined not to let Borzacchini through. The two fought a pitched battle for a number of laps, at one point getting into a broadsided clash just beyond the village until it all ended, predictably enough, with Campari's Maserati trailing acrid-blue smoke that abruptly dried up about a mile out of Tajura. A lap later, Borzacchini suffered an altogether more explosive fate down the main-straight when a piston came shooting out of his Alfa like a firework. The two retirements left

83

Birkin up front with Nuvolari trailing him comfortably and Varzi ten seconds back, his Bugatti now rasping fluently.

On lap twenty-one, Nuvolari and Birkin – separated by less than a second – chose the same moment to make a pit stop. Through my binoculars I observed mechanics vaulting over the concrete pit-counter, carrying jacks, fuel-hoses, and wheel hammers. A flame-resistant blanket was hurriedly thrown over Nuvolari's head and shoulders as thirty gallons of fuel pumped into the stalled engine in less than forty seconds. The starter was then jostled into the nose of the car, the blanket removed from Nuvolari by a mechanic holding a bottle of mineral water, and while Tazio guzzled, the motor kicked over and then he was off, back into the race in less than a minute.

Things did not go so smoothly for Birkin: while jumping from his cockpit during refueling, he had slipped and scorched his arm on the exhaust pipe that trailed down the flank of his Maserati. After a tourniquet had been hastily applied, Birkin rejoined the fray in third place. The crowd applauded the brave Englishman as his mechanics strode nonchalantly back behind the concrete counter, seemingly content to have confirmed their plucky reputations.

'So you fixed the race,' said a voice behind me.

I turned to find Campari standing with a bottle of beer in one hand and his race jacket in the other, his face streaked with oil and dust. He was a big man, Campari, and I was suddenly all too aware of how alone we were out here in the desert. He pointed his bottle at Nuvolari, who was just then roaring past us. 'He never even spoke to me about it,' Campari said, throwing his coat onto the hot soil and sitting on it with a grunt. 'He only spoke to Borzacchini – his bitch – and that idiot Varzi.' His eyes fell on me. 'And you of course.' Campari took a long swig from his bottle. 'You don't look so well, Finestrini. Birkin buggering up your plans?'

'I'm just a journalist, Giuseppe.' I placed the binoculars over my eyes and followed Birkin, who was still in third place.

'So how come you didn't write about the fix?'

'Because there is no fix. Did someone ask you to throw the

race?' I asked nervously, glancing back to gauge his reaction.

Campari said nothing. And really, what could he have said, when it was clear that his friends had excluded him from their little agreement? Campari was about to turn forty; he was a long way from his glory years in the early '20s, and Nuvolari's betrayal must have felt like the final confirmation that he was yesterday's man, that grand prix racing had moved on and left him behind.

In the distance we could see Varzi heading toward us, his hands anxiously rummaging around the cockpit. Since he hadn't made any stops yet, he was now leading Nuvolari and Birkin by over a minute.

'He's looking for his reserve tank,' said Campari. Varzi's attention remained focused on something within his cockpit as he counter-steered distractedly out through Tajura. 'He's got a lever in there connected to the reserve tank – it's probably stuck. Seems like your man's about to run out of fuel. And that's two criminals down, Finestrini. Now it's all up to Tazio, eh?' Campari laughed as Nuvolari sped past us. 'Tell me, did you guys actually script this? It's like something out of an American movie.'

As if to prove Campari's point, Varzi's Bugatti ran out of fuel right under the grandstands. Nuvolari had swept into the lead by the time Varzi managed to budge the lever, the fuel-starved engine finally bursting into life to the cheers of the crowd.

'What drama,' said Campari. 'And like the best of them, it's turning into a fucking tragi-comedy. Your boys are born actors, Finestrini.'

Nuvolari's lead was up to ten seconds, but from the fierce look on Varzi's face I could see that he was ready to fight. Instinctively I set my stopwatch on the two men. Two laps later, Nuvolari came in at 4.33 and Varzi at 4.27. Campari, glancing at my stopwatch, drained the last of his beer and let out a fearsome burp. 'Five seconds faster than anyone this weekend,' he said. 'So what happens next?'

I stood up then as Varzi raced toward me and began waving both my arms, imploring him to slow his pace. He was oblivious to my entreaties. Nuvolari, on the other hand, kept gesticulating wildly and pointed an accusing finger at me. So much for fixing the bloody race, I thought.

'Don't tell me the two idiots are actually racing each other?' shouted Campari, roaring with laughter.

That was exactly what they were doing – and now they were speeding past us, side-by-side, at over 260kph on their final lap. Varzi had the advantage into the braking zone for Tajura, leaving his brakes unbelievably late before committing to the turn with a scraping gear shift. Nuvolari locked up all four tyres in response, running Varzi wide into the dirt right there in front of me. Rear tyres were trailing crimson dust as both men struggled to nail the power down on the grimy surface. And just like that, with Varzi's Bugatti in Nuvolari's slipstream, the two men rocketed towards the chequered flag a couple of miles up the road to Tripoli. 'Varzi's got him,' said Campari, grabbing my binoculars in disbelief, 'he's bloody got him!'

Varzi crossed the line less than a second ahead of Nuvolari, the closest finish in history, with a clearly delighted Birkin in a distant third place. Campari slapped me on the back. 'Quite a show you crooks put on, Maestro,' he said, handing me the binoculars. 'So much for *i signori senza quatrini* … ' Gentlemen without a dime – I had once used that expression to describe the *fratellini*. It seemed like a lifetime ago.

I returned to the hotel right after the race and collapsed on the bed, my body burning with fever. Somewhere, the velvet-voiced Gea della Garisenda was singing *Tripoli bel suol d'amor*. When I woke up, the sun was blasting through the room and my sheets were damp with sweat. I felt weak, my head swimming and body aching as I drew a steaming bath in the claw-footed tub, but whatever disease had consumed me that weekend had dripped away with the night, and I was soon overcome with a painful and most welcome hunger.

I was heading towards the hotel restaurant when sturdy fingers seized my shoulder. Borzacchini stood there behind me with a radiant smile on his face. 'Finestrini, do you know what t-t-today is?' he asked, holding my shoulders tightly as he blinked back his tears. 'I'm th-th-thirty-five years old and today, today I'm finally an in-in-dependent man.' He then proceeded to tell me everything he would do with the money, from the house in Bellaria to the nest-egg for his kids. It took a while …

◘

'He was floating on air that morning,' Finestrini tells me, 'and it made me want to weep because he was about the only good man I had ever met in that world of theirs. He was a good father, a good husband, and an honest, clean racer.'

'Did Nuvolari lift his foot?' I ask abruptly. 'Before the line, I mean? Did he lift, to give Varzi the win?'

Finestrini looks at me. 'Varzi asked me the same question.'

'Did he?'

'Yes, that very afternoon. I remember thinking, how could he be so insecure? He had lapped three seconds faster than Nuvolari on that last lap – three seconds. And now he was a millionaire to boot. Yet the only thing he could think about was whether Nuvolari had thrown the race.'

'Well, did he?'

Finestrini shrugs. 'With Nuvolari it's impossible to know.'

'What did he say?'

'I don't recall ever talking to him about it. He left Tripoli that same afternoon, after having been tipped off that the Supreme Sporting Authority were convening for a special session the following morning. They came to the conclusion that Varzi, Nuvolari, and Borzacchini had conspired to fix the race, but the punishment was nothing more than a rebuke, a warning that any future infractions of the sporting code would see them stripped of their racing license.'

'In other words – '

'In other words the lottery had been a great success. Everyone that mattered walked away richer, including the Party, and the blame ultimately fell on the innocent – in this case, the organizers who had made the error of assigning tickets to drivers days before the race. It was announced that from then on, the assignations would be broadcast no earlier than thirty minutes before the start of the race.'

'So everyone walked away a winner.' I assemble my cut-outs

and place them back into the folder in no order at all. 'But you wrote that the race was cursed, right?'

'I was quite taken with the idea of curses in those days,' says Finestrini wryly. 'But really, looking back, a curse is as good an explanation as any for what happened over the next few months. As I'd told Varzi, nothing good would ever come of Tripoli. It all started when Birkin died three weeks later as a result of the burn he sustained during his pitstop; it was a blood infection, if I recall correctly. Next, it was Sforza's turn: he was forced to resign from the Auto Club a month after the debacle, and his life went to pieces after that.'

'And then there was Monza.'

Finestrini nods slightly. 'Yes, in the autumn of 1933.'

'You never did file a story on Tripoli.'

'Didn't I?'

'No. Your next report was almost seven weeks later, at the French Grand Prix. You missed Nuvolari's win at the 24 Hours of Le Mans that summer. So what happened between Libya and France?'

'I don't rightly recall. Maybe I took a vacation.'

'You missed the AVUS race, too, when Varzi became the first foreigner to ever win on German soil.'

'Did I really … ?'

'So what happened to Nuvolari?' I ask, unsettled by Finestrini's sudden evasiveness.

'He left Ferrari mid-season – after Nîmes, if memory serves.'

'Did it have anything to do with Tripoli?'

'No idea. The fact that Nuvolari was now richer than Ferrari certainly didn't help. If you listen to Tazio's version of the story, he walked away when Ferrari refused to rebrand the team "Nuvolari–Ferrari".' Finestrini laughs. 'I remember Ferrari phoning me in a towering rage. "Imagine," he had shouted, "not even Ferrari–Nuvolari!" '

'And Campari won in France …'

'Yes, his final victory. I remember that he wanted to thank the spectators but he didn't speak a word of French, so instead he sang a stirring rendition of *O Sole Mio* over the PA before drinking

88

himself into a stupor. That's when he announced his retirement. After Monza, he said, he was out – he was done with the rotten sport and would dedicate the rest of his life to his one true love: Opera.'

'And then they all came to Monza.'

Finestrini glances down at his wrist-watch. 'And then they came to Monza, yes, in September – with Campari scheduled to retire, Nuvolari without a team, and Varzi – well, no one knew which five-star hotel Varzi would turn up at in those days.' Finestrini pushes back his chair. 'I'm supposed to take a walk every morning – doctor's orders.' He stands up gradually and stretches his arms a little. 'Let me fetch my coat from my room. We'll have a nice little *passeggiata ala Italiana.*'

Finestrini has donned his gray loden coat and woollen hat, with his gloved hands deep in his pockets. I open the frosted-glass lobby door to the mid-morning chill and follow him out into the murk. The Bora wind is tired, breathless in the hush. Bleak oyster clouds race across the sky, the sunshine glinting over the spires and steeples of Venice.

'The Bora is born in Senj, marries in Fiume, and dies in Trieste,' Finestrini tells me, pulling up the collar of his heavy coat. All sports writers probably have a coat like this. There's salt in the air, settling on my lips, the water from the lagoon cresting the Riviera and flushing across the cobbled street. 'Aqua Alta,' Finestrini side-steps a nest of seaweed, 'they'll be swimming in San Marco by tonight.' I follow him through constricted streets where shuttered houses rise beyond moist stone walls, palm trees dripping globules of water. We're in a maze of streets now, a labyrinth borrowed like time over bridges and alleys, the wind an afterthought upon our backs. After a while, I can't hold back my question any longer. 'So were you there?' I ask.

Finestrini takes a few slow steps before replying. 'September,' he tells me, 'is the devil's month. And for Italian motor-racing, September the 10th, 1933, was the end of everything. There were two races scheduled for that day: the Grand Prix d'Italia in the morning and the Monza Grand Prix in the afternoon. The

Monza Grand Prix was supposed to be held earlier that summer, but work on the track's safety had been delayed. The layout for the two races was different; the Italian GP was run on the full ten kilometre track, whereas the Monza GP would run on the shorter speed-circuit (also known as the oval) and would comprise three heats and a final. The whole thing started with an innocuous incident in Heat One, when Count Trossi left the transmission to his battleship-sized Duesenberg on the South Curve.' He glances at me. 'You know who Trossi was, right?'

'The president of Ferrari,' I reply.

'Yes, exactly. His family's bank had underwritten Ferrari's purchase of racing Alfas from the defunct Alfa Romeo works that year. Anyway, Trossi dumped a tanker's worth of oil on the track and that would prove to be catastrophic. But I'm getting ahead of myself …'

◙

Monza terrified me. I feared the speed, the awful, wide-open speed in those confined spaces, and I feared, more than anything else, the ghosts of this place. Monza, they said, was the home of Italian motor-racing, but to me it had always been our mortuary, and I couldn't set foot in the place without remembering Materassi and that charming late-summer day in 1928. This place killed men.

From where I was sitting in the grandstand, I could see the six foot ditch that Materassi had vaulted over before torpedoing into the grandstand. I had been in the pits that day, and I could still hear the screams as his Talbot had viciously ploughed into the crowd. Twenty-one people had died that afternoon along with Materassi. The horror was always there for me when I came to Monza, and I struggled to keep the memories away as I focused my attention on the grid and the seven cars scheduled to dispute Heat Two. Borzacchini was sitting in the shade of his Maserati (alone in a field of Alfa Romeos), sipping on a bottle of Pellegrino. Campari, meanwhile, was standing on the grid surrounded by well-wishers and flashing camera bulbs. He was chatting intimately with Hellé Nice, a female race car driver who, if you listened to Chiron, had once moonlighted as a stripper in Paris. Through my binoculars, I saw Borzacchini stand up and walk up the grid. As he passed Campari, he paused for a moment, as if unsure what to do next. If Campari saw him, though, he didn't let on, and after some hesitation, Borzacchini finally headed towards the garage for what I knew would be his pre-race ritual vomit.

During the summer I had tried to get the two of them to make their peace, but Campari would not hear of it. The one time I had dared to press the matter, he had started in on me, and since then I had steered clear of both him and the subject. Time, I thought, was the only thing that would ever bring the *fratellini* back together again. With Nuvolari, though, things had been different. Tripoli would never be forgotten of course, and it would always remain there like an infidelity, but Nuvolari and Campari had renewed their friendship at Le Mans in the summer. This didn't surprise me, as there had always been a simplicity to their friendship that had somehow eluded Borzacchini.

The race, delayed for over an hour already, showed no sign of getting underway as clean up of Trossi's oil continued, and soon the entire grandstand over the mainstraight was on its feet, stomping and whistling and shouting impatiently. I glanced down at the Royal Box. The Crown Prince, who was sitting next to Galeazzo Ciano, kept tapping on his wrist-watch as if he had to be somewhere else. The rumours of his homosexuality had never really been put to bed, even after his marriage, and I wondered how true it was that Mussolini and Ciano had compiled a secret dossier on the young man's dalliances. Suddenly, a voice boomed over the PA, interrupting my thoughts.

'Piloti, to your cars.'

Moments later, all seven cars due to take part in Heat Two were on their starting berths, enormous engines puffing and huffing; the vibration shook the foundations of the grandstand, and I felt my heart beating in my chest. I trained my binoculars on each one of the drivers: Campari, Balestrero, Borzacchini, Barbieri, Castelbarco, Hellé-Nice, and Pellegrini. The cars were running with special shaved tyres for the ultra-quick circuit, and I knew that the front-runners, undoubtedly Campari and Borzacchini, would have dispensed with their front brakes too, to save on weight. Raw speed won races here at Monza, along with brute force. I rubbed the sweat from my palms on my trousers, holding my breath and listening to the shrill note rising from those seven stressed engines, all waiting for that flag to fly in the afternoon breeze.

The shrill pitch suddenly dropped to a dense growl, and they were off, racing toward the North Curve. The cars ducked and dived then funnelled into an orderly row at the approach to the banking, the slipstream propelling them to over 200kph.

I stood among the crowd, listening to the cheers as Campari took the lead, Borzacchini jostling for second place, ahead of Barbieri and Castelbarco. They entered the North Curve in that order and rapidly vanished beyond the tree line. All eyes now turned to the exit of the South Curve, where the cars would return to our field of vision in less than a minute.

Balestrero, Pellegrini and Hellé-Nice came into our line of sight like little specks on the inside of that enormous oval. As they roared past the main grandstand, I heard a man beside me shout: 'Where's Campari? And Borzacchini?' We waited, but the cars that raced by two minutes later were the same three. Balestrero suddenly broke from the track and lunged toward the pit lane. I followed him down that narrow road with my binoculars, tracking the long-nosed Alfa as it came sliding to a halt. His mechanics seemed uncertain: a couple of them were running to the rear of the car, while another one listened to Balestrero, alternately shaking and nodding his head. After a short stop, Balestrero blazed down the pit lane, narrowly avoiding an ambulance parked at the exit. I could see three nuns climbing into the back of the ambulance before it drove away, vanishing through a set of rusted gates leading into the woods at the heart of the circuit. Christ, I thought, stumbling out of my seat and running down the rear of the grandstand, what the hell's happened?

I don't know how long it took, but I ran as hard as I could over the bridge that stretched across the track until finally I reached the pit lane. My heart was bursting by then. Balestrero's mechanics were speaking to the chief steward, their faces grim and taut.

Borzacchini's wife and kids were there as well, listening as the group of men discussed 'the accident'.

'What accident?' I asked, elbowing my way toward the steward. 'What fucking accident?'

'Campari and Borzacchini,' someone replied, and I recognized the voice of Giulio Ramponi, Borzacchini's chief mechanic. 'Castelbarco, too. Do you think they'll stop the race?'

'What kind of accident?' I insisted, grabbing Ramponi by the collar. '*What's happened?*'

Ramponi took a step back from me. 'They went off, that's all we know,' he said, surprised by my ferocity. 'They went off.'

I could hear the three remaining cars zip past the line. In their wake came a silence fraught with terror. I looked around the pit lane, lost in my own anxious thoughts. Mechanics and marshals stood about in a state of paralysis. Everyone was waiting for answers. Up ahead, I saw an Alfa sedan heading towards the same narrow road that the ambulance had taken only minutes ago. I broke into a sprint, chased it down, and dived into the rear seat.

'What the – ? Jesus, Finestrini!'

'Enzo,' I said, recognizing Ferrari's hollow eyes staring at me in the rear-view mirror. 'What the fuck's happened?'

The man in the passenger seat beside Ferrari turned around. I recognized him instantly; it was Guy Moll, the twenty-three year old driver Ferrari had hired to replace Nuvolari. 'I warned them,' he said, staring at me with glassy eyes. 'I warned them.' His face was blank, expressionless.

'It was Trossi's oil,' Ferrari said, driving on into the dark shadows of the woods that surrounded us. 'It spilled all over the entry to Vedano.'

Vedano, I thought, the cobbled South Turn.

'They put sand on it,' said Moll. 'It would have made the oil as slippery as ice.'

We were lost in the trees now, heavy amongst the ghosts. Suddenly, a figure in white materialized ahead, with goggles wrapped about his wrists, spectral, alone.

'Stop!' I yelled. Ferrari hit the brakes and came to a grinding halt.

'Is that – '

'Barbieri!' I shouted, jumping from the car and tripping over myself, 'Barbieri!' My voice was obscenely loud in the chilly silence. I heard birds take flight above us, and Barbieri froze as I stumbled over the damp undergrowth toward him.

'You saw?' he whispered to me when I finally reached him. 'You saw?'

'What happened?' I asked, wheezing. 'Tell me what happened.'

I heard Ferrari's footsteps crunching closer. I turned to him; he was carrying a metal flask in his hand which he handed to Barbieri. The driver took a long swig.

'What happened?' Ferrari asked, his voice as soft as the slanting sunlight.

Barbieri seemed to focus now. He looked at me, then at Ferrari.

'They're all dead,' he said. 'All of them. They're all dead, you see … '

I slapped him across the face. A stinging blow. Barbieri took it, blinking away his tears. And then he spoke slowly, deliberately, with his breath smelling of the booze.

'We came into Vedano,' he said, 'Campari leading, Borzacchini in his slipstream. Campari took the inside line, and I followed him down to the apron. And then Campari was gone. He lost the rear-end, just lost it like that.' Using his hands to demonstrate, Barbieri described how Campari's Alfa had slid into a tank-slapper at 200kph and smashed into the retaining guardrail, right in front of Borzacchini. 'Borzacchini had no choice, he tried to avoid him – I saw him steer hard to his right, but his car just began rolling, you see, and then he was sent flying through the air. He was flying,' Barbieri insisted, staring up at us now, and in his eyes I saw the horror unfold.

'Dio bono,' whispered Ferrari.

'And Campari?' I asked. 'Where's Campari?'

'It happened so slowly,' Barbieri said softly, 'so slowly.'

'What happened?'

'The guardrail seemed to hold him at first, but then – almost in slow motion – his Alfa just tipped over. He tumbled down the embankment. Castelbarco hit the rails too and was overturned. His car fell on top of him but he was still moving. I'm sure he was.

But Campari went over, you see?'

Ferrari placed his hand around the man's shoulder and steered him tenderly toward the car. He opened the rear-door and helped Barbieri in. 'You coming, Finestrini?'

Where, I wanted to ask. Where can we go to get away from *this?* Ferrari accelerated away with Guy Moll on the front seat staring at me with eyes that never blinked.

◻

We pause, Finestrini and I. He stares out at the lagoon as I struggle to light a cigarette.

'Something died that day,' he tells me. 'The sport lost its innocence – or perhaps I did, perhaps something in me died that day, I don't know. They still ran the final, you know, and Brooklands legend Count Czaykowski went off at the same place as Campari. He flew over the edge and his Bugatti landed on top of him and burst into flames. It took them three hours to extinguish the blaze, and who knows what they found in there ... '

Finestrini watches me smoke. 'Campari died instantly, of course. He was still in his Alfa when it collapsed into the ditch below the banking – must have been a twenty metre fall from up there. I suppose his size kept him trapped in the car until it smashed down on top of him. Borzacchini was not so lucky – he was thrown out of the cockpit and catapulted into the trees. He survived long enough to get to the hospital, where he died later that afternoon with his family at his side. Nuvolari, you know, stayed the whole night in the morgue with them, with their bodies. Carolina came eventually, having heard no news from him, she came with Ferrari's chauffeur and took Nuvolari home in the dawn. I was there, I saw him leave – the last of the *fratellini.*

'And that's how that awful year ended. The scandal at Tripoli soured everything ... it was a curse, I honestly believe that. Campari, Borzacchini, Birkin, Alfa bankrupt, Maserati on the brink, Nuvolari out in the cold ... everything we'd built after the war, all of it died at Monza. And poor Caracciola, he spent nine months in that hospital and a week after he was discharged he lost his wife, Charly, when she died in a fucking avalanche – she wasn't even thirty.'

Finestrini swallows, avoiding my eyes. 'But really, losing Campari and Borzacchini was the biggest tragedy of all. Chiron later told me about the time he saw Borzacchini arrive at the Reims track with a brand new leather briefcase; Chiron had asked him if that was where he kept all his millions. "Oh yes," Borzacchini had replied, "I carry it with me all the time. Then, at night, I close the door, make sure no one is around, and count all the bills before I turn on the fan and dance in the fluttering 1,000 lira notes."

'I met his son some years later. He lived in France and had that same shy smile, it truly broke my heart. Ah well,' Finestrini sighs as we start walking back toward the hotel. 'It was an awful loss, but the Party made the most of it, of course, especially with Campari's funeral. Everyone was there, even Ciano, and I'll always remember his words to me when he came to shake my hand after Campari had been laid to rest.

' "Finestrini, don't look so glum, my boy – think of the joy he brought us, the column inches he gave you, think of all the newspapers he sold in his lifetime, and the newspapers he will sell tomorrow – think of how he died. Think of the glory, Finestrini. There is no greater way to live and die than did Giuseppe Campari."

'You know what's ironic?' Finestrini asks me when we step into the lobby.

'What?'

'That in January '44, Mussolini had Ciano tied to a chair in a muddy field in Verona and shot in the head. There's a photograph of Ciano, just as he's about to be shot, twisting in his chair to face the firing squad. I suppose that he, too, had a glorious death in his own way.'

In the elevator, we set a time for lunch before going our separate ways. Stepping into my room, I throw the rucksack on the bed and lie down beside it. The clouds outside my window are dark and menacing, full of foreboding at what's to come. I lift the receiver and dial. Listen to the ring.

No one answers, and it's a relief when I replace the receiver and shut my eyes to the silence.

PART THREE
THE DEVIL IS TOO SLOW

We are on the extreme promontory of the centuries! What use looking back if we are to smash open the mysterious shutters of the impossible? Time and Space died yesterday. We already live in the absolute, since we have already created eternal, omnipresent speed.

– The Futurist Manifesto, F. T. Marinetti, 1909

A DECISION ON THE ROAD
TO BRESCIA

L'Isola Del Lido, February 15th, 1968

Finestrini is in a quiet mood as he leads me through a warren of alleys and cobbled streets. The Bora has left us now, and in its wake descends a moist chill that worms its way to my core. Snowflakes softly stumble and burn on the slick sidewalk. Finestrini had called from the lobby and given me five minutes to meet him, neither apologizing for his lateness (it was almost 2pm) nor for his sudden haste. I'd found him out on the street with his greatcoat buttoned and a silk scarf wrapped before his mouth, one boot stroking the sidewalk.

The restaurant lies beyond a rusted gate and a meandering path bordered by rows of palmettos. It spreads itself out within the confines of a sand-coloured villa, window-shutters the garish green of spring in the flatlands of the Veneto. The room into which I am led is grand, with its cavernous fireplace and polished oak floor over which an elegant man strides with a smile and a searching open hand.

'Johnny, *ma che piacere riverderla.*' The two men hug and exchange pleasantries until Finestrini turns to me and says, 'I think lunch first, Sergio.'

99

Sergio accompanies us down a narrow hallway that opens up into a dining room at the rear of the villa; the glass walls and lush plants remind me of a greenhouse.

'I've been coming here for thirty years,' Finestrini says when Sergio leaves us with a bottle of water and two menus. 'Legend has it that Hemingway wrote a novel here. But then, Hemingway wrote a novel in every bar this side of the Adriatic. Tell me, Deutsch, what have you written?'

'I've been working on this book for the past decade,' I reply.

He snorts derisively.

'Cheers,' I add, raising my glass.

'It's bad luck to toast with water.'

'I thought it was white wine.'

'Only if you're a Florentine.' Finestrini looks down at the menu. 'It's interesting: while I was sitting in my room this morning, hoping to fall asleep, I had a moment of clarity. Looking back on it, the deaths of Campari and Borzacchini symbolized the end of Italian dominance. In 1934, the world order was set to change with the new 750kg formula, which was specifically chosen to lure the Germans back given the advanced state of their metallurgy. Making matters worse for us was the fact that, of the four champions who had raced for Alfa in '32, Campari and Borzacchini were dead, Caracciola was crippled, and Nuvolari was no longer welcome. So instead, Ferrari kept faith with Guy Moll, and added Varzi and Chiron to his line-up.'

'All foreigners,' I venture.

Finestrini sips his water to mask his hesitation. 'I wrote an article for the *Gazzetta*, if that's what you're referring to, noting that it was unpatriotic of Ferrari to run two foreigners in its team at a time when Italy's primacy in the sport was being challenged. The 'paper had been out less than an hour when I received a call from Viganò, Varzi's secretary. He informed me that I had been invited to the Varzi estate in Galliate, and that he would pick me up from my apartment … at four a.m.'

'Hold on while I set up my recorder,' I ask.

Finestrini watches me draw the machine out and place it on the table with a patronizing smile.

The Varzi villa sat on a ridge on the fringe of Galliate, a minor town dominated by the Varzi-owned textile factory. The villa's red brick and limestone walls promised comfort from the bone-chilling cold that had seeped into me since my arrival. I followed Varzi, Chiron, and Benoist as they walked amidst the skeleton trees, chatting and smoking with their feet no doubt toasty in their mud boots, their cracked shotguns slung over their shoulders. Viganò followed in my tracks with two pheasants hanging limply about his neck, both victims of Benoist's marksmanship. The hunting dog ran toward the house and I listened to it bark excitedly, as eager as I was to escape the cold. Varzi slowed down, allowing Chiron and Benoist to walk up ahead, and waited for me to catch up.

'I read your piece in the *Gazzetta* yesterday,' he said, staring at me with pale, wet eyes. 'I was fascinated by your insistence that Ferrari ought to employ Italians. Did you forget that I was Italian?'

'Varzi ... '

'Did it not occur to you that Ferrari's decision was only logical, after what happened with Campari and Borzacchini? How would you feel if the media had accused you of murdering Italy's Golden Generation?'

I avoided his eyes, focusing instead on my mud-soaked moccasins.

'But really, I'm just a foreigner in your Italy, isn't that right, Finestrini? You and your friends – you decide who is Italian, yes?'

'Varzi –

'Tell me, Finestrini,' he said in a calmer tone. 'You ran a quote from Alfred Neubauer stating that Nuvolari was a hero and I was an artist. Did he actually say that?'

'Of course he did.'

'You spoke to him then?'

'Clearly.'

Varzi came to an abrupt halt and lowered his voice to a whisper. 'So Mercedes is back.' He poked me sharply in the chest. 'But tell me, are they fast?'

'I don't know.'

'What does he say?'

'Who?'

'Neubauer. Mercedes' boss, fat guy, been running their race division for a decade until they went bankrupt. You *have* heard of him, right?'

'He hasn't told me anything,' I said, ignoring Varzi's sarcasm.

'They don't have any drivers. It seems logical that they'd turn to foreign talent as well.'

'I suspect that won't sit well with their backers in Munich,' I replied.

'And Auto Union – will they be ready for this season?'

'I don't know.'

'Of course you do.' Varzi looked down at my sodden moccasins sinking into the rich earth. 'Jesus, Finestrini. You'll catch your death of cold.'

Inside the warm kitchen, Varzi, Benoist and Chiron sipped on espresso laced with grappa. I sat before the potbellied stove, my bare feet resting on a chair in the glow of the blazing wood fire, and sipped the espresso, the cup of pure grappa burning its way into my frozen gut.

'Signora Pina!' I heard Benoist say suddenly, and I quickly put my bare feet down. A woman in a worn coat and yellow muddy boots was easing her way through the kitchen door. I watched Benoist peck her on the cheek, as her arms enveloped him in a tender embrace.

'Robert,' she said, 'how wonderful – you know, Menotti and I were in Paris only last week and dropped by the Bugatti store, but they told us you were away.'

'Robert is a Chevalier,' said Chiron, giving the Signora his most charming smile. 'Work is merely a distraction for him now.' In his youth, I thought unkindly, Chiron's smile must have served him well in his profession as *danseur mondain* at the Hotel de Paris in Monaco. So well that he'd managed to fund his own racing career until millionaire Freddie Hoffman, in need of a top-line driver for his fledgling grand prix team, had come calling. In gratitude, Chiron had seduced his wife, Baby, with whom he'd been romantically engaged for years. He had learnt much from the rich who tipped his father so leanly at the grand hotel of his youth, had Chiron, and behind the debonair grace was a street fighter not restricted by any gentle manners.

'Dear Louis,' she said when he kissed her cheeks. Then her eyes darted towards me.

'That's Johnny Finestrini,' said Varzi, not looking up from the 'paper. 'The journalist from the *Gazzetta*.'

'Is it indeed.' She stepped closer and extended a warm, soft hand which I took into mine. She glanced down at my feet in dismay.

'I got mud on my shoes,' I explained apologetically.

Varzi sniggered. Signora Pina gave her son an admonishing look. '*Achille*. It's not funny – it won't do at all for dear Johnny to catch his death of cold.'

I chose that moment to release a vicious sneeze.

'Poor little man. Come with me.' Her grip on my hand strengthened as she marched me out of the kitchen and down the hall. She led me to a cozy sitting room where the curtains were still drawn and logs lay waiting in the hearth. 'Sit here,' she ordered before vanishing from the room. She soon returned with a pair of thick, woollen socks. 'These should fit,' she said, handing them over. 'You know, my husband, Varzi's father – oh, listen to me, Menotti, I mean, that's his name, and those actually are his socks – now what was I saying? Oh, Menotti, yes, he holds your work in much esteem – he insists that you have a unique insight into Achille's passions. But I must confess I don't share his enthusiasm.' She drew open the curtains with a practised curve. The day beyond remained filthy, and I shivered involuntarily, embalmed by the damp. 'Not your work, of course – I meant Achille's vocation.' She let her sentence hang like a question, her eyes – Varzi's eyes – doing the rest. 'I too have actually taken to reading your columns with a rather bewildering regularity.' She looked at me with curiosity. 'You seem almost – how can I say it – almost in love, yes?'

I blinked.

'With the sport,' she added, walking toward me. 'Perhaps that's what Signor Varzi sees in your work.' She kept staring at me until I felt the discomfort build around us. Finally, she said: 'We'd better get back before Louis starts getting ideas – he's an incorrigible man, that one, and a hopeless gossip.' I followed her back to the kitchen with an odd sense of relief.

Signora Pina deftly prepared us a meal of fresh eggs, venison and caffè latte. With four steaming plates on the table, she gave Varzi a quick peck on the cheek and left us to it. Varzi didn't touch his food. Instead, he idly flipped through the morning edition of the *Corriere*. Benoist and Chiron appeared to be as famished as I was, and the sounds of chewing and eating filled the silence.

'So where is the charming Baby Hoffman?' asked Benoist eventually.

Chiron gave him a look brimming with fury.

'Hunting,' said Varzi, 'is a man's sport. Isn't that so, Louis?'

Chiron chewed his food vigorously without replying.

Varzi tried again. 'Remember when we went hunting with Caracciola and Charly, back in '31?'

Chiron wiped his lips with a napkin, stood up, and headed out of the kitchen with a dejected stride.

'Did I say something wrong?' asked Benoist haplessly.

Benoist had become a Chevalier of the *Légion d'Honneur* in 1927, that fairytale year when he'd won the Italian, Spanish, French, and British Grands Prix. With his tough crooked nose and brooding eyes, he was a striking man, and one for whom Varzi had all the time in the world.

'Chiron's in a funk,' Varzi was saying. 'I wouldn't worry too much about it. Woman troubles from what I gather.' He led us into a delightfully airy room, with a cluster of mismatched chairs and sofas dotted about at odd angles beneath modest oil paintings. Benoist helped himself to Varzi's 'paper and settled into an easy-chair. He looked increasingly agitated as he turned the pages, until he finally blurted out: 'Himmler has taken charge of the entire German police force. Do you understand what that means?'

Comfortably ensconced in an armchair, I nodded drowsily in agreement.

'These Nazis are turning Germany into a police state,' Benoist insisted. 'It won't end well.'

'Won't end well for any of us,' agreed Varzi. He lay on a couch with his feet dangling over the edge, his eyes staring sleepily at the ceiling. 'Mercedes are going to eat us alive, aren't they Finestrini?'

'You've seen them?' asked Chiron, stepping into the room and moving towards the fireplace.

'He spoke to Neubauer,' said Varzi accusingly.

'So who's driving for them then? When will they make their debut? I'd half-anticipated them at Monaco actually.' Chiron's eyes fell on me.

'They're debuting at the AVUS,' said Benoist with the kind of authority that allowed no scope for doubt.

'But who will drive?' insisted Chiron. 'Surely not that cripple Caracciola – he made a fool of himself in Monaco, didn't he?' Caracciola had indeed returned the weekend before in Monaco, and there hadn't been a dry eye in the place when he slowly made his way around the circuit in the same Alfa that had almost killed him a year before. He did one lap, and even I was reduced to tears when the recently widowed Rudi Caracciola stood shaking in the cockpit, waving his arms and smiling through the agony of it all.

'I thought what he did was very brave,' said Benoist. 'And I was under the impression you were a good friend of his, Louis.'

Chiron turned his back to us, spreading his fingers before the flames. 'Don't forget I was the one who pulled him out of his wrecked car,' he said. 'And I was the one who told the doctors not to fucking amputate and wait for Putti. Rudi is broken; he was broken physically when he went into that fucking wall, and he was mentally destroyed when Charly went off skiing and never came home. The only thing he can offer now is his experience, his technical insights – isn't that right, Finestrini?'

I sighed. 'Look, all I know is that Mercedes have scheduled a series of tests at the AVUS for May.'

'Who told you that?' asked Varzi.

'What does it matter? Caracciola will be there.'

'Impossible,' said Chiron, walking towards Varzi's couch. 'He can barely walk.'

'That man has no nervous system left,' agreed Varzi, curling his legs up for Chiron to sit beside him. 'Lost it along with Charly – remember how he was that night when we got there from Zürs?' The night that Caracciola had been told of Charly's accident, Varzi and Chiron had received a call from Rudi's doctor, who'd asked them to come immediately to his home in Arosa. They had found Rudi in a bad way. They had called Baby Hoffman and abandoned Caracciola to her care while they went back to their ski lodge. She had somehow managed to get him back to his therapy, to his training, and she had been there by his side in Monaco when he'd returned to the circus. I wondered now what had happened between them in that villa. Charly and Rudi, Chiron and Baby; they had been inseparable back in the day, even founding their own team in 1933 when Chiron had been fired from Bugatti and Caracciola had lost his ride with the defunct Alfa works. The debut of the Scuderia CC at Monaco had only lasted a few hours – until Rudi smashed into that wall. Nothing had been the same since then.

'You'll be at the AVUS, won't you Finestrini?' asked Varzi, interrupting my thoughts.

'I hadn't thought about it.'

'Why not? The great Aryan champion returns – as does the mythical Mercedes team. Surely worth a headline, eh? It wasn't a coincidence that Neubauer let you in on his secret.'

'Neubauer is a cagey old bastard, always was,' said Benoist. 'Still, one wonders what he sees in those Nazi thugs.'

'Money,' said Chiron.

'Doesn't matter,' Varzi yawned. 'It's too soon for Rudi. He'd be crazy to do that run in May.'

◉

Finestrini pauses to sip on his Campari, and I seize on this opportunity to interrupt his story.

'Caracciola did the run, though, didn't he? At the AVUS?'

'Yes he did. And he was fast enough to persuade Neubauer to offer him a limited contract.'

'Were you there?'

'For the test?' Finestrini nods. 'And I'll tell you what, I've never seen a man endure such pain as Caracciola did that day. He was paper-white by the end of that run, shivering uncontrollably. It really was something – he had nothing, you understand… he had lost everything, and this was his last chance at redemption. And he seized it: he was faster than all the young guns that Mercedes were running that week.'

'Nuvolari was running for Maserati that season, right?'

'Yes,' Finestrini replies, running his finger around the rim of his glass, 'and he felt at home in Bologna, too. Maserati had a bigger shop than Ferrari back then, and they would always invite their drivers in to look over the drawings and the cars as they were being designed and prepared. There were no secrets at Maserati – all very socialist, of course, but then that's Bologna for you. Nuvolari would meet with the mechanics on Tuesday afternoons and they would swap ideas. He was a happy man at Maserati, but he was going nowhere fast, and he knew it. He was never sentimental when it came to winning, and come time for the Mille Miglia, he didn't hesitate for a minute to ditch Maserati for the race in favour of an Alfa Monza which he secured through Eugenio Siena, who had just started his own scuderia that year. It was identical to the one that Ferrari would enter for Varzi. However, Nuvolari couldn't get the Pirelli tyres that Ferrari was using, and he had to settle for Dunlops instead. As it turned out, that altered the course of the race.'

'Why?'

'Pirelli's chief technician, Cossatter, had developed a new tyre that had studs in it; in wet conditions, these tyres were far better than the Dunlops. Ferrari, you know, had positioned scouts ahead on the road, and he got word that rain was falling down in the Veneto, so he had the mechanics prepare the wet tyres for Varzi – even though the sun was still shining at the final stop on the Bologna-Imola autostrada. You can imagine Varzi's reaction, then: it was eight or nine hours into the race and he was trailing Nuvolari by about thirty seconds, and when he saw those wet tyres, he went ballistic. Accused Ferrari of wanting to sabotage him, of favoring Nuvolari, all kinds of crazy stuff – it was quite a scene, I can tell you. At one point, the two of them were actually pushing each other physically, and I was convinced it would all end in blows. But Ferrari, you know, never lost an argument. When he pointed out that Varzi's wasn't leaving until he took the wet tyres, the argument was pretty much done.'

'And did it rain?'

'Of course,' replies Finestrini. 'It was torrential. *Of course* it rained, why else would Ferrari have wanted him on the wets? But that was Varzi for you, his paranoia was contagious. The rain let up by the time they got into Brescia, but not enough for Nuvolari to pose a threat. Varzi won by three minutes, and I don't think even he would have dismissed Ferrari's role in that win. Not that he ever acknowledged it, mind you. For the rest of the season the two of them went about their business with mutual suspicion. Their business of winning. At the end of May, they went down to Sicily and swept up the Targa Florio. Varzi became the first man – and the last – to hold both the Mille Miglia and the Targa titles at the same time.'

'Nuvolari wasn't at the Targa, was he?'

'No, he'd injured himself at Alessandria. Badly.'

'Were you there?'

Finestrini glances up. 'We should order, it's getting late.' He looks at the menu and ignores me studiously.

'Nuvolari accused Ferrari of deliberately trying to kill him at Alessandria – was it true?'

'He certainly believed it,' says Finestrini.

'Did you?'

'Alessandria was a miserable place,' he replies, interrupting his thoughts long enough to entrust Sergio with our order. 'That track was a grim thing, flat and featureless and dangerous: It crossed over the Tanaro twice before winding its way through an awfully depressed part of town – and believe me, the rest of it was hardly worthy of a postcard. The race was named after Pietro Bordino – the driver who drowned in '28 when he got trapped under his Bugatti in a foot of water. That's the kind of place Alessandria was.'

'The 1934 race was the last time they went to Alessandria, wasn't it?'

'Yes, and good riddance, too. No one was in the least surprised when Nuvolari had the biggest shunt of his career there. As it was, he came out of it better than his team-mate, who left in a pine box.'

I retrieve an article from my folder and slide it across the table. Finestrini holds it up to the dim light so he can read the first few lines.

'I got into trouble for this one,' he says, smiling to himself.

"Count Trossi was yet again implicated in a serious incident here at the Bordino circuit this afternoon, and one cannot help but recall that it was his oil that played such a calamitous role in the deaths of Borzacchini and Campari at Monza last year. But before this controversial final heat, two heats took place in the morning, and it is my sad duty to report the tragic death of Carlo Pedrazzini – Tazio Nuvolari's young team-mate – during Heat One.

Heat Two was marked by two more accidents involving Roberto Malaguti, who crashed into the crowd, and Louis Delmot, who suffered a similar incident when his Bugatti veered off the track and ploughed into a house. Both escaped any serious injury.

It was therefore with much anticipation and an understandable sense of dread that the world's finest drivers assembled for the Final Heat beneath a stormy sky. The roads through Alessandria were packed by fans who had gathered to watch Nuvolari exact his vengeance for his Mille Miglia loss, but on the grid it was Varzi who sat calmly in his cockpit beneath an umbrella, while Nuvolari was a bundle of nerves. It was clear that Nuvolari was in for a tough afternoon, surrounded as he was by Ferrari's men. Alongside him on the second row was his chief rival, Achille Varzi, while Mario Tadini was at the very front, and row three featured Louis Chiron and

Count Trossi.

The start was shambolic and proved, yet again, that Nuvolari and Varzi operate in their own dimension. The moment the official time-keeper touched the shoulder of the flagman, Nuvolari and Varzi were already on their way, cutting through the field and diving into Turn One side-by-side, Varzi leading by mere inches. These two quickly separated themselves from the chasing pack on that first lap, with Nuvolari darting this way and that in a futile attempt to escape the spray of water and mist that poured from the rear-wheels of Varzi's Alfa. Desperate to get out of the spray, Nuvolari attempted an ambitious pass into the hairpin at the head of the back-straight. Varzi, in an overly aggressive move given the circumstances, chopped down on the Mantuan, and the two cars brushed bodywork as they did in 1930. Varzi managed to race ahead, while Nuvolari was thrown into a harmless spin. By the time Nuvolari sorted his Maserati out, the Ferraris of Chiron, Trossi, and Tadini had all sped past him.

His became a frenzied pursuit. While other drivers would have taken the series of fast switchbacks in classic oversteer, Nuvolari adopted an understeering technique, aggressively yanking his steering wheel with every turn. There are not many men brave enough to induce that level of instability in a car while racing lap after lap in the rain; but then, Nuvolari is no mere mortal. Today, he found a surprisingly effective way to get through those bends, and his courage paid off. In two breathtaking laps, he disposed first of Chiron, then of Tadini. Nuvolari's outrageous manoeuvres had now propelled him into third place, and soon he was hounding Count Trossi's Ferrari–Alfa Tipo B.

Nuvolari attempted to pass Trossi at the hairpin, but found the door firmly shut. He tried again the next lap with the same dismal result. On lap eleven, at the exact spot where Pedrazzini had lost his life earlier in the day, Nuvolari attacked again. What happened next remains shrouded in mystery. All we know is that Nuvolari lost control of his Maserati at close to 170kph. One of his wheels struck a ditch, and the Flying Mantuan – living up to his name – was tossed from the cockpit. His flight ended at the side of the road when his Maserati came crashing down onto his legs.

Up ahead, Count Trossi had also lost control of his car but his crash into a pole did not injure him in the slightest. Trossi maintains that his Alfa and Nuvolari's Maserati had absolutely no contact, but if that is the case, one is left wondering how the two drivers ended up shunting at the same time on the same corner.

Three nurses from the Red Cross were the first to reach the stricken and bleeding Nuvolari, who lay barely conscious at the side of the track. So grave were the champion's wounds that Varzi almost veered off the track upon seeing the blood on his rival, and witnesses report that Varzi slowed every lap thereafter to inquire after Nuvolari. The reply was non-committal as doctors battled to keep him alive trackside, while an ambulance was dispatched from the nearby hospital.

Varzi won the race by 1.2 seconds over Louis Chiron, and two minutes ahead of Tadini, making it yet another clean sweep for the all-dominant Scuderia Ferrari in 1934. Nuvolari, meanwhile, was transported to the hospital in Alessandria, suffering from a badly fractured left leg and numerous contusions to his face and upper abdomen. Doctors have declared his condition serious but stable as we go to press. The whole of Italy will no doubt keep Nuvolari and Carlo Pedrazzini in their thoughts and prayers.

Believe, obey, fight!"

Finestrini slides the article back across the table when Sergio appears with our starters. The two men share an aside in dialect which I'm unable to follow, before Sergio laughs and walks away with a quick glance back in my direction.

'So why did you get into trouble?' I ask.

'Count Trossi took exception to what I'd written, and Cristoferi raked me over the coals for writing "unsubstantiated rumours".'

'What rumours?'

'That Trossi and Nuvolari had touched. Trossi, I suppose, was worried about his reputation – and rightly so. If Nuvolari had died, he would have been implicated in killing all three champions of the Golden Generation. Not quite the reputation anyone would have wanted, especially in those days.'

'*Did* they touch?'

'Nuvolari believed they did. He was convinced that Ferrari had deliberately set out to have Trossi and Tadini block him to allow Varzi to get away. A week later, he wrote an official complaint to the Commissione Sportiva del Reale Automobile Club d'Italia, in which he alleged that Enzo Ferrari had conspired to physically harm him during the race. It was a serious allegation which, naturally, went completely ignored. Not that it was the first time Ferrari was accused of using his drivers as mobile road blocks – Caracciola had experienced similar at the Mille Miglia in '31 when Campari, Borzacchini, and Nuvolari had run three abreast for over fifty miles to block him for passing. Still, that was a bad shunt; I could hear his screams from a long way off, and those nurses holding him down, it was all … ' Finestrini clears his throat. 'It was a strange day, and it got even stranger by the end of it. After the race, back at the pits, Varzi sought me out. I assumed that he wanted to ask me about Tazio, or maybe swap an anecdote or two, but instead he asked, "Who is Paul Pietsch?" '

When I look up from my soup, I find Finestrini's gaze waiting. There is something there, in his eyes, an expression that I can't quite make out. I blink and focus down on my soup; not yet, I think. Not yet.

'Turns out,' Finestrini continues, and I can feel his eyes staring at me, 'Pietsch had run a privately-entered Alfa in Heat One and Varzi wanted to know who he was. I didn't have a clue, but promised to find out. I must confess, though, that I promptly forgot all about it by the time I reached the hospital.'

'You had a lot on your mind.'

'I certainly didn't have Pietsch on my mind,' he says, as if baiting me. He can't know, I reassure myself. He can't know, and I must play it cool. 'Actually, Deutsch, I paid Nuvolari a visit at his home, where he was convalescing, on my way to the Libyan Grand Prix.'

'How did that turn out?' I ask, checking to see if the Carry-Corder cassette is rolling, and lifting my gaze to meet Finestrini's.

His wife Carolina led me through the austere house on the Viale Delle Rimembranze.

'I told him not to be so morose,' she joked. 'After all, he's got a permanent set of wheels now, hasn't he?'

Nuvolari was out in the garden in his wheelchair, his injured leg propped on a wicker table. He sat still in the spring air, sipping on lemonade and watching his two boys kicking a warped soccer ball around the lawn.

'Come to commiserate, Finestrini?' Nuvolari asked when I walked up behind him.

'No,' I replied, resting my hands on his stiff shoulders. 'Just to amuse myself.'

He gestured towards the wicker chair beside him on which Carolina had left her sunhat, and I sat down, placing the hat on my knees.

'Does it hurt?' I asked.

'No more than a shattered leg should.'

'Prognosis?'

Something played in his dark eyes. 'No more racing, no more sex, no more walking, the usual rubbish, you know what doctors are like. They give you the worst possible news and then cure you miraculously. I'll be back at the AVUS to race in my pathetic car yet again, while Varzi wins everything.'

The chair creaked rudely when I settled back and gathered my coat about me. The sun was warm despite the nip in the air, but I had yet to shake the cold that had fallen like a malevolent shadow over my life.

Giorgio, Nuvolari's eldest, was growing into a man, all of fifteen and blessed with the easy-looks of wealth that his father could never have dreamt of in his youth, the son of a peasant that he was. Alberto, too, was growing fast, but he was, I thought, a pale and pasty boy.

'I'm sending Giorgio off to finishing school in Switzerland,' Nuvolari said, gazing at his kids. 'Near Lugano. Finishing school, can you believe it?' Nuvolari had left school at fifteen – eight years too late, as he related it.

'He's a smart boy,' I said, despite the fact that I had never even spoken to the kid.

'He gets that from his mother – from me he got nothing but a love of engines.'

'That and a future.'

'Yes,' said Nuvolari. 'There is that.' He paused for a moment. 'I was born not far from here, you know.'

'I know, Tazio. Everyone in Italy knows where you were born. It's practically a shrine by now.'

'A little farm,' he went on dreamily. 'That was meant to be my destiny: dirt and work, Finestrini, dirt and work – had it not been for this.'

I gazed at him for a while but said nothing.

'I hear Mercedes will be at the AVUS,' he said after a while.

'Yes I believe so, Tazio – and Auto Union, too.'

'Have you seen them?'

'I just got back from Berlin: Caracciola was testing the new Mercedes.'

Nuvolari turned to me. 'And?'

'It's fast,' I replied. What more could I add? That the new Mercedes looked and sounded as if it had come from somewhere in the future? That Italian dominance was a thing of the past? That I had seen Caracciola spin his rear tyres in top gear? The sleek and powerful Silver Arrows had taken an evolutionary step, and Alfa would not be able to compete unless funds were found to design a whole new car. But these thoughts I kept to myself as we watched Giorgio and Alberto play football through the afternoon.

After a while, I realized that Nuvolari had fallen asleep, and I left then, hailing a cab for the station and the night ferry to Africa.

Unable to sleep, I'd arrived at the track early on raceday and found a sombre mood had settled over the Ferrari pit. I soon discovered that Varzi had had a close call in practice the day before when, with the official session over, he had decided on a final lap at speed to test a new suspension setting. Count Brivio, meanwhile, had broken down just beyond a rise at the back of the circuit, and his team-mate Dreyfus – assuming the session was over – had decided to tow Brivio back to the pit, using a rope to link the two Bugattis. Varzi, encountering them at full throttle, had somehow managed to avoid a serious shunt by veering onto an earth bank. From there, his Alfa taken off over both Bugattis before smashing down on all four wheels, cracking its half shaft.

Under the noonday sun that glinted off the cars assembled on the grid, I found Dreyfus sitting in the shadow of his Bugatti sipping on a bottle of mineral water. He was a shabbily dressed, even-tempered Frenchman who had been friendly with Chiron for a decade, and was now enjoying the best season of his career. I squatted down beside him on the hot tarmac and listened to his version of events.

'Didn't see a thing,' Dreyfus said in perfect Italian. 'I was too busy making sure I didn't slip the clutch as I started to drag Brivio's car. Then I saw Varzi flying over my head.'

'Was he angry?'

'Probably. I'm sure he'd have been angrier still had his buddy Brivio not been there. Brivio was born an aristocrat and wants to forget it – Varzi is a commoner and wants to be an aristocrat.' An easy smile crossed his face. 'So anyway, I reminded Varzi that we were ten kilometres away from the pits, and I don't think he fancied the walk back. He calmed down quite a bit after that.'

Dreyfus's laughter still echoed in my ears as I made my way up to the press box over the main grandstand where I was treated to an unobstructed view of the thirteen kilometre track. From up there, I could see all the way to the airfield before the road veered to the right and drifted out into the desert. The press box was sheltered from the concussive heat, and cool drinks were proffered via barefoot boys who would vanish God knows where at the merest snap of the fingers, only to return with chilled rum and Coca Cola.

Ferrari was running P3s for the race – the same cars that had been so successful for Guy Moll in Monaco and for Varzi in Alessandria. They were malleable, powerful cars, with Dubbonet front suspension – precise weapons that were about to become obsolete at the very cusp of their dominance.

I watched Varzi's P3 being pushed onto the grid by two fez-wearing mechanics. Ferrari had flown in a new engine during the night, and Varzi was still fuming over the fact that he hadn't been permitted to take over Moll's P3 after his practice incident.

As the number one driver, Varzi always insisted on first choice of car, and an untested lump dumped into his Alfa at 5am by sleep-deprived mechanics was clearly not to his satisfaction. Varzi had phoned Ferrari repeatedly during the night, but the old lizard would not yield. Moll was not going to surrender his car, and that was that. It was typical Ferrari, pitting one driver against the other, but I sensed that there was something deeper at work here. Ferrari seemed to have real affection for Moll, an almost paternal fondness that I hadn't seen him express since his glory days with Nuvolari. He had once told me that it was Moll's mixed heritage – Spanish mother, French father, raised in Algeria – that made him the best talent he'd seen since Nuvolari.

Marshall Balbo, the new governor of Libya, was now mincing down the grid in all his finery. He walked from driver to driver, extending his hand and sharing some well-chosen thoughts in impeccable French, English, Italian, and German. When he eventually reached Varzi he did neither, pointedly ignoring Varzi's proffered hand. Even from up in the box I could sense Varzi's astonishment as Balbo continued his tour of the grid, brushing aside the reigning champion with deliberate indifference. He had clearly heard about the controversy surrounding last year's race.

With his grid walk complete, Balbo was escorted off the

track, amid loud applause from the crowd. The cars were now officially under starter's orders. The Alfa-Ferrari P3s sounded superbly tuned, but their noise was immediately drowned out by the thunder of Piero Taruffi's Maserati V5. The entire grandstand stood as one to gawk at this 16-cylinder monstrosity that sounded more like a squadron of Balbo's planes than a race car, and we could feel it rumble mightily beneath our feet. Maserati's mythical *sedici cilindri*, I thought, back from the dead. First conceived and built in '29, it had taken Borzacchini to 401kph at Cremona, but it had proved hopelessly inept on any track other than those with open, wide straightaways, and it'd been shelved after Ruggeri, chasing the world 1-Hour record at Montlhéry in '32, had lost control and killed it along with himself. I could see it still ran diminutive drum brakes, and I felt for poor Taruffi – it was going to be a short and brutal afternoon for the Roman.

Weighing just under a ton, it shot off past everyone including a hapless Varzi when the flag dropped, sailing off into the heat as if someone had injected it with an explosive. It ran on full grooved tyres while the rest of the field ran on slicks to lessen the friction on the flat, fast circuit, but the V5 had enough brute hate to chew through its tyres in a matter of laps. Here, though, on the fastest circuit on earth, Taruffi just might have a fighting chance – provided he could keep the thing on the track. I wiped my brow and watched the cars vanish into the desert. The race would last about three hours, and would be decided, as always, on the last lap, since it was improbable that any car would break from the pack. I grabbed my straw hat and headed out of the press box. By the time I got down to the pits, the PA had announced that Taruffi's V5 had gone off the track near the salt pond at Saline Mellaha.

◼

Sergio has brought our main course: polenta baccalà. 'The Venetians,' says Finestrini, 'despite practically living in the sea, can't cook for shit – the only thing you can trust them with is salted cod from the bloody Atlantic.' He waits until I take a bite

117

before continuing. 'The race became the customary procession, with the three Ferraris in tandem until Chiron's car developed a misfire, leaving Varzi and Moll to fight it out between themselves. I don't know what happened out there during that final lap in the desert, but Varzi crossed the line inches ahead of a visibly angry Guy Moll.

'I caught up with Taruffi as he was heading back to the pits, and he confirmed that he had killed the Beast of Bologna once and for all. We chatted about Varzi's narrow win for a while, and by the time I got to the Ferrari garage, the celebrations were already long over, the grandstands emptying out, and the silence palpable. Varzi was leaning against a wall in the shade of the concrete garage, with a few mechanics serving as a make-shift cordon in front of him. I assumed that this was to keep the press at bay, until I followed Varzi's surreptitious glance toward the opposite end of the garage, where Moll was engaged in an animated discussion with Bazzi. I watched as Bazzi placed a restraining hand on Moll's shoulder but Moll broke away from his grip and started striding toward Varzi.

' "Here comes trouble," whispered Taruffi at my side.

' "You dirty little bastard!" shouted Moll, shouldering past the ring of mechanics surrounding Varzi. "You almost had me in the wall!" He raised his clenched fist and was about to start swinging when Viganò intervened, wrapping his forearm around the French-Algerian's neck and dragging him away. Moll continued shouting obscenities in Italian and French and God knows what as he struggled to break from Viganò's grip.

'Varzi offered nothing aside from that empty stare of his, that vacant, sarcastic glare. Until Moll was a safe distance away, that is, and behind a screen of mechanics. Then Varzi started to laugh – a shrill sound so vicious that even the mechanics were taken aback. Moll, shamed and enraged, strode out of the garage, making sure his shoulder smashed into mine as he walked past, almost knocking me off my feet.'

Finestrini inserts a fork into his yellow polenta and nudges the mush about. 'That was a long trip back to Italy, I can tell you. Fraught, I think you would say. But that was Varzi for you, wasn't it, 1934 vintage anyway, when he dominated the grand prix racing scene. Only Moll seemed capable of giving him a run that season. He was Varzi's new enemy, and I doubt Moll really appreciated how far Varzi would go to destroy him. Didn't help matters much either that Moll was such a hot-head: he went off to the French press and insisted that Ferrari had interfered with the result, that Ferrari was favoring the Italian and so on. Truth was though, if there was any favoritism, it was Moll who had been the recipient at Tripoli, as he would be at the AVUS where he was resolved to settle matters with Varzi. And I almost missed the race.'

'Why?'

'The world's inaugural World Cup was scheduled to begin in Rome the same day as the AVUS race, and Cristoferi was less than keen to pack me off to Berlin, claiming the expense of sending nine journalists around the country to cover the football games had sapped the 'paper's travel budget.'

'And?'

'And I took him for a long boozy lunch to persuade him, much as you're doing to me, young man. It usually works.'

○

'The Germans are determined to crush us,' I told Cristoferi, pouring him another glass of Barolo. 'That's the story, you see?'

'No, I don't see.'

'The Germans are coming,' I said. 'And they want to defeat us. And I – that is, the *Gazzetta* – will chronicle their failure.'

He signed off on the trip that same afternoon. On the night-train to Berlin, I started reading through a series of articles on the history of the AVUS, the world's first purpose-built race track. At least, that had been the plan when it had first been conceived and designed back in 1907 by the operating company *Automobil-Verkehrs und Übungs-Straße* – the initials of which would give the track its name. When the track had finally been built in 1922, Brooklands and Indianapolis had already been around for over a decade. The AVUS was, in essence, two sections of autobahn running north and south for two-and-a-half miles, with a hairpin corner at each end. The simple layout served to create races that were inevitably tight affairs, and the race in 1933, the first sports event held beneath the swastika, had seen the closest finish in motor-racing history, when Varzi had pipped Count Czaykowski by less than a tenth of a second in front of 170,000 fans.

Up in the stands that day, watching Italian and French cars take the first five positions, Adolf Hitler had resolved never to suffer a similar humiliation again. That weekend had been a particularly bad one for Germany, with legendary driver Otto Merz dying from wounds he sustained during practice. Merz had been chauffeur to Count Boos-Waldeck in Sarajevo in 1914 when Archduke Franz Ferdinand was assassinated, and it had been Merz who'd carried the wounded Archduke from the scene and watched him die.

This year's race was the first of the new 750kg formula; it was also scheduled to mark the return of Mercedes (with their W25), and the debut of the newly-formed Auto Union (with their Porsche-designed, rear-engined Type A). Both cars had been built courtesy of a one million Reichsmark subsidy from Dear Uncle Adolf who had, at the 1933 International Motor Show in Berlin, assured the world's press that in twelve months, Germany would dominate the motor racing world. Come race day, though, neither he nor Mercedes were present, Mercedes having withdrawn due to fuel pump issues. That left only Auto Union in the fight with the Italians.

The idea that the German industry could destroy fifteen years of Italian dominance in twelve short months seemed, to me, a little optimistic. Still, I must confess to having felt a sense of anticipation when I first reached the track, knowing that I was finally about to set eyes on the Auto Unions. Even before I had seen the car, I had a hint of what to expect when, passing their garage just past dawn, I'd caught a glimpse of the mechanics heating oil on little stoves. The engines, I assumed, needed thicker lubricants, and that had me wondering what the hell they were running in those cars of theirs.

Standing on the grid that afternoon within touching distance of the quicksilver Auto Union with the *Horst Wessel* song ringing in my ears from 200,000 throats and a pale May sun gleaming off the coachwork, I began to suspect that it was I who was suffering from over-optimism. The Alfas cowering there beside the three Auto Unions looked like metal bathtubs sloshing with toxic, combustible fuel. Even Moll's special 'slipstream' P3 Alfa seemed out of place beneath the endless rows of swastikas wafting in the cool breeze. (Varzi, needless to say, was furious that he had been denied the slipstreamer, as its aerodynamics made it far quicker on the straights than his regular grand prix P3. When we had spoken at the hotel after Thursday's practice, he'd informed me that his relationship with Ferrari was now beyond salvaging, and that he was officially on the market for the 1935 season.)

Auto Union had entered cars for Hans Stuck, Hermann zu Leiningen, and August Momberger – these last two pretty much unknown novices and looking every bit the part. I walked past Momberger on the grid and noticed how terrified he was, sitting there with his goggles shielding his eyes a full twenty minutes before the start. He had that stare, unblinking and terrified, already projecting his fate into the Grunewald forest with that vicious and mighty V16 behind his head intent on murder. I had watched the Auto Union mechanics conduct a full pit stop that morning, and it had been a sobering experience. They had specially designed pressure hoses capable of pumping five gallons of fuel per second. Just one small error by those highly-skilled mechanics would have been enough for gallons of highly toxic and flammable fuel to spray over the car with unimaginable consequences.

Hans Stuck, meanwhile, was taking it all in his stride, his six-foot-two frame positively gleaming in spectacular white overalls. He towered over a fedora-wearing Ferdinand Porsche, and team boss Willy Walb in the Auto Union garage, where the world's press was hanging on to their every word. Behind them, in full Nazi regalia, stood a short, blunt skinhead who was introduced as Korpsführer Adolf Hühnlein, the National Socialist Motor Corps leader. Rumour had it that his job was to file personal race reports for Geliebte Führer, and I couldn't help thinking that, by comparison, dealing with my cantankerous boss, Cristoferi, was a piece of cake. Hühnlein, by all accounts, had spent the Roaring

Twenties smashing up commie heads with much relish, and he looked tough enough to cope with a few thrashings from Dear Adolf.

I eased into the scrum of journalists and listened as Dr. Porsche explained some technical details about his mid-engined Auto Union. 'We are running a Roots supercharged 4.4-litre V16 engine capable of producing around 280bph at 4500rpm with a five-speed gearbox and independent suspension front and rear. Zenith carburretor and valves are operated off of a single shaft. The stub exhausts – I know some of you have asked – are for aesthetic purposes only, because we believe a fast racecar needs to look fast, too.' He laughed, and the German press, encouraged, laughed with him. 'We completed work on the first Type A in October of last year, but only as a result of a team of highly-specialized German technicians working for six months on a twenty-four hour a day, three-shift schedule. I'm reliably informed – given that I designed it – that the car has over 1,622 differing components, all of them quite useless without one crucial element.'

Porsche seemed comfortable in his own skin. Not surprising, of course, since this was the man who had been head-hunted by Stalin to oversee the industrialization of the Soviet Union. Instead, Hitler had offered him a new project in the service of the Reich – to design not only the Auto Union, but also the People's Car. I watched him give Stuck a thumbs up. 'Ready, Hans?'

Stuck, with that infectious, crooked-toothed grin of his, led us onto the grid, a blitz of cameras capturing this moment for tomorrow's newspapers. He strode toward his Auto Union, waving at the cheering crowd. After ensuring that the German press corps had been given plenty of time to snap photos of him posing with one foot on the cockpit, he finally slid into the blood-red leather seat.

'You will notice,' Dr. Porsche said, 'how far forward Hans is sitting; the seat has been molded to fit his, and only his, frame.'

'Like a second skin,' said Stuck, sitting in a tub over the front axle with the arched bodywork streaking behind him as if carved by speed itself. Even standing still, the car seemed in motion.

'The advantages of a mid-engined configuration,' Dr. Porsche continued, 'are numerous, but I won't elaborate since we're here to win, not give pointers to our opposition.'

The German journalists tittered. It was common knowledge that Porsche had left Mercedes under somewhat of a cloud after his pet project – a lightweight, rear-engined car that could be easily and cheaply manufactured – had fallen out of favour with the Daimler-Benz board. In 1929, Porsche had been shown the door, and he had started his own design company in 1930 with a fellow named Rosenberger, a one-time driver who now owned twenty-five percent of the firm. Bradley had told me that they had designed armoured combat vehicles in violation of the Treaty of Versailles, along with the self-propelled 88mm 'Ferdinand' gun, and the Tiger Mark I tank. Cristoferi had nixed an article I had written in the fall of '33 that revealed the military implications of a German motor sport project. 'Who gives a crap?' had been Cristoferi's reply. 'So what if the Germans are arming themselves to the teeth? They're fucking Germans, no one expects anything else.'

I stepped a bit closer to the car, about to touch the glistening silver machine when Porsche's voice stopped me. *'Nein, Signor* Finestrini, do not touch please. That shell is made of duraluminium – it weighs less than forty-five kilos – you can dent it simply by pressing too hard. Step away please. *Weggehen, weggehen!'*

I stepped back from the car with a sheepish smile. I could not imagine how Stuck felt about propelling the Type A into the woods at over 300kph, but suddenly Momberger's fear seemed perfectly reasonable to me. The Alfas may have been from a different era, but their skin could hardly be dented by a stray finger. A mechanic fixed Stuck's steering wheel onto the naked steering column as he sat with his hands on his lap. Dr. Porsche checked the stopwatch hanging from his lapel. 'Gentlemen, I think it would be prudent for us to step off the grid right about now.'

We followed Porsche back over the make-shift pitwall from where we watched Auto Union's mechanics wheel the starter battery to Stuck's Porschewagen Type A. The starter was the size of a small wheel barrow, and I could see the Ferrari boys watching in astonishment. Stuck consulted his instruments like an aviator before his finger clipped the ignition switch that released a small amount of ether directly into the fuel tank. The V16 wheezed, drank up fuel and spat out an eruption of smoke from those stubbed exhaust pipes pointing up at the sky like a battery of canons. And then hell opened up. The note was profound and resonant, a hollow menacing growl from the supercharger that was located between the carb' and the engine. The noise growled out into the grandstands like a virus where 200,000 stood transfixed to the sound of Stuck's telegraphing foot. I'd never heard such a sound before. Tightly wound, an elastic machine. The mechanics started up the sister Auto Unions, Momberger's last, and the fury that smelt of arsenic ripped the fabric right out of our world.

I glanced around the grid and spotted Nuvolari, who was here driving against doctors' orders. His leg was still in a cast, and he was smiling like a kid at Christmas. Moll, meanwhile, was already in his cockpit, and his eyes were watering from the fumes of Momberger's Auto Union. The fuel mixture of the German car smelled like poison gas, transporting many of us back to the trenches of 1917.

◘

'I spent the evening in Berlin filing my story,' says Finestrini. 'The next morning I found a copy of the *Gazzetta* at my hotel and took in the headline "Italy humiliates United States 7-1 in Opening Match of World Cup" before finding the motoring section at the back: "Italy Says Goodnight to Germany's Dreams". It wasn't quite what I had written, but Cristoferi was not far off with his edit. In the end, Momberger's Auto Union was the only German car that had finished the race a distant third, behind Moll and Varzi's Ferrari-Alfas. It was a far cry from the resounding German victory that Uncle Adolf had been counting on, and it wasn't until July 1st that the Germans would again do battle against the full might of Ferrari, at the French Grand Prix, where Chiron duly delivered for the Scuderia. Worse still, Ferrari swept the entire podium, the Germans outclassed and humiliated on French soil.'

Finestrini takes a frail bite of his baccalà and washes it down with a sip of white wine. 'After that debacle, Walb and Neubauer were summoned to Berlin for a little chat with Hühnlein in his office, which was less than a hundred metres away from the Führer's. Hühnlein made it clear that no further failure would be tolerated, and that their only option was to win at the upcoming German Grand Prix.'

'This was at the Nürburgring?'

'Yes. Hitler was again scheduled to attend. That, I should imagine, was about a good a threat as Hühnlein had in his arsenal.'

'Did Hitler attend?'

'Let's get some coffee, Deutsch,' Finestrini suggests, seemingly reluctant to revisit that day.

Sergio sweeps away our plates, and I notice Finestrini has done little aside from picking at his lunch. He waits for Sergio to return with our coffee, and remains silent as he watches me drop sugar into my cup. He waits for me to drink before continuing.

It was a dark day for Italy, July 15th, 1934. I filed my story an hour after the event, but it was a pitiful thing to write. I stood by the window staring out at the quaint village of Adenau with its sidewalks roped off by the military corralling spectators over the pontoon-bridges that crisscrossed the ancient cobbled streets, and felt ashamed as I went over the race in my mind. I had written a straightforward report, devoid of any humiliating analysis. Stuck wins for Auto Union in front of Adolf Hitler, Fagioli for Mercedes in second, Chiron for the Scuderia in third, Nuvolari in his privately entered Maserati in fourth. A triumph, I added, for Italy's drivers.

What I failed to mention was that Chiron had come in an astounding eight minutes behind the Auto Union, while Nuvolari had been *seventeen minutes* behind. Even the likes of Momberger had been lapping fifteen seconds a lap faster than Varzi and Nuvolari, and had Caracciola not blown an engine on lap fourteen, the beating would have been even more resounding.

In the dining room that evening I sat at a table with Caracciola, Varzi, Nuvolari, and Chiron – like the old days, except that we were now in a new age, an era of German efficiency and technology that would surely last for many years to come. The victorious Auto Union team had secured their own table, and Hühnlein was proposing another toast to Stuck, who was already half under the table. And who could blame him? In one short month, he had gone from obscurity to being Germany's golden boy.

Caracciola too was the worse for wear. He was looking worn out that night. You wouldn't have guessed from his sad, dark eyes that he was barely in his thirties. He'd come back to us, after his accident, after Charly's death, but we'd lost a part of him forever. There was a deep pain there that would always keep us at a distance. I turned to Caracciola and told him that he'd been on his best form that day.

'I manage the pain,' he replied, 'like I manage a race.' And that's how he managed his life too, I thought.

'Can't be too hard then,' Chiron said, masking his disdain behind that easy smile of his, 'with that car of yours.'

'Yes, Louis, I suppose so.'

'You're going to put us all into early retirement,' said Varzi, sipping on a glass of champagne.

'Well, you can always turn to journalism,' I suggested to Varzi. 'You seem to have an eye for spotting new talent.'

It was rare to find Varzi at a loss. He looked at me, furrowing his brow. 'What are you on about?'

I nodded toward the Auto Union table, on top of which Willy Walb and Neubauer were now standing, both singing *Ich liebe den Wein, mein Mädchen'* at the top of their voices. Meanwhile, a tall man in a smart suit was holding a sagging Momberger upright. I discreetly pointed at the man.

'Paul Pietsch,' I said.

Varzi glanced at Pietsch before turning to me. 'Yes, what about him?'

'He's been offered the Auto Union ride for next season – you asked me to keep an eye out…' My words faded as Varzi's face clouded over. He glared at me as if I had somehow betrayed his confidence, and the tension between us was so palpable that Chiron's eyes, forever alert, glanced first at me, then at Varzi, and then over at Paul Pietsch. Just then I was rescued by the sudden appearance of a sparse, sweating man who inserted himself in our midst with the conviction of the born salesman. Curly hair corkscrewed out from his shirt collar and sleeves, little maggots curling about his pale flesh like filthy thoughts.

'Ugo Ricordi, Auto Union's Italian representative,' I announced with a relieved smile.

'And Italy's most sought-after man after today, I should think,' Ricordi added, dragging a seat over and arranging it between Nuvolari and Varzi. 'So tell me, Finestrini, which of these men would you rate as the fastest?'

'Varzi,' replied Nuvolari instantly. 'Finestrini over here is the world's biggest Varzista – aren't you, Johnny?'

'Well,' I began, slightly put out, 'if we had to look at this season's record – '

'What about it?' asked Nuvolari, suddenly on the defensive.

'Tazio, do you even *remember* when you last won a race?' asked Varzi, and I was grateful for his interruption.

Nuvolari narrowed his eyes. 'And what do you know of my career, Achille?'

There was a slight pause. Chiron started to speak, but Varzi interrupted him in a clear, crisp voice. 'In 1924 you won at the Savio Circuit in a Chiribiri Monza: then at Polesine the same year, and at Tiguilio. In '27 you won in Rome and Lake Garda … ' For a full minute, Varzi reeled off Nuvolari's record as we all sat there listening with a mounting sense of discomfort.

When he was done, Ricordi broke the tension by turning to Nuvolari and playfully punching his arm. 'What a waste, Tazio! When are you going to find your competitive drive again?'

'You tell me,' said Nuvolari distractedly, staring at Varzi with a look that suggested something had just clicked in his brain.

That night, long after Nuvolari had retired to his room and the festivities had wound down, I caught sight of Varzi and Ugo Ricordi, along with a bespectacled man I didn't recognize, all huddled together in a corner of the abandoned dining room, voices rising and falling in a hush of secrets.

■

'That summer belonged to the Germans,' Finestrini says, sipping his coffee. 'They went from win to win, while Ferrari was left to feed on scraps. Sadly, no one told either Varzi or Moll, and their rivalry just kept on heating up. Moll was very much in the Nuvolari mould, you know: he was quick and brave, and I really believe he could have beaten anyone that season, anyone but for Varzi.

'But as the season wore on, Varzi seemed to find new and improved ways of getting under Moll's skin; his calmness, his methodical approach and his speed constantly got the better of Moll, and it ate at the man. There's nothing worse, I think, than unfulfilled vengeance. And Varzi was remorseless; he gave Moll every reason to despise him, and then come Sunday he would crush him out on the track. The more Moll ached for vengeance, the more indifferent Varzi became, almost as if beating him was a given – and Moll just kept digging deeper, pushing harder and harder, and going slower and slower because he was overdriving, you follow?' Finestrini swirls the espresso about its dainty cup.

'Moll was completely lost toward the end of that year. At the Coppa Ciano in Livorno, the Germans were a no-show, and that left Moll and Varzi to fight it out between them. And that's pretty much how it played out. I remember finding Moll in the box by himself, this after he'd finished ten seconds behind Varzi, sitting on his haunches behind the tools, shivering and rocking with exhaustion ...' Finestrini downs his espresso with one sip and sets the cup down firmly. 'We should have known then, looking back on it. Maybe a word, you know, a sentiment would have saved the boy from what happened in Pescara.'

'You were there?' I ask.

'Sadly, yes.'

The race was named after Tito Acerbo, a soldier who had died for the patria in 1918. He'd been a perfectly ordinary soldier, no different from the tens of thousands who'd perished on the banks of the Piave, but his brother Giacomo had risen to the upper echelons of the Party after the war, and he'd made the Coppa Acerbo the race of the season for Party bigwigs. On the front-straight that ran along the pastel seafront and tired hotels fronting the Adriatic was a massive billboard featuring Duce's profile in all its Olympian radiance. *Vincere e Vinceremo!* Win and we shall win, the dictum for this weekend and really, who could argue with that?

Ferrari himself had made a name here back in '24, his win prompting the Alfa works to offer him a ride at Lyon the week after, the race from which he'd famously withdrawn under circumstances he – nor anyone else – had ever adequately explained, and which had drawn a curtain over a promising career.

The Coppa Acerbo was run on Ferragosto, and the festival atmosphere would carry through the entire weekend, with a fair, air-shows, musical concerts, and the race itself drawing over half-a-million peasants from all over the province.

Despite falling on a holiday, I was forever forced to attend by Cristoferi who, I'd begun to intimate, had an inane sense of what rubbed me up the wrong way, for there was no event on the international calendar that I despised more than this. I dreaded the arrival of the *contadini* with their broken teeth and foul-smelling breath, these *zozzi di collina* with their jingoistic songs and incestuous, provincial ways excreting down from the Abruzzo once a year to Pescara, a wretched little town where the mosquitoes could eat a man whole if he didn't come invested with a FLIT spray. "The best blood will at some time get into a fool or a mosquito" – I didn't doubt Duce'd come up with that truism here in Pescara, perhaps on that brown beach on which the Adriatic lapped like a dying, stinking dog.

My hotel boasted a café on the trackside from where I had watched every race since 1930. The track offered little challenge aside from its length and the remarkable straight that ran from Cappelle all the way back down to the Adriatic, a five mile burst which saw cars reaching improbable speeds. That morning at breakfast, the waiter informed me that Henne in the Mercedes had been the fastest during practice, clocking in at 293kph. Nuvolari was the quickest of the Italians at just under 250 kph in his Maserati. Sebastian, Caracciola's legendary mechanic (who had first thought of using the steep drainage ditch on the inside of the Karussel at the 'Ring as a makeshift banking, this back in '31) and now at Auto Union, had been clocked at 277 kph, Chiron in the Alfa at 270 kph. It was, I thought, the perfect illustration of Germany's new-found dominance. The main thoroughfare, the Via Adriatica, was swamped by 20,000 soldiers marching to the collective apathy of the luminaries of the Fascist State. The soldiers had a glaze about them that afternoon as they marched past my seat on their flushed way to glory, the rain and the sweat dripping from their forthright faces, jackboots thudding past the royal box where Ciano saluted with a slack arm and a cigarette dangling from between his lips.

Avè. Boia chi molla!

Three hours later, the race had ended as it began, sopping with rain. The dire weather matched my mood as I headed back to my hotel room, wondering how to put into words the awfulness of what I had just witnessed. It was evening when I finally gave in to the need for a stiff drink and called downstairs for a bottle of whisky. I hit it hard, hoping the warm nectar would finally erase the memory of Ferrari's face when I had seen him walk past the café with two laps of the race remaining. I had known that face for a decade, and had seen it take on countless expressions – some faked, some genuine, all uniquely Ferrari. Today, I had seen a terrible sadness in his face that I had never witnessed before … Christ, I thought to myself, just write this race report, get on a train, and go home before this miserable place swallows your soul. I steeled myself and typed the headline that would run on the *Gazzetta*'s front page the next day: "Moll Dead at 24. Mercedes Triumph."

◘

'Moll's accident,' Finestrini tells me, 'was just fucking awful; there really wasn't much left of him to send back to Algeria. He hit Henne's Mercedes on the fastest section of the track and just took off. They say he cut through an electricity line, he flew so high. Such a horrific accident and a really grim death.'

Sergio delivers two Limoncellos, and rubs Finestrini on the

back. Finestrini smiles, and silently watches Sergio walk out of the room. 'It was inevitable, of course. Moll was too young to handle being in the same team as Varzi. Too young and too ambitious. He was a threat, and Varzi dealt with him as such. It didn't help either that Ferrari was so open in his admiration for the boy, comparing him to Nuvolari every time he spoke to the media.

'Ferrari took Moll's death hard, and that left the team in disarray for the rest of the season. Varzi, of course, was convinced that Ferrari blamed him for Moll's death, and began positioning himself for exile in Germany. And so, while Ferrari mourned and Varzi schemed, I was thrown into the bloody mixer. I had just gone to bed the night after the Italian Grand Prix at Monza – which Caracciola won in convincing fashion – when the phone rang in my apartment and an extremely agitated Ricordi pleaded for my help.'

'What did he want?' I quizzed.

The conversation began cordially enough.

'How are you Ricordi?'

'I'm in hell, Finestrini. Hell!'

'Are you in Pescara?' I asked, smiling slightly.

'Pescara? What are you talking about? I'm in Rome. Listen, Varzi tested for Auto Union at Monza.'

'Yes,' I said, lighting a cigarette. 'On September third.'

'How the fuck did you know that? Did Varzi tell you?'

'Everyone knows, Ricordi.'

'Everyone?'

'Everyone.'

Dio can',' came Ricordi's voice, clearly deflated. 'It's worse than I thought.'

'What is?'

'Nuvolari is also scheduled to test with Auto Union. On the twenty-fourth.'

'I see.'

'I don't think you do,' said Ricordi dolefully. 'Do you understand

131

what will happen if Italy's two top drivers both sign with Auto Union? Do you have any fucking idea what will happen to me? Ciano will have me carrying buckets of water in Abyssinia for the rest of my natural life!'

It struck me that he was probably being optimistic, but I kept silent and let him go on.

'Finestrini, you must help me.'

'I don't understand why you offered Nuvolari the test to begin with, Ricordi.'

'Why? Because the Germans asked me to! Jesus, Finestrini, don't be so naïve.'

'How much is Varzi's contract worth?'

'Fifty percent of winnings, ninety percent of appearance fees.'

'Christ. Well, I'm not really sure what I can do.'

'There must be something – *something!* Dear God, think of the patria – think what it would mean for both Varzi and Nuvolari to be driving for the fucking Hun! Don't you care about your country? Or your beloved Italian motor sport?'

I couldn't help but laugh. Nuvolari and Varzi together at Auto Union would inflict far more damage on the Germans than on us. All the same, I could empathize with Ricordi; as Auto Union's Italian representative, he was bound to be blamed for any loss of face on the part of Rome, and our two best drivers deserting the patria for Zwickau was the kind of shame and humiliation that wouldn't go unpunished. I promised him that I would sniff around, which meant calling Varzi the next morning at his hotel. Varzi was brief and to the point, suggesting that I wait until the winter for his official statement.

'What statement?' I asked.

'That I'll be leaving Ferrari,' he replied. 'Because Ferrari is a self-involved egotistical prick who likes to play mind games with his drivers. And you can print that now,' he added. 'Only don't quote me.'

'Look, Varzi, I know about your test with Auto Union.'

'Who doesn't?'

'So did you sign a contract?'

'Excuse me?'

'Did they offer you a contract?'

'What do you think?'

'Well, did you sign it?'

Varzi paused for a second. 'Maybe … why?'

'Just asking.'

'Nonsense. Tell me or I swear I'll never speak to you again.'

'I heard that Nuvolari will be testing for Auto Union in a couple of weeks.'

'Who told you that?'

'I can't reveal my sources, Varzi. But it's someone who is well informed.'

'Ricordi? Well informed? Don't make me laugh. And as for Tazio – surely he won't abandon Italy now, in her time of need? You'll make sure of that, won't you, *Johnny* – you and your Roman chums.'

And with that parting shot, Varzi hung up.

I sat there on my couch for a good hour, perturbed by what Varzi had said because he was right. Ricordi's problem was sure to become mine – it would simply not do for Italy's two biggest names to desert the patria for Germany. It would make our motor-sport tradition look infantile, parasitic, defeated, and worse still, mercenary. On the other hand, since neither Alfa nor Maserati were able to provide a competitive ride for our champions, it was only right that Varzi and Nuvolari should move on to a winning team. Auto Union had their yearly stipend courtesy of the Nazis, and they would not hesitate to spend a fat chunk of it to entice Italy's champions. Their technical ability alone was worth countless months of research and development. Varzi was actually a perfect fit for Auto Union: he had shown no loyalty when he had switched to Bugatti back in '33, and his coldness would be perfectly suited to the German way of racing. The more I thought about it, the more I realized that for Nuvolari to leave Italy would have been unthinkable, a crushing blow for our industry. It would be far better if Varzi were the one to do it – after all, he was always the anti-hero, wasn't he?

◘

I slide an *Auto Week* article towards Finestrini. 'It's dated September 23rd, 1934,' I tell him. Finestrini bows his head and reads the article:

"After the 1928 season when Varzi and Nuvolari founded their own team – Scuderia Nuvolari – both men pledged never to repeat the experience that had threatened to end their friendship. When, in 1930, they tried again at Alfa, it did nothing but confirm the obvious – theirs was a doomed love affair. And yet now we hear rumours that Varzi the Nobleman and Nuvolari the Flying Mantuan will be reunited again at an un-named German race team in 1935. I am reliably informed that, instead of despairing over this turn of events, Italy's big teams are in fact jubilant at the prospect."

'I take it that this is your work?' I ask when he finally looks up. He points at the byline. T.V. Bradley.

'So you had nothing to do with that story?'

Finestrini shrugs.

'You pushed Varzi into the arms of the Germans.'

'I don't think I was in a position to do that, Deutsch. Was I?'

I steel myself. 'To have done so,' I tell him, 'would be an act of betrayal, wouldn't it?'

Finestrini sits forward and places both elbows on the table, meeting my gaze steadily. 'You want to know about betrayal? Let me tell you about something that happened in Czechoslovakia.'

◎

It was a viciously hot September day when Richard Völter, Auto Union's Press and Sports delegate, sought me out at my hotel the morning before Wednesday's practice.

'Is it possible,' he asked via the house phone, 'for us to have a private word?' He suggested a café away from prying eyes, tucked down a cobbled alley leading up to the Špilberk Castle, and I joined him there an hour later, at a table in the shadows back near the kitchen. Völter produced a gold box of cigarettes and attempted to ingratiate himself with that awkward humour and clumsy chumminess that the Germans alone seem to possess. Despite that, I immediately liked the man; perhaps it was because I was intrigued by the fledgling status of Auto Union, which still seemed to operate in the shadow of Daimler-Benz and their Mercedes legend. After all, the Führer did not drive a car from Zwickau. Auto Union had been created to provide nourishing competition for Mercedes, and that seemed to inspire the boys from Zwickau to upstage their big brothers as often as possible.

'You are no doubt aware,' Völter began, 'that Auto Union and Mercedes have won every major grand prix since the 'Ring in July.'

'Your achievements haven't gone entirely unnoticed in Italy,' I assured him.

'We have won six races this season to Mercedes' five,' he continued, failing to notice my sarcasm. 'We expect Ferrari to respond of course. Only Ferrari – neither Maserati nor Bugatti have the resources to mount any significant challenge to our dominance. I hear that Ferrari have entrusted Bazzi and Jano with developing a new car, is that right?'

'Herr Völter, it's my habit to publish scoops for the *Gazzetta*, not to give them away over cake and tea – I find the *Gazzetta* keeps paying my bills that way.'

Völter's eyes grew wide behind his spectacles, and it struck me then that this was the man who I had seen with Varzi and Ricordi at Adenau.

'Yes,' he said vigorously, 'yes of course, it wasn't my intention to compromise your neutrality. I asked you here today because I spoke to Mr. Bradley at *Auto Week* about his source – I assume you read his piece in that magazine? – and he suggested that I speak with you.'

I cut a piece of cake with my spoon and placed it into my mouth. 'Why would he do that?'

'Unlike you, Mr. Bradley is not a discreet individual,' said Völter, clearing his throat.

'Did you bribe him with tea and cake then?'

'More like whisky,' replied Völter. 'And a lot of beer.' He attempted a smile, but it came out more like a facial tick. 'Let me ask you directly, Herr Finestrini – do you feel that Varzi and Nuvolari could be enticed to race in the same team?'

I took my time before replying. 'Undoubtedly, yes. You will find that both of them are partial to winning – and money.'

'Of course, of course, aren't we all. But tell me, if you were a team-leader, would you consider running both these men?'

'Herr Völter, I consider these men my friends.'

'Naturally. But you are probably the most informed journalist in your country, and since we're – '

'Herr Völter, if you're asking me, as an Italian, whether I'd want both these champions at Auto Union, the answer is no. If you're asking me as an Italian journalist, the answer remains no. However, if you're asking me as a patriot ... well then, I would say unquestionably yes, Herr Völter. I'd want both of them on a German team together.'

◻

'Nuvolari's test with Auto Union was carried out in secret on the Monday after the season-ending Brno race, and on the Tuesday, I accepted a ride back to Italy with him. He assured me that his test had been a great success, and invited me to stay at his newly-built summer house in Gardone. I could hardly refuse. With the season now over, there was nothing waiting for me in Milan but my empty apartment and the coming winter, and Nuvolari's villa, with its splendid garden overlooking the Garda Lake, and Carolina's quiet dignity, and the boys playing in the late summer sunshine, was just the tonic I needed. I wrote Cristoferi that I was working on a new profile on Tazio Nuvolari that would coincide with a major scoop sometime in the late autumn. It was a lie of course, but as it turned out,' Finestrini watches me tap ash into an ashtray, 'it proved a rather inspired one.'

'Why was that?'

◉

I spent the week down by the lake fishing with Giorgio in the afternoons. He was a serious boy with a good head on his shoulders. I tried to recall how I had been at that precocious age of fifteen, and could hardly imagine having the same self-assurance as Nuvolari's first-born. But then again, I was hardly the scion of the world's most famous racing driver. Inevitably, our conversations would always turn to papá.

'He has somehow got it into his head that I'm supposed to become a lawyer – a professional,' Giorgio told me as we sat on the white craggy shore of the Garda Lake. 'That's what he says all the time – *un professionista*. As if he were some sort of dilettante.'

'He wants the best for you,' I assured him. 'He cares about your future.'

'All I want to do is race,' Giorgio replied, throwing a stone at a rotting fishing boat anchored below us. 'I just want to be like him.'

'You are like him: you have that deeply ingrained desire to be the best, to achieve things. You don't need to risk your life to achieve greatness, son. Your father did it because an education was beyond his means, but what makes your father great is not his skill as a race driver. What makes him great is his heart, his spirit. Given a different set of circumstances – had he been born a Hapsburg in a castle and not a Nuvolari on a dust farm – he would have achieved greatness in a different field. A more important field. One that is now yours to conquer.'

'What's better than racing? Do you know that he receives letters from America simply addressed to Tazio Nuvolari? And somehow they always find their way here. He makes people dream, I've seen it with my own eyes.'

On the morning of the fifteenth, Giorgio left for his finishing school in Switzerland. Tazio drove him to the station, while Carolina said goodbye in the driveway. She gave her son a radiant smile before bursting into tears as soon as the car was out of sight.

While we were having lunch in the garden, Tazio asked: 'So, did you cry, Carolina? You promised you wouldn't, remember?' He turned to me. 'Did she cry?'

'And you didn't?' asked Carolina.

'Of course not,' said Nuvolari, keeping a watchful eye over his younger son Alberto, who was pushing a wooden racing car around the table. 'Not all the way to the station, not while he climbed onto the train, and certainly not when I watched the train depart.'

Carolina found his hand and squeezed it. Alberto squealed with delight as his car went flying through the air.

'Oh, I almost forgot,' she said suddenly, her mood darkening. 'You got some post from Zwickau.'

Nuvolari's head came up fast. 'When?'

Carolina went back into the villa; a moment later, Nuvolari had the letter in his hand and Carolina was comforting a distraught Alberto over the loss of his smashed racing car. It was poignant to see the world's most famous grand prix driver clutching that letter so tightly – a letter from a company in faraway Germany that remained his only hope for a competitive drive, after three years of useless machinery. A hope that could never be allowed to blossom.

My mind drifted back to Adenau, to Varzi asking when Nuvolari had last won a major grand prix, and I found that I genuinely couldn't remember. He'd spent a year fighting for a spot on the podium minutes behind men who had no right to even share a race track with him, and it seemed cruel that such a champion should find himself out in the cold. Nuvolari's eyes scanned the letter, betraying nothing. 'Here,' he said, tossing it at me, 'from Auto Union.'

"After our conversation and test at Brno," I read, "I believe I am in the enviable position of being able to offer you a ride with our team – Auto Union – for 1935. Please send along your proposal and desires in the matter of contractual obligations at your earliest convenience. – Völter."

I looked up at him.

'What deal did Varzi manage to negotiate?' he asked shrewdly.

'I don't know, Tazio,' I said, distracted by Alberto's increasingly loud wailing.

'What do you *think* he got out of it?' insisted Nuvolari, deaf to the boy's screams.

I shrugged.

'Come on, Finestrini.'

'What's an Italian champion worth?' I asked.

'You tell me.'

'I don't know, Tazio,' I said, but the lie was already formed on my lips. 'Two million on signing, and probably one hundred percent of appearance fees and, Jesus, seventy percent of winnings?'

'That much?'

'He is an Italian champion after all.'

'Yes. Two million lira,' repeated Nuvolari. 'Did you hear that Carolina?' He looked at her. She was too involved with Alberto's tantrum to have paid much attention and Tazio, in one seamless motion, lifted the boy from his seat and began to throw him up into the air. The boy choked back his tears and was soon lost in a long happy giggle that was like sunshine in the afternoon.

'Papà is back!' said Nuvolari. 'Papà is back!'

The mist rose off the lake as Nuvolari and I stood and smoked in the silence of the morning. I'd been a guest for seven weeks by then, and had settled in like the winter. Nuvolari had just passed me the latest letter to come from Zwickau, which he'd received the day before, and which he'd only now seen fit to share with me. I had read it twice and found, in its terse language, an unnecessary cruelty.

"Dear Sir,

It is with deep personal regret that I must inform you that, over the course of the last few days, our tentative agreement to offer you a factory drive for 1935 has met with some resistance. I believe it is my duty to be entirely open with you given your reputation and standing, both within the international motor-sport fraternity and our team at Zwickau, where your name is revered and respected in equal measure. However, it is precisely your reputation—your greatness—which has become an issue for our other drivers contracted for 1935. It has been asked why Auto Union would desire two number one drivers ... "

'*Varzi*,' whispered Nuvolari, with smoke blowing from his lips.

I could not bring myself to look at him.

'No, I don't think so,' I replied, regretting my lack of conviction. 'He doesn't have that kind of pull with Auto Union, even if they have offered him a contract. No, it must be Hans Stuck; he's the only driver with this kind of sway.'

Nuvolari looked at his cigarette before tossing it into the swelling mist that rose over our ankles. 'I expect that you'll be leaving this afternoon,' he said, walking back toward the villa.

■

'They said Nuvolari was finished, and he looked it that morning.' Finestrini watches me kill my cigarette in the ashtray. 'Mercedes was a closed shop, Auto Union was now Varzi's, and with Ferrari there was nothing but mutual antipathy. All that was left for him was another year risking his life for measly scraps, and I don't think even he could stand another season of humiliation. Not at his age, and not with Varzi winning at Auto Union. Carolina offered me a tender kiss when I left that afternoon. Tazio, she said, was asleep, but had arranged for a taxi to drive me all the way back to Milan.'

'So you lied to him. To Nuvolari.'

'About what?'

'Varzi's contract. You made him inflate his own personal worth. Why?'

'Why do you think?' asks Finestrini.

'For Ricordi?'

'Don't be stupid, Deutsch,' he says. 'Nuvolari couldn't be allowed to sign for the Germans, I told you: It was just not a possibility. For any of us, and that included Tazio.'

'So you betrayed both of them – Varzi and Nuvolari.'

'You're being dense,' he tells me. 'I wasn't responsible for what happened: I did what I could to ensure only one of them signed with Auto Union. Varzi was going anyway; I made sure it happened. And that's it. And it was lucky I did.'

'Why?'

I got back to my office in early January to find a letter from Achille Varzi in which he wrote of his persecution by the *Gazzetta* and that I, as a man of integrity (this phrase was followed by a series of question marks), should be grateful to be in possession of the truth contained in the second sheet. This turned out to be a 1,000 word rant aimed squarely at Enzo Ferrari:

"I would like to clarify the reasons why I believe I can no longer be a part of Scuderia Ferrari. To begin with, Ferrari did not see fit to renew my contract: Indeed, the two proposals I received from Ferrari offered terms far inferior to those of last year. In contrast, Ferrari has offered lucrative new contracts to all his foreign drivers. I must also make it clear that as an Italian patriot, I could not sign a contract with a team that employs more than one non-Italian. And finally I would like to state that I have never asked for preferential treatment with respect to cars, but merely a level playing field with the other drivers – a situation which did not always occur last season. I believe this is something I deserve due to what I have achieved ..."

The letter had not come out of the blue, of course: As rumours spread of Varzi's contract with Auto Union, public opinion had increasingly turned against him. Two days earlier, *La Stampa* had even gone so far as to ask whether an Italian who would abandon the nation in its time of greatest need was actually guilty of treason.

This letter, I knew, would not help matters much. It was an inescapable fact that Varzi was being disloyal to Italy, and I felt certain that his self-righteous monologue would be matched by an equally cold – and far more destructive – reply from Ferrari; but since Varzi had not returned my call by deadline, I left the office with his letter typeset for printing in Tuesday's *Gazzetta*, fully aware that he would live to regret it.

The reply, naturally, lay on my desk Wednesday morning, but

instead of being addressed to Finestrini, the blood-red envelope simply mentioned the 'Motoring Editor'. Within it, in Enzo Ferrari's purple ink scrawl, was a point-by-point rebuttal to Varzi's published letter, and it was both merciless and accurate.

Varzi had been offered the same terms as last season, as the Secretary of the Racing Commission would testify. Foreign drivers were contracted at significantly lower rates than Varzi, as would be expected from an Italian race team, especially one that had been flying the tricolore for a decade. There was only one foreigner contracted to Ferrari for 1935, and that was Renato Dreyfus – Chiron had only been offered an extension to his contract after Varzi had turned down the Scuderia's final offer. Varzi had often sought and received the best equipment, and he had always been given first choice of car for every race. Ferrari had concluded:

> "We have done everything in our power to retain the services of our Great Italian Champion, despite our limited position as a small Italian team fighting against the state-subsidized German motoring divisions. However, it must be acknowledged that it is not our fault that we are unable to meet Varzi's terms, given that the market has been inflated beyond what is realistic by the arrival of the German teams..."

Classic Ferrari – while he stuck the knife in Varzi with one hand, he still found time to hold out the other for any small change the state might send his way. I could hardly muster any sympathy for Varzi though – I didn't know if he actually believed in some vast conspiracy involving foreign drivers and Enzo Ferrari, but as things stood, he had just walked into what was probably the strongest team for 1935, and he had done so because he wanted to win and because they were paying him a small fortune to do so. That should have been his defence. But Varzi was capable of believing the most outrageous rubbish, wasn't he ...?

That night, after the *Gazzetta* had published Ferrari's response, I went to bed thinking that I would probably hear from Varzi in the morning, and I felt more than prepared to stand my ground.

Cristoferi was waiting behind my desk with his back turned to the door when I got to work the next morning. The snow fell steadily beyond the window, my desk lamp imprinting a livid mark over my papers. Papers that, I noticed with my heart skipping a beat when I stepped into my office, had been shuffled about in my absence.

'You're late,' Cristoferi said. 'We've been waiting for you.'

In the corner, smoking on my couch, sat Galeazzo Ciano. He wore a strikingly pale suit and dark tie, his dandy legs disdainfully crossed. I took off my coat and dumped it on to the rack, trying hard not to think too much; to think too much, I knew, would make me sweat and look guilty.

Cristoferi turned towards me with his white-knuckled hands throttling the back of my chair. 'We have concerns about how the Ferrari–Varzi affair was mishandled. By *you*. This was a situation that should have been dealt with through back channels.' Cristoferi stared at me accusingly. Back channels?

'You made us look like clowns,' added Ciano, blowing smoke in my direction. 'Disunity is our fucking disease.'

Us, I knew, was a term that included no one and everyone, depending on the context. The Party was Us, and anything that embarrassed the Party also humiliated its people and was therefore treasonous. I swallowed hard, found a cigarette, and tried to stay calm.

'We need Varzi to sign for Ferrari,' said Ciano. 'Italy is crying out for unity, for a collective front. Our patria cannot be made to suffer the ego of Achille Varzi. In private, this would have been tolerable, but now that you have made it public, there's only one option – Varzi and Ferrari must be reconciled. You follow?'

'It's not possible,' I said. 'Varzi has already signed with Auto Union.'

'You know this for a fact?'

I smoked harder.

'Are you aware of the terms of that contract?' insisted Ciano.

'I don't follow – '

Ciano blinked. It was enough.

'Yes,' I admitted.

'And yet, I have not read one word about it in the *Gazzetta*. Why is that?'

'Yes, why is that?' said Cristoferi, looking at me with disgust.

143

'It was only a rumour, told to me in confidence.'

'By whom?'

I cleared my throat.

'By whom?' repeated Ciano.

'Völter. From Auto Union,' I lied.

Ciano sat forward. 'I'm aware of who Völter is, my friend. I would strongly suggest that you do not patronize me.'

'Jesus, Finestrini,' whispered Cristoferi.

'What were the terms?'

'Fifty percent of all winnings, ninety percent of appearance fees.'

Ciano stubbed his cigarette repeatedly in my ashtray. 'That's a lot of cash for someone like that,' he said eventually. 'It strikes me that Varzi has placed his personal interests above ours. Would I be correct in thinking that?'

'Yes,' I said quietly.

'This is most upsetting,' said Ciano. 'It's almost a bloody provocation. But we can hardly force a man to be a patriot. Can we?' He looked at me, and I was about to suggest that yes, I was sure he could think up a few ways, when he uncrossed his legs and said: 'Something must be done to address this colossal cock-up, Finestrini.'

In the silence that followed, I reflected that betrayal was a lot like murder – it was seldom premeditated. Before I knew what I was doing, I blurted out: 'Tazio Nuvolari.'

Ciano's eyes fell on me. 'Yes,' he said, 'remind me why Nuvolari isn't racing for Ferrari?'

'There's a lot of bad blood between them,' I replied.

'Ferrari needs an Italian champion. And Nuvolari doesn't have a works drive, does he? It seems obvious that they need each other.'

'Yes,' I agreed. 'Except that the last time they spoke, Nuvolari accused Ferrari of trying to have him killed.'

'Surely a misunderstanding,' said Ciano. 'So how might we persuade them to reconcile?'

I hesitated for a second. But it was too late to stop now; Judas had already spoken. 'Ferrari is in need of investment funds; for instance, if Tazio's retainer were taken care of by well-meaning patriots – '

'Nuvolari will race for Ferrari this season,' Ciano said, cutting me off and standing with a grunt.

'Yes,' said Cristoferi, 'it's perfect, brilliant – our two great Italian champions reunited in the common fight against the Hun and the Traitor. Perfect!'

I had to admit that it would make quite a story.

'Il Duce will be informed that you, Finestrini, will sort this mess out.'

'You won't be disappointed,' said Cristoferi. 'You can trust Finestrini here to do the right thing. He's a good boy despite some of the crazy ideas that go through his head. It was the war, you know. He came back in a bad way from that.'

Ciano grabbed his coat from the rack. 'You fought in the war, Finestrini?'

'I was at Caporetto,' I told him.

He allowed Cristoferi to help him into his coat. 'We'll never suffer another Caporetto again, mark my words. Not with Il Duce to guide to us. Farewell, gentlemen.'

Cristoferi followed Ciano out of my office, leaving me alone with my thoughts. Only then did I realize I'd stopped breathing.

I spent an unpleasant afternoon in the café across from the railway station trying to rationalize my guilt. *Chi si impiccia resta impicciato,* that's what my teacher had always maintained at the liceo – he who gets involved gets implicated. I couldn't think of a more apt expression of my current predicament.

I wasn't too worried about convincing Nuvolari. His whole life was focused on family, pride, honour and – like all men from those back-breaking fields around the Po river – money. Count Brivio had once told me that Nuvolari's main reason for insisting on being a team's number one was so that he could reap the highest financial rewards. Indeed, while his team-mates would be obliged to share their winnings with him, he would never share a cent – that was the only contractual stipulation he had ever demanded. Nuvolari, I believed, would sign if the price was right.

Ferrari, however, was a far more complex animal. His casual brutality had always made me wonder about his motives and he was going to be the harder one to convince, for sure.

I wrote Nuvolari a short letter in which I asked him to consider his future. 'A champion,' I wrote, 'must either race to win, or not race at all.' I then wrote a letter to Ferrari, in which I made it known that Rome would look favorably on his Scuderia should he consider bringing back the great champion Tazio Nuvolari into his fold.

A day later, both sent replies suggesting a mild interest in whatever it was that I was peddling. The stage was thus set. The meeting place was a restaurant in Piacenza, a trattoria which both men could call neutral ground, since it was almost equidistant from Modena and Mantua.

Nuvolari arrived on time, and I welcomed him beside a blazing fire in the ancient fireplace with an espresso corretto. In the chill of the old stone house, I outlined his prospects for the coming season. Maserati was financially ruined. Yes, they were working on their new slipstreamer, the V8-RI, but that would only materialize in the late summer – if ever. Until then, they would have nothing but an upgraded and ageing 8CM monoposto at their disposal. Bugatti, meanwhile, was content to simply upgrade the Type 59, which was only a year old but already woefully out of date. It would not have independent suspension since Le Patron believed that was a solution for those who didn't know how to construct a chassis. All in all, the boys at Bugatti had no real hope of rivalling the Germans.

Nuvolari listened in silence, content to smoke and play with an errant strand of fabric from the green hat on his lap.

As for Mercedes and Auto Union, I continued, they were both out of Nuvolari's reach for 1935. It would be folly for a champion such as himself to waste time –

'Finestrini,' he interrupted, tapping my wrist, 'when does he get here?'

Ferrari arrived an hour later. His chauffeur had driven him down from Modena along with Vittorio Jano. Both men were sporting dark glasses and dark suits. Once lunch was served, I opened up my second line of offence, distilling Alfa Romeo's current situation. Nicola Romeo's departure had brought the curtain down permanently on Alfa's legendary racing programme.

His replacement, Ugo Ojetti, was a political hack who had been hand-picked by the Party to oversee the company's bankruptcy. Ojetti was loyal to only one man, Il Duce, and could be counted on to do precisely as instructed by Rome, now fully in charge of Alfa's purse strings. Ojetti's main objective, I stressed, was to break the trade unions and to trim the company down to profitability. Under his leadership, the military would soon become Alfa's biggest customer. In fact, Alfa was already producing engines for the S.79 planes that would be put to use in Abyssinia. This left Ferrari with rather bleak prospects – unless a solution was found.

I turned to Jano. 'Do you know that I attended the race in which your P2 made its debut, back in 1924? That day, Alfa and Campari beat the world's best drivers, humiliating them so badly that many of them almost quit the sport altogether.'

Jano smiled fondly at the memory.

A decade on, I continued, the time had come for Jano to once again triumph against all odds. But this time, it would be with Ferrari, not Alfa, and instead of Campari, it would be Tazio Nuvolari who would bring them victory.

'Your rhetoric is improving with age,' said Jano. 'But unfortunately, I don't think the P3 is anywhere near competitive enough to deal with the Germans. We've introduced independent suspension of course, which will make us faster, but still … '

'What about the *bimotore*?' I asked him. 'I heard that you and Bazzi had been working on it, is that true?'

Jano seemed to ignore my question, so I turned to Nuvolari. 'Maybe Ferrari can't beat the Germans in the regular season, maybe we have to accept that the grand prix world has changed, but that doesn't mean we have to abandon our legacies – we can still fight, still win – '

Ferrari cleared his throat. 'Tazio, are you tired of hearing this imbecile drone on like this?'

Nuvolari grinned. 'I did promise to drive Carolina over to Switzerland this evening.'

'You did?' Ferrari's posture now excluded me from the conversation entirely. 'And how is Giorgio coping?'

'He tells me he wants to focus on engineering.'

147

'He wants to be an engineer? You know he'll always have a job with us of course.'

'I think it would be best if he found a job somewhere else, you know.'

'Yes,' Ferrari smiled. 'Probably for the best, it's always inconvenient to have a father and son working together. Come,' Ferrari slapped his knees and stood up stiffly, 'let's take a walk.'

I was left alone with Jano in front of the crackling fire. Beyond the deep windows, I could see that Ferrari had linked arms with Nuvolari as they walked around the garden with heads bowed in conversation.

'Just between us, the *bimotore* project you referred to earlier is a monumental disaster,' said Jano. I sat forward. 'Two engines – only Bazzi would come up with something so idiotic. One at the front, the other at the rear. Pushes out about 540bph on the dyno', but the thing weighs more than a tank.'

'I imagine it would eat through the tyres,' I said.

'Yes, no doubt Bazzi will ask Engelbert to make tyres made of iron or something equally stupid.'

'Did you tell Ferrari?'

'I tried to. But he's spent the last three months telling me how re-signing Nuvolari will change our fortunes.'

□

Finestrini glances at his wrist-watch. 'I wrote an editorial that same evening for the *Gazzetta*, in which I asked my readers to try and understand Varzi's motivations. But more importantly, the *Gazzetta* had a front page scoop: the announcement that Ferrari and Nuvolari had joined forces to take on the Germans in the 1935 season.' Finestrini pushes his chair back. 'And now, Deutsch, I'm afraid you'll need to excuse me. I have an appointment this afternoon in Venice.'

'Oh – of course … '

'I should be back for dinner – perhaps you can call my room at say, seven? We can talk then, if you'd like. About Varzi, and how he self-destructed in six very short months.'

I stand and accept his hand. With the bill taken care of, and with nothing to do, I stroll down toward the sea, to the deserted rows of abandoned candy-cane coloured cabins, Roman legionnaires standing in symmetric rows on the sodden beach battered by a wintry, dreary sea. The beach is powdery and fine, mine the only bootsteps. I make my way past the cabins and the occasional warped mirror reflecting the snow, a ghost-town of forgotten summer romances, and stand at water's edge. The storm is a belt out there before me and feeling the chill, I wrap my anorak tight and head back through the ungiving streets to find refuge in my hotel. In the bar I order a whisky and find a comfortable chair by the windows. Finestrini had betrayed Nuvolari, he'd admitted as much, and had shown no regret. How will he react, I wonder, when I confront him with his betrayal of Achille Varzi? Because I need him on the record: I need him to commit to his lie.

PART FOUR
A VERBIS AD VERBERA

The Fascist accepts life and loves it, knowing nothing of and despising suicide; he conceives of life as duty and struggle and conquest, life which should be lived to the full, lived for oneself, but above all for others, those who are at hand and those who are far distant, contemporaries, and those yet to come.

– The Doctrine of Fascism, Benito Mussolini
and Giovanni Gentile, 1933

L'Isola Del Lido, February 15th, 1968

I peel back the dark curtain and accept the cold light of day onto the crumpled pages of my much-revised manuscript. I need to re-read the manuscript, I need to prepare for Finestrini. I flip through the pages and find the section I'm looking for – the section that begins in March of 1935. The year Varzi was the highest paid sportsman on the planet, perfectly positioned to become the greatest driver in the world. And then – I think, placing the pages before me in a neat pile – and then he had met Ilse. I begin to read through it again:

"Achille Varzi strides through the glass doors of the Hotel Savoia, a neo-classical edifice that dominates the leafy Piazza Fiume. He wears a double-breasted gray flannel suit and crisply polished brown handmade shoes, his slicked-back hair revealing a deep scar slashing down his forehead. A bright-white Lucky Strike dangles from the corner of a mouth set in a sneer of permanent distaste, square chin set to the fore in search of quarrel. He walks through the lobby and into the Veranda Room, indifferent to the countless eyes that are following his every step. Varzi scans the crowd clustered around Auto Union's chief, Willy Walb, and spots

151

her immediately. Ash blonde hair razored like a boy stripping her neck as naked as an erotic thought, a dirty-strand fringe over a despondent and vague face, features diamond-cut, set and cruel. Her mouth is strict, pert lips viscous, eyes vaguely anxious, distant, irreverent, afraid, moody, mocking – what, thinks Varzi, what hides in their cosmic-coloured apathy?

'Signor Varzi,' says Walb, breaking Varzi's thoughts. 'Finally.' Varzi allows Walb to guide him around the room, formally introducing him to the Auto Union team.

First up is Dr. Magneven, the team medic, a bearded man hiding behind gold-rimmed spectacles; Walb assures Varzi that the doctor will be conducting a full medical exam during his test at Monza. Next up is Hans Stuck, whom Varzi knows well and has long since consigned to the second-tier of grand prix racing, along with his wife Paula, the German tennis champ'.

'And this is Paul Pietsch,' says Walb.

Pietsch. Varzi feels his hand seized, feels the strong grip of the tall man with the oddly shaped nose, watches Pietsch bow. The man, thinks Varzi, is far too obliging. Finally, Varzi is introduced to Bernd Rosemeyer, Auto Union's young recruit.

'We plucked Bernd from the NSU works – they're part of the Auto Union concern, as you may know, Signor Varzi,' Walb says. 'He impressed all of us at our speed-test at Solitude over the winter. He has a lot of potential, and I'm sure he's dying to learn from you.'

'As long as he doesn't die while learning,' says Varzi, with Bernd's hand in his.

'Dying is part of our game, Herr Varzi,' Rosemeyer replies, vague blue eyes meeting Varzi's without a shred of nerves. 'There's no room for cowardice... not in our world.'

'Or in the Reich,' says Walb with a shrill laugh. 'Dr. Porsche sends his apologies for not being able to attend – he's with the team at Monza setting up for tomorrow's test. These soirées leave him rather cold.'

Varzi turns to Pietsch. 'May I be introduced?' he asks, trying to hide his agitation.

It takes Pietsch a moment to realize that Varzi has addressed him. 'Oh,' he says, 'but of course.' He turns and beckons her forward. 'My wife, Ilse. Ilse, this is – '

'Achille Varzi,' she whispers in a cracked voice.

'Ilse,' Varzi says. He is about to add something more, but when her eyes rise from her bowed face, his finds his voice had choked in his throat.

*

Varzi is off the pace. The V16 is a low-revving thug of an engine peaking at 5500rpm with uneven torque. In third gear, coming out of the temporary, tyre-defined chicane on the front-straight of the Florio layout at Monza, he feels the rear tyres lose traction. Sitting up between the front wheels, Varzi lifts, corrects, squeezes the throttle like a sniper does a trigger, and finds even more wheelspin. He keeps his boot in anyway, arms fully rotated, and races toward the first Lesmo turn. The car is spongey under brakes. He has a dead throttle for over a second coming out of the second Lesmo turn – a second wasted, inertia spent. The throttle to the right of the brake pedal is not an intuitive thing – for his entire career, he has been accustomed to finding the throttle-pedal in the centre with the brake to the right – and he must consciously think before feathering it. The tyres are overheating, the tread cooked off the rears.

He is unable to feel the car rotate, reacting more by sight than sensation, and he's in the middle of a tank-slapper before he even realizes it. Varzi shifts up through the gears, rattattating the throttle when fourth gear refuses to engage. He withdraws from the limit then, backs off entirely and heads past the empty grandstands sleeping in the March sunshine and onto pit-road. One hundred metres before the waiting mechanics – led by Rudolf Friedrich, who has been assigned to Varzi as his personal mechanic – he cuts the engine to prevent the plugs from oiling up and rolls the car to a halt.

Dr. Porsche and Willy Walb stand by the retaining concrete wall, caught up in a whispered conversation with the man from Continental Tyres, Dietrich. Rudolf steps over and unclips the steering-wheel before assisting Varzi out of the cramped cockpit and into the chilly morning air.

Every car has its logical, raw limit. To get there takes a rare combination of skill and guts. It's only there – on the limit – that a machine's character can be empirically assessed. Much like a man, thinks Varzi. Pre-season testing is not about speed: it involves technical trials to determine and confirm particular data. Last night, at his suggestion, the team had installed a new self-locking diff', and Dietrich had welcomed two trucks from Hanover carrying a new batch of specifically manufactured compounds.

Varzi peels off his Fowler leather gloves and glances around him. The carb' mechanic is already leaning into the rear of the Auto Union where slats have been peeled open, gloved fingers tinkering about in the steaming, clicking motor shed. Alongside him is the fuel man who will, armed with the carb' readings, head off to his test-tube at the back of the garage to mix fresh mixtures for the afternoon runs. Dietrich, meanwhile, is taking readings on all four tyres, diligently scratching notes on a clipboard. Each one is a professional, and the entire team is dedicated to only one goal – making Achille Varzi faster.

'It's too stiff,' Varzi tells Porsche and Walb when they walk over to him, 'and it has terminal understeer followed by snap oversteer. I'm also having issues with the driving position, I've never felt so out of touch with a car.'

Walb shows Varzi the morning times on his clipboard. 'You're five seconds faster than Stuck.'

Varzi looks up from the ruled paper. Mechanics' eyes meet his meekly, seeking tacit validation. Did they build a winning car? Varzi doesn't know, it's too early to judge, but he suspects it's too much of a handful to be competitive in its current configuration. He spots Rosemeyer sitting on a stack of tyres in the shadow of the garage. Rosemeyer stares back at him, welcoming his gaze with an impish smile. Varzi turns back to his car and points at one rear Continental tyre, the carcass blistered, the white breaker-strip visible on the left rear. 'Wheelspin in fourth,' he says, 'is impressive, but not the fastest way to go about racing. Either we need a change in stiffness, or we need to work on the diff'.'

Dr. Porsche is taking notes in a black Moleskine notebook. A strange man, thinks Varzi. According to Finestrini, he had never attended university. Instead, young Porsche had worked as a janitor at his local college in order to sneak into engineering classes, where he had learnt to translate the genius bubbling in his brain into precise numbers on paper. Varzi walks away, black-tinted triplex goggles hanging from his wrist.

'You seen Pietsch?' he asks Rosemeyer on his way past him.

The young man shakes his head. 'Achille,' he calls, standing up. 'Achille, what are you in for the Lesmos? Second or third gear?'

'What's Stuck using?'

'Second.'

'And he's five seconds off,' says Varzi, heading for his Alfa in the paddock.

*

Fresh from the Mario Bosisio boxing match, Baby Hoffman, Chiron, Caracciola, and Varzi take a late dinner at the Pidocchio. Varzi, without appetite, stirs at his Campari and soda with a swizzle stick, his gaze drifting to the specks of blood on Baby's dress.

'What's with you, Varzi?' asks Chiron, wiping his lips. 'You're acting like your image.'

Varzi ignores him. 'Tell me,' he says, the smoke from his Lucky drifting towards Caracciola, 'do you know Paul Pietsch?'

'Pietsch? Of course.' Rudi glances up from his stained bowl and takes a sip of beer. 'Don't tell me you're concerned about that bloke – Varzi, he's a plodder, nothing more.' He skillfully swivels bucatini onto his fork. 'Actually, if I were you, I'd be more concerned with that boy Rosemeyer.'

'Oh yes?' Varzi feigns interest. 'And why is that?'

'I hear he lapped a second faster than you this afternoon.'

'A full second?' asks Varzi.

Chiron washes down his bucatini with an audible gulp of wine. 'Varzi isn't inquiring about Pietsch's driving abilities, Rudi.'

Varzi takes a sip of Campari, aware of Baby Hoffman's

curious gaze.

'Her name is Ilse,' Chiron continues, 'and she rather reminds me of your buddy Nuvolari.'

'Tazio?'

'Fast and loose, Varzi, fast and loose,' says Chiron with a suggestive smile.

Hoffman raises one eyebrow. 'What's this, Louis? Did this Ilse turn down one of your advances?'

Chiron laughs vigorously. 'Not my type, Babylein. She's strictly middle-class – you know the type, right? All morals and high values, but maybe not so innocent, yes? They tell me she was married off early by her mother – not a difficult enterprise, as I'm sure you'll agree, Varzi.'

'What?'

'Has her beauty really escaped your notice, Varzi?'

'She's absolutely exquisite,' says Caracciola.

'Funny, I never noticed her.' Hoffman sips her wine.

'She's usually hanging about, quiet as a mouse though. Pietsch keeps her well in line. As he should.' Chiron lights one of his handmade cigarettes and hides from Baby's withering stare in the smoke. 'Anyway, she was married off to some traveling businessman from Frankfurt – chap by the name of Enge – when she was barely seventeen.' His eyes remain fixed on Varzi's face. 'You can imagine her then, can't you? Eh, Varzi?'

'Louis!'

Chiron feigns fright at Baby's stern expression. 'Turns out her husband was the doting sort too, and would often come home with a gift for his young bride.'

'The clap?' suggests Hoffman.

'Close. The scent of another woman.' He gives Baby a meaningful glare, and she smiles that American smile of hers. 'All the money in the world couldn't disguise the situation, though – a nineteen year old lass trapped in a loveless marriage with an unfaithful man. They tried to reconcile of course, and a month or two went by until, one afternoon, she accompanied him to the aerodrome on another one of his business trips. In the café, watching her husband fly off, she met an Austrian by the name of Jellen.'

Rudi frowns. 'Jellen?'

'The hillclimber,' says Chiron. 'Charlie they called him.'

'Yes, that's the man,' Rudi pauses with his beer at his lips. 'He was pretty fast, if I recall – raced a Bugatti, didn't he?'

'He was pretty fast with the ladies too – our Ilse fell for Charlie Jellen in a bad way.'

'First love,' suggests Varzi to his blood-red Campari.

'Whatever it was, she left her husband for him and the two quickly became a regular item on the hillclimbing circuit. It was all rather idyllic, with Ilse playing the part of the doting wife to Jellen's rising star.'

'I remember talking to Neubauer about Jellen back in '31 or 32,' says Rudi. 'He rated the boy highly at the time.'

'He thought highly of himself too, did Jellen. Enough to turn Ilse down when she suggested they tie the knot.'

'Why would he do that?' asks Varzi.

'No idea.' Chiron taps ash from his handmade brown cigarette. 'Maybe he was too committed to his profession, too focused on his career – he was a youngster after all, maybe twenty, twenty-one at the time. He was racing along with his best friend, a young man by the name of Paul Pietsch.' He pauses, waiting for Varzi to react. Varzi is too focused on splaying his fingers on the tabletop to notice. 'In '33, he and Pietsch formed Team Pietsch running Alfa Romeo 8Cs, hillclimbs mostly, and they were pretty successful too. But it seems our Pietsch had also fallen hopelessly in love with Ilse and, having heard that Jellen had spurned her offer of marriage, he offered his own hand – which she promptly accepted.'

'Why would she do that?' asks Varzi.

'Because,' says Chiron, 'she's a woman.' He studiously ignores Baby's disapproving stare. 'Listen, people overcomplicate this nonsense, my friend. Life is simple when you get right down to it. A man walks through life trying to worm his way back into his momma's womb, and a woman lies around deciding who gets to wriggle back into the sac. It's that simple, Varzi, there's no fucking mystery to it. As I said, she's a middle-class *hausfrau*, probably wants four snotty-nosed kids running around while she tends to the kitchen in her bare feet.' Chiron pushes his plate forward, warming to the subject. 'But I can see that my views haven't affected the randy look on your face one tiny bit.'

Varzi smiles.

'So what was Jellen's reaction?' asks Rudi.

'Jellen?' Chiron takes a measured drag of his cigarette. 'He took the whole thing rather to heart.'

'Typical man,' sniffs Baby. 'Too little, too late.'

Chiron clears his throat. 'He and Pietsch remained friendly by all accounts, but it couldn't have been easy having Ilse around. Jellen's form suffered, he lost something – well, we know *what* he lost, but it was reflected in his driving, and he became a bit erratic. Last year in May, on the Ingolstadt highway, he went off as he was going into Neuherberge – you know the turn, right? His car flipped over.' Chiron waits for Varzi's question.

'Dead?'

'Instantly,' he replies, raising his brows meaningfully at Baby's expression. 'He was only twenty-five.'

Varzi considers his pack of Luckys. 'So what are you suggesting, Louis? That she's dangerous?'

'More like a poor judge of driving talent. First Jellen and now this Pietsch fellow,' says Rudi.

'Sounds like you're far too good for her, Varzi,' adds Hoffman.

Chiron stubs his cigarette out and waves away the smoke. 'She's been opened by more men than a hotel elevator, is what I'm saying.'

'*Louis,*' hisses Hoffman.

Varzi sucks Campari from his swizzle stick. 'How do you know all this?'

'Neubauer.'

'Neubauer?'

'I was talking to him last week in Berlin and we ended up chatting about Auto Union and, well, one thing led to another. Kind of like Ilse and her men, come to think of it.'

Varzi places a pile of crisp fresh notes on the table. 'Call it a night?' he suggests.

Outside, Varzi watches Rudi and Hoffman kiss goodnight. The restraint of lips on cheeks is not mirrored by their tender embrace. Chiron pulls his Alfa kerb-side and Varzi stands beside Rudi, watching Baby slide into the front seat. As the Alfa's red tail-lights fade into the distance, Varzi lights a cigarette and watches Rudi limp away into the chill of a March night in Milan.

*

Paula Stuck sits on the chaise longue and reads the letter one more time. Its contents fill her with fury – and fear. Hans sits beside her, reading his newspaper dated May 30, 1935. 'German sport has only one task: to strengthen the character of the German people, imbuing it with the fighting spirit and steadfast camaraderie necessary in the struggle for its existence,' Hans reads out loud. 'Good old Göbbels,' he adds, turning to the sports pages. He informs Paula that Auto Union will finally be debuting three of its troublesome Type Bs at the AVUS this weekend. As she listens to Hans drone on about the race, Paula folds the letter warily along its pre-determined creases. She can't speak to him of this, she just can't … the shame of it, the consequences are far too ghastly to think about now, especially with his career –

There's a brief knock on the door and Hans, not looking up, says, 'Guess who?'

Paula slides the letter into her purse before walking irritably over to the door. Ilse is standing in the hallway, her short hair ruffled and spiky, blood-red lips forming a guarded half-smile. Sighing, Paula steps aside and allows the blonde into the hotel room. Paula watches those tanned long legs stride over to the couch and notices how Hans lowers his newspaper when Ilse sits down beside him. Later, she would recall that it was the look on Hans's face more than the letter that had incensed her the most.

'So how are you today, Hans?' Her voice is raspy, and no wonder, thinks Paula, little tart that she is. 'Excited about the race? Have the cars arrived yet?'

Paula slams the door and walks resolutely towards the couch. 'Hans,' she says, 'would you mind getting us a copy of the *Tatler* from the lobby?'

'I'll call down for it.'

Paula glares at him.

'Ah,' he says, folding the newspaper and tossing it onto the coffee-table. 'I'll just go and get it myself, shall I?'

Standing there over Ilse, Paula reminds herself of her own mother – and tries to keep the edge out of her voice. 'What are you doing, Ilse?' she asks as soon as Hans has stepped out of the room. Ilse frowns. The petulance of it annoys Paula even further. Who does she think she is? A virginal Marlene Dietrich, a perfect fucking Aryan – Paula catches herself then, and tries to quell her anger … After all, Ilse is just a naïve girl, probably not even twenty-five, provincial and yes, achingly beautiful for all that. Paula sits on the couch and places her hands sedately on her lap, steeling herself for what she's about to say.

'Ilse, you and I, we're friends, aren't we?' Ilse offers her a vague, almost indifferent stare, which Paula finds hard to reconcile with what she knows this girl is concealing. 'In March, in Milan, at the Savoia, you spent ten minutes with me in my hotel room during the afternoon. Do you remember?'

'Yes,' says Ilse, kicking off her shoes and tucking her feet beneath her. 'Of course I do.'

'And then in Adenau in April, you came by my room every day for a week – at the same time every afternoon, for no more than ten minutes. Do you remember?'

Ilse looks at her warily but stays silent.

'And then yesterday you came by in the afternoon. And here you are today, yet again.'

Ilse bares perfectly white teeth. 'Well, we are friends, Paula.'

'Yes, Ilse, we are. Which is why I won't be used as your alibi any longer.'

'Alibi?' Ilse sputters.

'When do you go to see him, Ilse? Before you come here?'

Ilse's face flushes.

'Or is it *after* you come?' Paula is surprised by the sharpness of her own voice, as if she were instructing an errant child.

'Paula – '

'Don't,' interrupts Paula. 'Please don't sit there and deny it.'

Ilse looks down at her hands. She is a beautiful creature, thinks Paula. Beautiful, and lucky to have avoided the curse of intelligence.

'I won't deny it,' Ilse says eventually, with a defiance that Paula suspects she doesn't feel. 'I sometimes visit with Achille, but we're only friends, nothing more than friends. And besides, he says he can get Paul a full-time contract as a works driver, not just a reserve – '

'So Paul knows about this, does he? Is he happy that you're fucking another man for his career?'

Ilse's eyes darken. 'That's vulgar,' she whispers, wrapping her delicate Hermes scarf around her neck. 'You have no business – '

'No, Ilse, vulgar is telling your husband you're coming here to visit your good friend Paula Stuck while you're out doing the nasty with Achille Varzi.'

Paula sees her hesitate. Would Ilse retaliate and risk alienating her alibi? Paula stares at her, waiting, curious. Ilse looks down at her flimsy summer dress, which she rubs with the palms of both hands. 'With Paul,' she says eventually, 'things are just not working out. All he does is talk about cars, about his big break...' She shakes her head and abruptly stands up. 'I should go, Paula, I'm sorry, I have to go.'

'Ilse,' Paula calls out to the girl – for she is a girl, Paula sees that now, a girl as aware of her beauty as she is unaware of its danger. 'You need to be careful.'

'You won't say anything?' Ilse, with her shoes dangling from one hand, has opened the door and walks right into Hans. Without a word, she darts around him and scampers off down the hall.

'Off to Varzi's I assume?' Hans throws a weather-worn copy of the *Tatler* onto the couch. 'He'll use her and throw her down the toilet like a used tissue, you know. He has his little *hausfrau* back in Milan, this one's just another plaything.'

Paula considers this. 'Has he had many? Lovers?'

Hans shrugs. 'Don't know, don't care. I have more important things to consider.'

Paula looks away from him.

'What?'

'Hans – '

He comes to her and runs a hand through her hair. 'What's wrong?'

Paula opens her purse and fishes out the envelope. She hesitates slightly before holding it out to Hans. He notes the official stamp, the eagle with the swastika in its talons, and that reassures him. 'What's the problem?' He skims through the letter. 'All they want is certificates for your blood relatives – this stuff is routine now.'

Paula stares at her hands.

'It's nothing, Paula, relax, we've all been through it.' Hans grabs her chin lightly and lifts her face. 'It's not as if you're a Jew or something, right?'

Paula does not reply.

'Paula?'

She just looks at him.

'Oh Christ,' says Hans Stuck.

*

Night has fallen in the Auto Union race factory in Zwickau. Four Auto Unions sit squat on the polished linoleum floor, two Type Bs and two streamlined Type As waiting to be disassembled and convoyed to Berlin in the morning. Bernd Rosemeyer climbs the metal staircase winding up to the rafters where glass-walled offices are suspended on a metal-floored catwalk. He pauses on the narrow walkway and gazes down over the factory floor.

That day back in October when he had received the invitation to the speed trials, he had sensed his time had come. Call it destiny – his mother had, albeit with a sense of foreboding – call it talent, call it what you will, but Bernd Rosemeyer had known this was his time. Still, he can't help but be astonished at how quickly his life has changed. Was it only three years ago that he had won his maiden race on two wheels, only a year since he had claimed his first German Championship? All is relative, he thinks: For the volk of his hometown in Lingen, his domination of the national biking scene was hardly a surprise, accustomed as they were to seeing the teenage Rosemeyer defy mortality on the Wall of Death ride at the local fair. And that too feels like yesterday.

The test in October had been Rosemeyer's debut in a grand prix car, but he had managed to clock the second fastest time on the first day. When Walb had inquired as to why he had arrived wearing a tuxedo, Rosemeyer had replied that, this being the most important day of his life, he had thought his Sunday best fitted the occasion. On the second day, Walb had offered him a contract as Auto Union's reserve driver for 1935, along with Paul Pietsch and behind regulars Varzi, Stuck, and Prince zu Leiningen. It was only possible in Nazi Germany, this meteoric rise of his. Pressure had been applied from Berlin, Rosemeyer had heard this from some of the mechanics, but how he got here really didn't matter. It has always been obvious to him that luck is more important than skill, than hard work.

But what happens from here on out will depend not on the Party, not on his blond hair or blue eyes, or even his luck. What matters now is conviction. In five days, the new Auto Union will do battle at the AVUS with a Mercedes team that has dominated the 1935 season. Bernd Rosemeyer is not about to miss his appointment with destiny.

When he reaches Willy Walb's office door, he turns the doorknob and steps inside. He grabs a pen and steps over to the calendar on the wall, a Walter Dexel twelve-month affair on which, for five days in succession, Rosemeyer has scrawled: *Will Rosemeyer race at the AVUS?* He is about repeat his message when he notices that someone has already written on the May 23 box in fierce red ink. *Rosemeyer will get his scrawny ass to Berlin today to practise for his debut at the AVUS on Sunday!*

*

For a man whose worth is measured in tenths of seconds, the hours he shares with his Ilse feel divorced: time evades him, mocks him on the confines of their imprisoned secrets. Varzi can sense her presence still in the imprint of her face on his pillows, the scent of Ilse a sentiment, a memory that survives

163

SANDRO MARTINI

only in resonating emotion. He imagines her but a few doors away, existing there beyond these walls in her Berlin hotel room but ten metres removed, in his hands … his hands, how can she stand it, Varzi wonders, being touched where she had been taken that afternoon.

Varzi heads out of his hotel room, must get away from her residue – she haunts him like a ghost. On the hallway, pain squirts across his abdomen. He stumbles, holding onto the wall until the pain loses its edge and leaves him sweating cold, leaves him staggering down to the bar and companionship – Chiron in a booth with a bottle of bubbly.

*

Adolf Hühnlein's head is enormous. It sits on his square shoulders like a light bulb, plump and luminous beneath a patina of sweat and bristles of iron hair. He is squeezed into a uniform adorned with medals – relics of a well-fought war. His pudgy fingers push the letter back across the table. 'It is purely a routine matter, Stuck. All of us – especially those of us privileged to serve the Reich as public representatives – must submit to a thorough analysis of our blood lines. We wouldn't want any rotten blood getting through.'

'The problem is that my wife,' says Stuck, tapping on the letter, 'has lost her papers.'

Hühnlein offers an expression that is indecipherable to Stuck. 'How is that possible?'

Stuck forces a laugh, hating himself for it. 'She's a woman.'

Ja, dogs and women, Stuck, dogs and women, they always bite your ass in the end.' Hühnlein bares his small, square teeth. 'Tell her to request the documents from her local municipal office. Those Jews have done a fine job of record-keeping.'

'For God's sake, she's Germany's number one ranked tennis player, why should she – '

'No one,' interrupts Hühnlein, 'is above the law.'

'She hasn't *broken* any laws.'

'Then have her submit her papers as requested.'

'This is an outrage.' Stuck leans forward. 'I won't have her treated this way. Let me remind you that I'm personal friends with the Führer – '

'Then why are you speaking with me?'

Hans bites back an angry retort.

'You know,' Hühnlein says, standing up laboriously, 'I think you ought to have kept your birth name, Stucki. The 'I' would surely have made you faster. Like those pasta-eaters, *ja?*' He looks at Stuck, whose eyes are downcast. 'My advice is to follow the law and not make waves. Surely,' he adds – is it an after-thought? – 'she has nothing to hide.'

*

Varzi watches as Nuvolari chats amicably with his team-mate Dreyfus, who had been in top form at the AVUS that afternoon. Nuvolari, meanwhile, had blown two sets of tyres and hadn't even made it into the final heat, and Varzi watches him laugh and drink as if seasons of failure don't matter. Hans Stuck's seat at the Auto Union table is vacant, despite him having had his strongest race since his win in '34 – Varzi had seen him leave the hotel with his wife directly after the race, both of them looking strained and anxious. Paul Pietsch, his hand draped over Ilse's naked shoulders, speaks to Rosemeyer, whose debut had seen him blow a tyre at over 300kph. He had failed to get into the final as a result, but if he feels any disappointment over this, his handsome face doesn't reveal it; he just seems happy to be here, in such illustrious company.

Varzi stares at Ilse, and she looks back at him, welcoming his lust-filled gaze. Fearing that is he being too obvious, he glances toward Pietsch – why this reaction, thinks Varzi? Why does he care whether Pietsch knows? – only to find him engrossed by his plate of sausage and liver. Rosemeyer observes Pietsch with a mixture of disdain and amusement, glancing first at Ilse and then back at Varzi with a look of understanding on his face. Varzi feels a sudden, stabbing pain in his gut – so sharp it seizes his breath.

*

Varzi weaves, ducks, and lashes out at Viganò with a clean uppercut that catches the shorter man just under the chin. Viganò stumbles back, stunned by his power. A vicious right smashing full into his face drops him cold.

Varzi stands over him, unstrapping his boxing gloves with his teeth. 'Did that hurt, Viganò?'

Viganò moans, a trickle of blood dribbling from his bottom lip. Varzi leans forward and holds out his hand to help Viganò up. Suddenly, Varzi sucks in his breath through clenched teeth and stumbles forward.

'What's wrong? *Varzi!*'

Varzi collapses onto one knee on the wooden floor of the hotel training room. 'I don't know, but it's time to find out,' he whispers, ashen-faced.

*

Viganò steps into Varzi's apartment on the Via Marchiondi, the pied-à-terre bought a month earlier and registered under Norma's name while Varzi continued living at the Hotel Cinque on the Piazza Fontana. Varzi he finds lying on a chaise longue by the open French window, his slicked-back hair caressed by a warm breeze that animates the linen curtains like ghost puppets.

'What did he say?' Varzi asks, looking up from his newspaper.

Viganò shuts the door and slides off his jacket.

'Out with it, Viganò,' says Norma, sitting behind a writing desk browsing through Varzi's mail. The apartment has been entirely decorated by Norma, and Viganò feels stifled by the dull colours she has chosen.

'Based on my symptoms, Dr. Losio suggests that I might have appendicitis,' says Viganò.

Varzi abandons his newspaper. 'And what does he intend to do about it?'

'He told me that I would need an operation. In fact, he was ready to do it right there in his office!'

Norma laughs. Viganò finds the pitch of it irritating, vulgar.

'Did you tell him I couldn't do it right now?'

'No,' says Viganò, 'I told him *I* couldn't do it right now.'

'And?'

'And he says we can wait – unless the symptoms get worse. He gave me these, to help with the pain.' Viganò shows them a box of pills.

Norma turns in her chair. 'Are they getting worse, Achille?'

Varzi ignores her look, which always seems to pierce his conscience. 'There's no way I'm going under the knife – not now – it will have to wait 'til the end of the season.'

*

Hühnlein sits at the desk in his room at the Eifel Hof in Adenau. Before him lies an empty page that is far more intimidating than anything he had experienced in the war. He is a man of action; the way he sees it, thought is the antithesis of action, and he has found the honour of writing these reports for the Führer vexing. He sits with his shoulders hunched, his pen hovering over an ocean of terrifying whiteness.

'Führer', he writes, before correcting himself, 'mein Führer, today, June 16, 1935, was a glorious day for both of our German teams. Auto Union and Mercedes crushed the foreign opposition. Caracciola triumphed over Bernd Rosemeyer, who has attracted much admiration from motor racing fans here in the heartland of Germany. Indeed, the biggest cheer of the day was saved for Rosemeyer when he had the temerity to pass Caracciola right in front of the grandstands three laps before the end of the race. Caracciola naturally fought back, and the master overtook the whippersnapper, seizing victory by less than two seconds. Of the top six finishers, mein Führer, five were German cars, with only Louis Chiron breaking our stranglehold, one full minute in retreat. It was a day of total domination for your Reich.

'However,' Hühnlein pauses with the pen held tight, 'there is one minor incident which I feel obliged to mention. At the bar this evening, Caracciola and Rosemeyer had a heated exchange when the latter accused Caracciola of blocking him; thankfully, Caracciola behaved himself like a true elder statesman, no doubt

167

mindful of the good example which he must set for the younger generation.' Hühnlein puts down his pen, his thoughts wandering back to that scene at the bar.

'You fucking blocked me.' Rosemeyer is in Rudi's face, his finger jabbing the older man's enormous chest. 'You could have made us both go off the track!'

Rudi gives him a withering look. He pulls out the swizzle stick from his cocktail and pokes it into Rosemeyer's chest. 'Listen my boy, you need to do more than just drive if you hope to survive.'

Rosemeyer strikes quickly, grabbing the stick from Caracciola and waving it in his face. 'Next time I come across you, just remember this: I'm in this game to win. Surviving is your job, old man. You just keep messing with me and you're gonna find me upsetting your retirement plans.' Rosemeyer walks away from Rudi with a satisfied smile, placing the swizzle stick in his lapel as if it were a captured battalion standard.

Hühnlein laughs to himself. Young cocks, he thinks, this is the way they are. Nothing a good horsewhipping wouldn't readily take care of. 'German cars have won every major grand prix this season,' he writes in conclusion. 'We are triumphant *mein Führer! Sieg Heil!'*

*

Varzi strides down the staircase from the villa that serves as Professor Losio's Clinica Evangelista toward a white Alfa that bakes beneath the relentless furnace of a summer's day in Milan. Adjusting his dark sunglasses, he throws the cigarette onto the melting tarmac beneath his spectator shoes and slides onto the passenger seat.

'So?' Norma asks from behind the wheel. 'What did he say?'

'He wants to operate.'

'Did you say yes?'

'I said I couldn't – '

'Achille – '

'This is not the time, Norma.'

'You can't continue like this – what about the pain?'

'He's given me stronger medication. I'll be okay.'

Norma slows down, turning to him. Varzi stares out the windscreen. 'Achille.'

'What?'

'Look at me.'

He turns to her. The chill in his eyes makes the words die in her throat.

*

Willy Walb has had the whole summer of 1935 to digest his failure – a sloppy meal of shame and humiliation. The lapchart on his clipboard has been updated as of five minutes ago, and the numbers don't lie – Caracciola and von Brauchitsch in the Mercedes are in a class of their own. Auto Union's Type B, with its larger fuel tank, continues to be prone to failure, and simply cannot compete with the Mercedes W25B. It has been this way all season. Walb is aware that the board back in Zwickau is clamoring for his head despite this only being July – he knows that the company is running at a loss, that funding for next season is dependent on this season's results, and that he only has two races to turn things around, beginning with tomorrow's German Grand Prix.

With the economic upswing in Germany, personnel working in the race department have been shifted over to the car production division, and preparation for race weekends is now shared amongst a handful of mechanics. It isn't enough, but Walb can no longer make requests of his board – he is a dead man walking, and they will not lift a finger to help him. All of which leaves Walb here, today, with three drivers, two cars prepped on pitlane, two out of the running, one hour left for qualifying, and Caracciola four seconds up on Bernd.

'Gentlemen,' he says to his three drivers assembled in the shade of the garage, 'we have a problem.'

'Indeed,' agrees Varzi, 'but while you work out how to share one car between two drivers, I need to get out there. The rain is coming, Walb.'

Walb stares at Varzi, who is standing between Stuck and Rosemeyer. 'Herr Varzi, we are in Germany.'

'Yes Herr Walb,' confirms Varzi, 'indeed we are.'

'I'm sorry to have to do this to you, but I've decided to send Bernd and Hans out first – you understand of course.'

Varzi blows a steady stream of smoke into Walb's face. 'I'm not sure I do, actually.'

'Our sponsorship and funding depend largely on our performance here, Herr Varzi. I wouldn't want to upset our sponsors by keeping our German drivers in the pits while favoring a foreigner.'

Varzi considers this. The clouds that roll over the track are pregnant with rain, and a lap here is over ten minutes long – at best, he would need to wait over thirty minutes before getting a chance at posting a time. By then, the circuit would be as slick as ice. He flips his cigarette down onto the concrete floor, watching it roll into a pool of raw, black oil. 'I'm sorry Herr Walb, but I think my contract stipulates that I'm entitled to first choice of car.'

Stuck strides away angrily; Varzi watches the tall man storm out of the garage before turning to Walb. 'It's decided then.' He steps past Walb and heads for pitlane beyond the open garage doors. Nuvolari scuttles past in his Alfa P3, the engine rattling. Rudolf, astride the Auto Union, holds Varzi's steering-wheel. His eyes, though, stare not at Varzi but behind him with a gaze that seems strangely transfixed. Varzi follows his stare. Ilse has stepped into the garage from the paddock, Pietsch by her side.

Varzi slows and abruptly swings back for the garage. 'Herr Walb, maybe you're right; I'm being unreasonable. Why don't you let Pietsch go out there?'

Walb doesn't wait for Varzi to repeat the offer. 'Pietsch!' he shouts, 'go find Stuck, and hurry the fuck up!'

Rosemeyer steps past with an amused smile. Varzi watches him slide into his Auto Union. The cheers rise from the grandstand like shotgun blasts, 'Bernd! Bernd!' Walb sticks fingers into his ears as mechanics shove the electric starter into the rear of the Auto Union. A moment later, with the rear tyres sweating a fine film down pitlane and the car fishtailing all the way up into third,

Bernd has the crowd on their feet.

Walb turns and sees Pietsch approach. 'Can't find him anywhere, boss,' says Pietsch.

Of course not, thinks Walb. Of course not. 'Varzi!'

'No, Herr Walb – really, I insist,' says Varzi. 'Get a German out there – Heil Hitler and all that, eh?'

Time is not Walb's friend today, and he can't waste time on another protracted argument with Varzi. 'Let's go, Pietsch. You can thank Varzi later.'

Paul Pietsch kisses his wife and strides toward the last of the Auto Unions, passing Varzi without even acknowledging his existence. Rudolf Friedrich allows him to settle in the cockpit before screwing Varzi's steering wheel on. It's only then that Varzi leads Ilse out of the garage and back out into the parking lot behind the paddock. The Nürburg castle stands guard over the circuit, almost lost up there in the hills where the clouds rush like a river.

'I thought you weren't coming?'

'Paul knows,' says Ilse, allowing Varzi to kiss her.

'About us? If he didn't, he's a bigger fool than I've taken him for.'

'Don't be cruel, Achille.'

'*This* is cruel,' whispers Varzi, touching her face. 'Seeing you like this – stealing moments, pieces of you like a thief, that's cruel. Isn't it time, Ilse?'

'It's time for you – ' She trails off, looking startled. Varzi spins around to find Stuck watching them from across the parking lot, a cigarette between his pursed lips.

*

Hühnlein sits at his desk and replays the start of the race at the Nürburgring in his mind. A series of lights have replaced the old canon-shot that had signaled the start of the race. Stuck is on pole, besides Nuvolari's P3, and von Brauchitsch and Caracciola in the all-conquering W25Bs. Chiron, Fagioli, Rosemeyer, creeping forward like miscreant schoolboys, make up row two, with Paul

Pietsch, Varzi, and Dreyfus, on row three. Fagioli's W25B has fire licking out of its exhaust, the revs shooting up when the lights flick from red to orange to green.

Hans Stuck reacts late, tries to make up for it when Nuvolari rushes past, and stalls. He lifts his arm out of the cockpit and waves it furiously as cars jink left and right about him. Behind the waist-high pitwall, Walb tries to grab the arm of an Auto Union mechanic, but he's too late, for the boy has already vaulted the concrete wall and is sprinting toward the stricken Stuck. Varzi, unsighted within the spray of Pietsch's Auto Union inches ahead of him, gets a narrow glimpse of an Auto Union – Rosemeyer – feinting right just ahead. He's in the process of working out why when the mechanic emerges before him through the mist.

The impact is violent, Varzi unable even to touch his brakes. The boy crumbles, snatched by the right front tyre and tossed into the pitwall. Varzi doesn't slow, locking up front tyres to pass Pietsch into the first turn and leaving behind in the bellow of the crowd a white-overalled mechanic lying still on the wet track. Dr. Magneven jumps the wall and is attending to the boy as two Auto Union mechanics push-start an agitated Stuck.

With pen – and schnapps – in hand, Hühnlein begins yet another draft of his race report. 'Mein Führer,' he writes, 'the race began with Caracciola and Rosemeyer offering the half-million German spectators a mouth-watering duel. It is my belief that Rosemeyer is set to dominate motor-racing in the next decade, and today he showed great maturity for a man competing in only his sixth grand prix. The rain was an intense affair, and as it thickened, Tazio Nuvolari, in his specially-tuned Alfa P3, began to close the gap between him and the two German leaders. On the wet circuit, the Italian's lack of power was proving to be an advantage. By lap seven, Nuvolari managed to claw his way back into contention, and on lap eight, somewhere near Klostertal, the Italian edged past Rosemeyer. By lap ten, Nuvolari had also overtaken Caracciola, and was now in the lead.' Hühnlein stops writing for a moment, squirming as he recalls the look on Göbbels's face when Nuvolari had roared past the two Silver Arrows. 'Caracciola and Rosemeyer responded with the true courage that is the lifeblood of our Reich. Their attempt to overtake Nuvolari ended up slowing everyone down, which allowed von Brauchitsch to close the gap – and by lap twelve, all four drivers were within inches of each other. Astonishingly, all four simultaneously took to the pits for fuel and tyres. Naturally, it was then that we seized command. In forty-seven seconds, von Brauchitsch's crew, led admirably by Hermann Lang, changed his Continental radial tyres and refueled his car, and it was he who came out in front, followed ten seconds later by Caracciola, and twenty seconds after that by Rosemeyer. Even Hans Stuck managed to get out ahead of Nuvolari. Thanks to the Italian mechanics' sloppy coordination during the pitstop, which took two minutes and fourteen seconds, Nuvolari was now in sixth place.

'We did not know it at the time, but we were about to witness an extraordinary event. Tazio Nuvolari drove like the devil on that damp track, consumed by an intoxicating disregard for his own life. In one lap, Nuvolari fought his way past Stuck, Fagioli, Caracciola and Rosemeyer. At the end of this lap – which is destined to go down in history as the greatest single lap ever driven by a grand prix driver – Nuvolari came past the start-finish line in second place, eighty-six seconds behind von Brauchitsch. On lap fifteen of twenty-two, the gap increased to eighty-seven seconds. On lap sixteen, Nuvolari broke the lap record, and did so again on laps seventeen, eighteen, nineteen, and twenty. With two laps remaining, he had managed to reduce the gap to just under thirty-two seconds. It was on the start of lap twenty that I saw Neubauer personally step over the pitwall and stand on the wet track to hold out a red flag for von Brauchitsch.

'It was an astonishing move, and one that was met with much derision up in the grandstands, but the decision to order von Brauchitsch to slow down was, in retrospect, the correct one. On lap eighteen, Caracciola had come into the pits for an unscheduled tyre change, and this had convinced Dietrich, the man from Continental, that von Brauchitsch would not be able to sustain his pace without compromising his tyres. Neubauer was thus left with a difficult choice: Should he pit von Brauchitsch and allow Nuvolari to take the lead, trusting that four new tyres would allow von Brauchitsch to overtake the Italian in two laps? Or should he simply order the Prussian to cool his pace? With a thirty second margin, Neubauer made his decision. However, it seems that von Brauchitsch completely ignored or missed Neubauer's signal, and his time on lap twenty-one was even faster than the one he had managed on laps seventeen through twenty.

'At the start of the final lap, von Brauchitsch had simultaneously extended his lead and lowered his chances for success; it was evident that the carcass of his Continental right-rear was blistering, the white breaker-strip visible even from up in the grandstands, and it was at the Karussell that von Brauchitsch suffered his catastrophic tyre failure. Yes it's true that they call the baron the *Pechvogel*, but today it was not misfortune that cost him and our proud nation our rightful win – it was, rather, his stubbornness that ultimately put pay to the victory that should have justly been ours.'

Hühnlein stands up and walks toward the window. He thinks about Nuvolari, who, in one afternoon, had rehabilitated his image, won his first grand prix in almost two years, humiliated the Reich, and driven the most balls-to-the wall race anyone had ever seen. He can still picture Nuvolari with the winner's laurel around his neck, his face filthy, looking like a gypsy in his blackened woolen pullover and baggy pants, with his handsome teenage boy Giorgio standing beside him. Hühnlein smiles at the thought of Nuvolari and Giorgio clinging onto the trophy, both singing the Italian anthem in the rain; and he realizes that it is impossible, really, to begrudge that little fucking warrior his due.

*

The hotel just off the Dietrichstein Palace in Brno is tragically empty. Varzi, sitting with his back to the lobby, yawns in the early morning and flips through the pages of yesterday's *Corriere* dated September 27. He reads that the swastika has now officially become the national flag of the Reich, but Caracciola, newly-crowned European Champion, will not have it on his Mercedes this weekend at the season-ending Brno GP. His Mercedes team has decided that winning every major grand prix of 1935, aside from the 'Ring which they preferred not to discuss, is satisfaction enough. Maserati has also chosen to stay at home, bankrupt and humiliated – pretty much, thinks Varzi, how Italy will feel in a few weeks when General De Bono completes his epic defeat in Abyssinia. Varzi glances at his Flieger Heuer chronograph, folds the newspaper, and listens to the approaching footsteps. Perfectly on time, he thinks, despite what must have been a distasteful invitation.

Hans Stuck, in a lightly creased woolen suit, collapses into a leather chair opposite Varzi without a word. He too looks tired. And no wonder, thinks Varzi: it can't be easy being married to a Jew nowadays, especially for a good Austrian. Varzi pulls out an envelope from his jacket and slides it across the coffee table. 'I thought you might want to read it – it's from Göbbels. I obtained a copy last night.' He waits for Stuck to pick it up. 'I'm sorry.'

Stuck slides the letter out and reads it without a trace of emotion. 'The Ministry of Propaganda requests that, in future, no lengthy articles be published about Hans Stuck's practice drives, but rather such tributes be reserved for the actual races, provided his performance is worthy of praise.– Göbbels, Reich Minister of Public Enlightenment and Propaganda.'

'A simple misunderstanding,' Stuck says, folding the letter pensively. 'I'll see to it. May I keep this?'

'Of course.' Varzi waves the letter away like an annoyance. 'Look, Hans, I need a favor.'

'I see,' says Stuck, the letter now buried in his jacket.

Varzi lights a cigarette. 'There's a bar on the way back to town from the track – there's a sign of a horse outside – '

'I know it.'

'I need you to bring Pietsch there, after Sunday's race.'

Hans Stuck sits back. 'Have you discussed this with her?'

'It's a simple request, Hans.'

*

175

Baby Hoffman lies naked on the bed in their Paris hotel suite, observing Rudi Caracciola as he sits on the window ledge. A solid, powerful man, she knows, built squat and hard. Whatever remnants of a Latin temperament had once shot through his veins, they had been bled from him at Monaco in '33, bled from him when he had lost his Charly. Two years it'd taken him, two years to regain his status as European Champion, and Baby hopes that this will be a new beginning for him. Rain is a sheet dripping off the chipped face of a gargoyle out there in the cold afternoon.

'*Gurgulio,*' she says, and waits for Rudi's distracted attention to shift to her. 'It means throat in Latin. They were invented as drain-pipes by the Romans. They're meant to frighten away evil spirits.'

He smiles.

'Norma called me yesterday,' Baby says.

'Oh?'

'She wanted to ask me if it was true.'

'If what was true?'

'That Varzi was having an affair of the heart.'

'Is there another kind?'

She licks her lips suggestively. Rudi swings one savagely scarred leg off the ledge. 'What did you say?'

'I told her the truth. That there are those who suspect that Varzi is seeing another man's wife.' Baby hesitates for a second as he sits beside her on the bed. 'Louis tells me that Ferrari won't renew his contract for next season – have you heard anything, Rudi?'

Caracciola plays distractedly with her nipple.

'He doesn't have a drive lined up for next year,' Baby insists.

'Times are tough,' Carraciola says. 'Chiron will sort something out. He always does.'

'Will you speak to Neubauer – if Louis asked you to?'

Why does she care, he wonders.

'Will you? Rudi?'

*

Willy Walb is hypnotized by all the empty chairs. The banquet he

176

has organized in Brno to wind down the season has turned into a perfect reflection of his year – a disastrous farce. Varzi, Stuck, and Pietsch are nowhere to be found, and Rosemeyer, who had finally won his first grand prix today, is busy chatting in a corner of the bar with an attractive woman wearing an aviator bomber jacket. At the long table in the centre of the room sits only Dr. Magneven, now on his fifth cognac, and looking the better for it. Walb takes a seat beside the doctor. 'Cheers,' he says, downing a glass of schnapps.

Magneven looks up. 'You must be relieved to have finally broken the curse, Willy.'

'Happy for Rosemeyer, yes – for me, I fear it's too late.'

Magneven juts his chin toward the bar. 'And who's the lady?'

'Elly Beinhorn.' Walb's gaze lingers on the woman, who is politely removing Rosemeyer's wandering hand from her leg. 'Do you know of her, Doctor?'

'Aviator, I believe.'

'Aviatrix,' corrects Walb. 'And not just a run-of-the-mill one either, as Völker was at pains to point out to me this morning when I asked why we paid for her to give us a speech. Only woman to have flown to Australia in '32 – she was awarded the prestigious Hindenburg Prize, no less. She is the German Amelia Earhart; a real celebrity, my friend. Survived a bad crash in the Sahara too.'

Magneven assesses her from behind his spectacles. 'Rosemeyer's in good company then.'

'Good for us too,' says Walb. 'Völker thinks she'll help with publicity in tomorrow's Berlin 'papers – you know I'm scheduled to speak to Hühnlein next week about our grant for next season.'

Magneven takes another swig of cognac. 'We did get our butts kicked rather comprehensively this season, didn't we, Willy?'

Walb smiles and pours another schnapps. 'And for that,' he says, 'someone will pay. Oh well – cheers… '

*

Across from a cigarette-scarred table, Paul Pietsch rubs the sweat from a pint of lager and gazes across at Varzi. 'Ilse tells me she loves you,' he says.

Varzi blows smoke toward the ceiling of the bar. 'And what did you say?'

'I told her what I'm going to tell you – she's my wife.' He watches Varzi flick cigarette ash onto the floor. 'I told her you'd both acted like common trash. How long has this been going on?'

'Six months,' replies Varzi, lazily returning Pietsch's stare. 'Or so.'

Pietsch inhales sharply, his nostrils flaring. 'You've humiliated me – both of you.'

'It wasn't our intention.'

'No? So what was your intention then? How did you think I would react when I discovered that you had seduced my wife?'

'I didn't think of you at all.'

'You fucking arrogant asshole.' Pietsch sits back in his wooden chair. 'Jesus Christ.'

'This isn't why I asked you here.'

'So why did you invite me here then? To gloat? Is that it? You – '

'I need you to consent to a divorce,' interrupts Varzi.

Pietsch tries to laugh. It sounds like someone has kicked him in the balls. 'Would that make you happy?'

'My happiness is irrelevant. It's Ilse that we should be most concerned with – her happiness.'

'Why? Was she thinking about mine, in your bed?'

'I would seriously doubt it, Pietsch.'

Pietsch draws his lips into a tight line, his fists clenched on the table.

'Pietsch,' says Varzi, leaning forward, 'you're making this about me, but it isn't – this isn't about me and it isn't about you. Ilse doesn't want to hurt you – neither of us do. We didn't ask for this – we fell in love. Can you understand that? We just fell in love.'

'You love her? Then act like a man and walk away. Ilse is my wife. She belongs by my side.'

'She doesn't love you.'

'That's my affair.'

Varzi allows that to sink in for a moment. 'I'm sorry for this – for your pain.'

'Shove your fucking sympathy, Varzi. She's my wife. You've had your fun – yet another conquest for the great champion. Now move on and leave Ilse alone.'

'That's not possible. We live in the same small world, you and I; we're in the same hotels for eight months a year. The only way that would work is if you gave up racing and disappeared. Are you prepared to do that? For Ilse?' Varzi's eyes focus on the German's face. 'Allow her to make her own decision. If you love her as much as you claim, you owe her that. Surely you can't in good conscience stand in the way of her desire.'

Pietsch stands up and leans forward, his shadow towering over Varzi. 'Good conscience? You fucking hypocrite. She's not a piece of meat, you, you – *she's my wife*!' He points a threatening finger in Varzi's face but his good breeding prevents him from going any further. It's this weakness that corrupts him, thinks Varzi. Pietsch kicks the table violently, shattering their drinks on the lice-infested floor, and strides out of the café, lonesome fury crossing the parking lot to Hans Stuck's waiting Horch.

*

A tinkling of a tea cup meeting a fine bone china saucer cuts the gauzy silence of the hotel lobby. Snow falls beyond the soaring, graceful windows, the December light dull and exhausted.

'So the operation was a success – Losio told me all about it when I called yesterday.' Norma stirs her untouched aperitif with a crimson fingernail.

Varzi takes a sip of his tea. 'Yes, it went perfectly.'

'I assume you're done with the pain killers, then?'

Varzi looks up, meeting her shrewd eyes. 'Norma – '

'Are you *done* with them, Achille?'

He finds a cigarette. Her chilly gaze is still fixed on him. 'Yes, Norma. I'm done.'

'And what about the woman? Are you done with her?'

Varzi's cigarette dangles from his lips. He says nothing.

'Is she upstairs, Achille?'

Varzi lights up. 'Yes,' he says, exhaling. 'Yes, Ilse is upstairs.' He expects a reaction, but her face betrays no emotion.

'And you're in love with this creature?'

Varzi picks a piece of tobacco from his lip, inspects it on his finger, and flicks it away.

Norma stands. Varzi does likewise. He leans forward to embrace her. She smiles and slaps him hard across the face, the sound echoing around the lobby. He watches as she turns away from him, heading toward the hotel's revolving doors, savouring the burn of his cheek.

*

Elly Beinhorn crunches through the snow toward her Mercedes Mannheim 380S, a leather satchel slung over one shoulder.

'That was an excellent lecture,' a voice behind her says.

She spins around, alarmed. A blond-haired man stands inches behind her, wearing a black leather trenchcoat. His smile is like sunshine. 'You remember me?' he asks. 'Bernd, the race driver.'

'Of course – how could I possibly fail to recognize Bernd Rosemeyer, the world-famous race driver?'

'Not exactly world-famous,' he says.

'Don't be so humble. My dear Bernd the race driver, you are the poster-boy of modern Germany. I read all about you in yesterday's 'paper. So what are you doing here?'

'I live here – this is Zwickau, home not only of Auto Union but also Nazi Germany's poster-boy. Now, how come you didn't tell me you were coming to town?'

'I didn't realize that I required your permission,' she replies.

'Permission?' His smile vanishes. 'Oh no, that's not what I meant – '

She looks back at him, containing her need to laugh at his sudden distress.

'Where are you going?' he asks, trying to regain his composure.

'I beg your pardon?' She slides in behind the wheel and tosses the battered satchel onto the passenger seat.

'I'd very much like to invite you to lunch,' he says, crouching in the ankle-deep snow.

'Lunch?'

'Yes. With me.' Bernd gives her his most charming smile. 'In Chemnitz – do you know it?'

She nods.

'Excellent. Shall I drive you?'

'No, I'll drive,' says Elly, wondering at what point in their conversation he had heard her accept his invitation.

'There's a lay-over just before you drive into Chemnitz – we can meet there perhaps?'

She watches him walk to a gleaming 5-litre Horch, exuding confidence with every step. Pretentious little git, she thinks, drifting her sports Mercedes onto the road to Chemnitz. Rosemeyer's car – with lights flaring – looms up quickly behind her. After a short burst of speed, he draws up alongside her, grinning like a madman; then he powers ahead, vanishing around the bend. Elly only spots him again an hour later, on the shoulder of the road that winds into the medieval town of Chemnitz. Bernd is sitting on the bonnet of his Horch with an umbrella over his head and a newspaper in his hand.

'I was worried about you,' he says when she pulls up beside him and rolls down her misted-up window. 'I've been here twenty minutes.'

God, she thinks, what an insufferable blowhard.

*

Chiron, Caracciola, and Baby Hoffman lunch at the Café *Les Deux Magots* overlooking the snow-capped terraces of the Place Saint-Germain-des-Prés. In an isolated corner of the café, Françoise Giroud and Saint-Exupéry share quiet words under the watchful gaze of Chiron.

'This is wonderful news. Isn't it Louis?' prompts Hoffman.

Chiron drags himself away from his people-watching. 'Yes of course,' he says. 'Five days into 1936 and it's already looking good. But I won't believe it until I actually sign the contract.'

Rudi sucks loudly on an oyster. 'Neubauer is waiting for your call, Louis.'

'And that's it?'

'As long as you sort out the financials, the drive is yours.'

Chiron lifts his glass. 'Your timing couldn't be better, actually – Ferrari officially fired me this morning.'

'I thought you had quit over Abyssinia.'

'Don't be an ass,' says Chiron. 'That's what I told Faroux, though,' he adds laughing. 'But really, I must confess it came as a bit of a surprise, getting fired. You heard Dreyfus quit the team in protest, right?'

'Did he?' asks Rudi, fully engaged with another oyster.

'Seems he's got it into his head that Ferrari won't be allowed to race in France, now that the League of Nations has imposed sanctions on Italy for its invasion of Abyssinia. Our Dreyfus is quite the liberal.'

'He's not alone. I hear Guaita and Orsi have fled to France: it turns out that Italy's World Cup winners weren't as keen to fight for Italy in Abyssinia as they were in a football game.'

'Well cheers then,' says Chiron. 'To cowardice.'

'And those no longer with us,' replies Rudi, stealing a glance at Baby Hoffman. Is she happy now?

*

Elly appraises her reflection in the mirror. She has three in her Berlin apartment, but this one, here in her bedroom, is the one she trusts most. She wears a crimson dress, off-red shoes, and her mother's unfussy pearl necklace. Not quite her regular look, but as the guest of honour for the German Colonial Society Ball, turning up in a faded pair of linen slacks and torn leather jacket would not go down terribly well with Göring and Göbbels, both of whom would be in attendance tonight. Just as she is putting the final touches on her makeup, she hears a knock at the door.

Bernd Rosemeyer stands in the hallway wearing a black tuxedo and a clip-on bowtie. He smiles in that infuriatingly confident manner of his, saying: *Wie geht es Ihnen*, Elly?'

'What are you doing here?' she asks sternly.

'I'm off to the Ball of course.'

'They invited you?'

His smile wavers. 'Didn't you read the 'papers today?' he says, trying a wink: it comes off as a nervous tick that enrages her further. 'I'm poised to bring a decade of glory to the Reich.'

'I have a taxi coming, Bernd. I'm late,' she says impatiently.

'I have my car downstairs.'

'And what, you just decided that you'd come around and pick me up, is that it?'

'Elly – '

She is about to lecture him then, on his impertinence, his arrogance, but instead finds herself saying, 'Did you actually think I'd turn up at the Ball, where I'm the guest of honour, with *you?* I'm not a bloody kindergarten teacher, you silly little boy.' His smile is still frozen on his face, and for some reason this makes her laugh. It's a sarcastic, vicious laugh, and it shames her.

'I didn't realize that it was so painful for you to appear in public with me', she hears him say. 'I'm sorry, I have clearly been presumptuous – I just thought, after our wonderful lunch at Chemnitz … Anyway, I hope to see you at the Ball,' he concludes weakly, turning away from her.

Elly slams her door. Why is she so angry? Is it because of how he makes her feel? What is he, five years her junior? And what's wrong with him anyway: why isn't a good-looking, famous daredevil like Rosemeyer out dating all the eligible beauties of Berlin instead of wasting his time here, with her? After this brief internal battle, she slips on her coat irritably and rushes out of the apartment. Bernd is still waiting for the elevator, and if he has noticed the suddenness with which she has exited her apartment, he doesn't reveal it.

'You brought your Horch?' she asks.

Bernd glances at her suspiciously. 'Yes. The big one.'

'Well then,' she says nonchalantly, 'I suppose I can tolerate turning up at the Ball driven in a Horch by the Reich's finest grand prix driver in a generation – better, even, than some chap named Werner.'

'So you did read the article then.'

'Shut up, Bernd,' she tells him as he opens the elevator cage for her.

*

The stylist who pilots a 400bhp projectile, Varzi the taciturn, has lost all control. He knows it when he touches her pale skin still baring his marks.

'We ought to get married,' he says. 'We ought to have kids.'

Her face on his pillow whispers, 'I can't.'

'Paul will consent to a divorce, Ilse.'

'I can't have children.'

She tells him then, lying on her back naked in their hotel room in Cortina, tells him with her eyes staring at the ceiling. It's the first time that she speaks of her past, of the illness that had fed on her childhood, and the operation in Wiesbaden that had left her alive, yes, but barren, scarred, constantly in pain. She didn't know happiness, she says, because it was always suspended, always defined by the spectre of another week, another month of illness, alone and not, thinks Varzi, with her dreams, but with her crippling isolation, her resentment, her cold bitterness that echoes in remote, acquiescent disgust.

'My mother kept telling me to buck-up, to be strong – but it was the morphine that made me strong. It was my only friend.'

*

The white Packard that Varzi has bought becomes their home. It sails silently through the winter from the Dolomites to the Alps, adrift in an ocean of opulence and snow and crackling fireplaces in cognac-coloured nights, drifting like flotsam toward Monaco and the spring. They sit in the rear while Viganò chauffeurs them from Italy to Switzerland, from Austria to Bavaria, from France to here, and breakfast with *Paris Match* between them on the terrace of the Schloss Elmau Hotel with the morning sun veiled by a glass-bottle sky.

'You look so dour, Achille,' Ilse says, and Varzi glances down at the photograph of him and Ilse standing on the slopes of a resort now lost somewhere in the winter.

'And you look like death,' he replies. 'A man-eater. Here,' he pushes a basket of warm croissants at her, 'do you ever eat?'

'Do you want me to be a fat Italian mamma, Achille?'

'We can afford it,' he says. 'I got the telegraph from Zwickau last night. Auto Union has confirmed me for this season.'

'And Paul?'

'Paul has left the team,' says Varzi. 'Walb is gone, too. A chap by the name of Dr. Feuereisen signed the cable. He tells me they've cured the oiling problem: scraper piston rings, he says. What a name – Feuereisen.'

'I know him,' says Ilse. 'They call him *Feuerschlucker*. It means fire-eater.'

Varzi observes Ilse for a moment, and his breath catches in his throat. He is compromised by his own mortality, his own weakness. He aches. Her obedience in his bed, her obedience to his desire is a passion that he cannot quell. This is love, he thinks; it consumes a man, making a fool of him. And there is no relief.

*

Rosemeyer sits at Elly's diminutive work-desk, writing a letter. His left foot is in a cast, signed by friends and family, and his face and hands are a sickly yellow. It has been a disastrous winter. It had begun with food poisoning, which had kept him in hospital for three weeks; and it had ended two days after leaving that bed, when he had gone up to Kreuzeck to ski with Elly and friends and made the fateful decision to attempt the descent with them. ('What's the problem?' he had asked, 'it's all downhill, isn't it?') Halfway down the mountain, he had fractured his left foot. Rosemeyer can't help but smile at the memory of Elly's reaction that evening in the hospital ('Feuereisen will have my skin for this!'). The framed photograph of Elly on the desk – standing beside her Messerschmitt airplane somewhere in the Australian outback – spurs him on to complete the letter with a flourish of the pen.

'Bit young to be writing your memoirs, Bernd the race driver,' Elly says. 'You've been at it for two hours.'

Rosemeyer turns in the fragile chair. Elly sits on her couch with a cup of chamomile held between both hands.

'It's a letter to Himmler,' says Rosemeyer.

'Himmler?'

He hobbles toward her, holding the letter out. 'I've addressed it already,' he says, 'and I'll leave it here, for you to post when you're ready.'

'Bernd.' She watches him sit beside her. 'What is this now?'

'I'm a member of the SS.' She holds the letter up to the mellow light of her apartment. His writing is clear, slanted, animated. 'So you know I'm of pure Aryan blood.' She is distracted by his smile. But really, she thinks, a specimen closer to the Führer's ideal man probably doesn't exist. 'You understand that, as a member of the SS, I can only get married with the direct blessing of Reichsführer Himmler.'

She sips her tea. 'Married, Bernd?'

'Elly, I love you. The moment I first met you I knew I was destined to spend my life with you.' He falters under the intensity of her gaze. 'Didn't – '

'Bernd, is this your idea of a proposal?' she interrupts.

'What? Oh, no, I – well – actually I didn't think of it quite like that,' he admits. 'But surely you felt it too, the first time we met?'

'The first time I saw you, Bernd the race driver, was at the AVUS.'

'During my first race?'

'Yes.'

'Oh,' he says, flustered and confused. 'Well, you know, I was so much younger then.'

'That was less than a year ago!'

'Yes, but I hadn't won anything yet.'

She sees that look again, the Bernd face – the one she imagines him wearing out there playing race driver. 'I thought you looked like a knight, Bernd Rosemeyer, a shining white knight that day at the AVUS. I was in the stands when you burst your tyre, and you looked so adorable with all your snot and tears.'

Rosemeyer blushes.

'Oh Bernd,' she whispers, kissing him full on the lips. 'I would be honored to be your wife.'

*

Nuvolari is bandaged and wounded. He has four broken ribs, contusions to the face, and a lost tooth, the result of an accident during practice when Jano's Alfa 12C-36 had shed a tyre at the exact same spot where Taruffi had come off the track at Mellaha the year before in '35.

'But at least,' he tells the *Gazzetta*, 'I didn't go through the billboard like Piero did – you know they charged him for damages!' Nuvolari had been fortunate: as he veered off the track at 200kph, he had been hurled from the cockpit into a mound of grass that had been scythed and piled only the night before. It had taken the marshals ten minutes to find him; when they finally did, he was crawling about on all fours searching for his gloves. And then, finding one, he had lost consciousness.

The 12C – a stock Tipo C into which Jano had contrived to squeeze a fat-12 – was proving a reluctant beast to tame. Nuvolari had not been its first victim: Dr. Farina, who had tested the thing at Monza the week before, had been bitten too, and for Farina it was the second big one in as many weeks; at the Deauville GP he'd tangled with Marcel Lehoux's ERA, the two cars balleting-off together into the scenery from whence Lehoux was destined never to return. Brivio, meanwhile, had had an enormous off a few short minutes after Nuvolari, he too thrown from his cockpit to sail over 100 hundred metres before he'd been found staggering around of the track wearing nothing but his goggles and one sleeve.

Nuvolari (racing against doctors' orders) is down in a distant eighth position at the Libyan Grand Prix with two laps remaining. He catches sight of a silver blur in his mirror and moves off the line to allow the leaders through – Stuck in the Auto Union, followed a breath later by Varzi. Nuvolari keeps glancing at his rear-view mirror, but there's no sign of Rosemeyer. A pity, he thinks, because the young lad would have learnt a great deal today from Varzi. Instead, Stuck will be the one forced to learn the lesson that Varzi had taught Nuvolari back in '34 – and at Stuck's age, the lesson will probably taste a tad bitter.

Varzi is poised, eyes veiled beneath black-lensed Triplex goggles. He runs out of Stuck's wake, ensuring that his radiator swallows fresh desert air. He has nursed his V16 all day, allowing Stuck to dictate the pace. This is a tactical battle; a battle of wits more than desire or skill. Behind the pitwall, Rudolf holds out a flag with Varzi's number and a green dot below it. It means, keep pushing. This instruction is hardly necessary, thinks Varzi: All will be decided on the final turn, a turn he had spent the entire practice session on Thursday exploring. He visualizes this turn now, imagining his exit in a deliciously controlled powerslide. He imagines victory – which isn't too difficult, considering how many times he has won here. This is his track: he owns this place, this Italian place in the sun.

Varzi follows Stuck into the final double right-hander, his line impeccable. He comes out in an expansive drift inches behind Stuck, his eyes concerned not with the road but with his rev'-counter. The V16 has a narrow powerband and the white face of his tachometer, when he enters the straight, reads 3200rpm. Perfect, he thinks, drawing into Stuck's wake like a shark. Perfect.

Stuck's V16 is a thumping, menacing beast spitting fuel and oil and fire, the noise a physical wave that skitters beneath Varzi's vibrating hands. Varzi eases off the throttle in the near-vacuum of the slipstream and feels himself sucked right onto Stuck's rear-end. He must wait; he has an inch left in the travel of his gas pedal. That inch is worth 10kph – enough for him to win.

The rear of Stuck's Auto Union suddenly rises. A fraction, but it's enough to panic Varzi into instinctively flinging his wheel left, scarcely missing Stuck's rear tyre as the German slows down. Varzi gets into a nasty tank slapper at over 280kph, corrects this way and that, his hands laser-quick, foot flat on the power. His car keeps threatening to spiral out of control. Varzi doesn't operate on instinct. He keeps his boot in, trusting in the power of his

V16. In a moment, all is sorted. He checks his mirror. Stuck falls away rapidly, chasing without much conviction.

Varzi is barely aware of the chequered flag, of the crowd up there beneath the sheltered concrete grandstand. He forgoes the victory lap, heading directly for the pits instead with the ignition already killed. The car is still rolling when he jumps from the cockpit, indifferent to the mechanics sprinting after the fleeing Auto Union. Viganò appears with a lit cigarette which he thrusts between Varzi's lips. Varzi throws off his goggles, tossing them onto the hot tarmac with such force that they shatter into pieces. He focuses his attention on the slight man standing by the concrete pitwall, behind a desk strewn with lapcharts and chronographs. Varzi rushes toward him.

'Varzi,' says Feuereisen.

'That filthy *fotze* tried to kill me!' yells Varzi, shaking with anger.

Feuereisen blinks, astonished. His bland eyes shift fretfully beyond Varzi's shoulder. Varzi spins around: Hans Stuck is ambling toward them. Sensing Varzi's next move, Feuereisen seizes his arm. 'Varzi, wait, you don't – '

Varzi breaks free from his grip and strides off toward Stuck. 'You!' he shouts, one finger pointing up at the tall man's face. 'You *fotze!* Why the hell did you slow down?'

'Don't be a clown,' says Stuck, his buck-toothed smile enraging Varzi further. Varzi winds up a punch, and Stuck takes a step back. Varzi realizes that something in Stuck's attitude isn't quite right. He almost seems ... righteous. On the hot ground by his feet, Varzi spots a flag with Stuck's number on it – 10. On it is a red dot. Red for slow down. Varzi looks at it for a long while. He feels an arm grip his elbow and drag him away through a tunnel of people sticking programs and paper in his face until he finds himself in the garage. There, amidst the tyres and tools on makeshift tables, Feuereisen whispers, 'Stuck was following orders.'

'*What* orders?' asks Varzi. Stuck, hovering beside Feuereisen, lights a smoke.

'Von Neurath's orders. It's been decided – by the Ministry of Foreign Affairs.'

'*What* has been decided?'

'Italian drivers will win in Italian races, Germans everywhere else. I'm sorry – this comes from high up.'

Varzi spits on the floor. 'Are you mad? I won't accept that – what is this shit? I don't need your fucking charity to beat Hans Stuck.'

'Please, Herr Varzi,' begs Feuereisen. 'I implore you – you mustn't make waves. Think of the team – this is bigger than you, bigger than us.' Varzi notices Stuck walking away into the sun. 'It's all politics now,' Varzi hears Feuereisen say. 'Please.'

'You didn't need to do this,' Varzi says.

'I had no choice.'

'Yes,' says Varzi, turning away, 'yes you did. I would have won anyway.'

*

Marshall Italo Balbo surveys his home, the Royal Palace of Tripoli, with barely contained rage. On the boulevard stretched before the palace, Bedouins on white horses welcome a flotilla of elegant cars that deposit drivers, team principles, and the toast of Tripoli society for the post-race banquet that doubles as North Africa's biggest party of the year.

Balbo turns away from his bedroom veranda. God alone, he thinks, knows how deeply he despises this place. Had he not marched with Mussolini to Rome – actually fucking *marched,* while dear brave Benito led three days from the rear from the back seat of his American limousine? Had he not been Il Duce's confidante and friend? Yes, he had been all of that – he had also fought at the battle of Vittorio Veneto, where he had liberated Italy from the very scum with whom Mussolini was now sharing his bed.

And what has been Balbo's reward? Exile in fucking Libya, that's what – because Mussolini is afraid of him, of what he stands for, afraid of Marshall Balbo, a loyal footsoldier in Fascism's endless war for freedom. Balbo now considers Il Duce to be an embarrassment, a liability.

The introduction of the Roman salute, that asinine straight-armed jab, is yet another imbecility, as farcical as the invasion of Abyssinia. Yes, Italian troops had finally marched into Addis Ababa last week, but the war had been waged so badly that Mussolini had been forced to bomb the bastards with chemical weapons. And therein lies the true price of victory in Abyssinia: Not the sanctions imposed by the League of Nations, but the break from Italy's traditional allies, Britain and France, in favor of Mussolini's new-found friend in Germany.

Today he had received the latest communiqué from the Grand Council. Il Duce's new idea was to join up with the Nazis in the impending Spanish civil war. Balbo is certain that no good will come of an alliance with the Germans – the mockery at the grand prix today, which had humiliated and enraged him in equal measure, only served to demonstrate the arrogance of the Hun. And someone was going to pay for today's shameful trickery.

Balbo strides into the banquet room, slowing down to allow his guests to stand as one and salute. He stares straight ahead, still enraged that Rome and Berlin had decided to fuck with his grand prix, his colony. Today, they would discover that no man fucks with Air Marshall Italo Balbo, heir-in-waiting to Italy's empire.

Balbo bows his head once. Men and women sit at that simple command. He takes the opportunity to survey his guests: to his left is the lottery winner, Italy's newest millionaire, and to his right is Achille Varzi, who Balbo singles out for a withering stare. Balbo knows the type, knows him for what he is – a bourgeois little prick. 'Quite a show you put on today, Varzi.' Balbo listens as everyone falls silent around him. 'But then again, I heard from De Bono that putting on a show, here in Libya, is something of a specialty of yours.'

Without waiting for a response, Balbo claps his hands for the feast to begin. Bellydancers jingle out from hidden recesses in the wings, along with Arab boys burdened by silver trays. After a few minutes, Balbo, irritated, turns to Varzi again. 'What the Ghibli gives, the Ghibli takes away – have you heard that expression?' Varzi shakes his head politely. 'No? Probably because I just made it up.' He pauses, and everyone laughs on cue. 'This place has been good to you, hasn't it, my friend – this fucking desert, it's

191

been kind to you.'

Balbo stands up with a flourish, holding his crystal wine glass. 'Ladies and gentlemen – a toast, please, a toast – to the victor!' He waits for his guests to get to their feet. In their haste, they sound like a storm of water buffalo. He watches as Varzi stands up last, head bowed as if to appear humble. Pompous little clown, thinks Balbo. 'Ladies and gentlemen, the winner of the Gran Premio di Tripoli … *Hans Stuck.'*

The silence is deafening.

Balbo wonders who will dare to defy him. He takes in all the faces around him, mocking their unease: Varzi swallowing air and choking on his self-importance; Nuvolari frowning with his black eyes glinting fire; Caracciola whispering to Chiron, who smiles delightedly. Finally, words pierce through the silence. Balbo darts his head like a cobra – yes, he thinks, yes it would be him.

'You have the wrong man,' says Bernd Rosemeyer. 'Varzi – '

Balbo smiles coldly. 'I'm aware, my German friend, of who crossed the line first. Because I myself had the dishonour of throwing the chequered flag to end that fiesta of shit you gentlemen served up for me today. I'm also aware of who won the race. They say only winners get to write history; but here in Italy, I am the one who writes history.' He points at Hühnlein. 'How do you Germans say it again? Hail victory?'

'Sieg Heil!' shouts Hühnlein. *'Sieg Heil!'*

Balbo is seated before Hühnlein's stiffened arm collapses by his side. Let them feast.

*

The Carthage circuit stretches out of the dozy village of El Aquina, heading north to Soukra before cutting back east to the coastal village of al-Marsa and its flotilla of fishing barges. On that twelve kilometre stretch there is a naturally-banked right-hand bend, a rough and dirty turn bordered by an olive orchard that rises improbably from the parched, dry soil of the desert. Raymond Mays cannot imagine a more desolate spot.

Mays has been tagging along with the circus for the North

African rounds of the season reporting for *Auto Week*, on special assignment as a personal favor to the editor, an Old Etonian with whom he'd shared the usual rounds of ritualized floggings, buggery, and cold showers. Mays, who had formed the British ERA team some years back, and who was a man not impervious to a spot of eye-liner when dining with his friend Peter Berthon, had gladly accepted the invitation to witness Europe's finest drivers and teams in action while *Auto Week*'s regular motoring correspondent – a chap named Bradley – recovered from a bout of malaria, gout, or an atrophied booze-liver (the editor had been rather vague on that score). And now here he is in Tunis, sitting in the shade of an olive tree on a fine mid-May afternoon. His white linen suit and baby-blue shirt, crumpled and sweat-stained, bear testimony to the blistering heat. He sips on warm beer from the stash in his wicker picnic basket and waits for the cars to race past him.

It was here, at this spot, that Nuvolari had insisted that a man could distinguish the great from the good. Nuvolari, who Mays had met back in Blighty a few years earlier, had chosen not to race this weekend, his broken ribs from Mellaha still not healed and causing him obvious discomfort. 'There's nothing better for a battered body than the massage of a grand prix car,' he had told Mays last night, 'but my ribs don't seem to agree.' This meant that old Tazio was amenable to a few beers at the hotel bar which led – as these things did – to a protracted discussion on the current state of motor-racing.

For reasons Mays was unable to recall this morning, their talk had ended with a thorough dissection of Achille Varzi's mood – which, admittedly, had been a tad sinister all weekend, strange even for someone as habitually strange as Achille Varzi. Varzi had hardly spoken a word to anyone since his arrival on Saturday morning. That afternoon, he had climbed into his Auto Union and proceeded to lap the circuit three seconds faster than Rosemeyer, eviscerating the lap record in the process. Job done, he'd parked his Type C and vanished back to his hotel, aggressively avoiding any contact with his team, the press, and everyone else.

Mays listens to the familiar whine of superchargers in the distance. He is alone out here, his little white rental Bianchi abandoned on the access road about half-a-mile away. Through the heat-haze, the cars suddenly burst from behind a burrow. Mays watches, transfixed. The air shatters like glass as the Auto Unions rumble past with their low-grumbling V16s. Behind them, the Mercedes' high-pitched whine, a screaming, unnatural wail, give chase. As Mays embraces the ear-piercing noise of the engines, he reflects on what Nuvolari had told him the night before. Not once, in a career that now spanned over a decade, had Varzi ever had what Nuvolari called 'the big one': while so many drivers around him had been maimed or killed, Varzi had just kept on winning, cocooned in a balloon of apparent invincibility. According to Nuvolari, true courage could only come after the big one – never before. And since Varzi had never had that experience, he continued to take risks that other drivers had learnt to avoid long ago.

Mays sits in wait now, prepared this time to detect the individual engine-notes that had brought him to this forsaken spot. The bend, here before Mays, appears as nothing unique. The banking is perhaps thirty degrees, the road narrow and pock-marked with blistered tarmac. It doesn't even warrant a name, unlike other sphincter-clutching turns of lore – the Masta chicane at Spa, the Flugplatz at the 'Ring. And yet Tazio had insisted that here, Mays would be educated as to why a man like Varzi would always be faster than a man like Dreyfus.

Varzi's Auto Union flashes through the burrow and into sight, punching through the haze. Mays watches the silver Type C run onto the banking. The rear skips out, caught by a quick flick of the wrist, and the Italian is through and gone. And not for an instant had that engine faltered. Not even a feather. Varzi had taken the turn absolutely flat, entirely in command of his fear and over ten seconds up on the chasing pack led by Bernd Rosemeyer who – here he comes – can't dissuade his mind from breathing on the throttle, an all-too-human confidence-lift. Yes, thinks Mays, beginning to understand.

Varzi's gap keeps climbing, twenty-five seconds by lap thirteen when finally Rosemeyer works the turn out and he too begins to arrow through without lifting. Nuvolari, thinks Mays, was right in his estimation of the young German.

On lap fourteen, Varzi enters the banking with the engine note flat, his edge delightful, the man himself relaxed in his seat, his immense wooden wheel inches from his chest. He is, Mays considers, the supreme stylist of his generation, and it would be a wasteful man who'd bet against Varzi winning the European Championship by the summer in that Auto Union. On the exit, caught by a sudden gust of wind, front wheels ascend from the track. At 300kph, the rising front-end inverts the car's aerodynamics and the silver arrow becomes its own wing. It takes flight, nose pointing up at an endless blue sky, and sails off the track as if made of paper. It soars into the olive orchard, this 700 kilogramme projectile, weightless and graceful. Until the rear digs into the sterile earth. The velocity slams the nose down a fraction of a second later, and then the car is cartwheeling away amidst a thunderstorm of ragged metal and mountings and shards of sheering aluminium all buried within a tornado of red dust.

Mays is running between the gnarled branches of the olive trees when Varzi's Auto Union finally comes to a stop in a cloud of dust. There's nothing much left: All four wheels have been ripped off, the engine severed, the frame destroyed. Mays, spotting Varzi slumped in the cockpit lying impossibly still, becomes aware of the silence. Dead, thinks Mays, as he rushes toward the wreckage. He's almost upon it when he sees Varzi's body stir, his gloved hands releasing the steering wheel. Mays slows, and watches in disbelief as Achille Varzi worms his way out of the cockpit.

'Varzi!' The Italian doesn't acknowledge Mays' shout. Instead he rummages through the pockets of his white overalls to eventually find a crumpled pack of Luckys. With trembling hands, he pulls a cigarette out. 'Varzi,' repeats Mays, looking at him in awe.

'Ah,' says Varzi. 'An Englishman. How charming. And in the desert.'

'My name is Mays.'

'Would you happen to have a light, Mays?'

'Of course,' says Mays, trying to hide his amazement.

'Excellent.' Varzi takes one step forward before collapsing like a puppet, his eyes rolling back in his head. As Mays carries

Varzi back to his rental car, he can't help thinking that the Italian certainly has style – even while fainting.

Varzi blinks, trying to see through the dim light. 'Can you hear me?' a voice asks.

'Yes.' Varzi focuses on the man's features. He sees a closely-cropped beard, and green reptilian eyes gleaming behind gold-rimmed spectacles.

'Do you recognize me?'

'Dr. Magneven,' whispers Varzi, his throat raw.

'Welcome back. You've been through the meat-grinder I'm afraid, but I can't find anything physically broken, you'll be glad to hear. How do you feel?'

Varzi ponders this question. He eases himself gingerly up onto his elbows. He is sitting on a stretcher in his underwear in the Auto Union garage. An engine screams past somewhere in the afternoon – a Mercedes, he recognizes the yowl. He looks down at his trembling hands. 'Can someone drive me to my hotel?' he asks.

Dr. Magneven does so himself. He accompanies Varzi all the way to his room and instructs him to call in four hours. 'We want to make sure you won't get a concussion,' he explains to Varzi before closing the door behind him."

*

Varzi is not quite sure if he has actually slept. On rubbery legs, he walks from the bed and draws the curtains shut to a throbbing sunset. He steps naked to his suitcase, rummages around impatiently, tosses his pressed clothes out until he finds a trivial tin box. With hands that won't cease shivering and sweat running chilled over his body, he clips the box open. It is, he thinks, sitting on the bed, a miracle. But the anxiety is eating at him, and he must consciously remind himself to breathe – to breathe.

Ilse – he must speak with Ilse, she won't understand, can't, even if he were able to express what it is that he feels, but it doesn't matter, her voice is like foam, like marmalade, a velvet blanket for the cold night.

L'Isola Del Lido, February 15th, 1968

Night has fallen beyond the window, the bobbing lights of drifting buoys on the ink-black lagoon dancing across my walls, shadows and masks. It's not yet seven. I lift the receiver and dial, listen to the electronic ring in my ear. It keeps beeping without reply. Strange. I find the number scrawled on the back of my notebook, and dial it carefully again. The ringing goes on until it jars my senses. I replace the receiver and stare at it. Why is there no reply? It's just gone seven when I head out of the room down to the check-in desk where the night manager is busy reading a crumpled copy of the *Gazzetta*.

'Is Signor Finestrini in his room?' I enquire.

'You're the gentleman from room 307?' he asks.

'Yes.'

'*L'Americano?*'

I shrug. A long story, so this will do.

The man extracts a manila envelope from a pigeon-hole on the wall behind him. 'Signor Finestrini left this for you.'

I accept the envelope. I consider returning to my room but find myself walking toward the hotel restaurant instead. I sit at the table where we had shared a meal, Finestrini and I, and it feels familiar to me. The envelope contains sheets of time-worn writing paper along with a message written on hotel stationery. I turn the page toward the light and decipher the spidery letters:

"Dear Mr. Deutsch,

I'm unable to meet you for dinner this evening. I do apologize. Perhaps we can reconvene for breakfast — I'll be sure to call your room in the morning. I hope, in the meantime, that you find this helpful.

Yours,

Johnny Finestrini."

'Do you need anything?' The night manager stands above me, moustache twitching.

I look at the moustache. 'Do you have a menu?'

'We don't serve dinner at this time of year.' To not accept inconvenience in Italy is to be driven mad. 'If you need anything else, just come call me – I'm behind the desk all night.'

He leaves me there at my table, perhaps reassured that somewhere near him another man sits awake on this snow-laced night on the Lido. I flip through the pages. They are letters, yellowed with age. I bow my head and allow the folded letters to stumble out into the light.

PART FIVE
TRACKS

Come to the edge, He said. They said, We are afraid. Come to the edge, He said. They came. He pushed them ... and they flew.

– Guillaume Apollinaire

November 7, 1946,
Graaf-Reinet, South Africa

Johnny,

I must confess to my astonishment upon receiving your letter last week. How you managed to obtain my address is a mystery I hope you will clear it up when you reply. I read, also, that you're now writing a book—that, I suppose, is a little less surprising ...

The last time we met was indeed in North Africa in 1940. You were there with Dr. Farina, and as we parted (you'd just received your call-up papers), you asked me whether I'd ever reveal what had happened to Varzi after his crash at Carthage in '36. You were always one to hold Varzi dear, weren't you, and I think of you now, you and Varzi, and wonder whether I ever really lived that life. In your letter, you have again asked me to speak of that strange year in the life of Achille Varzi. Johnny, it will no doubt amuse your sense of irony to learn that I was attached to a column composed mostly of your Italian Alpini, the Tridentina Division, during that awful winter of 1943. I treated your boys on that retreat from the Don – the maladies of a lost war, do you like that turn of phrase? It sounds so much more poetic than an accurate description of the hundreds of amputations I performed using a butcher's knife. I mention this because I have a memory of us sitting together in that hotel in North Africa, discussing our mutual love of motor racing. Do you remember what you said that day? That it was the men, and not the sport, who captivated you the most? Johnny, I must tell you that the frozen Steppe – littered by the dead – has forever changed my perception of what came before. Human life is not at all precious, we got it wrong, you see. We thought our heroes were risking something valuable – but here is the bitter truth:

the dead are all alike. Horseshit is good for frostbitten toes, and far more useful than a human life, even that of a doctor operating with a butcher's knife. And so, Johnny, the answer is yes: I see no reason, anymore, to protect the reputation of one flawed man.

Let me take you back, then, to the spring of 1936. Feuereisen suggested that I accompany Varzi to Milan, this after his massive shunt at Carthage. Considering it meant flying to Europe on a Junkers, rather than that distasteful ferry trip back to Genoa, I accepted with gratitude. Feuereisen had expressed his concern that Varzi might experience a delayed form of anxiety, since this had been his first major accident. However, I found an altogether unaffected man waiting for me at the aerodrome in Tunis that Thursday morning. Varzi was dressed as impeccably as ever in his pressed linen suit, silk scarf, and dark sunglasses. I remember that, while ascending the stairs leading up to the silver Junkers, his impenetrable gaze had fallen on a pair of photographers standing on the tarmac. I still have that photograph, of Varzi and me, somewhere here in my files. We looked so very self-important back then, didn't we?

It was while sitting beside him on that flight that I was reminded of how strained conversation always was with Varzi. I played out various ways in which to broach the subject of Tripoli and the Balbo imbroglio with him— conscious all the while that an ill-chosen phrase, particularly after Carthage, would have had serious consequences for his morale. In my hesitation to dig too deeply into his state of mind, I must confess also to my own anxiety – that of alienating Auto Union's number one driver. Feuereisen had been adamant on that score. Had I been given carte blanche, I'd like to believe that I would have probed that strange man's mind a little deeper that day. And had I done so, Johnny, do you think anything would have changed?

In your letter, you write that it's your belief that the seeds of Varzi's downfall were sown at Balbo's banquet. You're correct, I believe. The accident at Carthage and the Balbo affair were not two random incidents; they were connected by Varzi's

paranoia, and his delusions of persecution. Carthage was a loss
of confidence that led to a full-blown identity crisis. I say loss
of confidence because Varzi was determined to humble those
who had taken pleasure from his humiliation in Tripoli. I recall
Feuereisen's awe at Varzi's pace in Carthage – he was driving,
and I say this literally, like a man possessed. Such was the depth
of his insecurity, Johnny. What I gathered from my brief time
with Varzi on that flight back was that he was a melancholic
man with a tendency toward depression. I have always
maintained that such men are starkly unpredictable, and Varzi
would prove to be no exception.

Ilse was waiting for him in front of their white Packard when
we landed in Milan. Varzi embraced her. She held him insipidly,
and it was she who broke first to give up the wheel for him. Varzi
had beckoned me over then, and with those dead gray eyes, he
looked straight through me and said, 'You can't fear what you
don't feel. Now, you'll kindly inform Feuereisen that I won't be
available for the test next week. I'll see him for the grand prix
instead.'

Varzi didn't give me a chance to reply and abandoned me
there without even a ride to the train station.

Feuereisen had sounded me out back in Zwickau, and I
warned him that we would find a guarded Varzi in Barcelona. It
was, I explained, a strange process, a man crashing at speed. First,
he sees it happen in slow motion and will know that he's about
to have the big one. Depending on the severity of the impact,
chances are the driver won't remember much, if anything at all
– and that was the second thing: Amnesia. Varzi would awaken
in the morning feeling exhausted, but would, in all likelihood,
be unaware of the nightmares that were triggering his delayed
lethargy.

You can imagine my surprise, then, Johnny, at the Varzi
who turned up for the Penya Rhin Grand Prix held up in the
Montjuïc hills, this almost a month after Carthage: his clothes
un-ironed, his shoes without their customary sheen, and a

wide smile plastered on his face. Varzi the reticent had been transformed into someone as chatty as a teenage girl drunk on bubbly. You remember that? I had expected that Varzi would be altered by his massive shunt – but this caught me entirely off guard. Should I have suspected then? Perhaps – but I was distracted, for it wasn't only Varzi that I found in an altered state. The city too was brewing something toxic, and there was talk of revolution and war, which perturbed me greatly. You'll remember Varzi did three laps in the morning practice before telling Feuereisen he was unable to continue. I did a full physical on Varzi that morning, on Feuereisen's orders, and it was, I concluded, my opinion that Auto Union's number one driver was in good physical shape.

'So what's the problem then?' Feuereisen asked me on Sunday evening, after Nuvolari had won the grand prix in his Ferrari, and Varzi had already gone home.

My reply was that Varzi's loss of form was psychological in nature, well aware that I was treading down a risky path with Feuereisen, a man not forgiving of weakness.

He told me he wanted Varzi back and winning by the summer.

Good old Feuereisen. Not a man with a light touch, was he, Johnny! Varzi I saw again a couple of weeks later when we went off to the Nürburgring for the traditional early-summer grand prix dubbed the Eifelrennen – I remember, Nuvolari launching his Alfa into the rain with that wolverine face of his all set and white teeth grimacing ... In that particular section of the track, Johnny, you'll remember, most of the cars would get airborne as they came off the narrow chute where the slick road, falling away, acted as a ramp. Nuvolari got the landing wrong almost every lap – no surprise, he was never particularly gifted when it came to technique, was he? – and his rear end would drift about, his hands twisting this way and that, correcting under brakes, and then the car was racing through the right-hander at an improbable angle. These were drivers at their

peak, Johnny, monkeys trained for this specific highwire act.
Lesser drivers operated on the premise that a bend has three
parts to it – the turn-in, the apex, the exit – but these men had
discovered multiple phases. For them, where they hit the brakes
didn't mean as much as where they came *off* the brakes; not a
matter of braking and turning-in, but of softly coming off the
brakes and rolling into the turn. I always found Varzi's style to
be quite unique, actually: a stingy, almost effortless exercise in
car-control. No doubt he was brave and fast, but he coupled this
with the smoothness of a Caracciola and an acute sensitivity to
how the race was playing out that only Chiron dared imitate,
and it was this Varzi who came punching through the Flugplatz.
And yet, by lap two, he had surrendered over a minute to the
front three, and had even been overtaken by his good mate
Count Brivio in his Alfa V8.

Rosemeyer, chasing hard in third, was a customary bundle
of uncoiling energy. There was a joy in the way he attacked,
Entangled in that raw talent of his was a deep sense of glee,
and the way he launched himself off the Flugplatz was quite
mesmerizing. He too would often get the landing wrong, and
the only thing that prevented him from going off into the trees
was his astonishingly deft touch. As I informed Feuereisen after
the race, it was an exhibition of style and courage such as I had
rarely witnessed before.

Feuereisen had agreed with my verdict, especially since
Bernd had ended up winning the race after Caracciola's engine
had swallowed itself. The mist that'd descended down from the
Eiffel Mountains had proved decisive for Bernd: As the track
faded beneath that gray cloud, the field had slowed – all, that
is, except for Bernd, who just kept going around like a Katyusha
rocket. For a man at speed, time must always slow. It's the irony
of the race driver: In order to go quicker he must physically
decelerate time, and this is achieved only when the driver is on
autopilot, leaving a mind free to impose itself upon the machine.
Bernd was simply phenomenal at that.

Varzi had finished a distant seventh, and I was at a loss to explain his lack of pace. I told Feuereisen that Varzi had seemed as committed as ever, before noting that he had beaten both Stuck and von Delius in identical Auto Unions.

'Ja,' Feuereisen had replied – you remember the way he spoke, Johnny, as if he was chewing someone's liver – 'ja, but he was also eight minutes behind Bernd.' Feuereisen had nodded toward Rosemeyer who, with the delightful and pretty Elly beside him, was being interviewed by state radio, his laurel still hanging around his neck. He told me a story then, one that Elly had related to him: Apparently she and Bernd had been driving through a fog-bank on their way to the track and she had asked him to slow down. 'Oh,' Bernd had replied, 'don't worry, I see him.' 'See who?' Elly had asked a second before a man on a bike had appeared out of nowhere. She'd said it was almost supernatural, the way he'd been able to see through the fog.

'Supernatural?' I repeated, shivering in my wet clothes in the garage after the race. 'I think it was more psychological.'

'You mean his eye-sight?' Feuereisen had asked.

'No,' I'd replied. 'His vision.'

I wonder, Johnny – you weren't terribly specific in your letter – will you be writing of Bernd? And will your book feature Louis Chiron?

I never liked that man much. There was something of the night about him, something so obviously self-serving and egotistical that I never felt at my ease around him. And I wasn't surprised when Baby Hoffman finally gave up on him. She turned up at Dreyfus' apartment one night in a dreadful state, while I was staying there. Chou-Chou gave her some whisky to calm her nerves, her face was puffy and swollen, she'd obviously been through hell. She was quite formidable, wasn't she, Johnny? Not someone who'd take anyone's shit, except of course for Chiron's. Dreyfus suggested she go to Lugano, to see Caracciola.

'Charly will always be there between us,' was Baby's response.

Dreyfus and Chou-chou then took it in turns to persuade her of Caracciola's unrequited love (yes, Chou-chou actually said that). This went on until Dreyfus, exhausted, suggested we take a drive to the train station to check out the schedule.

It's true, we were all a bit light-headed with the dawn and the drink when we waved Baby goodbye on the 7:37 a.m. train to Lugano. When we returned to the apartment, we discovered Louis Chiron waiting for us in the lobby on a carpet of his own handmade cigarettes. Chiron told us that Baby had gone mad. Dreyfus uncorked a bottle of chilled Prosecco right about then and, suitably fortified for what we both knew was coming, told Chiron we'd just come back from the station where we'd seen Baby onto the Lugano express.

Chiron mulled that one over for a while. 'Lugano? She didn't even pack her bags – why would she...' And then it hit him – harder than either Dreyfus or I could have anticipated. 'Caracciola? She's left Louis Chiron? For a fucking cripple?' And with that, he charged out of the apartment, slamming the door with such violence that one of Dreyfus's modernist paintings fell right off the wall to shatter at our feet.

Which, I suppose, leads me on to 'The Beinhorns', as they were referred to by the press (much to Bernd's amusement), celebrating their wedding vows with the team on the Friday night before the German Grand Prix. You'll recall that Bernd and Elly had tied the knot two weeks earlier in a low-key affair in Berlin.

Looking back on it now, Johnny, that weekend at the end of July 1936 was to be the acme of Auto Union's success. I believe that it was also the weekend when Feuereisen became convinced that the team had no further need of Achille Varzi. He was in good spirits, our Bernd, playful and charming as ever that weekend, enjoying a wave of success that had seen the Berlin press nominate him as the most recognized sportsman in the country. Rosemeyer's image had become synonymous with Hitler's can-do spirit and the youthful promise of his Reich, but privately, Johnny, I must tell you, Bernd was increasingly disturbed by his fame. He had gone from being an unknown racer to an international phenomenon in a matter of months, and I don't think he'd ever really considered the consequences of his meteoric rise. Bernd was a small-town boy with honest values, and he just couldn't get his head around his own myth – the one that was shaped for him, Johnny, and the one in which he would be entombed.

Elly it was who shielded him and guided him without her, I'm convinced he'd have been swallowed whole by the press, by the Party, by the constant requests for his time, his face, his quotes, and his thoughts. Elly looked resplendent that Friday night, I still remember her wearing her bandana emblazoned with the number thirteen on it, Bernd's lucky charm. She, Bernd, and Tazio made an unlikely threesome as the evening wore on. I had been watching the three of them for a while from the bottom of my vodka glass when a voice in my ear interrupted my thoughts. It was Feuereisen, and he said something like, 'I see Bernd has invited an Italian, which is just as well, since he's the only Italian here.' Varzi, you see, was a no-show for the grand prix – hadn't even bothered to send a telegram. Feuereisen wasted no time informing me that 'we' would need to deal with this. That, of course, was his way of telling me that I had misdiagnosed Varzi's condition. It was an accusation that was not too far from the truth, actually.

Varzi's season had gone from the crash at Carthage to this – AWOL for the all-important German Grand Prix. In my defense, Johnny, it had appeared, through the early summer, as if Varzi had been rehabilitating his frail, injured psyche. He had run two average races post-Carthage, it's true, but I had anticipated a fully rejuvenated Varzi in Germany after the summer break. His vanishing act was the last thing I had expected.

In contrast, Rosemeyer's runaway victory that Sunday, in front of 300,000 spectators chanting his name, hardly came as a surprise. The boy who had driven his first grand prix scarcely a year before was now poised to clinch the 1936 European Championship, and Mercedes' humiliation that weekend had us feasting on a rich banquet of red meat. We were like vultures, I must admit; but isn't grand prix racing a blood sport? The Mercedes W25K was a debacle, their season had been a disgrace, and now, in Germany, their drivers, too, began to unravel deliciously. Poor Neubauer, the longer the weekend progressed, the redder his face became from a combination of shame and rage, and I must say I was rather concerned over the fat man's health.

I remember Caracciola and Chiron spending the weekend swapping icy looks when their paths invariably crossed in the garage, and despite René Dreyfus's heroic efforts to try and force a reconciliation, the situation just got worse. Meanwhile, Fagioli was pacing about like a panther, apparently enraged that no one had yet apologized to him for his woeful season, and von Brauchitsch was suffering from the pain of an alleged horse-whipping he had received in Berlin after an incident involving a girl with questionable morals. Neubauer must have been grateful that the Summer Olympics, scheduled to begin the following week, meant that the Party bigwigs had remained in Berlin.

But if the build-up to the grand prix was a debacle, the race itself was an absolute tragedy for those shits from Mercedes. It got so bad that Fagioli actually brought his car into the box after being lapped by Rosemeyer. 'This thing's going to kill someone!' he'd shouted, and Neubauer had responded by physically hoisting the Italian out of the car to replace him with Lang – you remember Lang, he'd been promoted to a race seat after working as von Brauchitsch's chief mechanic. Anyway, Neubauer and Fagioli were still exchanging words in three different languages when Caracciola came in with a terminal misfire. Five laps later, he took over the ex-Fagioli–Lang car (after Lang dislocated his finger shifting gears), but that too expired from an overheated engine. Von Brauchitsch then pulled out, complaining of an ailment, which left Caracciola, in the baron's car, to salvage some sort of pride with a distant fifth place finish. The only driver who didn't bring his Mercedes to the pit that afternoon was Chiron. He came back on a stretcher after going off the track on lap thirteen in a foolish attempt at chasing down Caracciola. He had missed being scalped by an inch, you remember, Johnny? A lucky man indeed.

Neubauer it was who summoned me over to the Mercedes garage, where I found Chiron barely conscious and in earnest pain. He had taken a pounding, thrown from his car at around 200kph, and his face was covered in a filthy mask of blood and mud. His shoulder was clearly dislocated, hanging limp off the side of the stretcher, and I figured that was as good a place as any to begin. I asked for two mechanics to hold him down and snapped the shoulder back into its socket. To his credit, Chiron's screams only lasted until I administered a shot of morphine. En route to the ambulance, Chiron had managed to express his feelings for me in no uncertain terms before telling me: 'It's supposed to happen in slow motion, but it happened so fucking fast.' I assured him that, as far as I could tell, a mild convalescence would be all that was required for a full recovery. 'Tell Neubauer,' he said, 'that I won't be driving for Mercedes again. You tell him that Louis Chiron has quit the team.'

'What team?' was Neubauer's reaction when I told him that night at the hotel bar. It was all delightfully delicious, wasn't it, and that feeling lasted until the Tuesday after the race when, back in Zwickau, I met with Feuereisen in his office. If Rosemeyer's win had done anything to elicit joy in that grim face of his, it had long since expired by the time I arrived for the promised 'Varzi-chat'. Feuereisen handed me a copy of 'The Motor' – an English weekly – and the 'Grand Vitesse' column written by Rodney Walkerley. I have found it in my files, and I quote from it for you.

'Story running about Italy that Achille Varzi, who was missing from the Auto Union team in the German Grand Prix, is neither unhappy with the team nor disappointed with the car, but simply in love. A German lady, moreover. Whole thing very complicated. All Italy hopes that the course will run smooth.'

Feuereisen went on to tell me he'd sent Varzi four cables, and had received no reply. He'd had his lawyers look over Varzi's contract, and it was watertight. 'Which means I can't fire the little shit until the end of the year,' he told me, before revealing that Hühnlein had called him that morning. Turned out your old buddy Ciano had attended the race at the 'Ring, and had not been impressed to find no Varzi on the grid for Auto Union.

Out here in South Africa, Johnny, they have a charming saying: Shit flows downhill, and that's exactly what happened next: Ciano spoke to Mussolini, who then called our beloved Führer, who, in turn, called Hühnlein, who had then called Feuereisen and told him precisely what was going to happen at the Coppa Acerbo. First of all, Varzi would race at Pescara. Second of all, Varzi would win. And that's when Feuereisen had asked me exactly how I proposed to make that happen.

I just sat there stunned. It got worse when he began questioning me about the physical I'd conducted on Varzi in Barcelona. The file was sitting there on his desk like a confession, and I distinctly recall starting to sweat while the rain kept pouring outside his window behind his desk. He asked whether I was ready to stand by the diagnosis, and of course I said I was. That's when, and I remember this like it was yesterday, Feuereisen had leaned back into that green leather chair of his, and said, 'I assume that analyzing Varzi's love-life rests outside your purview, ja? But I do wonder though —is love the reason behind Varzi's unprofessional behaviour?'

'Varzi's a wealthy man,' I told him, 'and now he's fallen in love. He's realized how much he has to lose, and how little he has to gain. He's won everything already, so what was left for him?'

Feuereisen had listened attentively, his head nodding as if in agreement. And then he'd said, 'I see where you're headed with this ... Except, of course, that it's a whole lot of bullshit.

Twenty years,' he went on, and I still recall him sitting forward and lighting up another of those foul smelling cigars of his, 'I've worked with drivers in one capacity or another. I realize, since Walb's departure, that it's fashionable for the boys in the garage to say that they replaced the Great Willy with a company man, but I'll tell you this –Varzi is not afraid. I know drivers, and I'm telling you, they're all the same, deep down they're all made of the same stuff. You put them in a racecar, and they're going to drive it as fast as they can. No, Doctor, there's something else at the root of Varzi's behaviour.'

'Such as?' I asked, instantly regretting that I'd just walked into Feuereisen's minefield.

'That is what you're going to find out. I want you to find him, and I want you to give him a complete physical. Convince me that Achille Varzi is suffering from nothing more than love and fear.'

Simple enough, I suppose, except no one seemed to have the vaguest idea of where Varzi was. The last anyone saw of him had been in Milan, on the twenty-eighth of June, when he'd raced a Type C at the Milan GP. He had lost to Nuvolari, and while the car had come back on June thirtieth along with its crew, Varzi had vanished.

I will write of how I came to find Varzi in my next letter, Johnny. Not that it will come as any revelation to you, given what I expect was your role in that farce. Maybe you ought to write back and explain, come to think of it, what precisely you knew in July of that year.

I leave tonight for Windhoek, to attend a seminar on genetics. It seems people here assume that, given my position before the war, I should be well versed in all that eugenics nonsense.

Mit besten Grüßen
Dr. Magneven

~

November 12, 1946,
Swakopmund, South West Africa

Johnny,

I have decided to take a week's vacation here in Swakopmund,
and will take this opportunity to reply to your letter. I've learnt
that there was once a concentration camp here. In fact, they tell
me it was the first of many, as we are now sadly discovering.

Anyway, back to Varzi. And back to Milan, in late July 1936.
You'll be happy to learn that I kept a diary of those days I spent
in Italy looking for Varzi, knowing that Feuereisen would want
a detailed report. I attach here the relevant pages. It begins
with my chat with Brivio at the Tre Marie bar on a hot summer's
morning.

'Please call me Tonino,' Brivio said. 'I'm a direct descendent
of the Sforza family who ruled this little city for two centuries,
but let's not let that spoil our afternoon, eh?' He poured me a
glass of bubbly. 'I take it you're here to find Achille, yes?' He
handed me a napkin with names and addresses written on it,
mutual friends of his and Varzi's and their known hang-outs.
'Of course,' he added, 'I doubt any of them will be in Milan at
this time of the year ...'

I found my handkerchief and wiped the sweat off my
brow. 'You've been very kind, Tonino. Would it be a massive
imposition if I were I to ask you a few questions?'

'Oh no, not at all,' he replied. 'It's like a detective novel, yes?'

I smiled at his open, warm face. 'How would you explain
Varzi's loss of form?'

'Is that what you're calling it?'

'What would you call it?' I asked.

'We Italians don't really go in for euphemisms, Doctor. We

like to call things as they really are – which is probably why our language has more words for "fool" than for virtually anything else. And this leads me quite nicely to the topic of Achille. I met him for dinner a few weeks ago, actually. The moment I saw him I knew he was in one of those dark moods of his, and when the meal came – the steak was undercooked or something, I don't rightly recall – he went savage on me. Literally ran into the kitchen, he did, and by the time I'd got in there after him he had the chef pinned against a wall. I managed to pull him away, but that's Achille, you understand?' Brivio considered what he had just said. 'Not that I want you to get the wrong impression here; he's also capable of the most generous acts, and he can be a real gentleman when he wants to. But sometimes he's capable of believing the most extraordinary nonsense. He gets it from his mother.'

'His mother?'

'Do you know she has a shrine in one of those rooms in that gothic house of theirs? She goes in there whenever Varzi is racing, prays to the Madonna to keep her son safe.'

I let this drift between us for a moment. 'What do you think about what Walkerley wrote the other day – that Varzi is simply in love?'

'What do you think?' he replied.

'I don't buy it,' I confessed. 'I don't see how love can affect a man so negatively.'

'Yes, but you're German. You have a natural fear of passion'. He stared at me for a while. 'You're also not Achille Varzi,' he said eventually. 'Nothing is simple for that man. Some people mistake him for a dandy, don't they, but he's a strong personality, though not always in a positive way. You know his mother used to dress him up like a girl when he was a baby? ... Very finicky is our Achille. Nervous. I remember back in '32, he was at Ferrari then, this was at Pescara, and he'd decided there was something wrong with the seat of his car; kept fidgeting, you know, sitting in the cockpit, getting out, ordering his mechanics to adjust this and that – went on literally for half-an-hour until Ferrari – who'd been monitoring this pantomime – came over and suggested Achille go get a drink while he sorted things out. With Achille out of the way, Ferrari grabbed a copy of someone's 'Gazzetta' and jammed it under the seat. Ten minutes later, Achille gets into the car and expresses himself delighted – moved to tears, he was, literally in tears such was his happiness ... His nerves, Doctor, his nerves.'

'You take a man like Nuvolari, and you know what you'll find in his soul? Desperation. For guys like that, speed is a natural extension of their beings. They crave it; it's almost as if the closeness to death is what gives their life meaning. For Achille, it's the reverse; speed is his way to escape his own self. In that cockpit, he has no time to reflect, no time to analyze. At speed, Achille is content because he can finally outrun himself. By the way, you do know the lady in question, right?'

'Oh yes,' I said, and we shared a knowing smile.

'Yes, well, it's easy enough to understand how a woman like that could gnaw at any man's soul.'

After Count Brivio had rushed off to another meeting (trying to organize a world championship for drivers, he said, for 1940), I was left with nothing much to do that afternoon aside from chasing down the leads that he had given me. By mid-afternoon, I began to understand why private eyes did this kind of legwork in the rain – with the sweat pouring off my face, I stuck my head into the Pidocchio and was informed that no one had seen Varzi for a couple of months. At the Hotel Cinque on the Piazza Fontana, the concierge admitted to keeping a suite for Varzi's private use, but apparently Achille hadn't made use of it since May. He suggested I try the Sport Club on via Maddalena, but they hadn't heard from Varzi in months, and at the Hotel Commerciale, they hadn't seen him since 1935.

'Perhaps you should try his apartment,' suggested the concierge at the Commerciale. 'He doesn't live there anymore as far as I know, but his wife does.'

'His wife?'

'Norma. Norma Colombo.'

'I didn't realize that they were married,' I said.

'A man doesn't need to take vows to be married, does he? I thought you Germans were a little more progressive than that.'

'I'm Catholic,' I told the guy as he scribbled out the address in exchange for a large bill. I went and sat in a café outside her building until I saw her leave, then I pounced. But she wouldn't tell me anything. She was still totally loyal to Varzi, even though he was with another woman.

When I went back to my hotel room, I discovered a message from Ugo Ricordi and he arranged for me to meet Varzi the next day, who, it turned out, was staying at a villa in Rome. I remember the visit well as it was when I had my first inkling that Varzi was up to something – that I was being lied to.

The villa sat a few miles down the Via Appia Antica, half-hidden behind an ancient wall. Its wisteria-lined driveway meandered through a park-like garden, at the end of which glinted a velvet-blue swimming pool. The villa seemed asleep, its windows ajar and its balcony, raised upon fine pillars of marble, devoid of life. The wicker-chairs around the pool were abandoned too, and crisp white towels were carelessly scattered about. Lizards darted up the walls as I approached the door in the deafening silence. I found it open and entered the villa, feeling the coolness immediately settle around me. The entrance hall was a vast expanse of marble from which an elegant staircase rose. On the left side of the hall, a series of doors led further into the villa, and it was through one of these that Vigano appeared, barefoot, wearing black swim-trunks. He led me up the marble stairs, down a hall and into a vast room in which fine white linen curtains stirred in the sunshine. Beautiful, ornate furniture was scattered about with no particular care or scheme, and I counted five men sitting about in various stages of undress and sleep, the distance between them allowing for no intimacy. There was a smell there, in that room, perfume mixed with tobacco and something acrid – joss sticks, I soon realized.

Achille Varzi lazed on a velvet chaise longue, wearing a white silk dressing gown, purple swimming shoes, and a derisive smile. 'How was your trip?' he asked.

'Long,' I confessed, staring into those eyes of his. He lit a cigarette and blew smoke into my face. His hands were steady, the fingers stained yellow by nicotine. He looked healthy, strong even, and his voice was perfectly calm as he inquired: 'To what do I owe this honour, Dr. Magneven?'

'Dr. Feuereisen has been desperate to contact you.'

'I was unwell – surely my cable was specific on this matter?'
'Your cable?'

Varzi frowned. 'Yes, my cable.' When he saw the puzzled look on my face, he shouted, 'Viganò!'

Viganò hurried over.

'Do you remember that cable I had you send Dr. Feuereisen?' Varzi asked him.

Viganò blinked.

'What?' asked Varzi.

'Oh Christ,' mumbled Viganò sheepishly.

'Don't tell me ...' said Varzi.

'Christ, I'm sorry, in between getting this place sorted and, with Ilse, I – O Dio, I completely forgot, Achille, I'm sorry!'

Varzi glared at him dismissively. Then, turning to me with a tender smile, he said, 'Dr. Magneven, how embarrassing for you. I can only imagine Dr. Feuereisen's annoyance.'

I swallowed my reply and gave myself a moment to compose my thoughts. 'You say you were unwell?'

Varzi tipped ash onto the tiled floor. 'Yes. Quite.'

'You look healthy.'

'I am. It was a minor complaint.'

'Did you consult your personal physician?'

'No. It wasn't necessary.'

A sudden gust of wind parted the curtains in the room, revealing a veranda facing the rear of the villa. I caught a glimpse of a naked woman tanning on a deck chair. Unsettled, I glanced back at Varzi.

'I assume everything's all cleared up then?' he asked, studying my eyes.

'There is just one more thing,' I replied. The curtains spread open again, and I valiantly tried not to look in the woman's direction, much to Varzi's amusement. 'Since I'm here, would it be an imposition if I – that is, would you consent to a physical examination?'

'Now?'

'If it isn't too much to ask.'

'Of course, Doctor. Come, there's an office over there that will afford us some privacy.'

The exam was over in an hour and showed up no organic issues. Johnny, I have thought about that hour with Varzi many times since I received your letter, wondering whether I missed something, anything, that afternoon, and I can honestly tell you that my conscience is clean on this front. Of course, I phoned Feuereissen to update him that Varzi had been found and he asked for a full report.

That official report would come back to haunt me, of course, because Varzi had indeed played me. Hadn't he, Johnny? But at least he turned up for Pescara in August, as promised. Such was the heat that year, that Feuereisen even burnt his hand on a stopwatch that had been left out in the sun, and out on the track, the tarmac was melting into chunks.

Looking tanned if a bit scrawny, Varzi had turned up on his own for the weekend, explaining that Ilse had chosen to remain in Rome. He was in good spirits though, and much to my relief he was on form too: in qualifying, he became the first man in history to break the sacred ten minute mark, an astonishing twenty-six seconds faster than Rosemeyer. He asked for a water bottle to be stashed under his seat before the race, with a rubber pipe leading directly to his lips – an invention that was soon copied up and down the pitlane.

I sat beneath an awning down past the makeshift pits to watch the race. The Fascist big-boys were out in force up in the packed grandstands, and I recall your friend Ciano sitting with his wife Edda; how Mussolini, with that Olympian head of his, could ever have produced anything so resplendent as Edda, Johnny, remains a mystery to a man of science like me. The thermostat that the Continental boys always stuck onto pit-road to judge the track temperature was up to 50C that afternoon, and I could feel the heat rise through the soles of my shoes. Nuvolari's engine was also cooked by lap three, allowing Varzi to seize the lead. He immediately broke the lap record twice, clocking the fastest-ever speed recorded in a road-race – 295kph. Five laps later though, he peeled into the box complaining of brake-wear issues. Feuereisen ordered the mechanics to alter the brake bias, leaning it to the fore, and while this solution enabled him to continue, the balance chewed through his tyres, and it was an exhausted Varzi who finally finished the race in a distant third, Bernd Rosemeyer notching up yet another win.

It had taken two mechanics to lift a shivering and semi-delirious Varzi from the cockpit. But this was typical of race drivers: natural endorphins had cloaked the physical damage his body had endured. I examined Varzi in the garage but found little wrong with him aside from dehydration, a condition which had also affected Rosemeyer, half a decade younger.

But you were right when you mentioned to me that Varzi's indifference to losing due to mechanical problems seemed out of character. What did you suspect?

I have another week here in this lovely spot and nothing much to do but drink Windhoek Lager and watch the fishing boats out in that ocean of blue.

Mit besten Grüßen
Dr Magneven

~

November 18, 1946,
Swakopmund, South West Africa

Dear Johnny,

It has been a week that I have been trying to get back to writing to you. Since last I wrote, I have met a rather sweet young girl from, of all places, Wiesbaden, and have enjoyed a delightful few days in her company. She flew home yesterday, and I promised I would look her up should I ever get back to Europe. But I should push on, now, and finish what I began – I've left you hanging long enough! It's time to write about where it all ended. Berne. How far away it seems to me now.

The circuit at Berne was a mighty thing, though, wasn't it? The track twisted around the splendid Bremgarten Park like a diamond cut within a primeval forest, tunnels composed of ancient trees and lost meadows winking in the sun. From Forsthaus corner, the track began to wind its way back to the permanent pit facility behind the goods yard on a road that was constructed of timeworn cobbles. Watching the grand prix cars power over those streets is a sight not easily forgotten – here, tonight, the memory can reduce a man to tears. From the pits one could see the banked turn where the drivers were sucked in by an invisible magnet, before being spit out at all sorts of wild drift angles. They were going in flat and bouncing out at over 250kph, and one single error going through the bend would've resulted in them being blasted into the trees. Bremgarten was a frightening place where you could really feel the speed and commitment of those men.

We had spotted Varzi on the Thursday night having dinner at the hotel with Ilse, but as Friday morning slowly drifted into the afternoon session, there was no sign of him, despite Feuereisen's repeated calls to the hotel. It was a haggard looking Varzi who eventually sauntered into the pits at just past 3pm. His flesh was pasty, his white race-overalls were un-ironed and stained with oil. A shadow of bristles covered his sinewy face, scruffy hair falling over dark and menacing eyes despite his smile.

'Sorry, had a late night,' was his explanation when he walked past Feuereisen. I watched Varzi walk over to the number eight Auto Union and slide into the cockpit. He dropped his hands onto his lap, allowing Rudolf to screw in the steering wheel before clipping the ignition switch. After a moment's hesitation, his arm came up, one finger in the muggy air circling like a vulture for the mechanics to fire up his engine. That's when Feuereisen came striding up to the car. 'Varzi, you've forgotten your goggles!' he shouted.

Varzi shrugged. He lifted his arm yet again. A test of wills, I thought. Feuereisen was about to speak when Elly came rushing down from the garage to squat beside the Auto Union. She handed Varzi a pair of goggles.

'Bernd's,' she said. 'Same make as yours, Signor Varzi.'

Varzi looked at her; if he felt any gratitude, he hid it well. He grabbed the goggles and wrapped them around his neck before staring down the pitlane. Feuereisen's mouth was set in a thin line when he nodded at the mechanic squatting by the starter battery, his hands covering his ears. The V16 exploded into life in a cloud of smoke. Varzi engaged first gear, dropped the clutch and accelerated away, almost stalling before a boot-full of raw power drilled the Auto Union onto the track in a perfectly executed powerslide.

Feuereisen just stood there for a while, listening to the sound of the engine rise and fall through the trees. Then, as if making up his mind, he stormed toward me and grabbed my elbow. 'Come,' he said, dragging me along, 'I've had it with this shit.'

I followed him through the garage out to the paddock and into his white Horch. He drove us into central Berne, picking his way through traffic on the Amthausgasse with a determined and deft touch before he pulled up outside the Bellevue Hotel on the Kochergasse. He hadn't said a word since we'd left the track, and I thought it best just to keep quiet. He strode into the lobby and up to the main desk with me firmly in tow. I had the misfortune of having seen Feuereisen in this mood before, and the concierge's attempt at putting up a fight was short-lived. Defeated, the clerk handed over the key to Varzi's room.

'Signora Varzi's still in there,' he cautioned, apparently mystified by his own weakness.

Feuereisen punched the floor-button in the elevator and we rode up in silence. When we arrived in front of Varzi's room, Feuereisen stuck the key into the lock and banged one fleshy palm on the wood. His knock was merely a formality, because he was already turning the key and flinging the door open like a cop on a bust. I stumbled in behind him, flushing with embarassment.

Ilse was standing by a vanity, and in the mirror's reflection we could see her staring at us with a mixture of confusion, alarm and anger. She was such a beautiful creature, Johnny. Do you remember her as I do?

'We need to talk,' said Feuereisen, impressing me with his conviction. I was perhaps too young and impressionable to have much going through my mind other than an overwhelming desire not to unduly upset Ilse. She must have sensed this because she glanced my way as Feuereisen stormed past her to the windows where, with one fist, he ripped open the curtains and exposed us all to the bright afternoon light.

Ilse sat down calmly on a red velvet Ottoman and crossed her legs. I looked away as she pulled her silk dressing gown tightly shut, and it was at that moment that I noticed it: a mini electric pan on the floor beside the bed, plugged into the wall and filled with bubbling water. When I looked back at Ilse, her eyes betrayed something akin to fear.

That's when Feuereisen let her have it. 'Tell me what's going on with him,' he demanded. 'Ilse, look at me. Look at me. I understand your desire to protect your man. But your man is a racing driver and right now he's not capable of defending himself. You may think you're protecting him, but let me tell you something my dear – you're exposing him to danger. This isn't a game, this isn't about his job, do you understand what I'm saying to you? This is about his life – this is about him staying alive. How would you feel if something happened, Ilse, how would you feel then?'

'I know the risks,' she whispered.

'You don't have a fucking clue,' Feuereisen said. 'Varzi's going to come back to you in a pine-box, my lovely – do you understand this? Do you?'

She closed her eyes, and I felt for her then, Johnny. She was so fragile, wasn't she? So fragile, and swimming in a tank full of sharks. She told us it had all started in Tripoli, and she'd been in Milan that night when he had called her after coming home from the Balbo affair, distraught and angry. Her immediate thought was that he'd hurt himself because he just kept saying, 'They want to take it from me'. A week later, she told us, he'd had that awful crash at Carthage and he came back – I'll never forget this, Johnny, the way she said this, 'he came back to me a changed man.'

Feuereisen, perhaps realizing how threatening he appeared, sat down on the bed and leaned forward to hold her hands.

Achille's not what people think he is, she told us: 'You all think of him as some sort of machine, but he's not – he's the most human man I've ever known.'

While she was charming Feuereissen, I went into the bathroom to hunt for the obvious explanation. I locked the door behind me and methodically searched the cabinets, the weekend bag on the floor, the mirror-shelf. Nothing. I blew my nose loudly, to give myself some cover, and tossed the tissue into the waste-paper basket, and just as I was about to unlock the door, my mind processed what my eyes had seen. I squatted there by the waste-paper basket and lifted my tissue. And there, in the belly of the frosted-metal basket, lay a small phial of glass, as spent as a bullet casing and just as deadly.

I stepped back into Ilse's room to witness a touching scene. Ilse was sobbing quietly into her hands, with that ogre Feuereissen on his knees next to her. Relieved to see me, he ruffled her hair gently and stood up. She hid her face from us and, do you know, Johnny, I don't even remember if I even said goodbye as I followed Feuereisen out into the twilight.

Feuereisen traced his way back toward the circuit in silence. I still remember – this memory is so vivid – I remember staring out at those imperial buildings drifting past, solid and immutable, and feeling the phial between my fingers, and thinking how easy it would be just to toss it out of the window. It would have just disintegrated, just ... bits of shard glass forgotten in the dark that parachuted about us. Instead I found myself running my mind over Ilse's body. It was not an altogether challenging exercise, as you can imagine; the swell of her breasts, her thighs spread open, and then it came to me.

'Tracks,' I murmured distractedly.

'We're almost there,' Feuereisen said, misunderstanding me.. 'Varzi's afraid, that's all there is to it. I don't blame him either – with a girl like that...'

It was then that I lifted the phial out of my pocket and placed it onto my palm.

'What's that?' he asked.

'A phial.'

'Ja, I can fucking see that,' he said in that annoyed tone of his. He parked his car haphazardly, seized the phial from my hand and examined it as if it were a bug. He squinted, struggling to decipher the fine print. And then it hit him.

'Morphine?'

Monoject ampule, Johnny. Standard issue for the Italian armed forces in Abyssinia.

It didn't take Feuereisen long to connect the dots. 'You got this from his room?' he asked and I felt nothing but a deep sense of shame. 'The boiling water,' he continued, and I explained it was to sterilize a syringe.

Feuereisen lit up his half-chewed cigar, and I listened to the poison crackle about us. We sat in silence watching the night stretch about us sleepily. Eventually Feuereisen asked if this squared with Varzi's recent behaviour. What could I say? Of course it explained his mood changes, his demeanour – all of it was explained by that little phial there in Feuereisen's hands. But none of it could explain why a man addicted to adrenaline should choose to dull himself with morphine.

Did I feel shame, Johnny? I don't have an honest answer for you, not even now, ten years later. I can tell you I spent an uneasy night with only my guilt and a bottle of whisky for company; and as I watched the sun rise, I tried to mentally prepare myself for the day ahead.

When I arrived at the track, Rosemeyer was being interviewed by a sea of reporters, and the brooding, almost ferocious look on his face made me instantly suspect that he had been appraised of the Varzi situation. As I was thinking that, he unleashed a scathing remark aimed at Elly, when she was asked – and had begun to give her opinion – on who was the fastest driver in the world.

'Elly, it's best if you just shut up and don't talk about things that are beyond you.'

Elly had smiled in response. She was used to the press. But if damage-control was what she was after, Bernd wasn't playing along; he stalked off instead, leaving poor Elly to apologize as the cameras snapped away at her shame.

Feuereisen, meanwhile, was so busy with race day prep' that he had no time to spare for me. I sat around the garage waiting for Varzi's arrival, playing it all out in my mind. Would Feuereisen fire him publicly?

The Varzi who appeared that morning was radiating joviality. He spent a few minutes talking things over with Rudolf before sauntering over to the Ferrari box, where he embraced Nuvolari and exchanged pleasantries with Dreyfus – a man for whom he usually had little time.

I breathed easier when he walked straight past me, contenting himself with a dour nod in my general direction. We were in stasis, I thought, each waiting for the other to fire the first shot. But as morning drifted into afternoon, it began to dawn on me that Feuereisen had no intention of confronting Varzi. This filled me with an overwhelming sense of relief, and as Varzi went ahead with his usual race preparations, my attention fell on Elly, who appeared far too occupied with her lapcharts to disguise her discomfort.

It had become something of a ritual for Elly and Bernd to banter with each other before the start of every race. That day, however, Bernd was nowhere to be found, and I could feel both Elly and the team's growing anxiety. Meanwhile, my anxiety was being fed by the spectre of Varzi – was he actually unstable enough to inject himself with morphine before the race?

Five minutes before the start, Bernd and Varzi appeared together fully suited-up, both men striding to their cars on the grid in their crisp white overalls and shiny leather shoes. With one foot in the cockpit, Bernd had suddenly hesitated before sprinting all the way back to Elly. He embraced her to the cheers of the crowd. She seemed relieved by this gesture, but whatever worm was infecting Bernd's mind had returned the moment the flag dropped. Caracciola seized the lead immediately with what looked like a false start to everyone but the chief steward. It was soon obvious that his Mercedes had no business leading the race, but this did not deter him in the slightest. Caracciola fought off a horde of Auto Unions: Rosemeyer, Varzi, Stuck, and von Delius (a young man from Plessa with whom Rosemeyer had developed a friendship), blocking them even after the chief steward had gone onto the track to wave the blue flag at him. If Rudi saw the order to let Rosemeyer by, he certainly did his best to ignore it: for another six laps, he blocked and frustrated Rosemeyer, who had dented the nose of his Auto Union by ramming it into the Mercedes. These two were out for blood, that much was certain.

225

Hühnlein had then made his way down from the grandstand, speaking first with Neubauer before striding over to Feuereisen. The two had a chat until Hühnlein, apparently satisfied, went off in search of the chief steward. With horse-whip in hand, he barked his orders and the poor man, visibly cowed, grabbed hold of the black flag and hastily attached Caracciola's number to it. He leaned over the pitwall and was about to throw the DQ flag when Rosemeyer raced past us in the lead. A minute later, Caracciola rolled into the pit with a snapped rear-axle. He shared a terse conversation with Neubauer before limping away, leaving the circuit with Baby Hoffman. He looked old that day, Johnny. He looked every one of his thirty-five years.

I must confess to an inability to place what happened next in any sort of context. Rosemeyer won, Varzi came in a splendid second, Stuck completed the podium for Auto Union; Rosemeyer threw his laurel away in disgust, his bloodied fists aching to smash something up; Neubauer announced that Mercedes were withdrawing from racing for the rest of the '36 season; and I hitched a ride back to the hotel with von Delius. And amidst all of that, Achille Varzi was lying in the sun with his Ilse, both sound asleep in a meadow of their artificial dreams.

As I rode the elevator on my way down to dinner that night, I made peace with myself. Yes, I still felt as if I had betrayed Varzi, but what if he had raced in a morphine-induced stupor and ended up killing himself? Or someone else? I had done the right thing by revealing his secret: I had done the right thing for Varzi, and the right thing for my employers. And anticipating your question, Johnny, yes, I still feel as if I acted appropriately. That's not the same, though, as absolving myself of the shame. But with hindsight, I also feel a certain amount of anger for those who knew. It should never have come to that, it should never have come to me discovering his secret.

Anyway, so there I was in the elevator when the doors slid open on the third floor and Bernd and Elly climbed in. One look at Elly and I knew that Bernd's mood had not altered much. She smiled bravely and inquired whether I'd take a look at his blistered hands after dinner. I was about to reply when the elevator dinged again, on the second floor, and I watched in silent horror as Rudi Caracciola and Baby Hoffman climbed in.

The air was sucked from the elevator. Caracciola met Bernd's eyes and promptly turned his back to him. And that was enough for Bernd.

'Your scarf is beautiful, Babylein,' he said, his voice impossibly loud in that little box. 'Blue suits you, what do you think, Rudi? Oh, wait, you don't recognize the colour blue, do you?'

Caracciola stared ahead at his reflection in the elevator doors. 'In my day, Bernd, a man fought his own battles— he didn't need the officials to help him win.'

'In your day? I didn't know they even had cars in your day.' Not content to leave it at that, Bernd added: 'They showed you the blue flag because you're slow, Rudi. Slow.'

'So why were you behind me, Bernd? As you are now; is there something about my ass that attracts you?'

Bernd clenched his fists in anger. Elly pinched his arm, trying to restrain him. The doors to the elevator peeled open invitingly right then, the lobby spread out mercifully before us like the Promised Land. Caracciola allowed Baby Hoffman to exit first, motioning for Elly to do the same. And then, with one step, he blocked Bernd with his big barrel chest. 'You need to learn some fucking respect,' he said.

'And you need to get the fuck out of my way.'

Bernd rammed his shoulder into Caracciola as he exited the elevator. Didn't help him much because Rudi was built like a brick shithouse, wasn't he, and poor Bernd bounced right off him. I watched him grab hold of Elly's hand and lead her into the dining room.

I'll never forget what Caracciola said to me then. 'You'll be scraping that boy off the tarmac one day.'

You know, Johnny, when I was withdrawing from the Don along with your Alpini in '43, we were all infested with lice –

these fat things swollen with our blood that we would take by
the fistful and throw into a fire just to watch them blister and
explode. We never needed to check when a man died: the lice
running from a body like blood was all the confirmation we
needed. I say this because that's pretty much what happened to
Varzi after Berne.

I don't think Feuereisen spoke of Varzi's morphine addiction,
and I certainly never revealed it. But still, the team gravitated
away from him after Berne, and when we got to Monza for the
last race of the season, we came as if attending a wake. I had
spent the week back in Zwickau waiting for Feuereisen to make
his move. Every time I saw him I was on the verge of asking
him what would become of Varzi, but my words always failed
me in the end. And then we arrived in Monza, and I felt deeply
unsettled by the lack of resolution concerning Varzi, made
worse when I actually spotted the man during Friday practice.
His demons were feasting fervently on his soul, Johnny. He
arrived without Ilse, but he looked sick: his eyes were glazed,
and his face had a yellowish tinge to it. I had seen that look
many times before, in other men. I thought then that Berne had
been a release of sorts for him. He must have known that we
knew, and since he no longer needed to hide his illness, he had
given free rein to his addiction.

After his first session out, he came back to the pits smoking
a cigarette, and listened with indifference as Feuereisen
explained that he was four seconds off Rosemeyer's pace. He
shrugged, nodded, smoked. Feuereisen and I exchanged a
glance and what I hoped was a shared concern: Were we really
about to knowingly allow a morphine addict to take part in a
grand prix, allow him to race wheel-to-wheel with other men at
300kph? Adrenaline, that lucid hormone, was a racing driver's
closest ally – it was also morphine's first victim. I couldn't
believe that Feuereisen would let Varzi out onto the track in
that condition – the man was clearly doped up. I kept thinking,
When will Feuereisen get him out of the damned car?

On the eve of the race, I finally worked up the courage to corner Feuereisen in the hotel restaurant. Our whispered conversation was as short as it was savagely instructive. I told him he couldn't surely be contemplating allowing Varzi to race.

'It's the last race of the season,' he told me. 'After that, he's no longer our concern.' Seeing my alarmed expression, he asked,

'So what would you have me do, Doctor?'

'End it, before he kills himself or somebody else.'

'If we break his contract, he'll be the one wronged. It could make it worse.'

The race, mercifully, was nothing more than a formality, marred only by Hans Stuck's epic smash on – what else? Lap thirteen. Ironic, given he'd been whining all week to the German press about the chicanes.

Anyway, the next morning, I received a phone call from Feuereisen, who ordered me down to the lobby. I found him sitting behind a colonnade along with Achille Varzi, whose face was eclipsed by those dark sunglasses he had worn on the Junkers all those months before. Feuereisen nodded toward the empty chair opposite him and I took a seat, trying to ignore the violent pounding in my head.

I will try and capture the scene for you, Johnny, exactly as it happened, given that you were so insistent in your letter that I reveal the precise way in which Achille Varzi lost his ride with Auto Union. And, I suppose, looking back on it, we can say he lost his career that morning too, didn't he, in the lovely surrounds of the Savoia.

I stared at Varzi and couldn't help but wonder what had possessed him – what kind of madness coursed through those cold veins of his? No doubt the same madness that would see him idolized by millions, while I, Johnny, am destined to fade away as just another footnote in a great man's life.

'We have had two exceptional seasons together,' Feuereisen told him. 'When you first joined us, Signor Varzi, our car was as new as our problems. You brought your skill, your experience, and your incomparable acumen to bear on our youth, and the result has been witnessed this year – a season in which we not only dominated, but humiliated those shits from Mercedes. I realize that Rosemeyer has bested you throughout the year; however, unlike some of my colleagues, I don't entirely ascribe his victories to his innate talent. As an engineer, I understand all too well that Bernd only wins when he has a car capable of winning. Your contribution to creating a winning car, and a winning mentality at Auto Union, will never be understated, not by me.'

Varzi lit up a cigarette and vanished behind a halo of smoke. When he rematerialized, his face was still devoid of any expression.

'It is therefore with a great deal of esteem, respect and gratitude that I must inform you that the board of directors in Zwickau has come to the decision that we are unable to offer an extension to your contract for next season.' In the deep silence that followed, I had to remind myself to breathe.

Varzi had leaned forward to crush his cigarette in the ashtray. 'You realize,' he said, his voice as calm as the syrupy sunshine that fell about us, 'that Rosemeyer won't last. He will fail you eventually, and where will you be then? Are you pinning all your hopes on von Delius? Stuck?'

'Mi dispiace, Herr Varzi. You need to appreciate that this isn't my decision. We are a German race team, and we race at the pleasure of the Party. Having an Italian in our team is not ...' he trailed off, trying to find the right words. 'We have Bernd Rosemeyer, that's all there is to it.'

Varzi took off his sunglasses, revealing those eyes of his. Dark they were, Johnny. Dark and bloodshot. He stood up slowly and gazed down at Feuereisen. 'It would have been better for all of us if you had chosen to be honest. We all know,' he said, looking down at me, 'what this is really about. Don't we.'

Feuereisen had stood up then and offered Varzi his hand. Varzi considered it as one does a fresh, ripe piece of excrement.

And then he was off, striding across the lobby and out into the piercing sunshine.

Feuereisen had sat back down dejectedly and asked what I thought would happen to Varzi. I had wondered about this myself, and I chose to share my guilt with him. Without a top level drive for next season, he'll sink, I said. He's already an addict.

Feuereisen had let out a deep sigh and asked the inevitable question. Why? Why the drugs? Why morphine? Why did he choose to throw away his career, his life? Why?

'Because,' I replied, 'he needs to escape. From himself.'

And there you have it, Johnny. Varzi's life, of course, just spiralled out of control after that, from what I heard, but I suspect you know more about that anyone else. Perhaps one day you'll tell me about it. And that reminds me! You won't believe who I met here at the hotel yesterday. None other than Giulio Ramponi. He sends his best wishes, and tells me he has a lovely house in South Africa, up north near the Crocodile River. I have promised to spend my Christmas break with him there. You ought to come, too. We could talk about Varzi and the old days. Yes, I think I would welcome that very much.

Until then,
Viele Grüße
Dr Magneven

~

It's past midnight. Outside the window, a fine mist is masking the silent streets. The letters end here. I browse back through the pages, marvelling at how Dr. Magneven's words have survived against all odds. His name triggers a faint memory, and I pull out my folder containing all the articles from that period. I spread the clippings out on the table, examining the red-ink dates scribbled in the margins. Where have I seen this Dr. Magneven before?

"SUPERB WIN BY NUVOLARI IN THE VANDERBILT CUP CLOSES THE 1936 MOTOR-RACING SEASON
Motor Italia, October 11, Anno XIV
Nuvolari's triumph has closed the racing season in an honorable way for us. Nuvolari has again demonstrated that, despite his age, he remains in the prime of his career. Those across the Atlantic did not doubt this for an instant, which is more than can be said for many of his domestic critics. The Vanderbilt Cup was a superb affirmation of European engineering, with Nuvolari winning by 12 clear minutes over his American rivals. Well done to Nuvolari, and well done, too, to Alfa Romeo. Technically the car was perfect, and it gave great honour to its creator, Vittorio Jano. This car is lighter than the Auto Union, enjoys a superior road holding than the Mercedes, and is also more manageable and secure than the car designed by Dr. Porsche that so dominated this past season.

Earlier this year, we mistakenly believed that raw power was not necessary for success—but at the end of this season, we have now learnt that creating harmonious cars will not be enough to see Italy triumph in the years to come. Indeed, power is crucial now."

"LUX MEA DUX
Johnny Finestrini, October 18, Anno XIV
It was in 1906 that they held the last international Vanderbilt Cup Race: The track then ran from Brookville to Jericho in Long Island, and then on to Lakeville and back again. This year the track was brand new, and measured precisely 6,437 metres with 14 interesting and quick turns.

Nuvolari decided to hole up, as they say here, at a hotel in Garden City and one night, two men of distinct Italian origin turned up uninvited, attaching themselves to our entourage and, in particular, to

Nuvolari's shadow. Who they were, no one quite seemed to know, but they acted as Nuvolari's de facto bodyguards until he left for Manhattan, the day after conquering the Vanderbilt Cup. On that Monday, Nuvolari received a cheque worth $32,000 from the mayor of New York. I was standing just under the podium, amid a crowd of at least 50,000 Italian-Americans, when I overheard Leon Duray, the famous Indy driver, say: 'He didn't even check the envelope to see if the money was in there!'

The 'Human Arrow' (as Tazio was dubbed here) then vanished for an entire afternoon. We from the press had been expecting him to appear at a dozen or so promotional and well-paid events that day, including a nationally syndicated radio show, but Nuvolari was nowhere to be found.

It was subsequently revealed to me that Tazio had decided to honour a strange request made to him via letter, which he had received some weeks prior to his trip. It transpired that an Italian immigrant had built a small dirt track in the state of New Jersey that was losing money hand-over-fist, and he had hoped that the great Tazio Nuvolari would help put his little track on the racing map. With the $32,000 envelope still in his pocket, Tazio Nuvolari had taken a cab from Manhattan all the way to New Jersey. Once he arrived there he had gone dirt track racing with 10 other Americans, who had no idea they were competing against one of the greatest racing drivers of all time. And yes, he won that race, too."

"GRAND VITESSE COLUMN
Rodney Walkerley, November 12, 1936
Varzi the taciturn has gone hunting and shooting. When asked whether he was leaving Auto Union next year, he smiled and said nothing."

"GRAND VITESSE COLUMN
Rodney Walkerley, December 12, 1936
Varzi the inscrutable is many miles away from his
native land. Speculation mentions two possible
reasons—a love affair, or merely winter sports."

"THE ECSTASY & THE AGONY
Der Stürmer, February 23, 1937
Bernd Rosemeyer and his wife Elly moved into
their new apartment in Berlin this week, after their
return from a triumphant tour of Africa on behalf
of the Reich. Elly had flown with Bernd from Berlin
to South Africa, where the European Champion
competed in three races on the dark continent. The
couple travelled to South-West Africa on their way
back to the homeland; it was there, amidst fellow
Germans at a banquet in Windhoek, that Rosemeyer
was given the news of his beloved mother's death.
Further sad tidings awaited our champion upon
his return to Berlin, when it was announced that
his brother, Job, had been killed in a bizarre traffic
accident."

I keep rummaging through the clippings, just about to give up
when I spot a photograph dated May 19, 1936. There he is, Dr.
Magneven: a slender man in a dark suit standing next to Achille
Varzi on the stairs leading up to a silver Junkers.

I stare at this image for a long time, wondering what had
become of the doctor in the gold-rimmed spectacles.

PART SIX
STAINS FROM A WASTED WORLD

The proud motto of the squadristi, me ne frego , written on bandages covering wounds, is an act not only of stoic philosophy, the result of a doctrine not only political; it is the education of war, the acceptance of the risks that war brings; it is the new style of Italian life.

— The Doctrine of Fascism, Benito Mussolini
and Giovanni Gentile, 1933

'BURN THE GONDOLAS, THE ROCKING CHAIR OF IDIOTS'

L'Isola Del Lido, February 16, 1968

My packed bag sits beside the door to the hotel room. It is just past 7am and my train is scheduled to leave Santa Lucia in three hours. There has been no word from Finestrini. Has he decided to abandon me? Does he suspect why I have come? I grab the receiver and dial. It rings. And keeps ringing long after my anxiety has crawled up my spine. I slam down the receiver and sit on the bed. The manuscript lies there beside me, and I flip through the pages and begin to read, stilling my anxiety.

"It was March 1937 and Varzi's winter season had begun with a spot of skiing in Chamonix, a spot of hunting in Scotland, society balls in London, gambling in Monaco and all-night parties in Berlin. It ends at the Hotel Savoia in Milan, where he secures a three-room suite.

He spends his days and his nights there with Ilse, feeling neither pain nor hunger, suspended in the stillness of his drug-induced calm. He reads the sports pages with a scornful detachment, laughing at the rumours that he has signed with Ferrari for the upcoming season.

At thirty-three years of age, Varzi is effectively retired. Ferrari won't hire him, Auto Union is no longer an option, and Mercedes belongs entirely to Caracciola. It doesn't matter, he tells Ilse, when she stares at him with her bleached eyes, doesn't matter because he has never been able to enjoy his youth until now. He had dedicated a whole decade of his life to racing, and had been Italian Champion at twenty-two. But he had never felt twenty-two.

Varzi hears a knock on the bedroom door.

'Finestrini's on the phone,' announces Viganò.

'Tell him to fuck off,' says Varzi, groggily throwing on a pale cotton shirt. Viganò is saying something else, and he strains to hear the words from beyond the shut door.

'He says it's a personal matter. He asks if you've read today's 'paper.'

Varzi has no idea what day it is. 'Do you have it?'

'No. Should I – ?'

'No, it's fine.' There is an extension there by the bed. Varzi lifts the receiver to his ear. 'What do you want, Finestrini.'

'Varzi, how are you?'

'I'm no longer in the game – and no longer speaking to the press.'

'Yes,' says Finestrini, 'and the press is no longer speaking to you. I have some bad news. About Tazio.'

'He's finally killed himself, has he?'

'His father passed away yesterday morning. Tazio asked me to extend an invitation to attend the memorial service. It's scheduled for the morning of April 1st in Gardone.'

Varzi hangs up the phone without replying.

*

Varzi is alone on the open road, Ilse having felt too ill to travel. He hardly recognizes the man with the odious grin staring back at him in the rear-view mirror: his face is cadaverous, his flesh a sickly shade of yellow, and his eyes have been reduced to pin-pricks. He looks like a lemon, he thinks. As he steps on the gas pedal, he feels his leg muscles tremble. He had left Milan much later than he had intended, and he has already missed the service.

SANDRO MARTINI

He heads directly to Nuvolari's villa instead, his Packard lost and anonymous amid the glittering coupés parked in Tazio's driveway. He pushes a greasy strand of hair off his creased forehead. He can smell himself, smell the sweat beneath his tailored black suit that no longer fits.

The door to the enchanting villa stands ajar, and he is soaking wet when he finally gets to it, dabbing at his face with a handkerchief that smells of Ilse. Carolina stands beyond the threshold along with Nuvolari's uncle, Giuseppe. She senses Varzi's presence and turns to greet him, trying to hide the consternation in her eyes. 'Achille,' she says, forcing a smile, 'it's so kind of you to come.' She pecks him on the cheek. Varzi holds her close for a moment too long. 'He's in there,' she says, gently pulling away from his embrace.

Nuvolari strides down the hall in his black suit, heading straight for him. 'Varzi,' he says. 'Finestrini told you, did he? He's around here somewhere.' Tazio squeezes his shoulder with a grave expression, as if Varzi were the one in need of consolation. Louis Chiron, Rudi Caracciola, and Baby Hoffman stand in one corner of the room, engaging in a tense conversation. Nuvolari steers Varzi in their direction.

'This isn't the time for it,' Baby is saying.

'What, you're suddenly concerned with etiquette?' Chiron's laugh is caustic. 'Seriously? You? And *this* prick?'

'I didn't steal her from her husband, unlike you – '

'Don't talk about me as if I'm not here, you're both – ' Baby interrupts herself as she catches sight of Varzi. 'Achille?'

Chiron swings around, spilling liquour from his tumbler. 'Christ,' he says. 'Talk about fucking ghosts. Did Tazio's old man bequeath you his stash of morphine?'

'Louis, that's enough.' Baby pushes past him. 'Do you need some water, Achille?'

Varzi just stands there.

'What he needs is a fix,' Chiron says, slapping Varzi on the back. Varzi stumbles.

'*Louis,*' whispers Baby, her eyes wide with shock.

'What? Everyone knows he's a fucking addict,' mumbles Chiron.

238

Varzi feels a soft hand feather his shoulder. He turns to find Finestrini standing behind him, pale as a ghoul and just as chilling.

'Could we talk for a moment?'

Varzi nods, welcoming the excuse to escape from Baby's unbearable sympathy and Chiron's hostility. Finestrini leads him to the opposite end of the room and pulls out a sealed envelope from his jacket. 'I'm sorry about the timing, but getting anything past Viganò nowadays is proving to be impossible.' Varzi slides the envelope into his pocket. 'So how are you keeping, Achille?'

'Keeping up,' replies Varzi, the sweat now pouring down his face. He walks away – does someone call out to him? – and heads up the stairs, locking himself in the bathroom. He notices Nuvolari's hairnet on the cabinet and smiles. He splashes cold water on his face, feeling a deep sense of relief. His syringe is in the same pocket as the envelope – one quick jab through the fabric of his trousers is all it takes. Bernd Rosemeyer stands at the base of the staircase speaking with Nuvolari and his boy Giorgio in fluent Italian. Varzi sucks in his breath and aims his chin down the stairs and out into the sun. It was pity he thinks, ambling into the Savoia like a fog to find his Ilse beneath cotton sheets with her marshy eyes staring up at him, pity, those looks he left behind in Gardone.

Ilse tries to focus on his face as he bends down to kiss her. 'I missed you,' she says. 'Where have you been?'

'The funeral,' Varzi replies, taking off his suit.

'What funeral?'

'You don't remember?'

Her eyes look dead. 'Come here to me,' she says listlessly.

*

The hotel suite's violent stench makes Varzi gag, sending him to the toilet to cough up bile. When had he last eaten? It must have been a day or two ago, not since the wake – and when had that been? He suddenly remembers his encounter with Finestrini. He wipes the bile from his lips on a soft white towel, finds the jacket he had worn that day, and rummages through the pockets. It's gone. '*Viganò!*' He marches into the living room, where Viganò is idly paging through the *Gazzetta*. 'The envelope in my jacket. What have you done with it?'

'What envelope?'

Varzi snatches the newspaper from Viganò's hand and waves it around menacingly. 'Don't play games with me, you halfwit. Where did you put it?'

'What are you – oh wait, you mean that?' He points to Varzi's work-desk, on top of which lies an envelope. 'You put it there when you – '

Varzi ignores him, grabbing the envelope and ripping it open. In the bloated light of the afternoon, he reads Finestrini's words.

"You must have no illusions, dear Achille. The path you've chosen has no end unless you can turn back now. Do you seriously believe that any firm or racing team will engage you again as a driver as long as they know the sort of life you are leading? I beg you as a friend: forget everything – and I mean everything – and try to regain some of your former self-discipline and self-control ... "

Varzi scrunches the words in his fist, as he had once done with the *Gazzetta*, and tosses the letter into the waste-basket. 'You fuck with my shit again and I'll kick you out,' he tells Viganò. He strides into the bedroom and snaps open the curtains irritably.

'Can you get the stuff?' Ilse mumbles behind him. 'It's in the bathroom.' As he walks over to get it, he can still hear her murmuring: 'Will you give it to me, Achille?'

*

The reprofiled Nordkurve hairpin has transformed the AVUS into the world's fastest race track; here, finally, a race car will approach terminal velocity, and to discover precisely what that is, the organizers have scheduled a Formula Libre event in May to enable Auto Union and Mercedes to run their purpose-designed streamliners. During practice, Rosemeyer's 6-litre V16 Type C

Stromlinen had cut through the traps at 374kph. Lang had come very close to passing the mythical 400kph mark when his Mercedes was suddenly swept up by a gust of wind and tossed around like a plaything. He had returned to earth a half-mile down the road, miraculously unscathed but not a little shaken when he climbed out and suggested Neubauer unblock the enclosed wheel flares.

The latest news at the AVUS is that Ferrari has withdrawn from the race. Losing has become routine for Ferrari, and left with nothing to do, Nuvolari spends the day popping his head into the various teams' garages. He is struck by how much things have changed: How had he failed to notice the ridiculous black fezzes on the heads of his mechanics, or Hühnlein scrutinizing the German drivers as if they were military recruits? Indeed, how had he missed Neubauer and Feuereisen acceding to Hühnlein's demands on strategy and the order in which the German teams sent out their drivers? Nuvolari feels a sense of loss, too, for his friends Campari and Borzacchini, but also for Chiron, Varzi, Dreyfus – the old guard is no more. He feels out of touch, out of date. Old.

He sees the young Englishman Seaman standing shyly in the Mercedes garage, and realizes that the boy was still in diapers when he was fighting in the war. Everyone has moved on: Ferrari, six years his junior, now a successful team-owner, Dreyfus dabbling with his restaurants, Chiron living the life of the bon vivant in Monaco, Varzi – well, Varzi was always going to be Varzi. But Tazio had never wanted anything more than this. His ambition ended here, on these tracks.

On Saturday evening, with no desire to return home, Nuvolari had bought himself a Leica II camera and talked Finestrini into hiring him as the *Gazzetta*'s photographer for the weekend.

The PA system announces that 515,000 people have come to watch the two preliminary heats and the final, which is scheduled for a 3pm start. Nuvolari amuses himself by taking snaps inside the Auto Union garage where Dr. Porsche, spotting him, comes over to express his admiration.

'The greatest driver of the past, present, and future,' he says in impeccable Italian. When Nuvolari asks about the possibility of running a Volkswagen franchise in Italy when he retires, Porsche reveals, loud enough for Finestrini to overhear, that Hitler, who had designed the Nordkurve banking, had also focused his artistic ability on the front-end of the soon-to-be unveiled Volkswagen Type 1.

'Looks a bit like a beetle now – he came up with a brilliant idea. But really,' Porsche says, 'why would you retire? You can always find a new challenge here, in a German car.'

The first heat features Rosemeyer, Caracciola, Seaman, Von Delius, and Balestrero. The race proceeds at a sedate pace because Continental are afraid the elevated speed will tear their tyres apart until, with two laps remaining, Caracciola finally darts past Rosemeyer and makes a break for the Südkurve. Rosemeyer responds, easily pulling away from the normal grand prix cars of Seaman and von Delius; Balestrero, in the Alfa, is already two minutes behind, left to race against his own shame.

The two silver cars peel out from the Grunewald and hurry into the banking one final time. They come in virtually abreast, Rosemeyer nose-diving down toward the apron, Caracciola heading toward the outside of the flat, banked bend. Nuvolari is struck by the bravery of the old master. Rosemeyer has the correct line, his angle is shorter, and he has better grip than his opponent. And yet Caracciola thinks nothing of skating the outer edge of that narrow strip of brick. If he gets it wrong, there's nothing – not even a barrier – to prevent him from flying off the track. Just as Caracciola's front right wheel is about to spill out of the arena, the main-straight accepts the grateful Mercedes, and Rosemeyer is powerless to stop Caracciola from claiming the win by less than a second.

Nuvolari is left with an indelible impression of Caracciola's daring pass. Caracciola is thirty-six now, ten years younger than Nuvolari, and the man Tazio considers to be the most complete driver on the grid. As the two men share a drink at the Roxy later that night, Nuvolari turns to Caracciola and says: 'We're the last ones left, you know, you and I. The last ones standing from the golden days.'

'Tazio,' Rudi replies, 'these *are* the golden days, my friend.'

*

The shrill sound of a phone cuts through the still summer Milan night.

'What?'

'Finestrini, this is Nuvolari. I need your help.'

'Tazio? – what – what's wrong?'

'I need a train. I need a train to take me from Lugano to Gardone – I've tried everyone, Finestrini, everyone.'

Finestrini sits up in the darkness, his fingers groping for the lamp switch. 'Christ, Tazio, it's not even morning yet.'

'They say Giorgio won't survive a car-ride, but in a train he can be made comfortable; only in a train, do you understand? I need a train, Johnny.'

'I don't – *what are you talking about?*'

After Nuvolari hangs up, it takes five minutes of controlled breathing for Finestrini to summon the courage to call the only person who can help them.

'Ciano,' says a rough voice.

'Good morning sir, this is Finestrini – '

'Who?'

'Johnny Finestrini, sir. From the *Gazzetta*.'

Silence.

'We met – '

'You're calling me at four fucking a.m. from a *sports 'paper?*'

'Sir, I'm sorry, Tazio Nuvolari – '

'Are you fucking *mad?* I'll have you shot, you son of a bitch.'

'Sir, Nuvolari's son is ill. He needs your help.'

Silence.

'Sir, I'm – '

'*What* does he need?'

*

The dawn is breaking when Finestrini parks his Bianchi behind the station and walks up to the platform. Two soldiers and Nuvolari's personal physician are waiting beside the locomotive. Sitting by the window in the train's only coach, Finestrini watches his reflection erased by the pale dawn coming up over the Alps.

When they arrive in Lugano, Nuvolari is waiting for them on the platform, looking much older than his forty-five years. He welcomes the doctor with a curt shake of the hand before leading him away into the station. They return a short while later. Behind them – lying on a stretcher – is Giorgio. The boy is carried onto the train by the two soldiers and transferred onto a bench that has been converted into a makeshift bed. He holds his hand out for his father, and Tazio comes to his side, stroking Giorgio's forehead as the doctor gets to work on a syringe. The train is already pulling out of the station when the boy sinks into a synthetic sleep.

Nuvolari sits down across from Finestrini. 'Giorgio was playing football, and he just collapsed.' Nuvolari tries to hold back his tears. 'Myocarditis,' he says in a dull voice. 'I've never even heard of it.'

'What do the doctors say?'

'They're doctors, they had me dead twenty years ago.' He looks out the window. 'All I ever wanted was for the boy to be happy – and you'll see, Finestrini, one day you'll be writing about Giorgio Nuvolari. I've seen it in his eyes, you know, I've seen the Nuvolari hunger.'

This is a man who suffered few affectations. And he had of course – lived – despite the destiny everyone had written for him. Forty-five he is, his father dead, his son – all of eighteen, dying back there in the room under the stairs in Gardone surrounded by his toy cars and planes and little plastic soldiers.

Nuvolari won't accept the diagnosis. When Giorgio wakens, sweating and feverish, it is Tazio's hand that he reaches for in the dark; and when he whispers, 'Daddy, I'm scared,' Tazio is the one who comforts him, saying: 'A Nuvolari never dies in bed – you're a Nuvolari, son, none of us will ever die in bed.'

Nuvolari has commitments; one is to defend the Vanderbilt Cup in July. The man who wins it twice gets to keep that enormous trophy. He speaks to Carolina as they stand just outside Giorgio's door, both acutely conscious of the silence.

'You must go, Tazio.'

'I can't.'

'You have no choice.'

'Of course I do.'

'You have no choice,' she tells him again. 'A father shouldn't see his child like this, it's unnatural.' She touches his face, gently tracing the path of the tears he has shed. 'Tazio, you're the bravest man I've ever known and I can't have you here like this.'

He shuts his eyes.

'Just go, Tazio. Go to America.'

'He'll be okay, you know,' Tazio says that night, hovering over Carolina as she packs his suitcase. 'I know he'll pull through. Auto Union will be there too, and Bernd suggested that it would be a good time to speak to Feuereisen about next year. Anyway, Giorgio will be all right, I know he will ... Doctors, they don't know anything, and it's only two weeks, I'll be back – '

'Yes, Tazio.'

*

Viganò has a ritual. It begins with the two-mile drive through central Milan, from his little apartment near the Porta Romana to the Savoia, bringing with him yoghurt and cottage cheese – now about the only food that Ilse and Varzi can stomach. He will leave the food on the breakfast table outside Varzi's bedroom, accustomed by now to the stench.

Of Varzi's addiction he knows too much: of Varzi's weakness he doesn't want to know any more. Having deposited the cheese and yoghurt, Viganò will then head north to the Tempio della Vittoria, that perplexing octagonal memorial to Milan's war dead. Across the piazza from the memorial squats the Garibaldi barracks, and behind that a tired bar where Viganò will meet – as arranged – a military doctor whose name he does not know. Viganò will exchange money for morphine – after four months, the transaction is mechanical, in a hostile way – before driving back to the Savoia with his tin-box of tricks.

Varzi, awake by then, will vanish into the bedroom with the junk. Abandoned, Viganò will stand on the balcony and observe the world below the Savoia. Eventually, bored, his thumbs ink-stained from a *Gazzetta* read front-to-back, he will peak into the bedroom and, certain that Ilse and Varzi have succumbed to their fiesta of fantastic dreams, will leave the room for a stroll or a chat with the doorman downstairs. On Tuesdays, he will meet Finestrini for drinks at the café across from the Savoia. In Finestrini, Viganò has found an unlikely ally. It had been the man from the *Gazzetta* who had convinced him to retain his job when, sickened by Varzi's addiction, he had considered leaving. Finestrini had told him that his sacrifice protected Varzi – and by extension, Italy – from shame.

The journalist sits at his usual booth with white wine and a panino when Viganò slides in opposite him.

'You look exhausted,' Finestrini says.

Viganò rubs his eyes. 'When does this end?'

'How's it going up there?'

'It's the same. Always the same – though it's as you said, his tolerance is getting higher. Do you know how much money he's burning through? With the junk and the hotel? And he keeps forgetting things – he's always bloody searching for something, even his stash.'

Finestrini lifts his sandwich, regards it with distaste and throws it down on the plate. 'You hungry?'

'No.'

'I'm going away for a while – two, three weeks. To America.'

'Two weeks?' Viganò is troubled by how alone he suddenly feels. Despite having made it clear that he could not get involved, Finestrini was at least a sympathetic ear. Viganò can't quite recall when he had first encountered the journalist in the lobby of the Savoia. Was it shortly after Varzi's return from Gardone? Finestrini had warned him of this – that he too would lose snatches of time, fragments of his life. Addiction, Finestrini had told him, was contagious. He was right.

*

The SS *Normandie* departs at 8pm sharp on June 24, 1937, its horns blasting through the tangerine-coloured hills like a February wind. Up on the bridge, Nuvolari analyzes the latest charts from the *Bremen*, the ship that is transporting the Auto Union team to

America. Nuvolari and Rosemeyer have taken bets as to who will arrive in New York first. That evening, in the impressive dining room, Captain René Pugnet assures Nuvolari that he is sure to win the bet. They call the *Normandie* the 'ship of light', and she steams through the cold dawn in colossal silence, slashing the ocean apart with the remorseless determination of a butcher.

Nuvolari spends his mornings on the upper-deck, idly watching the children play. He had instructed Giorgio's nurse to allow the boy to send as many messages as he wished; as he sits on a deck chair, smoking, he reads the first one.

"Daddy, please come back. I feel I will drift away without you. Please stop and come back."

The *Normandie* is four days away from New York. The Italian liner *Rex* is scheduled to head back to Genoa on the same day that the *Normandie* is arriving. Nuvolari can be home in nine days …

'Sir, the captain reports that, despite our half-day handicap, we have just surpassed the *Bremen.*'

Nuvolari glances up at the first mate and smiles at the Frenchman's Italian.

'Excellent. Tell the captain I'm a thousand dollars richer because of him, and to please accept my invitation to dinner in New York.'

Nuvolari procures a warm blanket and a cosy spot on the deck and sleeps the afternoons away. In the evenings, he takes his dinners in the not-quite-so ostentatious café-grille, away from the pomp of the main dining hall. He suspects that it's the rich French cuisine that keeps him awake at night. In the chapel down in the bowels of the *Normandie,* Nuvolari prays on his knees. He doesn't want to go back to his dark, airless cabin, which reminds him of a coffin. Up on the deck outside his first-class cabin, the night is ruptured by an elated panorama. The lone man standing in the fog holds a teletype in his fist. It must be Giorgio again, pleading for him to come home.

"Dear Signor Nuvolari, it is our painful duty to inform you that your son Giorgio has passed away."

*

Nuvolari is standing on the bridge when the *Normandie* arrives in New York Harbour, waving mechanically at the thousands – tens of thousands – who have come to welcome him back to America. As they disembark, the captain tells him that Amelia Earhart has gone missing on the final leg of her circumnavigation, her Lockheed L10-E Electra having disappeared somewhere between New Guinea and Howland Island. Nuvolari recalls that Elly had once met Amelia in Hollywood. He feels completely numb as a group of policemen escort him from the *Normandie* and into a waiting patrol car, pushing through the crush of people chanting his name.

'You're like royalty,' says the cop, driving.

'The King of the Guineas,' says the other.

Nuvolari, who speaks no English, assumes that they're speaking of New Guinea, of Amelia.

'At least they're peaceful; wait 'til the *Bremen* comes in – we've got twenty thousand Jews waiting for that Nazi ship. Gonna be hell to pay.'

Nuvolari looks out of the car window, thinking of Giorgio. The tears roll down his cheeks as he smiles and waves at the crowd lining the streets to catch a glimpse of the legendary Tazio Nuvolari. As he passes through Little Italy, flowers rain down onto the patrol car from the tenement apartments above him.

*

A mob has gathered around the Waldorf-Astoria, clamoring for blood. Bernd Rosemeyer, ensconced in his suite on the fourteenth floor, stares down at this swell of people through a gap in the drapes. He and Elly had been transferred from the *Bremen* amidst violent scenes between cops and demonstrators, entering the hotel via its secret underground platform in the hope of throwing off the mob. But they had been tracked down anyway, and he listens to the roaring voices outside their window. 'Nazi killers!' the crowd is shouting.

'Would that be us?' Bernd inquires, turning toward Elly and von Delius, who are reading newspapers in the air-conditioned suite.

'That would be us,' confirms von Delius, with the *New York Journal* open on his lap.

'They seem angry.'

'They hate us for our freedoms – here, look at this.' Von Delius shows Elly a column written by Bill Corum.

"This Rosemeyer family is in the deuce of a hurry. He drives at almost 250mph on an autobahn, she flies almost as quickly around the world: what will happen if one day they have a son? There will be nothing left for him but to visit Mars in a rocket!"

'Have either of you seen Tazio?' asks Elly, changing the subject hurriedly. 'I promised Carolina I would speak to him – '

'He's here somewhere in the hotel. I saw Finestrini earlier this morning; he told me that the mafia has asked Nuvolari to throw the race.'

'The mafia want *us* to win?' asks von Delius.

'Obviously not the Jewish mafia.'

'Bernd please, as if we don't have enough problems already,' says Elly. Today's front page news is all about Amelia's disappearance, and Elly considers her fellow pilot's fate an unwelcome reminder of her own sacrifice. Whatever happened to her and Bernd sharing their lives, their passions? In the first few months of their relationship, she had tried to keep up with her commitments – her book tour, her frequent lectures – but it had soon became clear that Bernd could not bear to be separated from her. She had given up everything for this poor lost boy, who also happened to be the world's greatest racing driver. Or second best apparently, now that Bernd had expressed his feelings of insecurity to her about Nuvolari's recent triumphs. When Bernd had been informed that the *Normandie* had overtaken the *Bremen*, his mood had soured. He had told Elly that he had been trying to coax Feuereisen into signing Nuvolari for next season: that way, when he beat Tazio with equal machinery, no one could ever again dispute his supremacy.

'Why are you looking for Nuvolari, anyway?' asks von Delius.

Bernd turns from the window. 'We want to ask him – '

'Bernd!' hisses Elly.

'What?' asks Bernd, shutting the drapes. 'We can tell Uncle Ernst, for God's sake.'

'Tell me what?' Von Delius looks from one to the other until Elly sighs in resignation.

'We want Tazio to be the godfather of our boy,' says Bernd, beaming.

'Your boy?' Von Delius feels the tenderness of their embrace, as Elly melts into Bernd's chest. 'You mean – Bernd, you're *pregnant?'*

*

Viganò walks into the Savoia with his leather briefcase.

'Viganò!' The concierge beckons him over, waving an envelope in his hand. It's a telegram from Finestrini in New York City. Viganò tears it open in the elevator. The sentence is terse, yet conveys a whole world of misery. As Viganò draws closer to the suite, he wonders how he will break the news to Varzi, whose moods were already bordering on the hostile.

'You're late,' Varzi says accusingly when he walks into the room.

Viganò holds up the telegram. 'It's from Finestrini.'

'Telling me that Nuvolari has failed in his conquest of America? He's a bit late, then.' Varzi points at the *Gazzetta* with an unsteady hand. 'Bernd Rosemeyer wins for Reich and Homeland,' he says, and Viganò knows better than to even bother checking to see if he's quoting the *Gazzetta* precisely. 'Nuvolari's Alfa catches fire, and the Flying Mantuan is forced to drive with only his feet to keep the fiery car from crashing into the crowd. Always a hero, our Tazio, even when he fails. *Especially* when he fails, the little prick.'

Viganò holds out the telegram as if it's infected. Varzi accepts it; reads it. Once. Again. Viganò says nothing, placing the valise on the coffee table and drawing out the tin box. He thinks he sees a trace of emotion flare across that impenetrable face, but it vanishes instantly. Varzi wanders off into the bedroom, carrying telegram and junk in the same hand. Viganò starts flipping through the newspaper. Voices trickle out from the bedroom – which is odd, since Ilse and Varzi usually carry out their ritual in sanctified silence. Viganò has come to realize that the life of a junkie is orderly, in its own way. He stands up and approaches the door.

' – no more, Ilse. I need to get clean.'

'Don't be stupid Achille – we'll never give up, you and I.'

'We'll find a clinic, we can do it. I want my life back.'

'What are you talking about?'

'Giorgio – Tazio's boy. He's dead.'

'Why do you care?'

'What's wrong with you? Don't you care about anything at all besides this?' Varzi's voice carries loudly, and Viganò quickly backs away from the door. Varzi bursts into the room in a whirlwind of rage and grabs the phone. In one minute, he has secured a bed in a clinic in Switzerland. Once this is done, he sits with his head in his hands, steeling himself for the return to his bedroom. Viganò watches him go.

'What are you doing, *Achille?*' Ilse asks when Varzi steps into the bedroom. Silence. 'Achille, what are you doing?'

'Come with me.'

'Where?'

'Switzerland.'

'Achille, look at me.' Still no reply from Varzi. 'Achille! Don't you fucking walk away from me.'

Varzi, dressed in a charcoal-black suit, strides out from the bedroom. Behind him comes Ilse in nothing but her briefs, her hand latching onto his jacket. He spins around and breaks away from her grip. She looks stunned.

'You leave me here and you never come back. You never come back, do you understand!'

Varzi grabs hold of the front door-knob.

'You *fuck,*' she whispers. 'Look what you've done to me.'

Varzi opens the door. She kicks it shut and places her body between him and the hallway. Varzi, as swift as he is cruel, picks her up and drags her away under an assault of punches that thud miserably in his face.

'Viganò!' he hisses, stumbling into the bedroom to heave Ilse onto the bed. She rolls off it, determined to go after him again. Varzi slams the door shut just as she gets to it. 'Stay with her,' he tells Viganò when she begins slamming her hands on the locked door. 'And make sure she doesn't leave.'

Viganò leans his weight onto the door: Ilse is kicking at it now. Varzi walks out of the suite without even a backward glance. After five minutes, Ilse's assault on the door finally eases up. Viganò – standing with his back to the cool wood – gives it another hour before he chances a look inside. Ilse is lying on the bed, with a syringe abandoned in her thigh. He leaves her there to the night.

*

Nuvolari parks his Alfa in the driveway. He sits in the car listening to the comforting click of the engine in the still summer night. He had driven directly from Genoa, slowly, not wanting to be here, not wanting to come home. The lights in the villa are all out. He kills the engine and steps out onto the driveway, shoes crunching over the gravel. The front door is unlocked; he stands on the threshold, acclimatizing to the darkness. Nuvolari can't bear the idea of going into his bedroom right now – he can't face this house. He walks into the conservatory and pours a whisky instead. Drinks it. Pours another. He walks over to the glass wall and stares out at the garden. It's summertime, and Giorgio would have been home from school now. The German Grand Prix is in two weeks; it's been two years since his win there, a win that he had celebrated with Giorgio. He had promised to take the boy this year too. He had promised too much.

Nuvolari knows where his feet are taking him. The door to the room below the stairs is shut. The knob is cold. He hadn't spent much time with Giorgio: he had been too busy with his career, too busy risking his life out on the track. He hadn't been here, in this room, when his dying boy had reached out for him in the dark. What had he said? 'Daddy, come home.'

I *am* back, thinks Nuvolari, fumbling about blindly in the dark. He triggers the light switch. Above the small, white bed is a wooden crucifix with an ivory Jesus dying naked and alone. Nuvolari's trophies are there too, but where are the toys? Where are Giorgio's toys? He leaves the light on and heads up the stairs.

Carolina sits up in bed and switches on the bedside lamp in one alarmed motion. 'Tazio.'

'Where are his toys?'

She stares at him, at his shadow melting into the dark behind him.

Where are Giorgio's toys? he repeats, unable to step into the bedroom.

'Tazio, don't raise your voice.'

'Where – ? '

'Papà, *you're home,*' says a voice behind him. Nuvolari spins around. Alberto stands in his shadows, barefoot and fragile. He runs and jumps, oblivious to fear, complete in his trust. Nuvolari snatches him out of mid-air, the energy steamrolling him back into the bedroom.

'Papà!' Nuvolari brings Alberto's face up to his. Giorgio, he thinks. Carolina heads downstairs and leaves Tazio to put Alberto back to sleep. In Alberto's bedroom he finds Giorgio's toys scattered about: his cars, his planes and his plastic soldiers. He sits beside his boy's bed, reading for a long time before Alberto finally falls asleep. It happens so suddenly that Tazio, concerned, touches his face – it's warm. Before he kills the light, he checks to make sure that Alberto's little chest is rising and falling under the blanket.

In the kitchen, Carolina sips on a cup of chamomile. He sits opposite her, staring at that honest, open face, and all he remembers is the day that she had come home with Giorgio. It's his tears that keep them up through the night, and when the dawn comes, Nuvolari tells her that he has agreed to help test Jano's new 4.5-litre V12 at Monza. It's a big job, it will keep him away from home, he will take an apartment in Modena, he needs to focus on his career, he loves her, he needs space, he needs time, he cherishes his time with Alberto, with the family, he needs to win again; he has to stop losing.

'You do what you want,' she tells him, 'but before you leave, you're to take Alberto to Giorgio. Do you understand me? You and your son will say goodbye to Giorgio together. After that you do what you want. Now go, get some sleep; Alberto will be up soon and he doesn't need to see you like this. You're still his hero.'

'I was Giorgio's hero.'

'Yes, you were.'

'And I let him down. He needed me. And I wasn't here.'

'No, you weren't.'

Nuvolari wants to lash out; but he swallows the angry words that are about to spill from his lips. 'I'm sorry, Carolina.'

She takes his face in her hands. 'Alberto needs you, Tazio. I need you. You go do what you need to and then you come back – you come back home to us,' she says, her voice choked with emotion, 'because Alberto needs a father, Tazio, and I need my husband.'

His tears mingle with hers on the cold kitchen table. The birds chatter in his garden, and he hears Alberto pattering down the stairs, looking for his father.

*

'She called again.'

Rudi Caracciola sighs. Lying on the couch with his eyes shut, he feels Baby brush his chest hair. 'So much for our honeymoon,' he says.

'So much for our new house.' He can hear the exasperation in her voice.

Their commanding new villa is poised on a ridge below the Alps in Ruvigliana. Out in the garden, fast asleep in a wicker chair under a heavy blanket, is Achille Varzi. He had turned up four days earlier, fresh out of a detox' clinic not ten miles from the villa. Baby had welcomed him in, chilled by his deathly complexion; the Varzi who had come in the night was a walking cadaver, his body consumed by twitches over which he had neither control nor awareness.

'Any idea when he's leaving?'

Caracciola leans his head on Baby's shoulder. 'He tells me he's borrowed a Maserati – he's going racing.'

'In that condition? At the *'Ring?*'

'Christ, no. A local race in Italy – same day as the 'Ring though. It'll be good for him.'

'And what about her?'

'He tells me Viganò is looking after her needs.'

'Her needs.' Baby tastes the words on her tongue. 'She's a morphine addict. Are those her needs?'

'Probably.'

'And he just lets her stay there, in that hotel.'

'Seems like it.'

'And buys her drugs.'

'Yup.'

'Why would he do that?'

'I don't know, Baby. What does she say?'

'She wants to speak to him.'

'And what did you say?'

'What I always say: That he's out. I need this to end. I'm sick of lying.'

'He leaves in a few days.'

'I just don't understand it.'

'You mean you don't understand *him.*'

'Do *you* understand him?'

To explain is to admit his own fear, so Rudi keeps his eyes shut and tries to enjoy the sunshine.

*

Guidotti – Nuvolari's co-driver at the Mille Miglia in 1930 and now Alfa Romeo's chief test-driver – stands bare-chested in the fading light of day. He shares a cigarette with Nuvolari as they had done on that glorious afternoon in May so many years ago. The mechanics are busy working on the new 12C-37 in the garage beneath the empty Monza grandstands. The car is a brick, but Guidotti is paid to run it day in and day out, all the while knowing that his best lap is six seconds slower than the Auto Unions had managed a year ago.

'It's a good thing that they decided to move the Italian GP to Livorno,' he says. Nuvolari gives him an enquiring look. 'They did it for you, you know,' Guidotti adds.

'For me?'

'They think the slower layout there will give you a chance to defend our colours.'

'And what colours are those, Giova'?'

'What they've always been, Tazio: the colour of money.'

Nuvolari smiles, squinting into the embers of the warm June day.

'Anyway, you did beat the Germans there last year, didn't you?'

'My last win,' recalls Nuvolari. 'Will the car be ready by then?'

'Maybe.' Guidotti glances back at the garage, where the mechanics are still hunched over the unpainted black-metal car. 'Tazio.' Guidotti waits for Nuvolari to look at him. 'I've been trying all week to find the right words to say – '

'The priest said them all for us.'

'Why don't you go home? There's nothing you can do here.'

'Do you think there is any hope for this car?' asks Nuvolari.

Guidotti ponders this question before answering. 'Between us? It's too soft, it's down on power, it's fragile – Tazio, if you want to win again, you're wasting your time here with us. We're doing our best – Jano is doing his best, the boys are doing their best, God knows they work like animals to please you, but we just don't have the resources. We're behind, Tazio, and we're not catching up anytime soon.'

*

It's been years since Mercedes won the German Grand Prix at Nürburgring, not since the summer of '31. Today, Neubauer is determined to end the barren run despite Auto Union's pace that has been blistering all weekend. Neubauer, though, has been around long enough to know that, in the end, pace is never the determining factor. If it were, not many would turn up on a Sunday afternoon to race. He times the gap between the leader Rosemeyer and second-placed Caracciola. Eight seconds the gap on lap four. Bernd is too young, too impetuous, and today, Neubauer is going to use that against him. The Continentals, Neubauer had determined after sending Caracciola out for repeated tests on Saturday, need to be cooled after their initial cycle: Caracciola's experience is key today, he must exert pressure on Bernd while still managing to cool his tyres.

Bernd, ignoring Feuereisen's instructions to slow his pace in his determination to break from Rudi, keeps pushing until the inevitable happens: his hubcap shores off and slashes the right-rear tyre. Caracciola, von Brauchitsch, and Nuvolari all flame past the Auto Union as it bears down toward the box on three tyres and a rim that shreds the bodywork. Rosemeyer's anger is palpable, throwing the thing around sideways behind shards of aluminium and sparks as the crowd will him back to the pit where Sebastian and Ludwig take to it with hammers. Stuck, von Delius, and Seaman have all rumbled past when finally Rosemeyer darts back into the race down in eighth. It takes less than a lap for him to close up on the Mercedes of Seaman and the Auto Union of von Delius embroiled in their messy scrap for sixth. Coming out of the Karussell, von Delius – with his team-leader's silver arrow dancing large in his vibrating mirrors – gets a tow on the Mercedes ahead. There's one turn left before the cars punch onto the final straight, a fierce one taken at 260kph. It waits beyond two hump-backed bridges that destabilize the entry. Von Delius forces the issue. He brakes late, bounces off the second bump and, anticipating Seaman's move to block the inside, dives up the outside. He makes it stick, gets out ahead of Seaman, nails the throttle and then he's into a vicious tank slapper that comes without warning. Von Delius catches it, but fate will have him this day. A hedge sucks him in and spits him back out into Seaman's path. The two cars collide, Rosemeyer, without even a lift, slicing between Seaman rotating off into the trees and von Delius cartwheeling away into the scenery. Rosemeyer doesn't slow. In the distance he can see a black dot vanish down into the valley. Nuvolari tries to hang on for three, four turns, but Bernd won't be denied, diving up the inside and vanishing up the road in his desperate attempt at catching Caracciola. He cuts the gap from eighty seconds down to fifteen, but it's not enough. Rudi takes the chequers with a faint wave of his gloved hand at Neubauer, jumping up and down in delight.

The grandstands rise silent in the late afternoon, the sky a crystal-cool pool that spreads like blood over the abandoned track when Nuvolari arrives at the Auto Union box. He finds doors sealed and padlocked.

'They're all at the hospital,' says Finestrini, smoking in the shadow of the garage. 'Von Delius is in bad shape.'

Nuvolari turns to him. 'You headed to Milan tonight?' he asks. 'I need a ride home – I came on Elly's plane with Bernd.'

'I have my car,' says Finestrini. 'But I'm driving. That's the condition.'

Finestrini drives his Bianchi through the night, with Nuvolari asleep on the passenger seat. The news comes on the Motorola radio as they rattle through Bolzano. 'German Auto Union driver Ernst von Delius has died of an embolism from injuries suffered during the German Grand Prix today. Von Delius lost control on lap seven and was found trapped in his Auto Union a quarter of a mile from the track on the main Koblenz-Cologne road. Rudi Caracciola, with his win, is now ideally placed to clinch the European Championship ahead of his fellow German rivals, Bernd Rosemeyer and Hermann Lang. In related news, our own Achille Varzi returned to action in San Remo today, after a lengthy illness. He won his heat in convincing fashion, lapping the whole field in his Maserati 4CM. It has been ten months since Varzi last raced, and his return is most welcome.'

'Poor bastard,' whispers Nuvolari with his eyes shut.

Finestrini glances at him in the dark, but Tazio hasn't shifted, leaving Finestrini to wonder if Nuvolari had really spoken at all.

*

Elly confides her thoughts to Carolina as they take their tea in the shade of a lemon tree at Gardone. She tells her that Tazio has somehow managed to help Bernd cope with Von Delius's death. The two men had spoken late into the previous night, and whatever it was that he'd said, Bernd's anxiety had softened when he'd woken up in the morning. Uncle Ernst's death had affected Bernd in a way that Elly had not anticipated. She'd thought that he was inured to the dangers of the racetrack, but he had been inconsolable when he'd seen Ernst's corpse at the hospital.

'You know, Bernd learnt Italian in two weeks,' says Elly. 'I've been taking lessons since high-school, and in two weeks he speaks it better than I can.'

Carolina sips her tea. 'Ernst died racing,' she says. 'It's all men like this can ask for.'

'Is that what Tazio told Bernd?'

'No. He would have told Bernd that, if a driver needs a friend, he ought to get a pet. Like Caracciola's monkey.'

Elly smiles. 'And I always thought Italians were romantics.'

'Death is part of us, Elly.' Carolina stares into the distance, leaving the rest unsaid.

*

Bernd Rosemeyer is playing with his spaghetti. People, he says, ought to eat meat and the occasional vegetable, it's the way humans are engineered. Pasta is to him what dust is to a carburettor. Elly smiles as she watches him struggle with his meal. His white shirt has red stains on it, as if he'd been shot – it reminds her of the gangster movie she had watched with the Nuvolaris at the theatre in Verona the night before. 'Lucky Luciano was staying at our hotel in New York,' she tells Carolina.

Bernd looks up from his pasta. 'We saw him in the elevator, remember Tazio?'

'Actually, I had dinner with him,' says Nuvolari nonchalantly.

'You didn't,' gasps Carolina.

'A quick affair; he wanted to meet the other famous Italian staying at the Waldorf.'

'He lives there?'

'Oh yes – him and his whores.'

'What was he like?' asks Carolina.

'Varzi,' replies Elly, and they all laugh.

An August thunderstorm chases them indoors, and Carolina serves coffee in the conservatory with the hail machine-gunning down over the lake beyond the garden. Alberto has brought out two of Giorgio's metal-cast racecars, and Nuvolari – in the Bernd Rosemeyer Auto Union – races against his son, who has picked the Tazio Nuvolari Alfa-Ferrari.

'Nuvolari wins again!' shouts the boy.

'It's amazing, isn't it, how kids have such fantastic imaginations,' says Rosemeyer.

Nuvolari laughs. Alberto looks up at him, confused. 'You two should think about having a child,' Tazio says, stroking the boy's hair reassuringly.

'Who says they aren't?' asks Carolina.

'Aren't what? Thinking about it?'

'Having one,' says Elly.

Nuvolari takes a moment to register her words. Then he glances up from his Auto Union. 'What am I missing?' he asks. Carolina's look is all the reply he needs. 'Oh,' he says. 'And what, it's yours then, Bernd?'

'That's exactly what he asked when he found out,' replies Elly with a testy smile.

'Actually, that's why we're here.' Bernd sits forward in his chair. 'Tazio, Elly and I would like you to be our son's godfather.'

'Godfather to Bernd Rosemeyer's son,' says Nuvolari pensively. 'We're quite a duo for the boy to live up to.'

'He'll probably turn out to be an orthodontist,' says Carolina. She listens to Bernd laugh, but there's a dullness in Tazio's eyes when he goes back to racing Alberto on the carpet. He'd lost more than his son the day Giorgio left, she thinks. Death is always greedy.

*

Viganò steps quickly through the hotel room toward the bedroom door. The ritual, today, has been broken: instead of delivering Ilse her junk, he has spent the day at home, with a girl he'd met last night at the Pidocchio. Ilse hasn't had her arm fed in fifteen hours, and Viganò had been too late to meet the good doctor with the goods. Viganò slows at the bedroom door and listens cautiously; the silence encourages him to open it and step inside. He switches the light on. Ilse is convulsing on the floor, her lips discharging frothy vomit.

'Help me,' she whispers with eyes that are seeping wounds. 'Have you got it?'

'No,' he says, and he sees her flinch. 'No.'

'Get it,' she says, wracked by a violent spasm. 'Where is it? Why are you doing this to me?'

He heads back to the door, on the verge of throwing up.

'Don't leave me alone.'

'I'll be back in an hour.'

'I want to come with you.'

'Don't be fucking stupid,' he tells her. 'Just lie down. I'll be back.'

'Stay with me.'

'Do you want the junk or not?' he snaps. 'Fuck.'

'I'm coming with you.' Ilse tries to stand, groggily steps toward him until she falls into his arms. 'Don't leave me here alone,' she whispers.

He lifts her, so light in his arms, and dumps her roughly on the bed. 'Christ,' he says, grabbing for the telephone and dials. 'Achille,' he says after a moment, 'listen, it's me – I slept late and – yes I'm here now. No, she's not well, she's vomiting and has fever. She insists on coming with me – I can't do that, the doctor's not there – yes, okay, yes, that would be perfect. I could wait here until – okay – but please hurry – hurry for fuck's sake!' Viganò hangs up the phone.

'Is he coming?' asks Ilse weakly.

'He's sending over his doctor,' replies Viganò, disgusted by the bruises on her pasty naked flesh. 'I'll wait here with you.'

She lays her feverish head on his lap and shivers uncontrollably. 'You'll see,' she whispers, 'he'll come back to us soon.'

*

SANDRO MARTINI

Livorno was where the Italian Communist Party had been formed back in '21, but there isn't much equality on view in the plush surrounds of the Grande Palazzo Hotel and its strawberry-shaded marble columns and floors.

'It's not as easy as you think,' Feuereisen tells Rosemeyer as they share a couch in the lobby awash in frail September sunshine. 'We can't simply petition the board – '

'Why the hell not?' asks Rosemeyer with a plate on his lap. 'Surely you're in charge of running the team.'

'You know what Berlin wants, Bernd. Germans.'

'I'm German.' Bernd takes a bite of his chocolate cake. 'Look, with von Delius gone, and Stuck being Stuck – '

'Stuck won't be with us next season,' interrupts Feuereisen.

'If that's the case, then surely the board understands that you can't just buy a grand prix driver at the local department store.'

'They don't care, Bernd. They have you.'

'I can't be expected to fight against Mercedes on my own. You saw what happened this season.'

'Anyway, Fagioli is Italian – we can't have two Italians in the Auto Union team. Nuvolari won't fly, not with Berlin or with Zwickau.'

'Then get rid of Fagioli.'

Feuereisen sits back, exhausted. This fucking job, he thinks to himself.

'What if I speak to Hühnlein?' insists Bernd.

Feuereisen is about to reply when a waiter appears beside him, carrying a calling card on a silver tray. He takes the card, reads it, and frowns. 'Christ,' he says, 'what is it with Italians? Every time you mention one, another comes calling.'

'Who is it?'

Feuereisen nods toward the elegant man gliding across the lobby in a neatly pressed suit, baby-blue shirt and soft leather shoes. As soon as Achille Varzi has reached them, he holds out his hand to Bernd. 'Rosemeyer,' he says in a casual tone.

'Varzi.' Rosemeyer's grip is strong, dominant. Varzi allows it, glancing down at Feuereisen, who doesn't get up from the couch.

'Herr Feuereisen.'

'Signor Varzi. I could ask what you're doing here, but I suppose we do have the Italian Grand Prix on Sunday. I believe you've made something of a comeback.' Feuereisen waves a hand at the couch, and Varzi takes a seat.

'Yes, I did win at San Remo,' he says evenly, lighting a cigarette.

'I see you're still smoking.'

Varzi exhales a steady stream of poison. 'A man should choose his addictions with care, Herr Feuereisen.'

'Or not have any at all,' suggests Rosemeyer.

'Adrenaline is an addiction, Bernd – one that seems to afflict you more than most.'

'As addictive, I suppose, as any other drug,' Feuereisen admits. 'But not quite as destructive.'

'I know many who would argue differently, Herr Feuereisen – that is, if they were still around to make the argument.'

Feuereisen and Rosemeyer share a glance. 'I believe you were in a clinic?'

'In Switzerland, yes.'

'And Ilse, how is she?'

Varzi takes another drag. 'I've left her. Last I heard she was seeking treatment. I'm sure we all wish her the best.'

Feuereisen sips on his sickly-sweet drink. 'She is a devastatingly beautiful girl.'

'Yes, she is.'

Feuereisen places his drink on the coffee table. 'It's good to catch up, Herr Varzi.'

'I was thinking more of leading,' says Varzi. He stubs the Lucky out, lights another. 'I want to drive.'

Feuereisen remains silent.

'Naturally, you know what I am capable of,' continues Varzi. 'What happened last year was – a blind curve – '

'More like a blonde curve,' Bernd murmurs.

'Von Delius's seat is available.' Varzi shows no emotion when he meets Feuereisen's eyes. 'And I am available.'

Feuereisen stares at him for a moment. 'What guarantees do I have?'

'Doctor Magneven would be able to run some tests, would he

not? Or you could simply take my word for it.'

'I would welcome Herr Varzi back on the team,' says Rosemeyer. 'I imagine it's difficult to find a German driver to take over from Ernst now – running Italians is inevitable. I'm sure the board will fully support this, won't they?'

Feuereisen observes Bernd's mock-serious face, impressed by how quickly the young driver is learning about politics.

'Very well, Herr Varzi. You can assume that we'll have a car prepared for you this weekend – on condition that you submit to a full physical with Dr. Magneven. If all goes well, we may be in a position to retain you until the end of the season at Donington.'

*

Nuvolari is all the way back on the third row, squinting beyond the smoke from Seaman's V12 Mercedes ahead of him. He catches a glimpse of Varzi's Auto Union on the front row. Varzi had been second quickest in qualifying, fastest of the Auto Unions, and Nuvolari can see him begin to creep forward, with Rosemeyer and Caracciola on either side of him gunning their engines. The time-keeper gazes down at his watch, ready to pat the flagman on the shoulder to signal the start; when his arm moves, Varzi, Caracciola, Rosemeyer and Nuvolari dump their clutches, and they're already in second gear before the hand reaches the flagman's shoulder.

Nuvolari can hear the deafening noise of the crowd. They're here to watch him win; they will be disappointed. All the same, Nuvolari's start is a good one: he has matched the revs perfectly and sweeps past Varzi into the first turn. Then they're into the swift switchbacks through Antignano, where Nuvolari watches the Silver Arrows drive away from him. There's nothing to be done. Once they are outside the village of Antignano, the Germans stretch their legs, 200bhp up.

Varzi easily overtakes Nuvolari before heading into the hairpin bend. Nuvolari is surprised to find that Lang, too, is nipping at his heels. Nuvolari backs off, allowing the Mercedes through before clumsily shutting the door on another batch of German cars led by Seaman and Müller. The two rookies try to insert themselves into Nuvolari's line, but the old man from Mantua has had enough. He feels a sense of outrage at their impudence, and for fifteen laps he takes them to school, blocking and weaving, using Müller's impulsiveness against Seaman's caution. If this were anywhere else but Italy, and if this were anyone but Tazio Nuvolari, the black flag would have been flying after two laps; but this *is* Italy, and no race official will dare disqualify him. And rightly so, he thinks, for he has earned their respect.

Up ahead, one of the Auto Unions is slowing down. It's Varzi. The engine note on the V16 sounds crisp and clean, but Varzi's in trouble, his head tilting to one side. He must have no stamina left, thinks Nuvolari. It takes strength to hold onto these cars, it takes physical vigor to jam one's legs into that cockpit and hold on to 600bhp hell-bent on murder. Varzi's talent is not enough; Nuvolari passes him to the thunderous approval of the crowd. Nuvolari checks his mirrors: Seaman, Varzi, Müller, and behind them, the leaders closing in fast. He has lost three minutes in twenty laps to Bernd, Caracciola, and Lang. Three whole minutes. Enough, he thinks, enough of this shame. He raises an arm from his cockpit, fingers clenched into a fist: it's the signal for Seaman to pass him on the outside line of the track. Nuvolari heads for the pits and slows when he sees Bazzi race toward him.

'What's going on?' Bazzi shouts.

'Something's wrong with the car,' replies Nuvolari, climbing dejectedly from the cockpit and sliding off his goggles.

'What?'

'It's a piece of shit,' he says, walking away.

'Nuvolari!'

He ignores the call, making his way toward Elly, who is sitting beneath an umbrella with a stopwatch and a clipboard on her lap.

'How's my godson?'

Elly smiles when he pats her belly, kissing Nuvolari on both cheeks. 'God-daughter.'

Nuvolari listens as the Alfa 12C-37 driven by Guidotti rattles past. This, he thinks, is his future. Jano's new car has been entered by the Alfa Corse division, and rumor has it that Alfa is considering a return to grand prix racing for 1938. The 12C-37, though, is as hopeless as Guidotti had intimated: it had qualified last, and it now runs two laps down. It lasts another three laps before the V12 finally succumbs to a merciful death.

Lang has now forced his way past Rosemeyer, and is going after Caracciola. The championship battle is clear – if Caracciola outscores Lang, he will be crowned the European Champion. If Lang wins, the title fight goes on to Brno in a fortnight.

'What's up with Bernd?' asks Nuvolari. 'He's been off all weekend.'

'He's pissed.'

'About what?'

'Bernd spoke to Hans last night. Hans told him what he's getting paid.'

'Let me guess – '

'Yes, it's much more than what Bernd is making.'

'And I'll bet Bernd said something like – it's not about the money, it's the principle. He's Auto Union's number one and ought to be their number one paid driver. Am I right?'

Elly laughs heartily. 'So what should he do?'

'He should speak to Feuereisen,' Nuvolari shouts over the roar of the engines.

'But then he'll know Bernd spoke to Hans.'

Nuvolari looks at her. 'Exactly.'

'Oh,' she says.

Caracciola and Lang flash past the chequered flag, so close together that it takes a union of marshals, officials, and ultimately Hühnlein himself, to call a winner. It's Caracciola, by less than four-tenths of a second. Varzi comes in a distant sixth, so exhausted that Sebastian and Ludwig must collectively lift him from the cockpit. They stand him up like a marionette, and Varzi makes a brave attempt to accommodate them until, left to gravity and his own legs, he tumbles drunkenly onto his knees.

'Where's Magneven?' shouts Feuereisen.

'I'm fine,' says Varzi, on all fours. 'I'm fucking fine.'

'Jesus, why does he do it?' whispers Elly.

Nuvolari grabs a bottle of San Pellegrino and beats a path

through the scrum of onlookers to kneel beside Varzi. He jams the bottle into Varzi's mouth and pours until the poor sod has something to throw up. Varzi's pale face looks up at Nuvolari with a trace of a smile on his vomit-stained lips.

*

Feuereisen is not enjoying his breakfast. He has heartburn: a sizzling in his chest that hasn't been eased by those damned pills that Dr. Magneven had prescribed that morning. It's bad enough that Mercedes has won the championship, he thinks bitterly. But to have his number one driver berate him about pay, on the same day that he had filed a mandatory report to Hühnlein explaining this season's failures – well, that was just too much. And that was not even the half of it.

Feuereisen gazes over at Stuck sipping his coffee across the marble-topped table. Fluent in Italian, German, and French, tall, good looking, and the main reason why Auto Union's race department had been funded by the Party, a personal acquaintance of the Führer, a hillclimbing legend, and the man who'd gifted Auto Union its first win.

Hans Stuck and his toothy grin and flop of blond hair is a man of honour and about, thinks Feuereisen, to be fired right on his first-class ass.

'Varzi's talent was bigger than his ambition,' Stuck is saying. Feuereisen hesitates to speak.

Stuck detects something in the silence and glances up.

'Hans, this is not an easy thing for me to do,' says Feuereisen, taking a deep breath. 'I'm afraid I won't be able to offer you a contract for next season.' To disguise the distaste of his words, Feuereisen sticks a forkful of egg into his mouth. He remembers that Paula had always said that Hans was allergic to the thirteenth of the month.

Stuck watches Feuereisen chew on his food until finally he manages to frame his question. 'You're *firing* me?'

'I was rather hoping you wouldn't look at it that way. Donington will, nevertheless, be your final race with the team.'

'The *team?*' Stuck spits the words out. 'The team *I* got funding for, the team *I* carried on my back for three fucking years while Ferrari and Bugatti begged me to join them? *That* fucking team? Is that the team you're referring to?'

Feuereisen swallows hard. 'Calm down, Hans.'

'This is about Paula, isn't it?'

'No, Hans. This is not about Paula.'

'This is about Paula – this is about her being – being – '

'No, Hans.' Feuereisen sits forward and meets Stuck's anger with a challenging stare. 'This is about you finishing ninth yesterday. Three laps behind Bernd.'

'My brakes were shot.'

'We checked, Hans.'

'You *checked?*'

'Your brakes were in perfect condition.'

'*Bullshit.* This is despicable, Feuereisen.'

Feuereisen isn't a man accustomed to being defied by his drivers, and certainly not twice in one day. Yes, he feels a certain sympathy for Stuck, but there comes a time when a man must compose himself, accept his destiny and be what he is – a man. 'Donington will be your final race with us, Hans. I'm sorry, but there it is.'

Stuck opens his mouth to speak, but no words come out. He takes his napkin and wipes his lips instead, pushing back his chair and striding away into the sun.

Back at the hotel, Varzi is waiting in the bar as arranged. 'You'll be happy to know that you have the drive for the rest of the season, Herr Varzi,' Feuereisen tells him. 'But only on condition that you spend the next two weeks with Dr. Magneven – he'll be responsible for your training.'

'I out-qualified Rosemeyer.'

'Yes, you did. But it doesn't add up to shit if you qualify on pole and finish last. You need to train, to get back into shape. Dr. Magneven will put you on a supplement of vitamins and oversee your physical regimen. That's the condition for your drive. Take it or leave it.'

*

In Brno, a few weeks later, the day's highlight reel swirls through Feuereisen's mind like a scream. It is only Dr. Magneven's little red tablets that calm him down, lulling him into a sleep that feels a lot like consciousness on the eve of the Brno Grand Prix. The day had actually started off on a positive note. News had filtered in from Milan that Vittorio Jano had been fired from Alfa Romeo. By mid-morning, Dr. Porsche was on the phone with Feuereisen, informing him that Nuvolari, enraged by Jano's firing, was threatening to quit the sport altogether. Dr. Porsche had therefore taken it upon himself to petition the board in Zwickau, who had decided – with Hans Stuck leaving and von Delius no longer on the roster – that Feuereisen should try to secure Nuvolari's services for 1938. Feuereisen had imagined that this task would be a no-brainer, until he was told that Nuvolari had refused to turn up for morning practice. Rosemeyer hadn't showed up either. Instead, he had sent Elly to the track, armed with a contract formulated by his private attorneys in Berlin. His new retainer was seventy percent higher than the amount that Feuereisen was authorized to offer him. After carefully reading through the document, Feuereisen had realized that this was nothing more than Hans Stuck's contract with added zeros.

'He's thinking of joining Mercedes,' Elly had explained when he asked her what the hell Bernd was playing at. Feuereisen had stormed off to the nearest telephone and buzzed Hans Stuck's room. Paula had answered the phone, informing him that Hans was in the shower. 'You tell that turd he's fired as of this minute,' Feuereisen had thundered down the line. 'You tell that Austrian son of a bitch that if I see him when I get back to the hotel, I'll give him a hiding myself!'

That was before lunch.

A short while later, he had called Zwickau and presented the most relevant parts of Rosemeyer's new contract to the board. Naturally, they rejected it out of hand.

'Are we really going to lose Germany's greatest driver to Mercedes?' Feuereisen had asked.

'You will ensure that Rosemeyer accepts our initial contract. He remains our future.'

'What's my spread?'

'Ten percent above.'

'That's less than Stuck is making.'

'Stuck was senior.'

'Rosemeyer is a legend.'

'So make sure he stays with us.'

It was only Feuereisen's commitment to the firm that prevented him from telling the lot of them to piss off – that, and another helping of Dr. Magneven's red pills. Bernd had turned up after lunch, responding to the threats that Feuereisen had conveyed via Elly. Feuereisen asked him to remain patient, assuring him that negotiations would continue throughout the weekend, and that he was putting as much pressure on Zwickau as he could.

That was 3 pm. It was then that Dr. Magneven had delivered his final report on Varzi.

'He's not ready. I would recommend that you not allow him to start the race here. The addiction has sapped his strength. By next season, under a strict training regimen, we could see him back to full fitness, but as of now, there's no way he can complete a full grand prix.'

'Not even Donington?'

'I can't answer that with certainty: he's a driver, he'd probably get it done, but I can't guarantee what damage – '

'I want your report on my desk Monday morning, in triplicate,' was what he told Magneven before signalling for Varzi to pull into the box. He had delivered the news in a secluded corner of the garage, out of earshot of Finestrini, who was lurking about as always. 'Keep working, and we'll re-assess at Donington.'

'You're making a mistake,' was Varzi's reaction.

Feuereisen had noticed the sweat on Varzi's face, and his nervously twitching fingers. The real mistake, he had thought, was sending Varzi out to kill himself through exhaustion. 'Keep working, Varzi. We'll see you in Donington.'

'Is Pietsch here?'

'I beg your pardon?'

'Pietsch. He went off the track. I saw him climb out of his Maserati. Is he here?'

'We'll see you in Donington, Varzi.'

And that was 4pm. With the dark, sullen sky reflecting his mood, Feuereisen had offered Nuvolari – who had arrived at the track along with Bernd – a ride back to the hotel and a tentative contract for 1938. Nuvolari had been ecstatic, saying that he was just grateful for the chance to win again.

That evening, Feuereisen had called Rosemeyer to his hotel room to hash out a new contract. After eleven phone calls to the board, a deal had been brokered near midnight, which guaranteed that young Bernd Rosemeyer would become the highest paid sportsman in German history.

After this brutal day, Feuereisen had finally fallen asleep, courtesy of Dr. Magneven's little pills. The following morning, he is woken up by a call from the good doctor.

'How did you sleep, Dr. Feuereisen?'

'Like a baby, except I kept hearing other peoples' screams.'

'I have some bad news.'

Feuereisen opens his eyes. Another fucking day, he thinks.

'I spoke to Finestrini this morning,' says Dr. Magneven.

'News of Nuvolari talking to us has made the front page of the *Gazzetta*, has it?'

'No, sir. It's Varzi.'

'What about him?'

'He went back to the Savoia last night.'

'The Savoia? What's at the – oh … ' Feuereisen shuts his eyes, sighing deeply. He is certain this job will kill him in the end.

271

L'Isola Del Lido, February 16th, 1968

I can't wait any longer for Finestrini. It's time to leave. I've sorted the pages of my manuscript into some kind of chronological order and am about to file them in the folder when I notice an old article that I'd sellotaped to page 348 of the manuscript.

"ROSEMEYER IS THE WORLD'S FASTEST MAN

Giovanni Finestrini, October 25, Anno XV

Bernd Rosemeyer is now, officially, the fastest man in the world. The fastest man there has ever been. At the wheel of his slip-streamed Auto Union – the self-same car he raced at the AVUS Grand Prix in May – Rosemeyer reached an astonishing 422kph on the Frankfurt-Darmstadt autobahn. This was achieved during the *Rekordwoche*, the 'week of speed' in which Mercedes and Auto Union traditionally do battle. Such was his pace and Auto Union's domination of the *Rekordwoche*, that Mercedes and their star Rudi Caracciola packed up early and headed back home, leaving the autobahn all clear for Bernd Rosemeyer to sweep up another three world records and sixteen international class records by the end of the week.

As impressive as this was, though, I suspect it was the sight of Rosemeyer deliberately sliding his shining silver fish at over 200kph in celebration of his landmark record that will remain the highlight of the week for most observers; this was Rosemeyer in simply irresistible form, and who can blame him for show-boating after what has proven to be a difficult grand prix season?

But how does it feel to drive at 420kph on a public road? That's the question I asked the world's fastest man, and readers will probably be surprised to learn that Bernd's reply came in impeccable Italian. Perhaps Varzi taught the young German whippersnapper something after all!

'The speed itself is imperceptible. The car runs wonderfully smoothly in perfect obedience to the driver. The steering-wheel must not be held in a vice-like grip, but lightly, between the finger-tips, so as not to be influenced by the swaying of the body. At around 385kph, the joints in the concrete surface of the road are like blows, and cause a corresponding resonance in the car itself; this, however, disappears immediately at a greater speed. Passing under the road bridges, the driver receives a terrific blow on the chest, caused by the compressed air displaced by the car. Enormous concentration is required to keep the car in the middle of the road, for these blasts of air make the car swerve quite violently and have to be countered at lightning speed. After only a few minutes of this, the driver's nervous energy is simply exhausted, and although a ten-mile record attempt lasts only about two minutes and forty seconds, the strain is much greater than that of a grand prix."

I entrust the folder with the manuscript to my rucksack and take a final look around. Everything has been packed, the hotel room once more left to its ghosts. The number that I dial again just rings. Bugger it, I think, I will try again from the airport. I take the elevator down to the lobby. The man behind the reception desk seems genuinely sad to hear that I'm checking out.

'Has Mr. Finestrini left me a message?' I ask, inspecting the bill. This being Italy, I assume I've been screwed.

'Mr. Finestrini is in there,' he replies, motioning toward the restaurant.

I sign the bill distractedly, leaving my suitcase there in the lobby and walk with my rucksack slung over one shoulder. Finestrini sits alone, sipping on an espresso and reading the *Gazzetta*. He hears me arrive and stands to proffer a hand, his eyes revealing nothing much at all.

'I must apologize,' he says when I shake his hand. 'An unforeseen circumstance kept me away. Come, do sit down.'

'I'm actually late for my train. And I have a plane to catch from Milan.'

He places the *Gazzetta* down on the seat behind him.

'Back to America, then, Deutsch?'

Yes, I think. Back to America. Back to nothing.

Finestrini observes me for a moment. 'In that case,' he says briskly, 'I think I'll accompany you to Santa Lucia.' He grabs his coat and steers me toward the lobby. We step out into the freezing cold day, heading for the vaporetto stop on the Piazzale Santa Maria Elisabetta opposite the Hotel Riviera. When I ask Finestrini what he remembers of the record week in 1937, my words come out in great plumes of smoke.

'Not much,' he replies, hands at his sides, shuffling delicately along the icy promenade. 'I remember standing on an overpass, watching Bernd roar past. He went through faster than the blink of an eye, rushing faster than sound, so it was literally like watching a bullet. To go that fast on what was essentially a two-lane provincial road – it was mad really, looking back on it. Quite mad. That record took place on the Italian New Year – '

'New Year?' I interrupt him, puzzled.

'Mussolini decreed in '36 that we Italians were no longer to celebrate the traditional start of the year, but rather the start of the Fascist era that began October 28, 1922. So we were in the year XV.'

I shift my suitcase from one hand to the other. 'Varzi was a no-show at Donington at the end of '37.'

'He'd gone back to Ilse. There was nothing more to it than that.' Finestrini shields his face from the wind. 'And if there was, I wasn't aware of it; at the time, I was too busy reporting on Alfa Romeo's decision to return to grand prix racing, which meant that Ferrari was now taking on a new role as team manager for the Alfa Corse division. His first job was to entice Nuvolari back into the fold. Again. Despite my best efforts though, I couldn't get either man to confirm or deny the possibility of negotiations. Ferrari must have known that Nuvolari was holding out for a contract with Auto Union, and Nuvolari – being Nuvolari – probably didn't want to burn any bridges, given what had happened in '35. In early December, though, Nuvolari invited me to Berlin for the New Year celebrations.'

'Hold on, let me get this.' I grab the Carry-Corder in its leather housing from my rucksack and slide out the microphone. I pass it across to Finestrini. He looks at it and shakes his head.

'I think we'll go off the record from here on in, don't you?'

We welcomed 1938 in at the Esplanade Hotel in Berlin. Thousands of cheap balloons were floating around the main hall, but the mood that night was strangely subdued. Nuvolari's natural exuberance was usually a foil for his emotions, but tonight there was an irony to his smile that I put down to the loss of his son. Time doesn't really heal wounds: a man simply stops scratching the scab and moves on, stunted and scarred. Rosemeyer too was a father now, and he seemed to have aged since I'd last seen him; he looked stern that night, the way some men become when they realize the implications of fatherhood. Tazio, Bernd, and I decided to take a stroll in the Esplanade's courtyard garden sharing cigarettes in the cold.

'Driving for records is a smooth and easy task,' Bernd told us as we stood there smoking. 'The road is yours and yours alone: you don't have to worry about any other driver and what tricks he might play, or what might happen if one of the tyres on another car bursts and it zig-zags in front of you. I only have myself to think of, and that sits just fine with Bernd Rosemeyer.'

'He talks about himself in the third person now,' said Nuvolari. 'Does that make him a star, Finestrini?'

'I hear Mercedes will try to take your records back in January,' I said.

Rosemeyer glanced at me. There was that quiet certitude of his again that made him a champion. 'Record Week is in October,' he said dismissively. 'Running in January is not possible.'

'If Finestrini says it's a rumour, Bernd, you may as well make a note of it in your calendar.'

'I don't have one yet,' said Rosemeyer. 'It's still 1937 – it would be bad luck to have a calendar for next year already.'

'If you were Italian you'd already be in the year of our Duce fifteen,' Nuvolari said to me. 'Or is it sixteen?'

'Have you seen the schedule for next season?' I asked.

'No,' replied Nuvolari, 'I haven't even decided if I'll be racing next season.'

I looked at his toothy grin. 'Come on, Tazio, everyone knows that you've already signed for Auto Union.'

Bernd's head popped up.

'Everyone?' asked Nuvolari. 'I don't recall reading it in your comic. In any event, it's pure nonsense; I haven't signed anything yet. Dr. Porsche has offered me a VW franchise for when I retire, though. And that, you can print.'

'Retire? You?'

'What of it?' he asked quickly.

'Remember when you told me you'd never die in your bed?'

'All kinds of people die in their beds, Finestrini.'

Silently, we returned into the hall in time for the countdown. Carolina and Elly were waiting at the table, and I overheard Bernd say, 'Come, Elly, let's dance the New Year in, it'll give us good luck,' before leading her to the crowded dance floor. Carolina – who had aged so visibly over the last year – stood with Nuvolari away from the dance floor, hand-in-hand and watching the crowd count down to zero. They didn't speak, didn't even see each other anymore, I thought; and I left then, making my way back to the hotel through deserted streets.

◘

'In 1936,' Finestrini says, 'there had been forty international races; for 1938, only fifteen were scheduled. War was coming. We all felt it – not that anyone ever talked too much about it, except for Dreyfus, and that often made him the butt of our jokes. War, for these men, would have been nothing more than an inconvenience, and Dreyfus's "the sky is falling" routine did become a bit grating. But then he was Jewish, wasn't he, Jewish *and* French.'

'Was Varzi still at the Savoia?'

Finetrini looks over at the vaporetto that is skillfully drifting toward our jetty. 'None of us saw him again after October. Wait, no, that's not right; I remember speaking to Brivio in early January, and he told me that he'd seen Varzi in November, the two of them having decided to drive to Venice for the day. Here, actually, to the Lido. During the car ride, Brivio had seen Varzi inject himself in the leg, through his trousers. At the beach, they had played football with some friends before lunch, and Varzi had collapsed with exhaustion: he was in a bad way.'

We share a bench inside the vaporetto's main cabin that smells of rot and damp and sick, and we are alone when it begins to steam its way across the lagoon.

'Pietsch says Ilse never took drugs when they were married,' I say tentatively.

'He ought to know,' replies Finestrini, loosening his scarf.

'So was it Varzi who made her an addict?'

'Neubauer says it was Ilse who introduced Varzi to morphine, in Tunis, after the Balbo affair. I thought that was common knowledge.'

'She wasn't there, though. Brivio and Lunari both contend that Ilse was never at Tunis that weekend – she was in Milan.'

'It's a fact that she was ill, even with Pietsch.'

'Yes, she was no stranger to morphine. But it was Varzi – '

'Does it *have* to end in blame?' Finestrini interrupts.

'Even now, Elly still refuses to speak of her. Pietsch too. I can't help thinking that Ilse might have been the real victim here – the scapegoat for all of Varzi's failings.'

'Does a simple love affair between two fragile human beings not provide enough juicy material for your novel, Deutsch?' Finestrini asks scathingly.

I look away from him, away from his condescension. '*Do* you know what happened to her? To Ilse?'

'And so,' he replies, 'we come to Ilse. It's taken you long enough. But you know, if tragedy is what you want, I can give you better material.'

'She's pivotal to Varzi's story – '

'Nuvolari yet again screwed out of a contract by Auto Union for 1938, that was a tragedy.'

'Ilse – '

'But of course, the real tragedy was Bernd, wasn't it, Deutsch. With his month-old baby and new wife waiting for him at home while he went off to fulfill his destiny, that was tragedy, my friend.'

The weather in Frankfurt was awful; not only cold but windy too, and Rosemeyer was lucky his flight had even landed on the night of the twenty-seventh of January. That morning, Caracciola had broken the last of Bernd's records, the one that mattered most: He was clocked at 432kph, becoming the fastest man in history on a public road.

I'd been holed up in my hotel expecting Rosemeyer's run to be delayed when Dr. Magneven had phoned to tell me that Bernd was scheduled to begin his first attempt within the hour. I was still buttoning up my coat and not looking where I was walking when I collided with something wide and hard as I stepped out of the elevator in the lobby.

'*Bloß auf!*' said a voice.

I looked up to find Caracciola staring at me with amused hostility. Behind him stood von Brauchitsch and Neubauer. 'Pardon me, Rudi,' I said, rubbing my shoulder.

'Off on a world exclusive?' asked von Brauchitsch. 'Squirrels loose in the park?'

I grinned and started walking away.

'Your story is right here,' Neubauer shouted at my retreating back. 'Rudi Caracciola, the world's fastest man.'

'Not for long.' I waved for the doorman to hail me a cab and glanced over my shoulder. Three faces stared back at me, astonished.

'Bernd's going? In this weather?' Caracciola asked, with something akin to genuine concern.

'Surely not?' Neubauer pushed past his two drivers and took a step toward me. 'The wind is up, what are they thinking? Going out now – '

'He'll kill himself,' said von Brauchitsch. 'Let's go watch.'

We all climbed into Neubauer's white Mercedes that he'd just abandoned outside the hotel. Neubauer ground into first gear and bounced us off toward the autobahn.

'Your wife was right, Neubauer,' said von Brauchitsch sitting beside me on the back seat. 'You should have been a bus driver.'

'Yes, keep it up Manfred, and we'll see what *you'll* be driving next year.'

'So what was it like?' I asked Caracciola. 'Your record-shattering run?'

'It was hell.' Caracciola glanced away from the chaos unfolding beyond the windscreen, as Neubauer slipped past a tram with inches to spare. 'Those bridges give off minor explosive charges as you go through. They're unbelievably narrow too, so you just aim between them – and when you come out, there's nothing but silence before you're hit by this wave of sound that crushes your chest, sucking the air right out of you. At that speed, the mind is too slow to react, so you must compensate for that: you must hold the wheel as if it were a sword's foil, and project yourself ahead because if you get into any sort of trouble, you're in God's hands. A man at that speed doesn't have the ability to control the car, and I don't care who that man is.'

'Not even Neubauer,' said von Brauchitsch with a wide grin. Right on cue, Neubauer shifted into third gear with such a thud that I half expected the transmission to fall out from under us.

We arrived at the two-kilometre marker-point on the motorway leading out of Frankfurt at just past 11am. The autobahn had been sealed off by an army of soldiers. Bernd's Auto Union *Strumliniewagen* was just sitting there on the tarmac, poised for action. I had never seen anything like this sleek, silver projectile which hovered no more than an inch or two off the black tarmac. In the cockpit sat Bernd Rosemeyer in his white linen wind-helmet and white racing suit, staring ahead into the middle distance while Feuereisen squatted beside him, checking dials and making notes on his clipboard. Ludwig Wilhelm stood just behind the sloping rear-end, and from him we learnt that Rosemeyer had already returned from his first attempt, having failed to break Caracciola's record. The car had been running too cool, and Sebastian, Ludwig's twin brother, was busy sealing the radiator with tape. Caracciola hobbled over to the Auto Union and shared a warm embrace with Sebastian, who had been his co-driver during the 1931 Mille Miglia.

'Congratulations, Rudi!' said Bernd, spotting him.

Caracciola knelt down beside the Auto Union. Glancing into the cockpit, he seemed on the verge of saying something before contenting himself with a none-too-delicate slap across Rosemeyer's back. Hobbling back past Sebastian, I heard Caracciola whisper, 'You ought to wait until tomorrow morning.'

Sebastian spat on the asphalt. 'Bernd is adamant – he wants to get this over with and get back home.' Sebastian looked at Caracciola, and jibed, 'Congratulations on your record by the way – I guess you'll go down in history as the fastest man for the shortest amount of time.'

Rosemeyer, jailed in his aluminium rocket filled to the brim with fuel, glanced up at Ludwig. *'Du kannst versichert sein, ich merke es alleine, wenn es nicht geht. Ich will nur noch einmal rantasten.'* Ludwig nodded affirmatively: One more run and they'd all go home, record breakers or otherwise.

Communications were run out of a tent in which Feuereisen spoke to soldiers manning posts at every kilometre mark. Satisfied with the preparations, he signalled for Sebastian to begin the countdown.

It was 11:46am when Rosemeyer roared past us in a whirlwind

of noise and smoke. Caracciola watched him disappear into the distance. I found myself telling him: 'You should have said something.'

'It wasn't my place to put doubt in his mind,' replied Caracciola. 'Not now.'

Needing an outlet for my nerves, I stepped over to the tent. Feuereisen saw me, and I'm sure he would have told me to get lost if he weren't listening so intently to all the voices reporting back to him.

'Kilometre one, past, kilometre two, past, kilometre three, past, kilometre four, past, kilometre five, past, kilometre six, past, kilometre seven, past, kilometre eight, past … '

And then came the silence.

It should have taken Rosemeyer seven seconds to cover the kilometre between posts eight and nine. The seconds ticked away. Feuereisen waited, we all waited. Until, unable to stand it anymore, Feuereisen shouted, 'Kilometre nine! Kilometre nine!' I turned and stared at the Langen-Morfelden bridge far in the distance. 'Kilometre nine! Come *in*, damn it!'

A voice crackled through the static. 'Something's happened. He hasn't come past – we can see some dust and smoke back between us and post eight – we're headed there now.'

Feuereisen threw the telephone down and stormed out of the tent. Dr. Magneven was already at the wheel of his Horch. Feuereisen raced toward him and I watched the two men drive away.

'Bernd would never lose it on a straight road,' said Neubauer.

'Why not? I almost did,' replied Caracciola.

'He's probably playing one of his practical jokes.'

Caracciola shook his head. Moments later, when an ambulance took off down the autobahn, we knew something had gone seriously wrong.

We stood there waiting – for an hour, perhaps longer than that. The road was so narrow, the bridge ahead with its central pillar of concrete no more than three metres wide. Bernd would have aimed his car into that needle, travelling at one hundred metres a second. If his steering had been off by one degree, he would have been off the road in less than a heartbeat – a man couldn't be expected to endure such strain.

We watched them return from afar, the white Horch leading the ambulance. It all seemed so painfully slow. Feuereisen stepped out, ashen-faced, and was immediately surrounded by the press. I was about to join them when I noticed Dr. Magneven appear on the verge of the road. Caracciola and I encircled him as he lit a cigarette with steady fingers.

'He lost it just past the clearing,' Magneven said. 'Nothing left of the car: it's like it shed its skin. It sliced a tree down at the height of about a metre.'

None of us said a word.

'He was in the forest. Still had a heartbeat. He was just lying there, looking unscathed. Just staring up at the sky. We thought he was about to sit up.'

Caracciola turned away. I considered joining the scrum of reporters around Feuereisen, but instead I followed Rudi back to the Mercedes. It was left to von Brauchitsch to ask the question. 'Who's going to tell Elly?'

◘

'It was a lie of course,' says Finestrini calmly, watching a pack of tourists climb aboard our vaporetto.

'What was?'

'He collided with the bridge at 400kph – do you really think he looked unscathed, as Doctor Magneven suggested?'

'Why would he lie?'

'There were many lies told about Bernd's death – many. Then and now. What was poor Bernd thinking of in those final moments? His baby? Elly? Whatever it was, it would have lasted less than a second because the Auto Union had become a wing, taking off and somersaulting away before crashing into the trees. Six seconds is all it took to end Rosemeyer's one thousand days of glory.' Finestrini gazes at the tourists absently. 'Truth is, none of us understood what Auto Union had done to Bernd's car. We now know that Auto Union had created something along the lines of the world's first wing-car, but at the time, no one had any idea how it worked. Neubauer's theory was that the wind pressure on the body had been so immense that, once a piece was dislodged, the car had simply shed its aluminium skin, leaving nothing but the bare chassis – which meant that in the end, poor Rosemeyer had just been a man in a seat travelling at 400kph.'

'And the Nazis made a big thing of his death?'

'Even better than what we did for Campari. The SS came out in force; but all I remember is Neubauer saying, "To me, he is still alive. He simply climbed into his silver car one day and drove off to an unknown destination we must all make sooner or later". And Hühnlein at the graveside proclaiming, "He died a warrior, he died a soldier. He died for the Reich, *dulce et decorum est pro patria mori,*" and through it all Elly shed not a tear. And then we all left him there, poor Bernd, forever twenty-eight.

'I watched Nuvolari and Carolina accompany Elly and Bernd's boy to their car and lead the black-sedan procession back toward Berlin. Nuvolari had never driven so slowly. One thousand days: 26 May 1935 at the AVUS to the 28 January 1938: thirty-six grands prix, twelve wins, twenty-two podiums, European Champion in only his second full season, killed while going faster than any man before or since. He'd found a wife on the same day he'd claimed his first win, and he'd found death on the same day he'd lost his speed record. It was all so quick for Bernd, so quick and perfect it had to end in tragedy. You know, Caracciola's record remains unbeaten to this day.

'That evening I found Nuvolari in the hotel bar. He was already the wrong side of a few whiskys, and he looked exhausted. He told me he'd spent the afternoon in Elly's apartment along with Carolina who'd looked after Bernd Jr. while he'd helped pack Bernd's clothes into boxes; his suits, his racing gear, his black leather overcoat. First they throw away the man, Elly had told him, and then those who loved him throw away everything else.

' "Want one?" he'd asked when I shuffled quietly beside him at the bar. I ordered four. Nuvolari downed one and set to work on the second. "Quite a service," he said after a while, staring down at the rainbow ice in his drink. "Think they'll put me to rest like that?"

' "We don't have any stirring songs," I told him, "ours are far too romantic."

The vaporetto squeezes into the Grand Canal. 'The Palazzo Contarini-Fasan,' Finestrini tells me, pointing to a gothic building with a coat of arms on its pink walls. 'It's where Othello killed Desdemona.'

'I thought that was fiction.'

'Everything is fiction when you get right down to it,' he says.

'Nuvolari started the season with Alfa, yes?'

'Yes. Lasted only one race only though – one race that would end his decade-long partnership with Alfa and Ferrari.'

'This was – '

'At Pau, first race of the 1938 season.'

It was while I was admiring Dreyfus's fluidity around the houses in Pau that I spotted it from the corner of my eye; unexpected as it was sudden, like lightning on a clear summer's day. The Nuvolari who tore out of the tunnel was a comet. He was standing in the cockpit with his legs dancing in a bathtub of fire, the Alfa headed for a row of houses at a serious gallop. I watched horrified as he chose the only option available to him: He jumped.

Landing on his feet, his legs couldn't match the speed at which he'd hit the road and suddenly he was somersaulting away down the road like a rubber-man: the grotesque flight ended perhaps twenty metres later when he thudded into the wall of a house. I found myself running. When I got to him, he'd been stripped naked; his face was badly singed, his hair and eyebrows smoking fibrously, blood fleeing from wounds on his dirty face, the bottom of his seared legs carbonized by the burns. He was conscious and screaming when the ambulance carried him off to the hospital. I hitched a ride there with Bazzi later that afternoon. We found him in bed, his burnt flesh soothed by foul-smelling ointment. He lay with his eyes shut, clearly in some pain, moaning as he was, but the doctor had assured us there were no broken bones or permanent damage.

Nuvolari opened his eyes as we walked in. 'Finestrini,' he whispered. He looked embalmed, ready for the tomb. 'I have a good quote for your funnies – "better to die pasted on a wall than grilled like a chicken".'

Bazzi laughed. Nuvolari's look of contempt wiped the sheen clean from his smile. 'I'm done with it, Bazzi. I'm done with this shit. *You*,' he pointed that chin at me, 'here's your headline: "Tazio Nuvolari Retires".'

'Nuvolari, relax,' said Bazzi. 'We know what the problem is.'

'No.' Nuvolari sucked up breath, his bruised body glistening like underdone meat. 'No. I'll be dead before I drive for Ferrari again, do you hear me? You tell Ferrari that – you tell him I'll be a dead man before I drive one of his shit-boxes again.'

◘

To our right is the church of San Geremia. In it, Finestrini tells me, lie the remains of Santa Lucia. 'She refused to be married off, refused to have her dowry given to anyone but the poor. When her would-be-husband told her how much he loved her, how beautiful her eyes were, she tore them out and gave them to him on a plate: "Now let me live for God," she told him.

'The Venetians have a thing for corpses, you know, Deutsch; even St Mark was stolen and brought here.' The vaporetto makes way for a gaggle of gondolas passing us from the station: we are close now.

'The Futurists hated Venice,' Finestrini says, standing in anticipation, 'they wanted to burn the gondolas, "the rocking chairs of idiots" they called them.'

'Didn't Varzi make a comeback?' I ask, following Finestrini off the vaporetto.

'I wouldn't call it that,' he replies. 'He entered the race at Tripoli in a privately entered Maserati in May of '38 and managed eleven laps before pulling out.'

We are on the top step leading into the station. Behind me, Venice sinks into its own filth. I turn away from it, from that vista as tender as a butterfly and that brittle sky, turn from it all and walk into the buzz of the station.

'Were you there? In Tripoli?'

'No. Neither were Auto Union – they'd fallen apart after Rosemeyer's death, and rumour had it they were shutting down their race team. I couldn't go because Cristoferi had cut my travel allowance.' Finestrini laughs. 'Probably my own doing, because I had written an article entitled "The End of an Era", in which I'd suggested that Italy was no longer a player in international motorsports after Nuvolari's retirement. Cristoferi had agreed with me, and suggested that I explore new avenues.'

'Which you did,' I tell him.

'Sorry?'

'Varzi.'

'What about him?'

I turn to face Finestrini. He stands inches from me now. 'How did it end?'

'How did *what* end?'

'Varzi was at the Savoia. And then what, he just left? With Ilse?'

Finestrini points at my cigarette. 'Mind if I have one of those?'

'No one,' I tell him as we stand in the echoing main hall, 'ever wrote about it. I can't find any reports, any documents – '

'No one wrote about it because it doesn't matter,' he says, and his voice is loud enough to rebound back at us.

I lean forward and light his cigarette. 'It matters because – '

'So that's it, is it?' he interrupts.

'I'm sorry?'

'That's what you had planned for me. The antagonist, yes? In your little narrative?'

'No, of course not. It's just – how can I write about something I don't know?'

'By not writing about it at all.' He takes a drag, coughs, and throws the cigarette on the marble floor. 'What do you *think* happened, Deutsch?' he asks.

'I think you betrayed them,' I reply, crushing his cigarette under my boot. Finestrini shakes his head and walks away. I follow him silently through the hall. We come to rest beneath the departures board.

'Do you have time for a coffee?' he asks.

I have twenty minutes. I follow him into a café and we grab a pair of high-stools, he ordering a white wine and I a glass of mineral water. He knows. He knows why I'm here now. He looks at me as if perusing a menu before he licks his lips and places both elbows on the table. 'It was the end of May in '38 when Viganò called me.'

◉

Viganò sat opposite me in the café across from the Savoia. He'd been a soldier for Varzi, and a good one at that.

'She's leaving,' he told me, and I could see a bead of sweat make its way down his collar.

'Leaving? For where?'

'Home. Frankfurt. Her mother is ill.'

'When?'

'Today – this afternoon. She's on the three-fifteen.'

'And Varzi? Will he go with her?'

Viganò lifted his face and stared at me. He knew then, I thought, he knew when he shook his head and sipped his coffee.

I mulled it over on the tram on the way back to the office through a glorious day in May. Varzi had made a fool of himself in Tripoli, and despite Eugenio Siena having killed himself in his Alfa – poor Siena who'd offered Nuvolari a drive way-back in his Maserati team, Siena who'd won the Mille Miglia with Nuvolari in '34 – people had noticed. Balbo had noticed. The phone shrilled to life in my office and a woman's voice I couldn't quite place asked me how I was feeling.

'I'm fine – '

'This is Pina,' the voice said. 'Achille's mother.'

'Mrs. Varzi, what a surprise – it's been a long time – '

'Since you were here hunting, Signor Finestrini.'

'It's nice to hear from you again.'

'You won't think so,' she said, 'when I'm through talking to you.'

'Ma'am?'

'Don't pretend you don't know, Signor Finestrini .'

I found a cigarette. 'Johnny, please, Signora – '

'Do you know, how long she is gone for?'

'Who?' The silence was my reply. 'Oh. Her mother, I'm told, is ill, so – '

'Long enough, then, for something to be done.'

'I don't understand. What do you think – '

'Signor Finestrini, we're all aware of your connections in Rome.'

'Signora – '

'She's a foreigner in this country, isn't she?'

'Signora, there's nothing I can – '

'It'll mean the end of your friendship with my son of course,' she went on as if I'd not spoken. 'And it will no doubt get out; others, I imagine, will not trust you as once they did.'

◘

'What did you do?' I ask.

Finestrini looks at me.

'You called Ciano, didn't you?'

'I heard from Varzi maybe a week later,' replies Finestrini, his hand absently stroking the glass of wine. 'He called me from the Savoia to tell me Ciano's men had come and confiscated his passport.'

' "That,' I told him, "is not the half of it, Achille – they're going to take your license as well."

' "They've done that already," he informed me.

' "Your race license, Varzi. The RAIC confirmed it this morning."

' "Finestrini," he said after a moment, "I can trust you, can't I?" '

Finestrini watches me smoke. 'Viganò called me the week after, it must have been June sometime I suppose, to let me know Ilse was on the night train back to Milan. She'd been gone almost two weeks by then, and Varzi had bought all sorts of gifts to celebrate her return.'

'Did you call Ciano? Did you tell him?'

'She was stopped at the border,' he tells me, ignoring my question. 'And there her passport was confiscated, and she was turned back.'

'How did Varzi react?'

'He called me that night, asked me for my help. I suggested we meet in the café across the road from the Savoia.'

◉

'It was a bleached Varzi who entered the café just past 8pm. He was high, I could detect immediately the eyes that glanced about like a beaten dog before they spotted me sitting in the corner.

'What the fuck's happening, Finestrini?' he asked sitting down opposite me.

'Ciano,' I told him.

'What about him?'

'He's taken a personal interest in your affair.'

'What affair? Ilse?'

'Ilse, yes. And the drugs.'

'Why? What does it even matter anymore?'

I shrugged, set my drink down, 'Varzi, I'm sorry, but you need to accept certain things here.'

'What are you talking about?'

'Ilse is not coming back to Italy. And you are not leaving. Please, you must try and understand what I'm saying to you: Duce himself has decided this. It's done.'

Varzi tried to speak but what was there to say? Was it unjust? Madness? How could they just take his life from him? His lover, his racing, all of him – how could anonymous men take all of this from him? I imagined it all crossed his mind then. But none of it was destined to fall from his lips.

'Varzi, I spoke to Ugo today.'

'Ugo?'

'Ricordi – the Auto Union rep'.'

'Fuck him – what's he got to do with this?'

'Your name came up. With Bernd dead, and von Delius too, and Stuck gone, and Tazio out of the game, they're in the market aggressively for a top-line driver.'

'What are you on about, Finestrini?'

'I'm saying Ilse is gone,' I replied. 'I'm saying it's time for Varzi to return.'

'*Varzi to return?*' He squinted those eyes at me and behind the pin-prick pupils I could actually read his astonishment. 'What am I, a fucking marionette? You people have no fucking right to decide who – fucking – ' I said nothing. Something, though, must have registered then. 'What are you saying here, *actually,* Finestrini?'

'That unless Balbo follows through with his promise to lob a few bombs into Mussolini's office, you're simply going to have to accept that Ilse is gone. I'm sorry.'

'You're sorry?'

I looked away.

'How did they know?' he asked suddenly.

'What?'

'How did they know that Ilse had left for Frankfurt, how did they know that?'

I shrugged.

'How did they know she was coming back today? On that train?' His face had a feral snarl, eyes squinched and menacing. I'd heard stories, we all had, but I'd never come face-to-face with this Achille Varzi. This, I thought, this was the Varzi who rivals had encountered on a blind curve in the rain, the Varzi who'd intimidated a generation of equals. This was the Varzi men had learnt to fear and despise.

'You fucking Fascist piece of shit. You – *you* fucking did this.'

'Achille, you're – you misunderstand.'

'Then *help* me understand. Because they've taken everything from me, they've taken everything and now this. '

'No, Achille – you lost it all, you threw it away –'

His fist slashed out and collected me in the face. It was a short blow, a boxer's blow, what they call a cross. It snapped into my face across the table and I was on the floor holding my nose together as a waterfall of blood burst through my fingers before I'd even had time to react. When I looked up through my tears, I found the waiter staring down at me and Varzi long gone.

■

'You look,' Finestrini tells me with his face tilted just so, 'as if you're working up to asking me something , Deutsch.'

I stare into the darkness of his eyes. 'You forced them apart. Varzi and Ilse. Did you even regret that? Did you stop for a moment and think of Ilse? Alone? A drug addict, because of Varzi, penniless, stranded by herself in Germany? Shunned by everyone she had ever known – blamed for Varzi's failings? Did you stop for a minute and consider that? Consider *her?*'

Finestrini sniffs the dank air with lips pursed. 'No,' he says, 'but if you're going to judge, judge what I did by the result.'

'And what was that?'

'Varzi tried every contact he knew including his uncle the senator, but every call ended in one place: Ciano's Office for Foreign Affairs. And there every inquiry died. Ilse Pietsch was no longer welcome in Italy. Viganò, through some contacts I'd rather not divulge, sorted Ilse an apartment in Munich where she received a weekly supply of morphine hidden in perfume bottles; in return, Varzi received a stream of letters.'

'Once a week they would speak over the phone as spring turned into a bleak and indifferent summer. Varzi didn't leave the hotel. By the end of June, he gave up trying to secure a lift on Ilse's ban: the two were separated by less than three hundred miles, but the border was impenetrable. Ilse's calls gradually began to fade, stretching out interminably, and when she did call, it was only to tell him she was broke, she needed more money, more drugs, she needed – she needed, but times were difficult now, even for Varzi.'

'Viganò's doctor was arrested late that summer, and Varzi was in bad shape until Viganò managed to sort a new contact. By that time, Ilse had been on the phone seven, eight times a day, sounding more and more desperate. And then the calls abruptly stopped. When Varzi finally got hold of Viganò's contact in Munich, he was told the apartment had been abandoned. And then,' Finestrini glances at his wrist-watch and downs his glass of wine, 'it all came to a head.'

◙

Viganò had sounded more distressed than usual over the blower.

He sat before me on his third espresso. 'The manager at the Savoia called me this morning into his office,' he was saying with the elasticity of caffeine gushing through his sweating body, 'told me Varzi's credit-line with the bank has been cut. The Savoia wants payment for three months rent but there's no cash.' Viganò looked at me pleadingly. 'There's no cash at all. And Varzi's upstairs vomiting his guts out; what am I supposed to do? He tells me to go get dope but with what? Where? So I called you.'

I sipped my espresso. In his eyes, in those haunted eyes of his, I could see some sort of resolve building. 'Look, Finestrini, I can't do this no-more.'

'Then don't.'

'Don't what?'

'Why don't you go home?'

'Home?'

'Back to Foggia,' I said. 'Go home for a while. Rest.'

'Now? But what about Varzi?'

'Leave it with me.'

'I can't just abandon him.'

'You want to, don't you? For months you've been begging for a way out.'

'That's not – I can't just leave.'

'You're not.'

'I don't understand.'

'You don't have to. All you have to do is go.'

'Just like that?'

'Just like that.'

'What will happen – to Varzi I mean.'

'I told you – leave it with me.'

That was the same day I captured the front page of the *Gazzetta* with a story about Nuvolari signing up with Auto Union. "Nuvolari Returns!"

□

'So you left him there?' I ask. 'You left Varzi at the Savoia.'

Finestrini downs his wine and taps his wrist watch. 'Your train will be boarding by now. Come, let's walk and I'll tell you what I did.'

*

'I met her downstairs from her apartment on the Via Marchiondi. She came in the late afternoon smelling of the summers of my youth. I had my pitch worked out – had scripted it during the night, sleeplessly playing the scene out in my mind – and the words rolled off my tongue as we sat in the small café across from her palazzo.

'Ilse,' I told Norma Colombo, 'is no longer around. Things have happened. Varzi is at the Savoia, alone.'

'And his drugs?'

'He hasn't had any for three days,' I said. 'By now he'll be climbing the walls.'

'Why not?'

'I'm sorry?'

'Why doesn't he have drugs?'

'It doesn't matter, Norma.'

'Doesn't it?'

'All that matters is that he's alone and in a world of hurt. He needs friends now, and there aren't many of those around anymore.'

'So why,' she asked, 'are we here?'

*

'I drove her to the Savoia in my ailing Bianchi,' Finestrini tells me as we walk toward the stairs leading up to the platforms. 'She asked – and I was surprised by her interest – about Ilse, and my reply was vague. I assured her that Ilse was fine – at home, I lied, with her family. Truth was, I had no idea where Ilse was then – didn't know and didn't care.

'Norma told me not that long ago,' Finestrini pauses before the marble, indented stairs, 'what happened that afternoon. Varzi, she said, was in bad shape, shivering and smelling of almonds when he'd answered the door to the suite, his arms torn and bleeding, his eyes dark pools of rage.

293

' "What are you doing here?" Varzi had asked, and Norma had replied, "I heard they want you out of the hotel. So I've come to help you out." She said he'd tried to dismiss her, but she'd placed one finger on his parched, blistered lips and said, "Come, Achille. It's time."

'I saw them,' says Finestrini, 'saw them come through the doors of the Savoia while I sat in my Bianchi. He was wearing a seersucker suit, and it seemed to float on him, made him look a fool, a clown. Made him look what he was – a thirty year old drug addict with his life in a tired bag held in one sagging arm. She led him by the elbow into a cab. I knew where they were headed of course, having secured Varzi a room at the Villa Egea the day before with help from Dr. Magneven who'd assured me that it was the best detox' programme in Italy.

'They arrived in the night. The villa was perhaps twenty miles out of Modena, and a nurse had welcomed them, helped Varzi from the cab and there, Norma had kissed him chastely on the cheek.

'Varzi had stood there and watched Norma's cab flicker away like a summer firefly. And I had gone back to my office to find a press release courtesy of Auto Union confirming Tazio Nuvolari as their number one driver for the remainder of 1938. He would be wearing a red leather helmet in honour of his friend, Bernd Rosemeyer.'

We climb the stairs slowly, our shoes sinking in the hollowed imprints that have come before us.

'Varzi convalesced through the summer and into the autumn. He was released in January of '39. Norma told me he went straight back to Galliate, to his family home, and asked her to spend the winter. She accepted the invitation.'

'And Ilse?' I ask.

Finestrini lets the name hang. 'Why,' he asks eventually, out of breath, 'are you so obsessed with her, Deutsch? This book of yours – you tell me it's about Varzi, yes?'

'Yes.'

'And yet we always come back to Ilse. Why is that? Why always Ilse?'

'Because,' I reply, 'I made a promise.'

'What promise?'

'Do you know? What happened to her? Don't you want to know?'

'Hans Stuck, after the war – he'd divorced Paula by then, left her for another woman – told me he'd seen Ilse in '39, in Munich. She was living in a hotel, broke and drugged up. She tried to commit suicide – Stuck was there, saw it happen. It – she was a total bloody mess.'

'And you didn't feel responsible?'

He shrugs away the question. 'Tell me, what promise?'

'It wasn't her fault,' I tell him. 'She was the one who was abandoned, eaten up by your world. She's nothing in your story,' I tell him, 'she was always a nothing. And that's why I care.'

'So this is your chivalry speaking, is it?' he asks when we climb the final stair.

'What?

'This interest of yours in Ilse – it's not about her. This is about you, Deutsch. This is about selling this book of yours – the writer who finally discovered what happened to the German slut who destroyed the racing career of Achille Varzi – that's your interest, that's the only thing you care about. Because you have nothing else to sell, do you – it's as I said, it's all been told already, and you knew that the day you bloody sent me your first letter. It's all been told but for that; but for Ilse's fate. So please, save me your self-indulgent shit, my friend – you're using her as Varzi used her, as all the men in her life used her.' He laughs then, a wheezing thing rasping with contempt. 'And this is why you came? All the way from New York City? All the way from America? For this? For *her*?'

Before us, on the concrete ground, a colony of gulls peck away at a half-dead pigeon lying on its wing. Finestrini pauses to watch. 'You're looking for a bad guy, but what you've found, Deutsch, is a man who was just doing his job. I was a journalist…that's all.'

'You could have helped her.'

'How? She would never go home to her mother in Wiesbaden. She was a grown woman who made her own choices.'

'Her life fell apart because of what you did.'

'There are winners and losers in everything we do, Deutsch.'

'So you have no regrets about what you did?'

He feints a kick to clear the gulls away from their savagery. 'No… no, Deutsch, I don't. Ilse, my friend, is best left to her secrets. And none of it mattered anyway, not when the war came.'

'That's your excuse? The war?'

He walks beside me into the station, struggling for breath, but I'm in no mood to slow my pace as I listen to him speak.

◉

Nuvolari led in his Auto Union Type D. The track that rambled over the tramlines through the Kalemegdan Park in the centre of Belgrade was slick with the September rain, the gleaming, cobbled turns sharp and abrupt. This was to be Nuvolari's first win since he'd dominated the tail-end of the '38 season, and as I stood there in the makeshift pits watching him control the gap back to von Brauchitsch in the Mercedes, I could think of no more fitting end to the world we had created. That this was to be the last grand prix for some time to come, none of us that day had any doubts, not since Germany had invaded Poland two days earlier. Caracciola had seen it coming and had refused to fly in for the Belgrade Grand Prix. Von Brauchitsch, who had, had tried to flee the night before after hearing of the invasion, but Neubauer had cornered him at the airfield just as he was about to board a Junkers flight.

'When war calls, a von Brauchitsch will answer,' had been Manfred's line, but Neubauer wasn't buying his chauvinism – not when he'd discovered that old Manfred was booked on the evening flight to neutral Switzerland. So poor Manfred had been brought back to race, and there he was in a resentful second place. Not that it meant much, since only five cars had taken the start – two Mercedes, two Auto Unions, and a Bugatti driven by local lad Bosko Milenkowitsch.

The news came to me with three laps remaining. It was Dr. Magneven who called me over, and I could see what he had to say on his face like a headline.

'The United Kingdom, France, New Zealand, and Australia

have declared war on Germany,' he said.

'And Italy?' I asked.

He looked at me blankly.

I turned my mind to the race and Tazio Nuvolari. The last one standing, the man whose destiny it was to die for patria, but there he still was, the last one standing in the last grand prix of our cursed generation. I felt for him, for Tazio banging about in that Auto Union with its tail sliding around in merry delight like a sidewalk drunk milking the crowd for applause and a few cents. And then he was rolling down pitlane toward me, ignition cut, chequered flag dropped, gloved hand waving at the crowd one final time. By then news had spread amidst the spectators, and it was muted applause that heralded Belgrade's first-ever grand prix winner. Nuvolari climbed from the cockpit reluctantly, his goggled-eyes seeking me out. He placed his steering-wheel deliberately upon the red-leather seat of his cockpit. About him were the faces of our world – those who had survived – Neubauer, Feuereissen, Sebastian, Ludwig, Hühnlein, they were all there, silent under that cold Belgrade sky.

'Well, Finestrini,' Nuvolari had asked then, 'what the hell are we going to do now?'

◻

'I spent the war in Milan, at the Zona Territoriale Aeronautica, until the Germans arrived, then I fled to Berne, to work for the Americans. In October of '44 they bombed the Alfa factory – they'd levelled Ferrari's shop in Modena earlier that year – destroying it completely, and that was that, too.'

'Did you keep in touch?' I ask. 'With Varzi? Or Nuvolari?'

'No. Really, it was not possible. Gasoline had been rationed in '40, and trains re-routed for military purposes. Varzi started a trucking business, of all things, early on in the war, and churned out quite a profit; Nuvolari saw the war out in Switzerland, Caracciola did the same, while Louis Chiron became involved with the Resistance helping downed allied soldiers find their way out of France through Monaco. Or that was the legend he told after the war, anyway. And Elly, she wrote a biography about her husband. Her book was a runaway success, and became very much part of Nazi lore – sacrifice and what not.'

We walk along the platform toward my train, following the passenger cars back into the cold.

'The *Gazzetta* was back in business by early '46, and I was assigned my own editorial desk.' Finestrini smiles. 'A promotion based on the fact that I had enough money to allow me a bit of travel since the 'paper wasn't even paying a salary at that stage so, I could write pretty much what I wanted.'

I set one foot onto a metal stair leading up into the second-class coach. I turn to Finestrini and offer him my hand. He takes it into his. Cold.

'I'm sorry,' he says, 'for wasting your time.' He sniffs the damp, cold air. 'But tell me, how is Ilse? Is she still married?'

I hesitate with his hand in mine.

'You've met her?'

'Yes,' I reply. 'In December. She lives in Wiesbaden. She – no one ever told her, how it all ended between her and Varzi. She asked me to find out.'

He smiles. 'She always had that effect on men,' he says. 'I see you too were unable to turn her down. Why didn't you just ask me?'

'She said you'd lie. To protect Varzi. His legacy.'

If he is offended, he guards it well. 'I'm glad to see her paranoia remains intact. And you found her well?'

I shake my head. 'No. She's been ill for a while.'

Finestrini slides his hand from mine 'I'm sorry to hear that. She was never blessed with health, though, was she? And so now you know. Does it help?

'She always assumed it,' I reply. 'That you'd betrayed them. She loved him, you know. She still loves him.'

'It wasn't meant to be,' Finestrini tells me. 'They'd have killed each other in the end. I really believe that. I did what I thought was right.'

'For who?'

'For Varzi,' he replies. 'For Achille Varzi, Italy's great champion. But I never wished her any harm. I hope she knows that. Maybe you'll tell her that.'

I turn from him then and step up onto the coach, about to muddle my way down the corridor to my compartment when I sense his hesitancy. I look down at this old man standing there on the platform, watch his hand slither under his loden coat. He withdraws a dark blue Moleskine notebook and, after what seems an instant of doubt, holds it out with a resolutely stiff arm.

'I had this sent overnight from Milan. I – until a moment ago, I wasn't sure if I'd even give it to you. But I think yes. Take it. Here, Joe Deutsch. Take it and use it as you wish.'

Stunned, I accept the notebook just as the door begins to beep and shut, cutting us apart with a mechanical whisper. He catches my eye through the reinforced glass. I watch him shuffle away and dissolve into the crowd.

I find an empty seat by the window and gingerly open the notebook. The train bounces forward edgily before finding its drive.

OVERDRIVE
RACING IN RUINS

We glorify war—the world's only hygiene—militarism, patriotism, the destructive gesture of liberators, the beautiful ideas for which we die, and the scorn of women.

– The Futurist Manifesto, F. T. Marinetti, 1909

Genoa, May 1st, 1946

Achille Varzi I had not seen since the summer of '37. Almost ten years and still I could feel the impact of his fist in my face. It'd been a long goodbye, ten long years worth of injury, but when I saw him again on that filthy cold spring afternoon in Genoa, I couldn't help but feel a tinge of regret: ten years and forty million dead separated us, but really, it was always Ilse – Ilse who'd vanished in the spring of 1939, sucked-up into the fissure of the war, it was Ilse who'd always be between us.

Varzi's belly showed an indulgent paunch, his face rotund and dripping a little fat and no longer set in that self-satisfied smirk of certainty. Standing beneath a black umbrella with the rain determined to burn into his dark blue three-piece suit, he was, I had to remind myself, barely forty now. We stood on the deck of the MS *Vulcania* that would take us to the new world, a world that had never known the monophonic bray of sirens or the closing thump of bombs in the night, he on his way to the Indy 500, I on my first cross-Atlantic assignment since 1937. It was impossible not to remember that crossing – to remember Tazio's boy Giorgio, dead all these years – and not compare this rickety liner to the glory of the *Rex*. She had been another victim of the war, as had Bernd's *Bremen*, and the *Normandie* too. But I suppose the well-heeled had no need of a luxury liner now – either dead or long since fled.

Below us on the filthy dock stood an army of emigrants, Europe's flotsam cowering with their sallow hungry faces waiting to be straggled onto the *Vulcania* along with their bedraggled belongings. War had been kind to Varzi: addiction-free and married to his Norma, he welcomed me behind a sardonic, knowing smile that warmed my guts.

'Finestrini,' he said, beckoning me closer to share his umbrella, 'you're looking old – as is that coat of yours.'

That's all there was to it. That afternoon, after we'd set sail, he invited me up to the first-class salon to sip chamomile tea and smoke his American cigarettes, and it wasn't long before we'd settled into a rhythm of memories half-recalled and half-told all the while avoiding – whether by design or fortitude on his part

I do not know – any mention of Ilse. I wondered whether he had any regrets – the Indy 500 would, I reminded him, be his first race since 1938. He'd been a young man then, his best years ahead of him. Varzi merely shrugged. Sometime during the war I'd gone through the major grands prix through the 1930s, and I'd spent a good week tabulating results to finally draw up a definitive list. I wrote it out for Varzi on a napkin.

Wins: Caracciola – 21; Chiron – 15; Nuvolari – 15; Rosemeyer – 12; Varzi – 10.

'I thought I'd won more,' Varzi said before enumerating his wins, one by one, to miss none at all. Coming up with my ten, he noted that he'd won the Mille Miglia and Targa in the same year, and that those should count for more.

It sounded a bit hollow, and he quickly changed the subject to Balbo who'd been shot down by friendly fire over Tobruk in '40 together with his family while trying to land with the sun at his back. 'Assassinated,' Varzi said, and it was, he added, the only decent thing Duce ever did for us. We shared memories, Varzi and I, as the *Vulcania* sailed west over that ocean gray beneath a sky that promised little aside from misery.

In '43, Varzi said, Italy had finally dropped its veil and showed the world what a used-up sloppy old whore she had always been: You people have no honour and no shame, he said, you ran and left us to die, all of us, you left us all to die. 'But we knew already, didn't we, Finestrini, we knew back in '37 what kind of shits we were dealing with. *Didn't* we?' he repeated, and his eyes fell on me until I looked away.

We spoke of Hühnlein, 'that fat bastard' who'd been promoted to head of military transport before dying in '42 in the assured conviction of victory, and Varzi insisted on denigrating Italy, 'la patria' he called it, and it sounded as if he was about to wretch.

He told me of a friend who'd been at Rostov – do you remember Hasse, he said as an aside, you know he died in Stalingrad in '43? – and had returned from the Russian Front filthy rich – they'd all done it, he said, those behind the front lines, they'd all worked the blackmarket leaving the boys on the Don without food or weapons or boots – that's who we are, he said.

That's why he was off to South America, to Argentina after Indianapolis. 'I'm off to join the Nazis, Finestrini, at least they died fighting, not stealing from their own and fucking whining.' We spoke of those who'd not turned up for the Coupe Robert Benoist – neither Varzi nor I had made it either to the first post-War European race held on a cool Sunday in Paris in September 1945, and neither of course had Benoist.

In the salon sipping on American bourbon now that the night had turned ugly as it must when men assemble the crumbs of war, he recalled Benoist and his days at Bugatti with much fondness. The last time I'd seen Benoist was at Varzi's family home – when was that I wondered?

'When you came hunting,' he replied, lighting another Lucky. 'Last time you saw my mother too. You still have those socks?' I confessed I'd lost them in the war. 'For the best,' he said, and I quickly turned the subject back to Benoist. I suggested his fate had been an awful one but Varzi pointed one of his American cigarettes down at the carpet and the mass of people presumably huddled down below.

'A man shouldn't survive a war,' he said, 'either he gets rich or he dies gloriously. Surviving war is wasted opportunity.'

The *Vulcania* sailed into a storm, and I fought to keep my guts down. I'd heard of Benoist's war, but Varzi had the definitive tale, he said, told to him by Chiron that summer: How he'd been enticed into the British secret service, the SOE, by none other than his old Bugatti team-mate Willy Williams: How the Gestapo had trapped him in Paris in '44 while he visited his dying mother – betrayed, Varzi said, by his own brother. The Nazis had taken him to Buchenwald – there they'd beaten him for days before hanging what was left of him from a meat-hook, nothing more than a slab of meat, killed, murdered by nobodies who didn't know or care who he was, who he had been before the war. I imagined he went with dignity, that beautiful man, he was one of those, wasn't he, one of those who would look death in the eye and nod his consent.

And what of von Brauchitsch, Varzi asked. The baron, I said, had warred at the Ministry of Armaments between '42 and '45, and he'd taken a wife. It was with her that he'd fled to Bavaria when the Russians had come to Berlin – he was living there now, I said, having heard of it from Rudi, in a shack – a veritable shack without water or plumbing near Starnberg, utterly broke but, considering his family connections, mercifully free. Caracciola had offered to send him to Argentina for old times' sakes, an idea that von Brauchitsch was keen to take up: in post-war Germany, Manfred had discovered, the von Brauchitsch name that'd opened so many doors in the past now guaranteed only the opening of a cell door.

We spoke of Dr. Porsche who – in '45 – had been invited to Baden-Baden by the French Minister of Industry, Marcel Paul. Turned out to be a trap, Porsche – dear Uncle Doctor Porsche as Rosemeyer had insisted on calling him – arrested and charged with Nazi activities. It was nothing more than a kidnapping, and I'd heard a rumour Nuvolari was set to pay his ransom.

'He'll rot then,' was Varzi's reply. 'Not even God has ever managed to get a loan out of Tazio.' Not even Ferrari, I said, and we shared a good belly laugh reminiscing over Ferrari's mythical tightness as the *Vulcania* lurched and pitched off waves that burst over her decks.

Ferrari had bought two barren fields near the village of Maranello in '43 where construction had recently begun on a new workshop and factory. 'Bought if for less than the dirt was worth,' I said, and Varzi repeated that it was proper that a man of substance either dies or enriches himself from war.

'And we know Ferrari was never going to die for glory – not even his own. ... And what of Tazio?' Varzi asked then. 'He must be fifty now. Last I heard he'd taken his family to Lanzo d'Intelvi.' Fifty-four, I corrected. And then I told him about Alberto, his younger son, dying too. Only eighteen. When I'd finished, Varzi had averted his face, and I thought that perhaps it was to hide the tears that rolled from his eyes.

'Death has refused me for too long: Now I go and find him,' was what Nuvolari had said, and Varzi smiled that smile of his and, before we called it a night, told me there was nothing Tazio could do, he was destined to die in bed because The Flying Mantuan was too fast for the devil.

New York City, May 14, 1946

We stepped out of our hotel onto Sixth Avenue. New York City was unaltered from my last visit, untouched by the dead: colossal, anxious, energized, rude, self-absorbed and self-aggrandizing. They had won the war, Varzi observed, and hadn't even lost a building. It was through rotting valleys of trash between those steel-and-concrete cliffs that I led Varzi to W49, 55th Street. There, a green awning stretched out its sheltering welcome, with *René Dreyfus – le Gourmet* written upon it in large letters. Varzi had a good chuckle at that.

Behind the dark oak bar stood a balding René Dreyfus; he sported an enormous pair of bookish spectacles and a suit with massive wings. Varzi said that he looked like a failed magician. Varzi and Dreyfus had never been close, but when I'd heard that René had opened a restaurant in Manhattan, I'd thought it would be a good idea to reunite these two men. Dreyfus was holding court with three suited gentlemen on the wrong side of cocktail hour when Varzi followed me to the bar.

'Campari and soda,' said Varzi, interrupting whatever Dreyfus was saying to the men in fluent English.

Dreyfus's head snapped up. 'Good God,' he said. 'If it isn't Achille Varzi in the flesh.'

Dreyfus found us a table where, after our meal – a good one – he joined us with a bottle of aged cognac. His brother Maurice took over at the bar, but the lunchtime crowd had mostly dispersed by then, lubricated for another afternoon of empire building. Dreyfus told us that he been stranded in America when he'd come for the Indy 500 back in 1940, the weekend Germany had decided to invade France. He'd opened a restaurant in Closter, New Jersey, before, with the allied landings in Italy, joining the US Army as a translator. He'd entered Paris as a liberator, he told us laughing, and that's where he'd found Maurice: alive, yes, blessedly alive, but living like a rat in the liberated city. The decision to join his brother in America had not been a difficult one.

'Say what you will about the fucking Germans,' he said, 'but they could never be worse than the French. They sent us to the ovens with even more satisfaction.' He was still stinging from

305

Chou-chou's betrayal – she had divorced him in '43 citing both the fact that he was living in America, and that he was a Jew, as reasons – and Varzi, sipping his cognac, couldn't help rub some salt on the wound.

'What did you see in her anyway, René?'

'Before the war,' Dreyfus replied, 'she was enormously bloody rich. I'm afraid her family hasn't done too well since, though. Her father was the world's biggest laxative maker, did you know that? *Pastilles Miraton* – but the Germans killed that market. Who needed laxatives with the Nazis in Paris, eh?'

Somewhere West of New York City, May 17, 1946

As the train wheezed its way into the heartland, Varzi could not stop complaining about the snail-like pace at which we were travelling. 'Fifty hours for a thousand kilometres?' Varzi exclaimed, sitting in the dining car and picking his way through a most unappetizing breakfast. 'Finestrini, the Indians walked faster!'

'That's because they were being chased by the cowboys,' I replied. It had become rather clear – annoyingly so – that Varzi was less than enchanted with America. 'It's the land of the automobile,' I said, trying to mask my irritation. 'You ought to appreciate that.'

'Italians appreciate nothing,' said a voice behind Varzi, 'this one least of all.'

I looked up from my food and saw Varzi swivel in his booth. Standing above us with a smile on his square face was Rudi Caracciola, with Baby Hoffman at his side.

'Jesus Christ.' Varzi slid out of the booth and held his hand out to Caracciola. 'I thought they'd strung you Nazis up in Nuremburg.'

'Only the poor ones, my friend.' Rudi slapped away Varzi's proffered hand and embraced him instead. I caught the suspicious glances of our fellow diners and wondered what they thought of these two middle-aged foreign men meeting on a train. What would they say if they knew that these two men had once been fêted by Mussolini and Hitler, and idolized by millions?

'We were staying at the Gotham Hotel,' Baby said, once we were sitting snug in our booth, 'and you won't believe what happened: I looked out the window, and what did I see across the road?'

'René Dreyfus – le Gourmet,' said Caracciola. 'We couldn't go in, of course – '

'Tony Hullman warned us to keep a low profile – '

'He owns the track at Indy,' explained Rudi.

'He warned us to stay in the hotel,' said Baby.

'It seems that I'm a war criminal now,' Caracciola said, his nostrils flaring. 'Anyway, René was kind enough to visit us in our room, and he told us that the great Achille Varzi had dropped by his restaurant not three days earlier.'

'Did you know that Tony Hullman's grandfather was from Lingen?' asked Baby.

'Same town as Rosemeyer,' said Caracciola.

'He's spent a fortune refitting the oval – it apparently went to rot during the war – which is why he's invited Rudi: he's hoping to attract some media attention for his little track in Indianapolis.'

'By inviting a Nazi?' asked Varzi.

'They're a simple people, these Americans,' said Rudi, looking about him. 'They need bad guys to fight the good ones, see?'

Varzi smiled.

'I assume that you've entered the Indy 500, too?'

'The Maseratis are already there,' confirmed Varzi.

'Tony says he's got something sorted for us at Indy. Guess we'll see. I heard they kept building racecars in Modena during the war – is that true?'

'Apparently Maserati decided not to retire – just like us. But you're getting a bit long in the tooth for the game, aren't you Rudi?'

Caracciola bared his teeth. 'A man risks his life for many reasons, Achille, but none more pure than money.'

'It's the American way,' I said. 'Indy will be full of guys like that – they come to the 500 like gamblers to a casino. They'll pitch up with their home-made cars and home-spun dreams and the lucky ones won't qualify.'

'And the unlucky?'

I looked at Caracciola. 'The oval at Indy,' I told him, 'is like nothing you've ever seen before, Rudi. It's a daunting place. An American place: it sucks you in, makes a friend of you – '

'And then it kills you with a smile,' completed Varzi.

Indianapolis, May 20, 1946

Varzi sat beside me over the banking to Turn 1. It was getting late, the sunlight a warm and lazy veil over our faces. I wondered what it would be like to live here, to find a home on these plains, to raise a family here, in America: the local wood-paneled diner, the football matches on cold fall afternoons, the dirt-track under Saturday night lights – it was an intriguing thought fuelled, I suspected, by Varzi's planned trip to Argentina. He had informed me that he would leave from La Guardia airport the week after the 500, to explore opportunities for the European winter. Europe, he'd said, was dead. It was a sentiment that lay not too far removed from my own. He had missed the cut in his 8C Maserati that morning, having blown his engine. The Varzi of old, I thought, would have been inconsolable; but the man who invited me to watch the rest of the qualifying heat from the grandstands, along with a bottle of chilled bubbly and a limitless supply of genuine American Lucky Strikes, seemed wholly unconcerned by his failure.

'It's a bit mad, this,' he said, staring down at the oval wrapping around itself in all its enormity. A chap called Rex Mays buzzed around Turn 1, skirting up toward the wooden rails on his final timed lap. Up ahead of him on the track, the asphalt merged into the worn brick of the original oval. 'I think it more a test of balls than skill.' The three million bricks that had once made this place the 'Brickyard' had been, over the years, replaced by asphalt, but the war and lack of funds had resulted in stretches of track – the front-straight and a good portion of the back one too – retaining their original brick face.

Varzi nudged me with his elbow and pointed at the pit exit. It was time. Joe Thorne had entered two cars for the 500 – one for a man named Robson, the other for himself, but he had managed to injure his leg the week before qualifying, and with a little help from his friends, Caracciola had been maneuvered into his Thorne Engineering Special. Caracciola now roared out of the pits and came through Turn 1 on his warm-up lap, the engine crackling expectantly in the twilight. I looked up at the grandstand – a grandstand the size of a battleship on which perhaps a hundred spectators sat about in various stages of lethargy. No one applauded. Caracciola wore his usual white linen helmet and a white short-sleeved shirt, his biceps flexing as he edged around the turn, foot squeezing the throttle at the apex.

'Go home you Nazi bastard!' came a voice from behind us. 'Kraut son of a bitch!'

Varzi winked at me. We listened to Caracciola's engine drone away from us down the straight, rollin' thunder as the locals called it. George Robson, in the sister car, had qualified at just under 200kph and I wondered aloud what that would feel like for a man who held the world record at 432kph.

'Feels fast,' Varzi said as Caracciola came round again, this time looking as if he meant business, the Adams chassis leaning into the banking like a drunk clawing onto a railing. Varzi stood up and, raising both arms above his head, applauded loudly before sitting down – fully aware, I thought, that he'd just made a few more enemies on a whole new continent. Some things never changed. As Rudi crossed the start-finish line, he punched up a fist from the cockpit to indicate to the time-keepers that he was about to begin his timed laps. Behind us, three voices were singing Back Home Again as Caracciola, typically smooth, committed to Turn 1 with intent.

The accident must have taken all of ten seconds, from start to vicious impact. To me, though, it seemed an eternity. On the exit of Turn 1, Caracciola's Thorne lost traction at the rear. They told me afterward that he had done the wrong thing: He had steered instinctively into the slide in a futile attempt to catch it. This, I was told, is what Europeans did: This was why Europeans got hurt here. Because part of running the Indy 500 is to accept the inevitable – when a man goes into a slide, the American driver relaxes in his seat, shuts his eyes, and offers up a prayer. Leaving destiny to its own inertia usually ended with the car thudding into the wooden barrier rear-first, but Caracciola, in trying to dominate destiny, had over-corrected due to the ramp-angle, and the car had instantly snapped away from him.

He had slammed into the wooden barrier that lined the circuit nose first. Caracciola was thrown from the cockpit like a puppet, all flailing arms and legs. He flew through the warm afternoon, before smashing face-first into the tarmac and cartwheeling away into the infield with his car – now splintering pieces of engines and bodywork – following. He came to rest on the apron in an untidy sprawl, the Thorne Special bouncing one final time to die beneath a bodybag of white smoke smoldering up into a flax-coloured sky. Varzi and I got to our feet. Caracciola was like a butterfly that had burst from its chrysalis. We stared down at the body on the track. He wasn't moving. And there was that silence then – that silence Varzi and I knew so well.

'Only good un is a dead un,' said a voice behind us. We heard someone burp, the stench of regurgitated beer wafting through the glorious gold-and-crimson sunset.

Indianapolis, May 18, 1946

Varzi had left the next morning, his Maserati sold to a private West Coast collector. I had expected him to show some sort of emotion over Caracciola's fate, but he was as inscrutable as ever at the train station. When I pressed him about how he felt, he had turned to me with something akin to anger and said, 'Finestrini, forty million died to make people like you happy – why do you care about an old man stupid enough to risk his life for a little money?' His words had stung for reasons I wasn't prepared to contemplate; and yet, once he'd left, I felt the crushing loneliness of America like a dead-weight on my chest. And despite Baby having been here in 1929 with Chiron, I sensed that she too felt that overwhelming burden of alienation.

Varzi and I had driven her to the hospital in downtown Indianapolis where we found Caracciola in a deep coma, paralyzed on the right side. Varzi had taken one look at him and had left without even saying goodbye to Baby.

Caracciola's face was shredded, his body mangled and broken, his scalp shaved and swollen. Baby saw none of that. She refused to leave him – insisted that her place was beside her man. Still, she must have felt the desolation, for I had been back in my hotel room for only an hour when she had phoned me, and I assumed that it was just to hear a friendly voice she could put a face to. It was a ritual that would repeat itself numerous times as the days stretched into fearful nights in which she remained by Rudi's side, refusing to leave, refusing even to change her clothes. She was obviously in shock, and somewhere in her mind I suspected that she must have thought of Charly, Rudi's first wife, and what she must have endured after his shunt in Monaco in '33.

'It's what Charly would have done,' she told me on one of those nights from the payphone in the hospital. 'Charly would expect me to be here until he wakes up.' On the fifth night, she had finally been persuaded to leave. That decision, she would later tell me, was a demonstration of the Lord's providence. The cab that had taken her from the hospital to her hotel room at the Marriott was yellow, she had said to me, but it was from the Red Cab Company. That seemed to matter to her. She had mentioned this to the taxi driver, needing a distraction – what would happen if Rudi died alone, here in this strange land? – and that conversation had somehow taken on an almost mystical quality for her.

'You're not from around here, are you?' the cab driver had asked. 'Where you from?'

'I don't know,' she had replied. 'All over really. Even here, once, a long time ago.'

'You're with one of them drivers then?'

'Yes.'

'The German fella? With the eye-talian name?'

'Caracciola,' she had replied from the back seat. 'Rudi Caracciola. Two-time European Champion and the fastest man in history.'

'I don't know nothin' 'bout that – out here, they like them cars, but me, I'm a horse man myself. Name's McClean,' the driver had told her when he had pulled the cab up to the Marriott. 'Next time you need a cab, ma'am, you tell 'em to call McClean, day or night. It ain't nice being a stranger in a strange city – me, I'm from Kalamazoo,' he had said as she climbed out, 'so's I know what it's like to be a fur'ner.'

The next night, after Baby had spent the day reading *Arch of Triumph* to a still comatose Caracciola, she had done precisely that. The cab had rolled up to the hospital through a night chilled by a fine spring rain and McClean had climbed out, carrying an umbrella to open the door for her. 'Like a limousine driver,' Baby said to me. 'McClean is like an angel to me.'

Behind the wheel, McClean had looked at her through the rear-view mirror and asked, 'your husband – has there been any improvement?'

She told him that Rudi had moved his right arm for the first time since the accident that afternoon. 'The doctors believe he may not be paralyzed,' she had told McLean.

McClean had smiled. 'I had me a feeling,' he'd said. 'Me and my family, we all prayed for y'all last night, all last night we prayed. We prayed for your husband, the German with the eye-talian name. We'd have called him by name too, but we couldn't pronounce it. But the good Lord, He knows His own children, don't He.'

Indianapolis, May 30, 1946

The Indy 500 was won by George Robson, in Rudi Caracciola's sister car. Villoresi had finished a credible seventh, his purse guaranteed to pay for his and Maserati's cross-Atlantic adventure with interest. I had watched the race from the main grandstand and had been shocked at the sheer ferocity of the racing. It was, as I wrote for the *Gazzetta*, an exemplary manifestation of American life. Men – and there were no women at that race, not in the cars or the pitlane – hurtled their rattling, tired old cars at insatiable speeds through those towering bends.

Unlike what we were accustomed to in Europe, these men were not paid to show up; they were paid only on results. It made them take some astounding risks. There was violence brewing below the surface, with all these wretched people and their wretched histories racing around quickly in circles – a violence that would suddenly emerge when one of the men in the pack would fall off the rails and the grandstand would positively crackle with energy. It happened to Mauri Rose, the poor bastard who was ejected from his car and tossed off down the main-straight like a skipping stone.

His somersaults went on for ages, until eventually he came to a halt on his backside in the middle of the track, as cars sped past him at over 200kph, some sliding away into the infield in a cloud of smoke and tyre-shredding madness, others spinning away into the wall. And then, amidst the chaos, Mauri Rose had just stood up as if he'd only been taking a breather, dusted himself off, and sauntered away down the apron. Yes, I wrote, here was a faultless metaphor for the American Way, as seen in Indianapolis in May. And with that story filed, I had packed my bag and checked out of the hotel.

I called Baby from the train station. I had tried to ignore my conscience, but eventually I had given in to it – Rudi, I knew, had been released into her care that morning, after X-rays had revealed no pressing physical ailments. The fact that he had been caught trying to escape the hospital – for he was now convinced he was being held in a torture camp for Germans – probably an indication that he was ready to leave.

It was a medical mystery, the doctor had told her, even a minor miracle that he was able to leave so soon after the shunt, and while it may have seemed that way to the doctor, Baby's nightmare was just beginning. As she told me over the phone: 'He's convinced that he was never at Indy. He says he's been kidnapped by the Americans.'

'Show him a newspaper,' I suggested, looking down at my copy of the *Star* and its headline: "Stutthof Concentration Camp 13 Found Guilty".

'I have,' she said. 'He told me I was in on it – that I was an American. He's convinced himself it's all a fraud. And he's forgotten how to eat: doesn't even know how to use a fork or knife anymore. Christ, I'm all alone here, I don't know what to do. He's sitting in the corner of the room rocking on his haunches, he's just sitting there staring at the door – he says they're coming for him, but they won't take him alive.'

'Well, at least he'll have to learn to use a knife to defend himself then,' I told her, before wishing her well and hanging up. My conscience be damned, I thought. I was sick of it, sick of the death, sick of the futile heroism. Motor-racing was a meat-grinder, and those stupid enough to continue got what they deserved.

Milan, July 15, 1946

I spent the summer after my return from Indiana desk-bound, and I received one letter from Baby during that time. In it, I learned that Tony Hullman had taken Rudi and Baby to his country estate in Terre Haute, where Rudi had convalesced with the aid of a world-class doctor flown in from New York City. 'I was so afraid he would fall in the damn pool,' she wrote, 'because he has taken to sleepwalking every night now.' In July, I received a telegram from Dreyfus, informing me that Rudi and Baby had dined at his restaurant earlier that month and were on their way back to Europe. Rudi, he wrote, looked and sounded well, and Baby had rented a house in Sweden along with specialist care near her family home. 'All told, he looks healthy, but still suffers from confusion now and again. I am assured he has no brain damage, so perhaps it is psychological after all. Oh, and who knew,' Dreyfus added as a P.S., 'that Baby was from Sweden!'

I was itching to get away from that desk and report on some racing. Nuvolari had returned to action that summer. I had heard that Carolina had fallen ill after Alberto's death, but my repeated calls and letters to Nuvolari had all gone unanswered. From Brivio I learnt that he spent his weeks with Carolina, and his weekends 'chasing death'. Unable to attend any of the races now that the *Gazzetta* was flirting with outright bankruptcy, I was reduced to reading and redacting reports from our stringers around the country, most of whom were unpaid amateurs. The picture they painted was of a Nuvolari obsessed with risk-taking like never before.

In Como, he had made front-page news when he drove most of the race using only his right hand, his left having been fully occupied with quenching the stream of blood gushing from his mouth. In late July, he won his first race in a decade at Albi, in a Maserati 4CL. Two weeks later, at the Nations Cup in Geneva, spectators had seen him swallow a plume of fuel from one of the dominant Alfa Tipo 158 Alfettas – the same 158 that Jano had designed ten years earlier, and that had now become the strongest racecar in Europe. Apparently, Tazio had been taken ill because of the fuel, and I called his home repeatedly after that race, but his secretary would not budge. 'Signor Nuvolari will not be taking calls from journalists. I'm sorry, not even you, Signor Finestrini.'

As for Varzi, his South American tour had been both personally rewarding and financially successful. He had written of his determination to return to Argentina as soon as the European racing season was over. 'You should come,' he had written, 'Perón is a Fascist, you'd love the bastard, and you can't take a piss without hitting a Nazi.' It was an invitation that certainly had its merits. Yes, Italy had lost a war and won the peace, but really, when one came right down to it, Italy in 1946 rather resembled Italy in 1936. Except for Il Duce, of course, and for dear Cristoferi, who I had run into in the park across from my apartment feeding the feral squirrels, and who had not recognized me at all, even after I had introduced myself.

At the end of August, I received the official entry list for the Gran Premio di Torino, and there they were, side-by-side on the press release: Achille Varzi, Tazio Nuvolari. It was the first time since 1937 that Italy's two great rivals would begin a race together. It was an event that I wasn't about to miss, and despite the sorry state of my finances, I managed to secure a cheap hotel in Turin and started counting down the days. Heroes, I thought. Cristoferi would be proud, for I would write again of men.

Milan, September 4, 1946

I returned on the evening train to Milan with Turin besieging my mind. I had not seen the city since the early '40s, and what I had found was a blistered wreck through which a track had been created with our usual Italian flare. Varzi had suggested that they rename all of the track's many turns: The Bombing of '44 hairpin, followed by the Retilineo of Massacred Partisans. He had been in good spirits, and had come along with his Norma. She had given me a cool air-kiss and had cheered her man to victory over a determined Jean Pierre Wimille.

The post-war Varzi, I wrote, was a harmonious and deadly combination of craft and style. Despite the win, though, the day had been a bittersweet one for me. In the pits I had found Carolina sitting alone beneath an umbrella, completely removed

315

from all that was happening around her. She had greeted me with a flat smile, and we spoke a little about her Tazio.

'He keeps telling me we'll see them again,' she said, staring blankly ahead of her. 'That's what he keeps saying.'

'I believe you will,' I lied.

She didn't look at me, still kind enough to save me from my own shame. 'What can life offer us now, after all this pain?'

We sat there under that umbrella as the race wore on, her beloved Tazio outclassed in an ailing Maserati.

'Look at him,' she said. 'Fifty-six years old. And all he wants is to die – that's what he wants. And me? I sit here and pray for Alberto and Giorgio to protect him, because I don't want to be alone. A woman who married a good man and had two strong boys shouldn't be alone.' Nuvolari was ill, she said, but he just couldn't keep himself from racing. 'And that's the thing: even in death, he will always be *Il Tassio,* forever alive. Isn't that true, Johnny?' she asked, and it had sounded like a recrimination. The fans chanted his name as they had before the war; they cheered for Nivola in the rubble of Italy's Motor City, waving him on with fists and newspapers that every day tried to explain a world that no longer belonged to us.

Varzi's win, Varzi laughing with Norma beside him holding his laurel in the sun, Varzi throwing his laurel at his mechanics as if it were a discus – all of it felt like a stab in the heart, a pale reminder of our glory days. His win had come on the first of September. On the third, they had scheduled another race in Turin on the Valentino circuit. It was to be the debut of the tiny Cisitalia D46, which we all hoped would kick-start motor-racing in post-war Italy. As debuts go, this one was quite astonishing in the wondrous hands of Tazio Nuvolari. It hadn't looked that way at first when, on the fifth lap, the steering wheel had shorn right off its column. Tazio, ever the showman, had driven into the pits using nothing more than throttle and gears. We had all thought his race over then, and one could physically discern the crowd's disappointment, until suddenly Nuvolari – having obtained a wrench from one of the mechanics – had come rushing out of the pit using the damned wrench as a steering-wheel and gone on to finish an astounding sixth.

Nuvolari had always maintained that his apparent indestructibility came from the heart. He would always say that, 'if a man takes risks, he must do so with all his being,' and despite what I kept hearing, I was convinced that Tazio couldn't kill himself in a car because dying would prevent him from winning. I confess to having shed a few tears that afternoon. It was Nuvolari at his very best, and his drive was precisely the tonic for what had been, until then, an emotionally fraught weekend.

I suspected that most of the crowd had been reliving the pre-war years in this bomb-cratered city; Tazio had brought us a sense of joviality, a sense of can-do a la Italiana. They carried Nuvolari back to the pits on their shoulders as if he had won the race, and it made the front page of newspapers as far south as Rome: the photo of Tazio in a wild drift held by that wrench, echoing that afternoon twenty years before when he had beaten the world sheathed in bandages.

However, that particular story was not destined to run under my byline, for that weekend I had stumbled across Bradley at the hotel bar. Bradley had introduced me to a British publisher who had expressed an immediate interest in my pre-war writing. His publishing house was producing a series of books on motor-racing, and he suggested that the book that I had been trying to write for the past two decades would be an ideal fit. An advance had been discussed and deposited into my account by the time I had returned to Milan. It wasn't a lot, but in 1946 a man could get by with very little at all; and so, inspired, I had asked for a year's sabbatical from the *Gazzetta*, and set to work on the manuscript.

Pavia, June 14, 1947

I spent the winter and spring of '47 firmly enclosed in my apartment, working on the manuscript. A first draft had magically materialized by early June, and I had been lost in the process of editing – oblivious to the world – when there came a brief knock on my door.

'You look like shit,' said Varzi in the hallway. 'Come on, grab a shower, I'll meet you downstairs at the café.'

317

'Why?' I asked.

'Because we're going to do what Italians do on Sunday afternoons – '

'We're going to church?'

'We're going to a motor-race, Finestrini. The Mille Miglia,' he said, shooting me a curious glance. 'You have heard of it, right?'

In his lovely Alfa Coupé, with a packed picnic basket of champagne and sandwiches on the rear seat and with the roof down, Varzi drove us out of Milan into the sun. He was tanned and fit, his paunch gone, courtesy of having spent the winter in Argentina where he had been racing his own Alfa 308C.

He had won a few races, been fêted by the Perón who didn't matter and had flirted with the one who did, and had come away with a deep love of the country and its wide-open spaces.

'So much opportunity,' he said. 'And everyone knew me – it was like the old days, Finestrini. Buenos Aires is like Napoli, you know: we have our own neighborhood, they call it La Boca, there are millions of us over there. They tell me a third of Buenos Aires is made up of Italian children.'

He discussed his idea of launching a driving academy over there, and Norma had not expressed any reservations when he'd suggested they emigrate. 'I'm heading back there in October,' he told me. 'You know, while I was there I met a man – fat guy like a bull by the name of Fangio, but behind the wheel he's like a ballerina, all grace and style. Fantastic talent – bit old, he's my age I think, and he keeps popping these little red pills of his that I'm convinced is cocaine! He wants to come to Europe and I'm thinking of organizing it for him. You know he was almost in tears when he met me? He calls me his Maestro.' He looked over at me. 'I always considered Nuvolari to be an artist – but he could never teach anyone because he's not a master. You can't teach art, only craft. What do you think, Finestrini?' He glanced over at me. 'Christ you look unwell, you know that?'

And so we stood there on the bridge over the Ticino, with the evening buzzing about us. Tazio Nuvolari was leading the first post-war Mille Miglia race in his little 1100 Cisitalia, whose chassis had been designed by Porsche Jr.

'Porsche is a genius,' Varzi told me. 'And his son clearly inherited something from the old man.'

'Tazio paid a ransom to get Porsche out of prison after all,' I commented.

'How the world changes, Finestrini,' he said with that smile of his that had once been so irksome and was now sweetly endearing to me. 'When you think about the years that have flown by and the friends you've left behind, those still here and those you'll never meet again … '

I was about to reply when the voice on his car radio transferred over to race control in Rome. Nuvolari, the voice announced, was up by eight minutes at the Modena stop. Varzi didn't need to call my attention to the clouds that crept toward us from the north.

'Rain,' he said, popping another bottle of champagne. Sipping from the bottle, he was the first to spot Nuvolari not long after. *'Eccolo!'* he shouted with the enthusiasm of a child. 'Look, Finestrini, there he is!'

We watched the little Cisitalia shoot toward us in a whirlwind of dust. The car was a simple thing, a box with an open cockpit, and we could easily recognize Nuvolari's face. He looked exhausted, his silver hair tousled by the wind. Varzi and I both jumped like cheerleaders on that bridge when that little car hurtled past, its engine rattling away in a crazed crescendo. Tazio, his head set forward as if riding a bike, waved at us without even recognizing who we were.

By the time Varzi had dropped me off at my apartment, the race was done. Nuvolari's Cisitalia had been defeated by the rain; still, he had crawled home in second place. In my apartment, we listened to Tazio Nuvolari's interview on state radio drowned out by the crowd in Brescia chanting Nivola! Nivola! As Varzi and I were sitting on my floral couch, sharing the last of his champagne and cigarettes, it felt a little like the good old times. When Varzi left at 2am, he gave me a hug. 'This book of yours,' he said. 'It'll drive you around the bend in the end.'

Milan, May 2, 1948

The way in which Tazio Nuvolari – in his Ferrari
Tipo 166S – did battle in the XV edition of the Mille
Miglia offers us final proof of the place that he will
forever hold in the heart of the Italian people. Had
he had at his disposal a publicity agent – or indeed
a scriptwriter from Hollywood – it's doubtful that
either could have come up with a more captivating
story than his triumphant failure here this weekend.
Nuvolari's odyssey began two weeks ago when Enzo
Ferrari – having heard of Alfa Romeo's intention of
signing Nuvolari for the Mille Miglia – had driven in
secret to a convent in Salò, where the Flying Mantuan
was resting under doctor's orders. This being Ferrari,
Nuvolari was not permitted much argument when
he was whisked back to Maranello. There, in Enzo
Ferrari's new facility, Nuvolari was shown a scarlet
Ferrari, in which he would drive to victory at the
Mille Miglia if he so chose. Nuvolari had immediately
accepted the challenge, and the fifty-six year old
Mantuan turned up at the Piazza della Vittoria in
Brescia on May 1 for the second post-war running of
the world's greatest road race.

The rest, by now, you have no doubt heard over the
radio or from friends. You will have heard that Tazio
seized command of the race in Rome and managed
to extend his lead to over half-an-hour when the
cars arrived in Florence with two-thirds of the race
complete. You will probably have heard that his
searing pace had broken the will of his challengers
– mentally, physically, and mechanically. Such was
his violent desire to conquer this race one final time
that, just outside Rome, he had lost both his front
and rear bumpers in a wild ride through a field. Less
than 40 kilometres later, the spring shackle had
broken, his bonnet shorn off to expose the engine
to the elements; then his seat had collapsed (he
managed to procure a bag of ripe, bitter lemons on

which he would sit for the remainder of the race), his tyre had gone flat, and his throttle had stuck open. Through it all, Tazio Nuvolari kept increasing his lead. But with that mighty engine now laid bare, Nuvolari was fully exposed to the threat of rain that chased him through the night over the Somma. And yet, like the men who would pursue him, the rain was not destined to catch up with Tazio Nuvolari – not on this day.

In cities throughout Italy, sitting with radios turned up high, hundreds of thousands of people listened to every mile of Nuvolari's journey. With every update one could hear the chants of *Nivola! Nivola!* from the bars and cafés and houses throughout our land, as the little man in the canary yellow jersey swept ever northward toward Brescia, carrying with him all of our yesterdays. Down the breakneck descent into Bologna we pushed him, this fifty-six year old, ailing gray-haired man. Nuvolari had united us once, before the war: His power to do so again transcended our mutual suspicions, and together once more, we Italians had found a common cause in *his* cause.

Just past Reggio Emilia we woke from that splendid dream. In one abrupt moment, Tazio's Ferrari entered the village of Villa Ospizio and never left. It was here that Nuvolari had calmly climbed out of his car, asking for nothing but a bed upon which he could rest. His Ferrari had betrayed him: it felt no remorse, no empathy, it had felt nothing at all when it had come to a grinding halt; and with it, the XV Mille Miglia too, had come to an end. It no longer mattered, it no longer had a place in history. Biondetti, who won the race, could say only, 'Forgive me.'

All of us know that this was Nivola's final Mille Miglia. Despite his defeat, he gave us back our youthful hope and optimism. Nuvolari allowed us once more to feel a sense of pride, not only for our yesterdays, but for our tomorrows.

I sat back in my chair. The *Gazzetta*'s office was quiet, my watch reflecting the time, just gone 3am. What more, I wondered, could I say? Could I say that I had been with Enzo Ferrari at the Modena stop when Nuvolari had come hurtling past with his car shedding water and oil, the engine choking and the smell of fried brakes in the air? Could I say that Enzo Ferrari had turned to me then with a shake of his head, that he had known, that all of us had known then that Nuvolari would never make it to Brescia? Nuvolari's Ferrari was running on pure spirit. Ferrari had called ahead to the mechanics waiting in Bologna and instructed them to stop him – but Nuvolari would not hear of it; not now, he had said, not this close.

Could I say that he had just kept on going because he knew this was his final Mille Miglia? That his defeat, however inevitable, was irrelevant? That Tazio Nuvolari didn't know *how* to stop? When Ferrari and I had arrived at Villa Ospizio, the rain was torrential. A few local lads had shown us the way to the San Francesco da Paola church, where we found Nuvolari asleep on a hard bed, with a surgical mask flecked with his blood abandoned on the hardwood floor beside him. We had allowed him to sleep. Downstairs, in his small stone cottage, the priest had given us bread and cheese, and we had waited for Nuvolari to awaken. He had done so sometime in the night; he looked exhausted, his face a mask of defeat.

'There's always next year,' Ferrari had said when he had accompanied Nuvolari to his car.

Nuvolari had placed one lax arm around Enzo's shoulders. 'Ferrari,' he said, 'at our age there aren't many more days like this; remember that, and try to enjoy them if you can.'

Mantua, June 26, 1948

The Mantua Automobile Club had organized the race around the Villa del Te for June 13. It was called the Coppa Alberto e Giorgio Nuvolari. Tazio had been instrumental in securing many of the world's foremost drivers for the race, including Achille Varzi, and it was a most welcome sight when the two old rivals lined up on the grid side-by-side on that hot and sunny Sunday. Varzi had been in a sullen mood all weekend, and I'd heard it said that his mother was seriously ill. He had left her bedside to come and show his respect for Tazio, who sat in the cockpit of his Ferrari Tipo 125S with a surgical mask hiding his mouth and nose like a bandit. But the only thing that Nuvolari was stealing was time. His hair was silver, cut short, his face without a shred of fat, just muscle and wrinkle and bone. I had no way of knowing that this would be the last time these two men would do battle with each other. It lasted less than eight laps, until Nuvolari had pulled into the pit. I was later told that he had vomited blood in the garage before cleaning himself up with a cloth and coming back to present the cup to the winner, Bonetto.

That evening, at Nuvolari's villa, Varzi and I had sat with Carolina and Tazio and shared a light dinner in his conservatory. Carolina was, as always, a gracious host, but she could not quite disguise the bitterness of a life betrayed. When we had left after dinner, Varzi had commented that their house was macabre, with those bronze busts of Alberto and Giorgio mounted astride the front door: it was an old man's home, he had said, the antechamber to the cemetery.

Varzi and I spent much of the night at a café in central Mantua, sipping Campari and sodas. I wished to speak to him of his mother, of Ilse, of what had happened back before the war when we were so much younger, but nothing would come out of my mouth except for bloody motor-sport news. Had he heard, I asked, that Mercedes was making its comeback in Berne on July 1? Varzi nodded, saying that he had also heard that Neubauer had been appointed the team's manager again, and that Chiron would be making his comeback as well.

323

'What about you?' I asked.

'I'll be there,' Varzi said. 'And you?'

I nodded, Varzi nodded, and the night wore on.

Berne, July 1, 1948

Berne. It was here that Dr. Magneven had discovered Varzi's secret; here that Varzi's career had imploded a lifetime ago; and today, it was a tired Varzi who I found sitting in the pits, much affected by his mother's death. He had invited me to the service two days earlier, a respectful farewell where I had seen Varzi cry without any shame at all. I had suggested that he skip this race, but he had simply shrugged and said: 'What else does an Italian do on a Sunday afternoon?'

It was fitting that practice for the grand prix should be held beneath a somber gray sky that dripped cold rain upon the track. Chiron was circulating the track, looking lively in a baby-blue Lago-Talbot. Varzi, sitting in his cockpit in a white linen helmet and white overalls, smoked languidly as he observed two mechanics completing a spring change to his Alfa. I noticed a tall man in a black raincoat walk toward him in the fog and touch his shoulder.

'Christ,' I heard Varzi say, 'if it isn't bloody Paul Pietsch.'

Paul Pietsch. He looked older of course, but there was no mistaking the tall, lanky silhouette and that crooked nose of his. He squatted and the two men shook hands, Varzi's glove in Pietsch's naked palm.

'What are you doing here?' asked Varzi.

'My new job,' said Pietsch, gazing into the cockpit. 'I'm playing journalist nowadays, Varzi – I've started my own motoring magazine.'

'You ought to employ Finestrini,' Varzi said. 'I hear his book is not selling too well.'

'And you, Varzi, don't you think you're a bit old for the game?'

Varzi fixed his eyes on Pietsch's face. 'Is this for the record?'

'No, no,' said Pietsch, raising his hands in mock surrender. 'I'm here to cover the return of Mercedes.' A smile crossed his face. 'Good Christ but it's been a long time, hasn't it? No one even remembers the '30s anymore; it's almost as if we've expunged twenty years from our collective conscience.'

'I suppose it's convenient,' said Varzi. 'It didn't end too well, did it?'

'No, I don't suppose it did,' Pietsch acknowledged. 'She's remarried, you know,' he said after a short pause. 'To an opera singer from Wiesbaden.'

Varzi smiled that smile of his.

'They tell me she's very happy.'

Varzi tossed his smoke out of the cockpit. Pietsch nodded, and stood. I thought he was about to say something, but Varzi had already clipped the ignition switch.

Pietsch walked away down the sodden pitlane as Varzi gave a thumbs-up for his mechanic to ignite the engine. It gurgled into life and he eased out the clutch, cruising past me without even a glance to join the circuit with a smoothly applied throttle, the rear tyres slipping on the slick, greasy surface. He sped up, and I could imagine his two fingers shifting up the gears before he vanished into the distance.

That was the last time I ever saw Achille Varzi.

Louis Chiron was the one who witnessed the accident. He had been just ahead of Varzi as they came into the quick Jordanrampe switchbacks, a series of turns taken at close to 200kph. He had been aware of Varzi in his mirrors for most of that lap, and as the rear of his Talbot began to slide, he had countersteered and caught the rear, while noticing that Varzi had closed right up. He was amazed at the speed Varzi was able to bring into the turn. Having sorted out his Talbot, he had glanced into his mirror and watched Varzi tip into a slide of his own. It was a typical drift, Chiron said, a four-wheel drift that he had fully expected Varzi to ride out, but the 158 had suddenly snapped into a tank-slapper, and Varzi had been pitched head-first into the wooden barriers that surrounded the track.

It wasn't a hard hit – Chiron was insistent on that point – but the Alfa had dug its nose into the soil and the rear of the car had soared like a wave. Varzi's car had then collapsed upon itself. With wheels still spinning, the Alfa lay still, belly-up like a poisoned cockroach.

Chiron had pulled his Talbot over and run back to find Achille Varzi trapped under the Alfa. He couldn't remember how he had done it, but somehow he had dragged Varzi from beneath the car. A stream of blood bubbled from Varzi's lips. The blood ran over the cobbles to mix with the rain. I never asked whether it was true what they said – that he had kneeled on that track with Varzi's head in his lap and cried until the ambulance had arrived. I never asked if it was true that he had removed Varzi's goggles to stare into his lifeless eyes. No, I never asked whether it was true that Varzi's white linen wind helmet had been dyed red from his fractured …

I never did complete that sentence in my mind. I never wrote about it either. Hadn't I written about the deaths of heroes so many times before? But of this – of this I would never write.

I was the wrong side of a bottle of Johnnie Walker in my hotel room when the phone buzzed in the night.

'Finestrini,' she said.

I recognized her voice of course. 'Norma.'

'Finestrini, I heard that Alfa want to pull out of tomorrow's race. Achille wouldn't have wanted that. You will make sure they race, won't you?'

'Norma –

'And you will do the eulogy at his service.'

'Me?'

'He would have wanted that,' she said, hanging up.

Galliate, July 10, 1948

His body had been placed on an Alfa 158 for three days in the nave of the San Giuseppe church in Galliate. They said 15,000 people came to bid him farewell. I wouldn't know. Those days leading to his burial passed in a blur of booze that blunted the edge of my loss. I remember standing in that little church, next to Caracciola and Nuvolari; I remember standing there before the altar looking down at Carolina and Norma; I remember seeing Brivio and poor Viganò, who had survived the Russian Front but was now a cripple. And in this diary today, I have found the words that I probably read at the service. The eulogy for Achille Varzi, from the man who had ruined his career and the love of his life:

"Perhaps you were destined to die, Achille, because in your driving there was something of that genius which is one of Nature's greatest mysteries, and Nature strives to destroy those who come too close to her. Beethoven was struck with deafness when he seemed about to transcend man's power of musical expression. Galileo was blinded when he tried to probe infinity and its laws. Leonardo da Vinci's hands were crippled when he was about come nearer to perfection than any man before him. And you too, Achille, were destroyed when you sought to cross the known frontiers of man-made speed. Now you are preparing for another race, the last great race. A race without danger, without care, without sorrow ... "

I resigned the next day – I simply walked into the *Gazzetta* and delivered my resignation on a whisky-stained piece of paper. Varzi had had two serious accidents in his whole career: The first, in Carthage in '37, had ended his domination as a world-class driver. The second, eleven years later, had killed him instantly. I was no longer interested in writing about this savage sport.

Crocodile River, November 30, 1952

One week after handing in my resignation, I had boarded a flight to British East Africa and travelled overland to South Africa to begin a new life. Before leaving, however, and at the behest of Varzi's father, I had met a portly man at Milano Centrale, an Argentine who had just arrived in Europe. He had the eyes of a racing driver, clear, bright, and nervous, and he seemed to absorb everything as he sat beside me in my Bianchi. I had driven him in silence to Galliate and deposited him outside that fine old house where Varzi's father, looking tired and frail, waited with Norma by his side. Varzi's garage, as promised, would serve as his headquarters; and Varzi's mechanics would prepare his car in a team named Scuderia Achille Varzi.

I had read much about him of course, this Juan Manuel Fangio, while I lived in South Africa. He had made quite an impact in the new Formula 1 series that Brivio had dreamed of all those years ago, but I couldn't quite bring myself to follow the sport with any enthusiasm. Racing, in my mind, had become a wicked thing. It ate men; it fed on their desire, and once sated it simply devoured them whole. It was therefore with a sense of regret that I found myself in Europe again, enticed back by a cable that had been signed Rudi Caracciola. At the self-same turn that had ended Varzi's life, Caracciola, in June of '52, had endured yet another life-threatening crash when his Mercedes' rear brake had stuck and he had plowed into a tree with such force that the entire thing had been torn from its roots. Caracciola had somehow managed to survive, though he'd been seriously mangled.

'It's the left leg this time,' he was quoted as saying. 'It's gone – so maybe now it will be the same length as the right one and I won't need to limp anymore.'

It had been five months since his crash. Caracciola was now holed up at the Hirslanden Clinic where his doctor expected him to remain for at least another four months. In his cable to me, Rudi had written that it was just like 1933 all over again – but this time he was in no great rush to recover, for he had all he needed right there at his bedside: his Babylein. All that was missing, he suggested, was a project; and for that, he needed to see me at my earliest convenience. Along with the cable, he had enclosed a one-way ticket to Berne.

I found Caracciola in good spirits, and it took him no time at all to half-convince me to ghostwrite his autobiography, now that he had decided to retire. We chatted for a while in the garden of the hospital, and from him I learnt that von Brauchitsch had been accused of spying for the East Germans and had been thrown into prison. And Nuvolari? He was still alive: he had finally retired at Silverstone earlier that year, running his final laps in a Jaguar in front of the British public who loved him as much as the Italians. I thought back to Bradley and the Targa all those years ago, and couldn't help but laugh. I assured Rudi that I would give his proposal serious consideration, and then boarded the night train to Milan.

It was that evening, while I was tidying up my apartment, that the news had come through on the radio. Tazio Nuvolari, who had been driving to Modena for an afternoon jaunt, had fallen ill on the Via Emilia just before the Mantua turn-off. His old friend

Compagnoli – in the car ahead – had found his friend paralyzed behind the wheel, and had rushed Nuvolari home. The prognosis was dire, with his personal physician not prepared to disclose the precise nature of Nuvolari's ailment, except to insist that it was 'very serious'.

I discovered just how serious it was four days later. I was returning to my apartment after a quick visit with Brivio when I had found a man standing outside my apartment building. 'My name,' he said, 'is Professor Alessio.'

'Nuvolari's physician?'

'You're well informed.'

'How is he?'

'He needs to see you.'

'Me? Why?'

'For reasons that I have warned him will have serious repercussions on his health. All the same, he insists, and at this stage, to be quite frank with you, it will make little difference.'

I stared at him. 'How did you know that I was back?'

'Ferrari,' he replied and left it at that. 'Will you come?'

It was the same question Nuvolari asked me three hours later. I had found him in his bed, pale and sweating, semi-paralyzed and thin as a snake. He had always been the smallest of men, no more than five-foot-three and sixty-something kilos, but he had never seemed small, not to me, not until that day when I saw him in that white bed.

'Will you come?' he asked, and I did not know what to say. Beside him, holding his hand, Carolina had nodded her reluctant consent.

Somewhere Near Foggia,
December 12, 1952

It was snowing. Nuvolari, wrapped beneath a brown blanket on the seat beside me, dozed as I drove his burgundy Alfa ever southward, on this mysterious journey of his. It had not occurred to me to ask why Tazio wanted me to accompany him: I suppose it was an honour simply to be asked. I knew our destination and had penciled in a route on the Michelin map that was folded away in the gap beside my seat.

'I can't understand why you went to Africa,' Nuvolari was saying. 'I mean, what on earth could you have found to do there aside from straightening bananas? You know, of course, that a man cannot avoid his destiny. Mine, it seems, was always to die in a bed, yours to write of other men racing; even if we both pretended otherwise.'

Carolina had packed panini for us; mozzarella and arugula, Parma ham and fontina cheese. Nuvolari ate a bite or two, and offered me the rest. When I grabbed the thermos of warm espresso, Nuvolari's hand seized the wheel and kept us pointed straight.

'You remember that night when we drove back from the 'Ring?' he asked.

'The night von Delius died?'

'Yes, that weekend – I think that's when it all began to crumble, you know?'

I chewed on my panino in silence.

'I'm dying, of course,' Nuvolari said.

I stared ahead at the road, changing gears to give me something to do.

'It's the lungs. Alessio thinks it was that jet of fuel I received in Berne in '46, but I think it was the Germans.'

'The Germans?'

'That fuel mixture they ran, back in the day, you remember how it smelt? I think I sucked too much of it up.'

'Your own fault,' I said, 'you should have been leading.'

Nuvolari wheezed. 'How long have you known me, Finestrini?'

'Thirty years,' I said. 'Give or take a few.'

'I don't have even have one left to give.' Nuvolari watched me drive. 'I never did ask why you did it.'

'Did what?'

'Did what you did. They say those who know, do, and those who don't, write. Is that why? Were you a frustrated racing driver?'

I kept my gaze on the road.

'You created my public persona,' Nuvolari said suddenly. 'I thought you'd want to know that. Varzi felt the same way. The two of us spoke about you often – he was very fond of you.

Remember that motto you suggested he use for his official letters?'

'Aut Caesar aut nihil,' I replied. 'All or nothing.'

'Dear generous Achille – I miss him most of all.'

Night had fallen by the time I had navigated up into the Gargano Mountains south of Foggia. The village of San Giovanni Rotondo was fast asleep when I drew the Alfa over the gravel driveway to the Convento Frati Cappuccini, a nondescript friary improbably balanced upon a cliff. Nuvolari sat beside me with his bloodshot eyes staring out at it.

'We're here,' he whispered.

I nodded, unsure of whether to turn off the ignition.

'Help me out,' he said.

I opened his door and leaned into the car. Death smells, even from a distance. I felt his arm – so weak, weighing less than a butterfly – grasp my shoulder, and I dragged him out into the night like a toddler.

'Thank you,' he whispered, finding his balance but not his strength.

'What now?' I asked.

'Now,' he said, 'you wait in the car.' He shuffled away from me and limped toward the church. He had walked perhaps five or six paces before the church doors opened. A figure in a brown frock helped Nuvolari up the steps and inside the building.

I slept in the car and was woken in the morning by Nuvolari, who was accompanied by a white-bearded man whose face was hidden by a hood. In the dawn light, his eyes were moist black pebbles. They seemed to smile at me as I slid fully awake from the car into a bright and cold morning.

'Padre Pio,' I whispered.

The priest helped Nuvolari climb back into the Alfa. Nuvolari didn't say one word about what had happened that night. When I insisted, he replied, 'Padre Pio tells me God has no good news. But He hasn't had any for me since He took Giorgio.'

I dropped him off at home and caught the night train back to Milan. In my apartment, I called Caracciola and told him that I had decided not to accept his generous offer. I had decided to devote my time on a project that had occurred to me that very day.

'A novel,' I told him.

Milan, August 1, 1953

I heard from Carolina sporadically throughout that year as I secluded myself in my apartment to work on a first draft. Nuvolari had decided to spend the spring and summer at his villa on the Garda Lake where, in bed, he was attended to by a private nurse named Rosina Vincenzi. He would call for her like a child in the night and ask for his scrapbook, through which he would scroll to regale her with the echoes of his fading life. Ten years before, I thought, I would have killed my own mother to overhear those recollections. In late July, before he had fallen asleep with the dawn, he had said to her, 'Rosina, I don't count for anything anymore.'

'You're still Tazio Nuvolari from Castel d'Ario,' she had replied.

The novel was neither what I'd planned nor hoped for. August was upon us with a ferocity that had me sweating at my desk. I smelt the odour of the ink from my typewriter, smelt the odour of words branded there on the page.

The phone – it was always the phone.

'Finestrini,' I said.

'It's Carolina.'

'Hello,' I replied, looking away from my typewriter.

'Tazio has asked to return to Mantua this morning. He says it's time.'

'Time?' I asked.

'Tell me Finestrini – last year, when the two of you left, where did you go? Did you visit Padre Pio?'

'Carolina – '

'Last night I walked into Tazio's room – it must have been 3am – and I swear to you, Johnny, that I saw Padre Pio kneeling by his bed.'

'Padre Pio?'

'Yes. But he couldn't have been there of course – it must have been a vision. When I told Tazio this morning, he said the oddest thing: "Oh, then it's time."'

I stayed silent.

'We go back today. Tazio says he wants to be at home.' I could hear her voice crack. 'Will you come, Johnny? I know he would like that.'

Mantua, August 12, 1953

I visited with him three days before he left us. He lay in that bed below the stairs where Giorgio and Alberto had died, surrounded by their toys and their memories and their photographs. He had been too weak to speak, wracked by pain and a wheezing rasp that he was unable to expunge from his lungs. There was a scent of roses in his room when I had knelt by his bedside and kissed his cold flesh. He had stared at me with horror in his eyes. I don't know if he recognized me: If he did, he must have thought me the devil.

He died today with Carolina at his side. She called me this afternoon, telling me that his last wish was to be buried beside his children in that canary-yellow jumper of his. I listened to her maintain her dignity; I suppose it's all she had left then. When I dropped the receiver, my hand brushed the manuscript before me, the manuscript entitled *Tracks*.

It was their story, the men whose lives I'd documented and recorded and yes, sometimes even falsified and exaggerated. I lifted the manuscript, all five hundred pages of it, and walked to the window. Perhaps it was the heat, perhaps the weight of the words, but the paper crashed straight and true to the sidewalk below like a bomb. That afternoon, a thunderstorm had come to wash it all away into the gutters.

*

The PanAm N711PA flight to JFK is on schedule. I spot a bank of payphones up against a green tiled wall in the departures lounge, there by the massive PanAm posters with the legend *Chasing the Sun* emblazoned on them. In my pocket I dig out four gettoni and feed the box. The number rings in my ear. Come on, I think, come on. I'm about to hang up when a voice cuts the static.

'Ja? Hallo?'

'Hi. Who – who is this?'

'This is Doctor Muller.'

'Oh, doctor, I didn't recognize your voice.'

'I recognize yours. Are you still in Venice?'

'No, no I – left. This morning. Look, is Ilse there? I've been trying to call since yesterday. May I speak with her, please? I'm at Linate, at the airport – I have some news.'

'I'm afraid I, too, have news.'

'I'm sorry?–'

'Ilse passed away yesterday afternoon.'

'She – but that's not – '

'I'm sorry, I know you two had become friendly since you visited last year. She spoke often of those chats of yours. She was excited about your book.'

'I – '

'Not unexpected, of course. To be honest, I think your interest in her, in her story, probably gave her longer than any of us had anticipated. Her funeral will be tomorrow, I'm sure she'd have been happy for you to attend.'

'Yes, I – I can't, I – I'm on my way home … I'm on my way home.'

'That's a pity … Back to America then, yes, Joe? I suppose we all go back home in the end.'

I hang up the receiver and walk away from the bank of payphones. My shoes click on the linoleum floor, the rucksack slung on my shoulder dragging with the weight of words. On the large departures board, I spot my flight to New York's JFK. Gate open.

But the doctor's words keep running through my mind. And I realise I can never give her, give Ilse, the answers she'd so badly needed.

What was I doing here, after all? I can hear Finistrini's words replay themselves … that I was using Ilse too, like all the men in her life.

But was she really such a victim, after all? She'd exerted a powerful magnetism … even in her old age, I'd felt it still.

About me faces appear and vanish in the artificial light. Strangers with a common purpose. I slow my stride and look about. Ahead I can see the row of sales desks. I step toward the Lufthansa desk. There is still time, I think, to do what's right.

'When is your next service to Frankfurt?' I ask.

'It leaves in two hours,' replies the sales lady with a bright smile.

I swallow frigid air. But there's no turning back. It's time to pay my respects, and to say a final goodbye.

AFTERWORD

This novel is based on a decade of research. An attempt has been made to remain true to the actual events that have come down through the intervening eighty years. The need, however, to retain a narrative drive has resulted in some scenes being invented such as Varzi's 'lost' months at the Savoia. Therefore the only fact that can be comfortably assigned to this novel is that it is, ultimately, a work of fiction.

The protagonists of the motor-racing scene of the 1930s were the losers of World War II. This has consequences for what is available to the researcher eight decades on. Elly Rosemeyer's biography, for instance, lost all of its Nazi overtones (including quotes from Hitler at al) when it was republished after the war. Italian journalists like Colombo, and Canestrini (who remains the most important voice from that era), worked for an Italian Press that was completely controlled by the State. Their memories after the war often contradicted their pre-war reporting. These discrepancies led to compromises when deciding which 'version' to include – that told before the war (propaganda) or that told after the war (revisionist). The solution was to seek a balance based on secondary texts and sources. However, it is also the case that the novel's inner logic has occasionally held sway in any final determination of which 'version' was used. All of which is to say, any claims to 'truth' in this novel must come with reservations. There are those, for instance, who are convinced there never was a fraud at Mellaha: Canestrini, however, wrote of it (or perhaps confessed would be more accurate, considering his involvement), and it happened pretty much the way it is related in this novel. So whose truth is true? Aldo Zana, a current Italian journalist, has noted that Varzi's file in the Auto Union archive is stamped 'Not to be opened until 2025'. Meanwhile, neither Chiron nor Nuvolari ever got around to writing their autobiographies. Some mysteries, therefore, will endure forever. Carolina Nuvolari was run down by a hit-and-run motorist in 1981. She had lived for two decades with nuns, to whom she left everything.

WHAT HAPPENED TO ILSE?

Ilse of the four names – one of which is an invention, the other erroneous – Engel, Hubach, Pietsch, Fehringer. While researching this novel, I became mildly obsessed with discovering what, precisely, happened to our femme fatale Ilse. There are a few 'theories' running around – Turrini, for instance, suggested she died in a threeway Nazi orgy during the war (he claims he got this enticing tidbit from Enzo Ferrari himself), while Aldo Zana has offered an intriguing theory on Ilse being a transvestite. Elly Beinhorn refused to speak of her, and Canestrini never mentioned a word about her drug addiction (or Varzi's), while Neubauer, who did, changed her name in his autobiography – understandably, since his book was published by Paul Pietsch who himself suggested to Varzi's biographer, the dependable Giorgio Terruzzi in '91, that Ilse died in 1974. In most texts, she remains known as Ilse Hubach, this itself an erroneous spelling of her actual name. Many theories and much intrigue. The truth, however, as is often the case, is a little more mundane: After her attempted suicide in '39, Ilse went back to Bad Kreuznach where, whilst working as a teacher, she met and later married the minor opera singer, Franz Fehringer, in 1946. In 2010, I contacted Birgitta Fella from F.A.Z.-Research who managed to get hold of a privately published biography of Fehringer published in 2009. In that, it was established that Ilse Hubitsch (from an upper-middle-class family hailing out of Wiesbaden) died, childless, in 1968, after a lengthy illness.

For more information about this book and how it was researched,
see the author's website:
www. Sandro-martini.com